THE ENGLISH AIR

Franz von Heiden, son of a Nazi official and an Englishwoman who died when he was a child, comes to England in 1938 to visit his cousins — and to study them. He is welcomed and entertained by Wynne Braithwaite's family and friends. But the peace and abundance which he finds about him are not what he had been taught to expect. These people are not the decadent enemy; their casual talk and happy lives betray no weakness. Franz is disturbed and, finding himself in love with Wynne, he is further troubled at the thought of his mother's broken life in Germany. Is Wynne to suffer the same slow death?

As the world prepares for war, Franz's dilemma grows increasingly acute. The manner in which he finally resolves it provides a thrilling climax to a moving book.

Books by D. E. Stevenson in the
Ulverscroft Large Print Series:

KATE HARDY
ANNA AND HER DAUGHTERS
AMBERWELL
CHARLOTTE FAIRLIE
KATHERINE WENTWORTH
CELIA'S HOUSE
WINTER AND ROUGH WEATHER
LISTENING VALLEY
BEL LAMINGTON
FLETCHER'S END
SPRING MAGIC
THE ENGLISH AIR

This Large Print Edition
is published by kind permission of
COLLINS, LONDON & GLASGOW

D. E. STEVENSON

THE ENGLISH AIR

Complete and Unabridged

ULVERSCROFT
Leicester

First Large Print Edition
published July 1974
SBN 85456 273 7

This special large print edition is
made and printed in England for
F. A. Thorpe, Glenfield, Leicestershire

The characters in this novel are imaginary; the opinions expressed by them are their own opinions — the natural outcome of their circumstances and individuality — and must in no case be taken to represent the author's views.

PART ONE

Summer's Lease

CHAPTER ONE

"WE MUST be very nice to him," said Mrs. Braithwaite, looking up at her daughter with large blue eyes.

"Nice to him!" echoed Miss Braithwaite in some surprise. "Well, of course we'll be nice to him. I mean why shouldn't we?"

Wynne Braithwaite's eyes were quite as large as her mother's and of the same shade of periwinkle blue and, as if that were not enough, she possessed golden curls, and a complexion of milk and roses which was slightly tanned by the sun. She was wearing a short white tennis frock which displayed her pretty arms to the shoulder and her slim legs to slightly above the knee.

Mrs. Braithwaite sighed. "I don't know why you like sitting on tables," she declared.

"Why shouldn't we be nice to him?" repeated her daughter, disregarding the red herring.

3

"Of course," nodded Mrs. Braithwaite thoughtfully, "of course he's half-English — we mustn't forget that."

"Even if he wasn't," said Wynne quickly.

"You mean he can't help it."

"No, I didn't mean that at all. I don't suppose he wants to help it — why should he? We mustn't be so awfully insular," she added, shaking her head earnestly so that the golden curls danced and gleamed in the morning sunshine. "We mustn't think that just because we like being British, everyone else would like to be British too. I expect he's very glad he's a German and thinks it's the best thing to be."

"Yes," agreed Mrs. Braithwaite doubtfully. "And anyhow he *is* half English, whatever you may say, and a sort of cousin as well. I shall find it quite easy to be nice to him because of his mother, but it's different for you."

The conversation — if such it could be called — lapsed into silence. Wynne could not explain her point further, and, even if she could have done so, it was doubtful whether Mrs. Braithwaite would have bothered to understand. Mrs. Braithwaite

4

had the elusive type of mind which prefers to follow its own thoughts, and can rarely be roused to argument.

It was the spring of 1938 and the tennis season had just begun. Wynne was waiting for three friends to arrive for a practice game. She sat on the table and swung her legs and looked at her mother with affection. Sophie was an obstinate mule and an old-fashioned stick in the mud, but she was a dear darling all the same . . . Their eyes met and they both smiled.

"I couldn't say no when he wrote and asked me if he could come, could I?" inquired Mrs. Braithwaite. "Besides I didn't *want* to say no . . ."

"I think it will be rather fun to have him," said Wynne, with a thoughtful smile. "He'll be quite *different*, won't he? I wonder if he's a Nazi."

"It will be much better not to mention politics at all," declared Sophie.

"But Sophie — "

"We don't want any unpleasantness, Wynne. You must warn your friends about him."

"Oh dear, what a fuss!" Wynne exclaimed.

Sophie Braithwaite sighed. She was a creature of impulse and she had not considered the difficulties before writing to welcome her young relative to come and spend a long visit beneath her hospitable roof. "I do hope," Sophie began, "I do *hope* that everyone will be nice to him — "

"Don't worry," said Wynne kindly, "I'll warn everybody to treat him like eggshell. Migs always says what he likes of course but the others will do what they're told. . . . Tell me about him," she added, "tell me how we're related and all that. I'd better know all about it before he arrives, hadn't I ?"

Mrs. Braithwaite looked at her in surprise. "But I've told you so often — "

"I know, but I've forgotten," admitted Wynne. "I don't always listen to things . . . at least I do listen, but, unless the things are going to be useful to me, I don't *keep* them."

Mrs. Braithwaite was quite pleased to oblige. She enjoyed talking and it had always seemed unfortunate that her daughter was not a good listener. Her husband had not been a good listener either, but he had been dead for four years and she remembered his good points and had forgotten his failings — in any case a man was different, you did not expect a man to sit down and chat. There was no reason why Wynne should not sit down and chat — no reason except that she did not seem to want to. Wynne was very sweet, and very kind and considerate in lots of ways but she was not much of a companion. She was always rushing out, or rushing in, or else she was so deeply immersed in a book that no good could be got out of her.

"Elsie was my favourite cousin," began Mrs. Braithwaite with a little sigh. "She was four years older, of course, but we were tremendous friends all the same. We used to stay with each other in the holidays and share all the fun that was going. They lived at Lowestoft, and had a small yacht — it was lovely — and Elsie always came to us for cricket week, or anything like that. Neither of us had a sister, you see, so we used to tell each other everything. She got married first — it was in November, 1913 — and of course I was her principal bridesmaid. We were all in pink, with bouquets of pink carnations and big black velvet hats. I remember my hat was so big that I couldn't get into the Daimler without tipping it up sideways . . . it was the fashion of course and I must say we looked very nice."

"I'm sure you did," said Wynne kindly.

"It was a lovely wedding," continued Mrs. Braithwaite reminiscently, "but, somehow or other, it was very sad. Elsie was going so far away from everyone. You see, I had hoped that Elsie would marry my brother Tom, and then she would have been my sister, but things like that don't happen in real life. Of course they were cousins, which isn't supposed to be good, but it would have been lovely for me, and they would have been much happier."

"You can't *know* that," objected Wynne.

"I do know it," responded Sophie Braithwaite with some heat. "Neither of them could possibly have been more miserable than they were, and so, if they had not married each other, they would have been happier. Tom adored Elsie, and I believe she would have taken him if only Otto hadn't appeared on the scene, but of course the moment Otto von Heiden appeared nobody else had a chance. He was very good-looking — tall and straight, with broad shoulders and fair hair . . . but I didn't like him."

"I wonder why," said Wynne, thoughtfully. "You like most people don't you?"

"You couldn't get to know him," explained Sophie. "He was so stiff and polite and so proud of his family connections. He made me feel that he was condescending to us all the time. I suppose Elsie didn't notice — or perhaps she didn't mind, or perhaps he was different to her when they were alone."

"He probably was," nodded Wynne.

"He played the piano beautifully, of course, and he had a wonderful voice. Even now when anyone sings Schubert's songs it makes me think of Otto. There was one called 'Ständchen' which was Elsie's favourite. We had it the other night when we were at the Audleys' and I could almost *see* Otto . . . in fact I saw him quite clearly when I shut my eyes."

There was a little silence and then Sophie heaved a big sigh. "I missed Elsie dreadfully," she said, "I missed her all the more because I lost her completely — more completely than if she had died. We had always written to each other and told each other everything but after she was married and went to Germany her letters were quite different — I felt she wasn't Elsie any more. Otto always called her Elsa — well of course that was a very small thing but I didn't like it."

"You were jealous," Wynne pointed out.

"Oh yes," agreed her mother, "Oh yes, I was. But it wasn't only for my sake that I was jealous — I was jealous for Elsie, if you know what I mean. I had always thought Elsie quite perfect, but Otto wanted to change her . . ." Sophie was silent for a few moments and then she continued, "I never saw Elsie again. She just seemed to vanish. We had arranged that I was to go and stay with her at Freigarten, but I never went. Elsie kept on writing and putting me off . . . and then the war came. I believe she knew beforehand that the war was coming."

"How could she ?"

"I don't know, but afterwards people said that the Germans *did* know . . . they had been preparing for it."

"People said all sorts of silly things," declared Wynne.

Mrs. Braithwaite did not answer this. She was following her own line of thought. "The war must have been dreadful for Elsie," she said sadly. "She was so cut off from her own people. Franz was born in 1916 and I never knew about it until the end of the war . . . ."

"Why didn't she write and tell you ?"

"Because it was war, of course. You don't understand what it was like in the war and I hope you never will." The words were spoken with such force and bitterness that Wynne looked at her mother in surprise. It was most unusual for Sophie to be bitter.

"I was very unhappy about Elsie," continued Sophie after a little pause, "and it made me think of the war a little differently from other people. When we heard that the Germans were starving I couldn't feel glad about it, because of course it meant that Elsie was starving too."

"Why should you feel glad ?" inquired Wynne in horrified tones.

"You don't understand," Mrs. Braithwaite told her again. "The Germans were our enemies and it was a weapon — just like guns. When armies besiege a town the people in the town can't get food — sometimes they have to eat mice (they did that in Paris, but that was another war of course) and we besieged the whole of Germany in the same way. It's dreadful, but all war is dreadful. You don't understand."

"I don't want to understand," Wynne said firmly.

Mrs. Braithwaite left it at that.

"Well, go on," said Wynne. "What happened after the war? Why didn't you see Elsie when the war was over?"

"All sorts of things happened." replied Mrs. Braithwaite vaguely. "By that time I was married and I had Roy. I couldn't have gone to Germany even if Elsie had asked me and, as a matter of fact, she didn't ask me. I expect it would have been difficult."

"Why didn't you ask her to come here?" demanded Wynne, who was holding to the one idea with the persistence of youth.

"Everything was different then," replied Sophie, still more vaguely. "I can't explain it, but it just wasn't thought of . . . and there was so much to do. I wrote to Elsie several times when the war was over but she never answered, and then, when I had almost given up hope of ever hearing from her again, she wrote and sent me a picture of Franz in his bathing suit. *That* made me more unhappy than ever . . . I don't mean the picture, of course, because he was a dear little fellow, very healthy and sturdy with lovely curly hair, but the letter was dreadful. It was a hopeless sort of letter and it didn't tell me anything I wanted to know. Then, about a month later, I heard from Otto that she had died. I couldn't send even a wreath because it was too late and there were all sorts of difficulties . . . Oh dear," added Mrs. Braithwaite pathetically, "oh dear, of course I know it didn't matter about the wreath . . . but I had a silly feeling about it . . . I loved her so much, you see."

Wynne said nothing. She swung her legs a little and thought about the story she had heard. It was as unreal to her as a fairy tale. It was a glimpse into a world which she could not understand, a frightening world, a world in which people were deliberately cruel to each other. The pale golden sunshine streamed through the open windows on to the lovely old Persian rug and the parquet floor. The pretty chintzes, the polished furniture, the china and the pictures and knick-knacks, which were all so familiar to Wynne that she scarcely saw them, suddenly took a different complexion and became dear and reassuring and homelike. Outside in the garden the birds sang lustily and the spring flowers nodded in the faint breeze.

"So you see we must be very nice to Franz," Sophie Braithwaite said.

Mrs. Braithwaite was a widow. Her husband had died four years ago, leaving her with two children. Roy was sixteen when his father died and Wynne was two years younger. The Braithwaites were a comfortable family, they were pleasant and agreeable to each other and had no sharp corners or complexes of any kind. Mr. Braithwaite was the pillar of the house, he managed everything and kept his wife and daughter in cotton wool. When he fell ill, and began to suspect that he was unlikely to recover, he had some bad moments for it was obvious that his family was incapable of looking after itself. Who was going to look after his family when he had gone? — that was the question. He and Sophie were both very badly off in the way of relations — their parents were dead: Sophie's only brother was in the Navy and was in the East at the time: he himself had no relative living except his half-brother Dane Worthington. He turned it over in his mind, which despite his illness was perfectly clear, and decided that he must ask Dane if he would look after Sophie's affairs. He saw that in some ways it was unfair to saddle Dane with the responsibility of his family but he had no option in the matter. So Dane was wired for, and arrived.

Dane seemed to think it quite natural that he should be the one to take over the care of his brother's family.

"I'll look after them," he declared. "After all it was I who introduced you to Sophie, wasn't it?"

Philip Braithwaite had forgotten this interesting fact, but casting back his mind he began to remember...

"At Oxford," he said in a tired whisper. "Yes, of course it was when you were at Oxford, wasn't it? I came down for

Commem . . . we went on the river . . ."
He shut his eyes and the brightly-coloured
picture took shape: the blue sky reflecting
itself in the water, the arching green trees,
and the boatloads of young men in white
flannels and young girls in pretty frocks.
Sophie's frock had been blue, the colour
of her eyes . . . so pretty, she was. He had
fallen in love with her at first sight and
had no eyes for anyone or anything else
. . . "Before the war," whispered Philip.
"What a long time ago it seems!"

It seemed a very long time ago to Dane
for he, too, was seeing visions. He sat
quietly beside Philip's bed so that when
the sick man opened his eyes he could see
him, and be reassured. They had always
been friends in spite of the ten years'
difference in their ages. Philip Braithwaite
had been extremely good to his young
half-brother, and Dane did not forget it.
He remembered incidents long before
Commem. He remembered Philip coming
to Rugby for the school match; he remembered Philip coming to Sandhurst and
taking him out for huge feeds of bacon and
eggs. It was Philip who had come for him
and taken him home when his parents

had both been fatally injured in a railway accident; Philip who had comforted him and sustained him and given him courage to bear his loss. Philip had felt the loss too, for he was devoted to his mother and his step-father, and, although he had left home some years before and lived in London so as to be near his work, he had kept in close touch with his old home.

Dane thought of all this. It seemed cruel that Philip should die at the age of forty-five, but if he had to die then he should die in peace. Dane owed him so much . . . it was the least he could do for him.

After the funeral Dane stayed on at Fernacres for there was much to settle and arrange. Fortunately there was no difficulty about money. Sophie, although not exactly wealthy, was reasonably well-off. Roy was started in the Navy and Wynne was at a day-school in the neighbourhood. Everything would continue as before. Having settled matters as best he could, Dane suggested that it was time for him to go, but Sophie pressed him to stay. He stayed another week . . . and then another. Somehow or other, without anything definite being said, or any arrangements being made, it became obvious to all parties that Dane was remaining at Fernacres indefinitely.

Fernacres was a pleasant place, one of those sunshiny houses in which it is almost impossible to imagine gloom. It stood in about three acres of pleasant garden, facing south. There were houses on three sides, but the view from the front terrace was unbroken except for trees, and from certain vantage points it was possible to see the sea in the distance — the sea, and a piece of cliff, and a stretch of green turf. The house itself had been built about the beginning of the century, it was a white house, low and sprawling with a red roof and green shutters. It was too big for Mrs. Braithwaite and Wynne, but of admirable proportions for a joint ménage. Dane took over the west wing which gave him a bedroom, a sitting-room and a bathroom and a room for his man. He decorated the rooms to suit himself and installed his own furniture. It was now necessary to have a business talk with Sophie, and Dane pursued her to the garden where she was cutting off dead roses and explained to her that he would pay her so much a month in rent and so much a week for food. She had agreed to everything else that he had suggested without a murmur and Dane was somewhat surprised when she raised objections to his plan.

"No, Dane," said Sophie with unaccustomed firmness, "No, Dane. It's nice for us to have you here and you're so good at arranging things."

"But I must pay you, Sophie."

"I don't need the money," Sophie replied, "and I'm sure Philip would like you to be here."

Dane was sure of that, too, but he was determined to pay for the privileges he enjoyed and he got over the difficulty by paying his monthly rent into Sophie's banking account. He was pretty sure that Sophie would not notice the sums, and Sophie didn't.

The arrangement suited everyone concerned. Dane came and went as he pleased. When he wanted a week in town he shut up his rooms at Fernacres and went to his club; when he wanted to go abroad he could do so (Sophie accepted his comings and goings without question) and, when he had been away and returned to Fernacres, he thoroughly enjoyed his welcome. The menage was a trifle odd, of course, and Dane was aware that there was a certain amount of gossip about in Chellford, but that could not be helped and he knew human nature so well that he comforted himself by the reflection that the gossip would die a natural death. Sophie would not be affected by the gossip, bless her, for any veiled hints or allusions would pass her by and she would be the last person to hear any definitely unkind remarks. In any case Dane felt that he could not desert his self-appointed post, for Sophie was incapable of looking after her affairs and there was Wynne . . . and Roy . . . how could Dane keep an eye on them unless he was on the spot ?

Dane had reasoned it all out, and having done so, and chosen his course, he did not worry about it any more. The gossip died down as he had expected and everyone was happy. Dane had now been living at Fernacres for four years and was completely dug in. Just at the moment however, Dane was in Carlsbad and Sophie had not been able to consult him before she replied to Franz von Heiden's letter. She had consulted nobody but had replied with impulsive friendliness — Franz was Elsie's son, and that was a sufficient recommendation to Sophie's good graces.

CHAPTER TWO

WYNNE was quite pleased to be "nice" to her mother's guest. She had plenty of friends in Chellford, of course, friends of all ages and conditions of life, but it would be amusing to have somebody new, somebody different. She had decided to give him a good time. There would be lots of tennis, and bathing, and the cricket match next week. She would take him to Kingsport — about ten miles away — and they could see the ships and go to the Picture House. Perhaps he would like to see the Roman Villa at Ashbourne . . .

I wonder what he's *like*, Wynne thought, as she parked her small car in the station yard and strolled on to the platform to wait for the train.

The wind was boisterous this afternoon and a trifle chilly. She was glad she had put on her thick tweed coat. It was sapphire blue, with deep pockets, and Wynne put her hands into the pockets for warmth. She stood there, waiting for the train, with her feet slightly apart and her head thrown back. There was something brave and dauntless about her attitude, and the wind whipped her gold curls so that strands of them blew across her face.

It seemed odd to Wynne that she should be standing here waiting the arrival of this stranger. A week ago she had scarcely known that such a person existed. She had known of him only in a shadowy sort of way as the son of Mummy's cousin who had married a German. But now, all of a sudden, the tale had become real and she was to meet this son in the flesh.

"Franz von Heiden," said Wynne to herself. She said it several times and decided it was an ugly name — but of course he might think her name ugly. It was all a matter of what you were used to.

The train was late, and Wynne strolled up and down the platform thinking about her new cousin. She wondered what Dane would say when he heard — whether he would approve of Sophie's latest whim. He wouldn't interefere of course, because he never interfered with Sophie's whims. He had smiled and agreed at once when Sophie had conceived the idea of inviting

an Austrian refugee to stay at Fernacres
. . . "It's your house," he had said . . . (It
was Sophie's house, of course, but Wynne
was aware that practically everything in
their lives depended upon Dane). The
Austrian refugee had had to be put off on
account of Franz, for it was obvious to the
meanest intelligence that Fernacres could
not harbour a German and an Austrian
refugee at the same time, and Wynne
could not help feeling that it was a little
hard on the refugee, and wondering where
he would go . . .

The train steamed in and the passengers
descended. Wynne had no difficulty in
picking out her guest for there was a
foreign air about him, and he was tall and
straight and fair, like the picture of his
father in Sophie's photograph album. She
touched him on the arm and inquired,
"Are you Franz von Heiden?" and he
drew himself up and bowed.

"I'm Wynne," she said, smiling up at
him in a friendly way. "I've come to meet
you."

"That is very kind," he said solemnly.

His gravity was the first "difference"
that struck Wynne. He did not smile

easily, and this made him seem much older than his years. His English was good (though a trifle pedantic) and without much trace of foreign accent. Wynne discovered these things while they were getting his suitcase out of the van and putting it on to a barrow.

"I'd have known you anywhere," she told him as they went out to the car, "you're so like your father."

"You have seen my father?" he inquired in surprise.

"Sophie has a photograph of him," said Wynne.

"Sophie?" he inquired a little doubtfully.

"My mother," Wynne explained.

He was silent for a few moments and then he said:

"I should like to have the picture. I have not a picture of my father as a young man. It would be very pleasant if I could have it to keep."

"You must ask Sophie," said Wynne shortly.

"I shall ask her," Franz declared as he climbed into the car and curled up his long legs.

Wynne settled herself at the wheel. She was a little disappointed in her new cousin, though she scarcely knew why. Perhaps she had hoped for too much. Wynne was used to a good deal of attention from the males of her acquaintance and although Franz was polite and pleasant he had treated her as if she were fifty years old and had a hare lip . . .

They turned out of the station yard into the main street of Chellford. It was narrow and winding and the shops were small. Chellford was an old fishing village, but it had been discovered by a firm of property agents about the beginning of the century and the result of their labours was a very pleasant residential area upon the hill behind the village. Wynne did the honours of the place to her cousin. She pointed out the little river Chell which ran beneath an old grey stone bridge and spread out fan-wise into the sea. She pointed out the post office and the local cinema but she forbore to point out the fountain in the square which was, in reality a memorial to the men of Chellford who had fallen in the Great War. They turned out of the village and breasted the hill.

"The Audleys' live there," said Wynne, pointing to a large square house standing amongst some trees. "They're great friends of mine and they have lots of tennis. Do you play tennis?"

"Yes," replied Franz. "But I did not bring my racket."

"We can easily lend you one," replied Wynne.

There was silence for a few moments and then he inquired, "Your house is far from here?"

"We're nearly there," Wynne said. "It's pretty country, isn't it?"

They were half-way up the hill now, and could look down on the village, and the stream and the blue sea. Farther along the coast there were fields and trees and the cliffs rose up, jagged and bold.

Franz looked down. "Yes it is pretty," he admitted, "but my country is more beautiful."

"But you haven't seen England properly yet," cried Wynne, "and, anyhow, this is your country too. Aren't you excited at seeing it for the first time?"

"It is very interesting," he replied gravely, "and I am glad to have the opportunity of making the acquaintance of my English relatives."

Wynne chuckled — she could not help it.

"Please," he said in a hurt tone, "please, I have said something wrong."

"It was too right," replied Wynne hastily, "too marvellous for anything. I just thought you must have made it up beforehand."

She had hoped to raise a smile, but she was disappointed.

"It is true that I made it up before," he declared with solemnity, "but I can see nothing funny in that. Was it not natural that I should prepare myself?"

"How lucky it fitted in so well!" she exclaimed.

They had now arrived at the gates of Fernacres, and Wynne was not sorry for she was finding her guest somewhat heavy on her hands. She swung into the avenue, which was bordered on one side by a high hedge of rhododendrons — on the other side the avenue was open to a lawn which was shaded by fine old trees. Mrs. Braithwaite had been listening for the car and came out of the front door as they drove up.

"My dear boy!" she exclaimed. "What a pleasure this is! If only your dear mother could be here too — but we won't talk about that. You must stay with us as long as you can . . . did you have a comfortable journey? I'm afraid the train was late . . . you can hear it whistle when it comes out of the tunnel."

Franz looked a trifle bewildered. "Please," he said.

"Did you have a good journey?" repeated Sophie Braithwaite, raising her voice a little as if she were speaking to a deaf person.

"It was very good," Franz replied. "Your train went smoothly."

"It was the sea I meant," Mrs. Braithwaite explained. "I hope the sea was smooth too — but perhaps you like it when it's rough."

"I have a good stomach," he replied, not boastfully, but merely as if he were stating an interesting fact, "but I did not come by boat. I came by air. It is remarkable how quick the plane goes and the seats are very comfortable. I arrived at Croydon yesterday and stayed in London for the night."

"Where did you stay?" inquired Mrs.

Braithwaite with interest, "I hope you didn't stay at an hotel — so dreadfully expensive for you."

"I stayed with a friend of my father's. He is a secretary at our Legation," replied Franz. "He is a very pleasant man and that is fortunate because I am to go there and have a post when I have finished my holiday. It is a very small post," added Franz modestly, "but it will begin me nicely."

"You must stay with us as long as you can," Sophie said.

"Yes, that is nice, but I cannot stay too long or the money will not last. It was permitted me to bring more than the usual money but it will not last forever."

Sophie did not understand what he meant; she said kindly, "You mustn't worry about money, Franz dear, I can easily advance you money. I know how difficult the exchange is, and you can pay me back any time — so don't hesitate for a moment to ask for anything you want," and then, before he could answer or protest, she went back and picked up another thread. "You should have wired to us and come down yesterday," she told him. "You could have come straight here — your room was all ready. I've put you in the green room because the sun is so nice in the morning. Perhaps you'd like to see your room now . . . and then a glass of sherry before dinner . . . or would you like a bath ?"

They were half-way up the stairs now — wide, shallow stairs with cream-coloured banisters and a tall window through which the westering sun streamed in a golden beam — Mrs. Braithwaite was leading, Franz followed, and Wynne kept a little way behind so that if she were overcome by another chuckle she could hide it more effectively.

"This is your room," said Sophie, opening a door on the big square landing. "You will be happy here, won't you? Remember that your mother and I were like sisters."

"Thank you, Cousin Sophie," replied Franz, "it is very kind. I am . . . I am quite overcome by your kindness, I do not remember my mother, she died when I was six years old."

"It doesn't matter," Sophie told him, taking out a small lace handkerchief and blowing her little nose, "I mean you're

31

Elsie's son whether you remember her or not . . . although of course it would be very nice if you *did* remember her — nice for me, I mean — because we could talk about her, couldn't we? She was a dear, sweet creature, so gay and pretty. I must show you some photographs of her, Franz dear . . . we will look at them after dinner."

CHAPTER THREE

THE dinner gong boomed pleasantly through the house, and Mrs. Braithwaite took her guest's arm and steered him into the dining-room. It was still quite light outside, but there were candles on the table and this made the dark-panelled room intimate and cosy.

"We shall be able to play bridge when Dane comes home," said Sophie Braithwaite smiling happily. "I mean there will be four of us."

"Perhaps Franz doesn't play," put in Wynne, hopefully.

"We could teach him," Sophie pointed out. "We could easily teach him, and he would soon learn to play as well as I do."

This was true of course, for Sophie's bridge was vague and eccentric, but it did not raise Wynne's spirits. She was about to bring forth further objections to the plan when Franz leaned forward and inquired.

"Dane? But I thought your son was called Roy, Cousin Sophie."

"My brother-in-law," explained Sophie. "At least he is really my husband's half-brother. He makes Fernacres his headquarters."

"He is a military officer?"

Sophie shook her head, "Oh, no," she said, "it isn't that kind of headquarters. I only meant that he lives here most of the time when he isn't somewhere else. He isn't in the army now. Of course he fought in the war like everybody else, and he got the D.S.O., so he must have done very well . . ."

Her voice died away and there was a short, but somewhat strained, silence.

"There is no need to feel uncomfortable about the war," said Franz gravely, "it is over a long time ago. Tell me some more about this Mister Dane."

"He isn't Mister Dane," Sophie replied hastily. "Dane is his Christian name, I'm just telling you this so that you will know. He is Major Worthington, but he knew your mother very well so I expect you could call him Uncle Dane if you liked."

"Franz had better call him Dane," remarked Wynne. "I don't think he's particularly keen on being uncled."

"But he is not my uncle," objected Franz. "He does not seem to be related to me at all, so I think it would be more polite for me to call him Major Worthington. What is his work?"

"Oh, he doesn't *work*," said Wynne. "You couldn't imagine Dane working."

"He does nothing at all?" inquired Franz in surprise. "But that is very strange ... perhaps he is an invalid?"

"Not exactly," said Sophie. "He isn't very strong, of course, and he goes to Carlsbad sometimes and takes the cure."

"It is the kidneys, perhaps?" inquired Franz sympathetically.

Wynne stifled another chuckle.

"I really don't know," said Sophie in a flustered sort of voice. "He doesn't . . . I mean we don't talk about these things, Franz dear. I'm sure it's better for me to tell you this quietly while we are here by ourselves. Dane wouldn't like any mention made ..."

"Naturally," agreed Franz hastily, and Wynne noticed that he was pink to the ears. The joke was that Dane would not mind at all — Wynne was certain of that — he would be quite pleased to discuss the condition of his organs with Franz. Strangely enough Wynne had never thought of Dane as being delicate in any way, and now that she considered the matter, she felt pretty certain that he was not. She realised for the first time that she had no idea what Dane did. He did something, she was sure of that. Wynne had grown up under the same roof, and had always taken Dane for granted. He wrote letters: he telephoned constantly: he rushed up to town and back again: he disappeared for weeks on end. That wasn't exactly work, of course, but it certainly wasn't play . . .

"When in Rome do as the Romans do." Sophie continued, trying to relieve the obvious embarrassment of her guest, "and of course you can't know the sort of things we say and do, so you needn't mind if I tell you. If your mother hadn't died when you were little she would have told you everything, of course."

"I wish to learn," declared Franz earnestly. "That is the reason I have come. It is a great pleasure to make the acquaintance of my English relatives, but the real reason of my visit is to learn the English manners and customs and to learn to speak the language like an Englishman. How long will this take, Cousin Sophie?"

Cousin Sophie missed the point, "You speak very well indeed, Franz dear," she declared, smiling at him encouragingly. "I think it's very clever of you to have learnt to speak so well, and I'm sure Wynne thinks so too. Languages are very useful because if you go to a place and you can't understand what the people are saying, or ask for anything you want, it makes you feel stupid, doesn't it?"

"My ambition is much more," he replied in a bewildered manner. "It is surely easy to understand and to ask for what is necessary — "

"Not always," interrupted Sophie. "For instance if I went to Russia I shouldn't be able to ask for a cup of tea."

"Samovar," murmured Wynne, "or is that the thing they make it in? Anyhow, if you said 'Samovar' I bet they would know what you meant."

By this time their guest looked so utterly befogged that Wynne took pity on him.

"I don't know how long it will take to learn to speak like an Englishman," she said thoughtfully, "the trouble is you speak far too well."

"*Too well!*" he inquired, unable to believe his ears.

"Much too well," nodded Wynne. "You talk like a book and use a lot of long words. We're too lazy to talk like that."

"It is necessary that I should learn," declared Franz anxiously, "so will you please tell me the right way."

Wynne said she would try. "But it will be rather difficult," she added, "because nearly everything you say is just a little bit odd. For instance we wouldn't say "it is necessary that I should learn," we just say, "I really *must* learn" or something like that."

"I really *must* learn," he repeated obediently.

Wynne smiled at him, and, for a wonder, he smiled back. He had a rather charming smile and for the first time since his arrival she saw that there was something very nice about Franz . . . it must be frightfully difficult for him, she thought.

The rest of the evening was passed in looking at photographs. Sophie and her guest sat together on the sofa beneath the standard lamp and waded through several large albums with admirable thoroughness. Wynne, who was endeavouring to read a detective novel, found her thoughts straying from the tangle of clues . . . He's very decent, she thought, he *must* be bored, but he doesn't show it at all. She was aware that very few young men would spend a whole evening looking at old photographs.

But Franz was not bored, he was just as interested as Sophie, and Sophie was in her element . . .

"Yes, that's Roy," she was saying. "And here's one of Eric — isn't he a darling fat baby ?"

"You have two sons then ?"

"Oh no," she replied, "Eric isn't my son, although sometimes I feel that he is. Eric is my brother Tom's boy but his mother has always been rather queer so Eric used to come here in the holidays. It was nice for Roy to have another boy to play with, and it was really less trouble to have them both here together because they amused each other. You see," she smiled and added, "Eric looks on Fernacres as his home — which of course it is — because he hasn't got any other home. My brother is a sailor so he has no home either . . . and that's Ethel."

"Who is Ethel?"

"Eric's mother. She's very good-looking, of course," admitted Sophie a trifle grudgingly, "but good looks aren't everything in this world and poor Tom hasn't had much comfort out of Ethel . . . nor has Eric for that matter. Eric was such a dear little boy," she added sadly.

"He is dead, then?" asked Franz, misled by her tone.

"Oh goodness, no!" cried Sophie, "I didn't mean *that* when I said he was a dear little boy, I only meant that it was so funny of Ethel not to like to have him with her. Of course he's quite grown up now and we don't see him so often. He and Roy are both in the Navy but they never seem to get leave at the same time."

"Ah — the Navy!" said Franz, nodding.

"Yes, both of them," Sophie said. "Roy is in the Home Fleet at present so he may turn up at any moment, but poor Eric is at Bermuda, so you won't see him, I'm afraid . . . but I wanted to show you some pictures of Elsie. They're in that big red book."

The big red book was lifted off the table and opened, and they were off again.

"*There*," said Sophie, "that's Elsie — your mother — when she was fifteen. The dresses we wore in those days look rather funny now . . . and the hats . . . but you can see what lovely hair she had. It was golden, just like Wynne's, but she wore it down her back in a thick plait. Here we are on the yacht . . . that's my brother Tom, and that's me holding the tiller. What fun we had in those days," added Sophie with a little sigh.

Wynne could not get on with her novel. The detective had now proved to his own satisfaction that the tall dark young man had committed the murder, and, as Wynne had taken a violent fancy to the tall dark young man and was perfectly certain that he was blameless, she ought to have been on tenterhooks, but somehow or other she could not concentrate at all.

"This is you again," Franz was saying, "you have not altered much, Cousin Sophie."

"Yes, that was the time we went to Commem," agreed Sophie. "It was in 1913 when Dane was at Oxford and he invited us down. My mother came to chaperone us — there she is in the black toque. It had red roses on it, I remember — there's Elsie in the white dress, and those two young men were Dane's friends — one of them was killed in the war. That was first time I met Philip — Dane's elder brother — but I didn't get engaged to him until long after that. He seemed so much older, somehow. It wasn't until Elsie was married and the war started . . . "

Her voice died away and she was silent for a few moments thinking of the past. It was queer to look over these old photographs and to see these young figures and unlined characterless faces. She felt vaguely that here one ought to find the key to the riddle of life. Here they all were — herself, Elsie, Philip, Dane and Tom and many others all young and eager like themselves, and here their lives had been in the melting pot. They had not realised this at the time, for they were all too young and gay and inexperienced . . . and it seemed a little unfair that these gay young creatures should have had the frightful responsibility of choosing their own moulds, of moulding their own lives and characters. It was all such a toss up, thought Sophie, as she looked back, Elsie might easily have married Tom . . . and she herself might have chosen a different partner in the matrimonial stakes. As she had said to Franz it was not until Elsie was married and the war started that she had agreed at last to marry Philip Braithwaite — he was safe and sure and so terribly in love with her and she had wanted a refuge from the storm.

"Is this your husband?" Franz was inquiring.

"Yes," said Sophie, blinking a little and bending over the book. "Yes, that's Philip. He's very good-looking isn't he? And here's another photograph of us all together. It was taken at seven-o'clock in the morning after we had danced all night . . . and there's another of Elsie and me together . . . isn't she pretty?"

"You all look very happy," Franz said.

"We _were_ happy," replied Sophie. "That was really the last happy time we had. It was just after that that your father came over from Germany and he and Elsie fell in love at first sight, and nothing was ever the same again."

"You did not approve of the marriage?" asked Franz, turning his head and looking at her earnestly.

"Well dear," said Sophie, grasping the bull by the horns, "well, dear, to be quite frank, I was rather miserable about it. Of course it may have been that I was a little jealous — Elsie and I had always been such friends — or it may have been because I knew she would have to go so far away — although I didn't realise that I should never see her again — but whatever it was I didn't like it a bit."

"It was your instinct," said Franz firmly.

"My instinct?"

"Yes, it was a very bad marriage indeed. It was bad for both of them — *schrecklich* — "

"Franz *dear!*" interrupted Sophie a trifle breathlessly. "I don't know how we managed to get on to the subject, Your parents . . . and they were very much in love . . . but really . . . really I don't think we should discuss it, and so . . . and so . . ."

"We will not discuss it," he agreed. "There is no need to discuss it if it distresses you. Cousin Sophie. Let us look at some more pictures, shall we? Wynne told me that you have a picture of my father as a young man. I should like to see it, and perhaps you would be very kind and give it to me."

"Yes, of course," agreed Sophie at once. "Of course you shall have it. Give me that brown book with the brass clasps . . . I'm almost certain it's in that one. Perhaps you'd like to have one of your mother as well."

CHAPTER FOUR

DANE WORTHINGTON arrived at Fernacre two days later at six o'clock in the morning. He arrived in his touring car with his man sitting beside him and his luggage piled in the tonneau. They had crossed the Channel from Calais the day before, had spent some hours in London and had left London in the early hours of the morning. They had encountered a few lorries, and a string of carts with vegetable produce going in to the market, but apart from these there was little traffic and Dane had done the journey at a good speed. He drove up to the side door, opened it with his private key and went in. Hartley carried in the luggage, opened all the windows and prepared tea. Hartley had been with Major Worthington for so long that he knew exactly what to do — there was little need for words between them.

"Splendid run, sir," he said, as he came into the sitting-room with the tray of tea and breakfast biscuits and a jar of marmalade.

"Yes," agreed Dane, looking up from his paper, "yes, it was. I can't think why more people don't take advantage of a clear road."

"They don't like getting up out of their beds," replied Hartley as he put the tray on the table and arranged it neatly. "There's plenty of people would take a fit if you asked them to get up at four."

"Do *you* mind?" inquired Dane curiously.

Hartley smiled. "No sir, it doesn't worry me."

"I don't know what I should do without you, Hartley."

"No sir," agreed Hartley, "you couldn't get on without me, and to tell the truth I'd be pretty well lost without you, sir, if you know what I mean. We've been through a good many funny experiences, haven't we?"

"Starting with the war," agreed Dane, who was in an unusually reminiscent mood, "starting with that hellish day at Festubert where we met face to face in a German trench and nearly scared each other to death."

"I've been nearly scared to death more

than once since that day," Hartley said thoughtfully.

Dane smiled again. "You might get a job as valet to a nice fat old gentleman and settle down to a respectable old age," he suggested.

"I'd be bored to death, then," replied Hartley seriously, "and that would be worse . . . My old grandfather used to say 'Better wear out than rust out.' . . . Will you be wanting anything else, sir?"

"No," said Dane, "you had better have a few hours in bed."

Hartley had no intention of going to bed. They had both been up all night but he had slept in the car and he was used to unconventional hours. Dane often chose to travel by night for he always travelled by car and preferred a clear road. Hartley was a good driver and sometimes took a spell at the wheel — he liked to drive with the powerful beams of the big head-lamps cutting through the dark. The Continental roads were the ones for speed — the long straight roads of France, and those new German *Autobahnen* — but all the same Hartley was glad to be home again.

When Hartley had gone Dane poured

out his tea. He stood by the table and drank it slowly. He put a large spoonful of marmalade onto a biscuit and ate it with obvious enjoyment. Continental fare was extremely good, thought Dane, but there was something very refreshing about tea and marmalade . . . it was extraordinarily clean food. He also was glad to be home. He liked the room with its bookcases and deep leather chairs. He liked the view from the windows . . . the green lawn, the thick wall of rhododendrons, and above and beyond the little peep of blue sea.

Dane was still looking out of the window when a figure ran round the house on to the lawn. It was the figure of a young man — a blond giant in running shorts and a thin white vest — and, as Dane watched, he began to exercise himself in a con- scientious manner. He ran round the lawn with his elbows to his sides and his knees well up; he stopped and bent, touching his toes and then straightening his back and throwing up his head; he swung his arms upwards and outwards in wide circles. Dane did not seem unduly surprised at the exhibition, but he did seem interested. He stood to one side of the window and watched, and presently he was aware that Hartley was standing behind him.

"Pretty useful sort of a fellow in a scrap," he remarked quietly.

"Yes, sir," Hartley agreed. "Fine dorsal muscles, he has. Knows his stuff, too. It's nice to watch, isn't it?"

"It would be nice to watch if you didn't know what was at the back of it," replied Dane slowly, "if you didn't know that the boy is preparing his body for war. To me there's something pretty grim in that thought . . ."

They were silent for a few moments and then Hartley said, "It's very queer, some-how — I can't get over it — I've seen lots of queer things, but a Nazi in Fernacres garden!"

"Stranger than a sea-serpent," suggested Dane with an involuntary smile.

The display on the lawn finished with an exhibition of jumping. The young athlete took a run and cleared the white painted garden bench end on . . . then, picking up his towel, he ran round the corner of the house and disappeared.

"Well, that's that," said Dane, turning from the window with a sigh. "Remember what I told you, Hartley," he added, "not a word to the servants."

"Not a word, sir," Hartley agreed.

The others were at breakfast when Dane went down, and, as usual, his welcome left nothing to be desired.

"What a lovely surprise!" Sophie exclaimed, smiling at him from behind the coffee-pot. "I was simply amazed when Rose brought my tea and told me you had arrived . . . this is Franz von Heiden . . . you remember his mother, don't you ?"

Franz had risen and was bowing politely with his table-napkin in his hand.

"Why, of course," Dane said, "I remember your father, too. I hope he is well."

"Thank you, he is in excellent health," replied Franz solemnly.

(Franz had the feeling that he had seen Major Worthington before, but he found it quite impossible to remember the circumstances. When and where had he seen that tall slender figure, that thin humorous face, that thick dark silky hair ? He noted the grey eyes, the dark arch of the eyebrows and the firm lips which, at the moment, were curved into a half-mocking smile. It was not a face or figure that one would easily forget and somehow or other Franz associated it with flowers . . . with large pink roses . . .)

Dane was now at the sideboard helping himself to bacon and eggs. "Marvellous stuff, bacon and eggs," he was saying as he picked out the crisp rashers and laid them neatly upon his plate.

"I *hope* everything was all right in your rooms," said Sophie anxiously. "If you had wired I could have had them all ready. We didn't expect you until next week . . . the fire wasn't lighted or anything."

"A match put that right," replied Dane.

"Did you get my letter?"

"Which letter? I got one just before I left."

"Was your cure over sooner than you expected?"

"I was homesick," he replied, smiling at her. "I was homesick for Fernacres and bacon and eggs."

"You have been at Carlsbad, sir?" inquired Franz.

"You're looking thin," said Sophie anxiously. "Have you been having enough to eat? Was the cure very strenuous?"

"How long did it take you to come down from town?" asked Wynne.

Dane laughed. "What a lot of questions!" he exclaimed. "I'm always thin — Carlsbad or no Carlsbad — and you must ask Hartley how long it took us to come down. He always times us carefully. As a matter of fact we came pretty fast — there was practically nothing on the roads."

"There wouldn't be at that hour," declared Sophie, "and talking of roads, Franz wants to buy a motor bicycle but I told him he must wait until you came home. I knew you'd help him to choose it. The gardener's wife wants a gas cooker — "

"Soot had kittens yesterday," Wynne broke in, "and I want to keep two—they're such darlings — "

"The Red House has been sold," declared Sophie. "They're rather queer people, I'm afraid — different coloured curtains in all the windows — it's such a pity because the Red House is so nice and I *do* so like having nice neighbours. Of course they're at the back," she added somewhat cryptically.

Fortunately Dane knew exactly what she meant. The Red House was on the north side of Fernacres so that although the gardens of the two houses were adjoining, they faced on to different roads. "So the curtains don't really matter," Dane said.

"No," agreed Sophie, "but I mean—" She hesitated . . .

"You mean that people who neglect the outward appearance of their house are usually indifferent neighbours."

"Of course that's what I mean," nodded Sophie with a pleased smile. "How clever you are, Dane."

"And there's more in it than curtains," put in Wynne. "Horrid little Pekingese all over the garden and the tennis court going wild—I wish you could do something about it, Dane."

"I wish I could," he agreed, "but although I am extremely clever and noted far and wide for my tact and diplomacy there are certain limits to what even I can accomplish — the case of the people at the Red House seems to be definitely outside these limits I'm afraid . . . "

After breakfast Dane returned to his own rooms to do some writing and, shortly after, there was a knock on the door and Wynne peeped in.

"Are you terribly busy?" she inquired.

"Terribly," said Dane, laying down his pen and clasping his long thin hands on the table in front of him. "Much too busy to talk to you."

Wynne opened the door wider and came in. She perched herself on the edge of the table and looked down at him.

"The house feels quite different when you're at home," she declared, "even our bit of the house feels different."

"More pleasant, I hope?" inquired Dane gravely.

Wynne did not answer this ridiculous question. She said, "I knew when I woke this morning that you were home, knew it in my bones."

"Horrid," declared Dane with an elaborate shudder.

"Why did you come home?" she inquired. "Was it because of Franz?"

"I told you — I was homesick."

"Sophie was very determined to have him."

"Why not?" Dane inquired. "There's no reason why she shouldn't have him."

"I wanted her to wait until you came home," explained Wynne, "or at any rate until she wrote and asked you, but she said you knew his mother, too."

"Yes," said Dane.

"Of course we had to put off the refugee."

"Of course," agreed Dane, raising one eyebrow in a humorous manner. "I am glad you had that much sense."

"Are you fed up about it?"

"My dear lamb it won't worry *me*," Dane told her. "As long as I don't have to listen to Nazi propaganda — "

"Oh, but you won't, darling," Wynne assured him. "We needn't discuss anything at all . . . he wants to learn English."

"He seems to know a good deal of English already."

"But he wants to speak like an Englishman," Wynne said seriously. "He's very thorough, you see."

Dane sighed. "Sophie has a very tender heart, but it's you who will have to bear the brunt of entertaining him. You must tell me if it worries you, Wynne."

"I don't mind," she replied quickly, "honestly I don't. I thought at first he was going to be a crashing bore but now I'm not so sure . . . there's something rather

56

nice about him," she added thoughtfully.

"He makes you laugh?" suggested
Dane.

Wynne did not answer directly. She
said slowly, "He's a funny mixture, Dane
— so young and childish and solemn and
elderly. He knows a lot of things I don't
know, but he's frightfully ignorant about
things that everyone knows."

Dane smiled.

"All right," said Wynne with some heat.
"All right, you talk to him and see. Ask
him something about history or geography
. . . Heaven knows I'm no scholar, but even
I could teach him quite a lot."

"Is he an intelligent pupil?" inquired
Dane gravely.

"Don't be horrid," Wynne adjured him.
"Don't be sarky, Dane. It doesn't suit you
a bit. I'm only going to teach him things
he *ought* to know — after all he's half
English, isn't he?"

"Yes," agreed Dane.

There was silence for a few moments and
then Wynne said, "But I didn't come here
to talk about Franz."

"I hoped you had come for a nice little

chat," Dane told her. "After all we haven't seen each other for about three weeks . . . "

Wynne shook her head.

He looked at her, his lips grave, but his eyes twinkling with amusement. "Well?" he inquired, "well, what can I do for you, Madam?"

"Tell me what you do?" she said, looking down into the smiling eyes. "I mean what sort of work. It's funny that I don't know, isn't it?"

"Not very," replied Dane, "because I don't work in the sense you mean. My father left me enough money to live on with reasonable comfort. It was extremely thoughtful of him, wasn't it?"

"But Dane — "

"So I'm able to live like a lily of the field," added Dane gravely.

"Lilies don't rush about all over the place like you do."

"They have roots," he replied immediately.

"I wish you'd be serious," said Wynne, "I wish you'd answer properly — what do you *do*?"

He laughed. "That's rather a large question, isn't it? Let me see . . . I eat and sleep and talk. Sometimes I listen to other people talking."

"Dane!"

"Why this sudden interest in my doings?"

"It was something Franz said," she replied. "He asked what you did, what sort of work. I don't know what to say."

"Tell him I encumber the earth."

"But it wouldn't be true."

"No, it wouldn't really. Anyone who has to look after you and Sophie has a full-time job. I suppose you want me to come and see Soot's kitten's don't you?"

"Oh, Dane, you won't drown them, will you?" she cried, jumping off the table and standing in front of him with her head thrown back. "Dane, promise . . . I won't show you where they are unless you promise. Ellis said he was going to drown them and I told him he must wait until you came home."

"We can't keep more than two . . . "

"But if I find homes for them . . . " cried Wynne, "if I can find *homes* . . . and they're so awfully sweet. Come and see them, Dane darling."

They went out together to look at the

kittens, and Wynne did not remember until afterwards that her question had remained unanswered.

CHAPTER FIVE

THE education of Franz, which had been undertaken so blithely by his cousin, proceeded smoothly and rapidly. Wynne had said that it would be fun to have someone "different" and she found that it *was* fun. She enjoyed showing him everything and hearing his comments, for his comments were unusual to say the least of it. Wynne advised him about his clothes, corrected his speech and ordered his goings out and his comings in — it was rather like having a very large child to look after. She had discovered that he was sensitive and easily hurt, and because she had a kind heart, this endeared him to her. He was so solemn himself that he was suspicious of the smiles of others and often imagined that people were making fun of him when they had no intention of doing so. If he happened to make a "gaffe" he was miserable for hours and would return to the subject again and again with apologies and excuses. Wynne took him to a cricket match and tried to

61

instruct him in the intricacies of the game. He went with her to several tennis parties and acquitted himself very creditably. She introduced him to all her friends, taking care to explain beforehand who they were and so to smooth his path.

The Corbetts lived next door at a house called Cherry Trees. Franz had not met Mr. and Mrs. Corbett, but he had seen quite a lot of the young Corbetts for they were constant visitors at Fernacres. Miss Corbett — or Nina — was a thin dark girl, very pretty and amusing, and Migs, her brother, was tall and dark with an olive skin and lazy brown eyes. On the other side of Fernacres there was a small but very attractive bungalow which was occupied by a young married couple called Winslow. There were the Audleys who lived in the big stone house which Wynne had pointed out to Franz on the way from the station, and there was Ian Sutherland, a stocky fair-haired youth, who owned a racing model and a large white bull-terrier with a ragged ear. There were other people besides these, of course. People who rang up on the telephone or drifted in; and there was Roy Braithwaite whose ship had come into Kingsport and who appeared suddenly and unexpectedly at irregular intervals and brought various naval friends to tennis and tea. All these people were very kind to Franz but he did not feel at home with them. They seemed so young; they were so childish and gay and inconsequent; they strolled through life as though the world were made for them — as though they had nothing to do but amuse themselves and each other. Franz was very grave and silent. He listened to their chatter but did not join in it. The fact was he could not make them out. He understood what they said but he could not understand their real meaning. It was not that they used long words (as Wynne had said, they used the shortest and simplest words possible) but the words as used by them seemed to have a different meaning from that given by the dictionary. This was very difficult for Franz and it puzzled him a good deal, but it was not his only difficulty.

One day at tea Mark Audley announced that he was getting up a small dance — "just a few couples and the radiogram."

"Oh, Mark, how lovely!" exclaimed Wynne.

Mark looked at her gravely. "But we don't want *you*," he declared in a perfectly serious voice. "I mean, we decided from the very beginning . . . I said to Claire, 'we don't want Wynne, do we ?' and she agreed that we didn't. I'm awfully sorry about it, Wynne."

"Horrid of you," declared Wynne. "Just simple horrid . . . and I thought you were rather nice. No brains, of course, but rather nice all the same . . . but I don't mind a bit about the dance. Franz will take me to the pictures, won't you, Franz ?"

Franz replied at once that he would be delighted to take her to the pictures. He thought it was extremely unkind of the Audleys not to want Wynne, and he could not understand why Wynne was not offended. However, that was none of his business. He made up his mind to be as nice as possible to Wynne to make up for her disappointment. He would take her to Kingsport and they would dine together at the big hotel and go to the pictures afterwards — it should be a gala night and perhaps Wynne would enjoy it even more than if she had been invited to the dance.

There was no opportunity to discuss his

plans with Wynne that night, but the following morning he sought her out and issued his invitation. "It will give me great pleasure," said Franz in a solemn voice, "it will give me great pleasure if you will dine with me tonight. I will telephone and order a nice dinner at the Grand Hotel and afterwards we will go to the Picture House. I see in the newspaper that Norma Shearer is there, and it says the film is very good."

"Oh Franz, how darling of you!" exclaimed Wynne, looking up at him with her friendly blue eyes. "How perfectly sweet of you to think of it and plan it all out like that — but we can't go *tonight*, you know, because of the Audley's dance. They'd be frightfully upset if we cried off at the last minute."

"B-b-but you were not asked," stammered Franz.

"Not asked?" echoed Wynne in surprise.

"You were not asked," repeated Franz, flushing to his ears with embarrassment. "Mr. Mark Audley said . . . he said . . ."

"Oh, but he didn't mean it," explained Wynne, laughing at the absurdity of the idea. "Poor Franz, did you really think he meant that he didn't want us?"

"He said . . . "

"Yes I know, but that was just his way of *asking* us."

Franz looked at her in bewilderment. "But how do you know?" he inquired. "If Mr. Audley says one thing and means something else how do you know which he means?"

Wynne found this question difficult to answer. "Well, of course they want us," she said, "I mean — well — Mark wouldn't have said all that if he hadn't wanted us, would he? But it was really awfully sweet and kind of you to think of dinner at Kingsport. We'll go another night, shall we?"

"Yes," said Franz in a dazed voice, "yes, we will go another night."

He was even more bewildered when, later in the day, he found that Wynne expected him to accompany her to the Audleys' dance. "But they did not ask me," he objected. "Mr. Audley did not mention me at all . . . he did not say I was to come or not to come and perhaps he will not want me. I do not like to come where I am not wanted."

"Nonsense," said Wynne. "They know

quite well that I wouldn't go without you. Of course they want you to come — how could they possibly *not* want you, Franz, dear? Go and get dressed now or you'll be late for dinner — just your dinner jacket and a black tie."

He went reluctantly and dressed as he was told.

Contrary to his expectations, Franz enjoyed the Audleys' dance very much indeed. He danced well in his solemn and somewhat stately fashion and he soon became aware that he was extremely popular. There were too few girls to go round but Franz always secured a partner.

Wynne watched him a little anxiously at first for she did not want him to make any of the funny little mistakes which, to him, were neither small nor humorous, but soon she saw that there was no need to worry, her child was doing splendidly.

"He's so *funny*," said Nina, as the two girls stood together for a moment. "He's so serious and polite. It's amusing to have someone quite different, isn't it?"

"Yes," said Wynne.

"And he's rather a dear, too," added

Nina, as she was whirled away in Mark Audley's arms.

Claire Audley had just come home from Munich where she had been studying music and she was anxious to air her German. She succeeded in catching Franz and bore him off in triumph to the little room which had been set apart for refreshments. Franz was quite pleased to talk German to this pretty girl who smiled at him so attractively, and once he had started he found it very easy to go on. Claire was older than the others and had seen more of the world. He understood Claire better than the others — much better.

"It's wonderful," she was saying. "I have always wanted to study music, but I never expected to be able to go abroad and study seriously. I am going back again next winter, and after that I hope to get a post — a post in an orchestra — perhaps in the B.B.C."

"That is good," declared Franz, "that is excellent. In my country, as you know, we think it right that everyone should have a career."

"I suppose you think that everyone here is idle?" inquired Claire.

"Most of them are. They amuse themselves all day."

Claire shook her head. "You don't understand," she told him. "My sisters and Wynne and Nina and all of them are not idle in the way you think. In Germany all the social work is in government control. but here it is different. Britain is fortunate in possessing a large unpaid army of social workers."

Franz was interested; he inquired what sort of work was done, and Claire explained that there were Youth Movements here, much as there were in Germany, but that they were run with voluntary staffs. There were organisations such as the Boy Scouts and the Girl Guides; there were clubs for mothers and babies, and the large charitable schemes had unpaid presidents and secretaries.

"What does Wynne do?" asked Franz somewhat incredulously.

"Girl Guides," replied Claire. "She took them over from me when I went to Germany and she is doing very good work. The girls all love her. She has a tremendous influence over them," added Claire earnestly.

"Wynne ?"

"Yes, *Wynne*," said Claire more earnestly still. "She is much better with them than I was — perhaps I was a little too interested in my music to make a good captain — Wynne is not such a butterfly as she looks . . . "

There was no time for any more serious conversation (and Franz was sorry for there were many questions he would have liked to ask) the refreshment room was suddenly invaded by a throng of people clamouring for "something cool to drink".

"Who's finished all the hock-cup ?" inquired Mark Audley, turning an empty jug upside down. "Claire, how could you ?"

"Not guilty!" retorted Claire, laughing at his disappointed expression. "Not guilty, Mark . . . Oh, Mark, you are a fool, you've got the wrong jug. There was water in that jug."

"Water!" he exclaimed. "What for ? Somebody been having a bath ?"

"Not you, darling of course," Claire retorted.

"What d'you mean — eh ?"

"Didn't wash behind the ears, did you,

my pet?" she inquired, and she seized her brother by an ear and examined it with an assumption of disgust.

There was a scuffle and a good deal of laughter and shouts of, "Good old Mark!" and "Go it Claire!" as the guests took sides. For a few moments the room was like bedlam with Mark and Claire the principal maniacs . . . and then, quite suddenly the play was finished and done with and everyone had stopped laughing and was perfectly quiet and sane. Mark picked up a chair which had been knocked over and set it upon its legs and Claire produced her powder puff and a comb.

"Oh dear, what a life!" she said, as she powdered her nose. "Who would have brothers?"

"Who would have sisters if they could help it?" retorted Mark, taking Claire's comb out of her somewhat unwilling hand and using it to arrange his own disordered locks.

Franz had looked on and listened to the whole affair with amazement . . . once more he was left standing at the post. At one moment Claire had been a quiet, sensible young woman discussing her career, and dilating upon social conditions with a good deal of knowledge and acumen, and the next moment, without the slightest warning, she had changed into a boisterous school-girl . . . what could you make of people who behaved like that ?

"You enjoyed it, didn't you ?" inquired Wynne, as the two of them walked home together arm in arm in the starry darkness.

"Yes," said Franz gravely, "yes, it was on the whole, a very enjoyable evening . . . I behaved myself rightly, I hope ?"

"I was proud of you," declared Wynne, giving his arm a little squeeze. "You were a tremendous success, Franz."

Franz said nothing but there was a warm glow in his heart as he took the latch key from Wynne and opened the door for her . . . it was nice that Wynne had been proud of him.

CHAPTER SIX

IN SPITE of his mixed parentage Franz was endowed with a full measure of German thoroughness and industry, and, having decided that there was much more to learn about his new friends than he had imagined, he cast about for the best way to go about his task. He decided to ask the advice of Major Worthington and the next morning after breakfast he pursued Major Worthington to his sitting-room in the west wing and broached the subject without waste of time.

"I wish to study," declared Franz. "I could study for two hours every morning without interfering with the rest of the day. It is essential that I should make the most of my opportunities."

"Yes," agreed Dane, hiding a smile. "Perhaps you'd like me to engage a tutor for you. We could probably get someone in Kingsport who would be glad of the job."

Franz considered this. "I do not think it necessary," he said at last, "but if you would be so kind as to give me some books to read . . ."

"Books about the political situation?"

"No," said Franz, "no, I think I should study the mentality of the British people first. One should understand the mentality of a people before their politics."

Dane looked at him with some surprise, and his desire to smile vanished. "Why of course you're right," he said, "you're absolutely right . . . it would save a great deal of misunderstanding if more of your fellow countrymen shared your views."

"I have begun to see that," said Franz gravely.

Dane walked up and down the room once or twice. He seemed to be debating some point with himself and finding difficulty in coming to a conclusion. At last he said, "You've come here to have a look at us, haven't you?"

"I have come to visit my English relatives and to learn the language."

"Yes," agreed Dane, "and to have a good look at us as well."

Franz did not reply for a moment or two and then he said, "A good look! I do not understand that term. Naturally I look at the English people when I am here. What else should I do, Major Worthington ?"

"It would be interesting to know what you make of us," said Dane, smiling at him.

Franz was silent — for the question was difficult — and Dane, after a moment's hesitation, decided not to press the point.

"Well, what about these books ?" he inquired. "What sort of books would you like ?"

"Books about people, please."

Dane thought it was a good choice. He searched his shelves and, discovering a set of Galsworthy, he chose a couple of books at random and gave them to Franz.

It was a set of Galsworthy which Wynne had given Dane for Christmas and the books were large and beautifully bound in tooled leather and printed on thick paper. The appearance of the books impressed Franz greatly, he accepted them with delight and assured Major Worthington that he would use them with the greatest care. Then he retired to the drawing-room, which was empty at this hour of the morning, and settling himself in an easy-chair he began to read. Fortunately he had read a great deal of English so Galsworthy presented no difficulties to him and he scarcely required the aid of the dictionary with which he had armed himself.

The room was quiet save for the clock which ticked away unobtrusively upon the mantelpiece; the sun shone in through the open french windows. Franz read on industriously. Sometimes he raised his eyes from the book and thought about what he had read and looked round the pretty room . . . it was just the sort of room that the people in the book had lived in, and indeed Fernacres was just the sort of house . . . it was a house which seemed at home in that pleasant English country. The rooms were well-shaped and well-lighted, they were bright and pretty and extremely comfortable. Fires burnt cheerfully in the brightly polished grates — fires of good coal and fragrant smelling logs; there were comfortable chairs and sofas in flowery chintz coverings; there were tables with vases of flowers and ornaments; there were pictures on the cream coloured walls — not particularly valuable pictures, perhaps, but good enough to give pleasure to the most fastidious eye. There were pretty carpets, good china, and an abundance of excellent food; there were magazines and papers and books lying about, and boxes of cigarettes for anyone who wanted them . . . there was all this, but above all there was peace. *Peace*, thought Franz, peace and happiness — yes, that was really the keynote of Fernacres.

The house was like the house in the book in other ways too . . . in the free and easy life of its inhabitants, for instance. People came and went, arranging tennis, or other kinds of amusement, chatting, planning, drinking a glass of sherry or a cup of tea and drifting away again . . . their comings and goings did not interfere with that fundamental peace but seemed in some strange way to intensify it.

Franz was making good progress with his book when suddenly the drawing-room door opened and Barber, the parlourmaid, looked in. She did not see Franz for he was sitting with his back to the door, but Franz could see her reflected in the mirror over the mantelpiece.

"No," said Barber, speaking to some person not yet visible to Franz. "No, Miss

Wynne doesn't seem to be here. If you'll just go in and wait a minute I'll see if she's in the garden. She can't be far away."

"Look sharp about it, then," replied a deep gruff voice.

The door opened wider and in walked a large policeman, followed by another, slightly smaller. They stood in the middle of the pretty room, big and bulky in their imposing uniforms, and poor Franz was so terrified at the sight of them and at the implications of their unexpected visit that for a few moments he was glued to his chair. Then, summoning all his courage he leapt to his feet.

"Hullo!" said the larger of the two policemen. "We're not disturbing you, I hope . . . didn't see you just at first. Perhaps you know where Miss Braithwaite is — it's her we want."

"Miss Braithwaite is out," declared Franz.

"The maid said she wouldn't be far away."

"She's out," repeated Franz. "She went out some time ago and she won't be back for a long time . . ."

"Out is she?" said the large policeman,

taking his handkerchief from his pocket and wiping his large red face. "Well, that's a pity. We wanted to see her most particular."

"Yes, she's out," repeated poor Franz — it was the only thing he could think of to say — "She's out . . . and I'm afraid it would be no use for you to wait. We do not know when she will be home."

He tried to edge the man towards the door as he spoke but the man would not budge an inch. His enormous feet seemed rooted into the moss green carpet.

"We'll wait a minute or two," the policeman said. "We're in no special hurry . . . the maid said she hadn't gone out, so perhaps you're mistaken. It would be a pity if we had to come all this way again . . ."

"What do you want Miss Braithwaite for?" inquired Franz in desperation.

The large policeman winked. "Oh, what do we want her for!" he said. "That would be telling, wouldn't it, sir? People that are wanted by the police are sometimes wanted pretty badly."

Franz gazed at him in dismay and his heart thudded violently. What could Wynne have done to have fallen foul of the police? He had heard her utter the most alarming and subversive statements, of course, but everybody in this extraordinary country seemed to make a habit of abusing their Government, and he had been told that complete freedom of speech was allowed. What did they intend to do with her? He tried to remember whether there were concentration camps in England . . . but the important thing was to get these men out of the house . . . to warn Wynne . . . would Barber have the sense to warn her?

"She's out," said Franz again, trying to speak in normal tones. "Miss Braithwaite has gone out. She will not be back for hours . . . perhaps it would be better if you left a message. I will tell her when she comes in."

"I'd rather see Miss Braithwaite herself," replied the policeman. "If I can't get hold of her now I'll have to come back . . . Ah, here she is!" he added, and a satisfied smile spread itself over his large red face. "Here's Miss Braithwaite, herself. That's good."

Franz swung round and saw his cousin standing at the french windows with

Barber behind her on the path . . . so Barber had not warned her . . . and there was nothing that he could do . . . the wild beating of his heart almost choked him.

"Yes," said Wynne, coming forward with a smile, "yes, here I am . . . so you've found me out, have you?"

The policeman grinned. "We've found you out," he agreed. "We always get our man sooner or later — slow but sure's our motto — the game's up, I'm afraid . . . and best come quietly. It's the cells for you this time and bread and water for a week . . ."

Wynne seemed quite unmoved by these threats. She perched herself on the table in her favourite attitude. "Have I *really* done anything frightful?" she inquired in an interested voice. "I can't remember anything at the moment."

"No, Miss," he replied. "You haven't done anything that I know of . . . not since the time you knocked me down in the High Street . . ."

"Oh, Sergeant White!" cried Wynne reproachfully, "you know it was an accident and you know how terribly upset I was . . ."

"Not so upset as me," put in the policeman with a chuckle.

". . . and I thought you'd forgiven and forgotten *long* ago," added Wynne, looking at him with large sorrowful eyes.

"Forgiven but not forgotten," he replied, still chuckling, "forgiven but *not* forgotten . . . and not likely to. Even if I was to forget, nobody else would. It'll take me the rest of my life to live it down."

"How's Mrs. White?" Wynne inquired, changing the subject somewhat abruptly.

"Very well, thank you," he replied, "and the baby's doing splendid. Perhaps you'd look in and see them if you happen to be down our way. Mrs. White would take it very kindly."

"I'll go tomorrow," she declared. "I'd love to see the baby. Is it like you?"

There was a smothered chuckle from the younger policeman who had been completely silent until now.

"What's the joke, Wallis?" inquired Sergeant White, turning on his assistant with ferocious mien.

"Nothing, sir," replied Wallis quickly, "bit of a cough, I've got — that's all."

"You'd better get some cough mixture, then."

"Yes, sir," agreed Wallis, turning away and coughing in a strained sort of manner behind his hand.

"Cough mixture," repeated Sergeant White vindictively. "Nasty tasting cough mixture, that's what you need . . . but I'll see to that afterwards."

Wynne evidently thought that it was time to change the subject again. "I wonder if Mrs. White would like a dear little kitten?" she inquired with a ravishing smile."

"A kitten, Miss?"

"Yes, a *dear* little kitten," said Wynne persuasively. "I could take it to her tomorrow in a basket. It would be so nice for the baby to play with when he's a little older."

"Well, Miss . . ." began the sergeant doubtfully. "Well, Miss, to tell the truth Mrs. White's pretty busy just now. The baby takes up a good deal of time, you see, and I don't really know . . ."

"It's a *darling* kitten," declared Wynne. "It's all black with a sweet little white waistcoat. Nobody could help loving it and later on, when it's a little older, it would catch all your mice."

"Yes," agreed Sergeant White, "yes, I daresay, but you see . . ."

"It wouldn't be any bother at *all*," Wynne declared.

"No, Miss, but . . ."

"I'll take it anyhow," said Wynne. "I shall take it down in a basket and if Mrs. White doesn't like it I can bring it back. That will be much the best plan . . . have a cigarette."

"No thank you, Miss. I always smoke a pipe."

"Have some tobacco then," suggested Wynne hospitably, and she lifted Dane's special jar of tobacco off the mantelpiece and pressed a fill of the mixture on each of her visitors.

They were both a little doubtful about the acceptance of this, but Wynne would take no denial, so the two pipes were filled and put away to be smoked at a more convenient hour.

"Well, Miss," said the sergeant at last, "we mustn't waste any more of your time. It's really about the parking. You know that corner by the Memorial where you always park? Well, we've got orders there's to be no more parking there in future."

"Oh, what a nuisance!" Wynne said. "*Why* have you made such a silly rule — I've *always* parked there."

"It's orders," he explained in apologetic tones. "They're tightening up parking everywhere, and I thought I'd better give you the tip in case you didn't happen to see the notice."

"I shall just go on parking there," declared Wynne mutinously. "It may be orders, but they're silly orders. It isn't in anyone's way and it's much the most convenient place."

"Well . . ." said the sergeant uncomfortably, "well, Miss, I hope you won't. It's orders . . . and if you did happen to park there . . . well then, your number would have to be taken and that would be a pity, wouldn't it?"

"You mean you'd take it?" Wynne inquired incredulously.

"I'd have to," replied the unfortunate man, "I'd have to take it if I happened to come round that way and your car was there. I wouldn't have no option but to take it."

"I never heard such rot!"

"You can park farther on," Sergeant

White pointed out in a persuasive voice, "you can park in Fargo Lane — that's a nice quiet place for parking, isn't it? . . . and it would be just as convenient for the shops."

Wynne was quite a reasonable sort of person, so she realised that there was no help for it. "Oh well," she said, "I daresay Fargo Lane would suit me just as well."

"It isn't *us*," continued Sergeant White earnestly, "it isn't us that make the rules about parking. It's just orders, that's what it is, I'm very sorry, I'm sure . . ."

Wynne accepted the apology and assured him that she held him blameless in the matter, but she continued to inveigh against his superiors in a manner that made Franz's blood run cold.

"What fools they are!" she said. "Why can't they leave people in peace? Why are they always badgering people like this? Of course I see it isn't *your* fault," she added generously, as she accompanied her visitors into the hall, "and it was really very nice of you to come up and explain about it . . . I hope I shan't forget . . . I hope to goodness I shan't forget and park there as usual. I've always parked there, you see . . ."

"If you do happen to forget I daresay a lenient view might be taken . . ." boomed Sergeant White's deep bass voice. "After all you always *have* parked there . . ."

Franz sat down in his chair rather suddenly. His knees felt like brown paper and there were beads of moisture on his forehead. He was wiping them off with his handkerchief when Wynne came back into the room.

"They've gone," she said, smiling at him. "What did you think of our policemen, Franz? Aren't they pets? . . . Why Franz, what's the matter? Aren't you feeling well?"

"It is nothing," replied Franz hastily, "nothing at all, Wynne. I thought for a moment . . . but it was a foolish thought . . . things are different here."

"I suppose they are," agreed Wynne in a thoughtful voice. "It must be very hard for you to get used to things here. I suppose *everything* is different. I suppose even policemen are quite different here from what they are in Germany."

"Yes," said Franz, "yes . . . policemen are . . . quite different."

CHAPTER SEVEN

AS DANE had guessed, Otto von Heiden had sent his son to England with an ulterior motive, and not merely for a pleasant holiday. Von Heiden was a highly placed official in the Nazi Party, and he had the interests of his party at heart. He was a far-sighted man and it seemed to him that it might be extremely useful to have first-hand information as to the feelings of the better-class British people and their reaction to Germany's policy. He saw that his son was exactly the right person to carry out his idea — Franz was young, of course, but he was very intelligent, he spoke English well and, best of all, he possessed those English relatives at Chellford. It would be quite natural for Franz to go and stay with them for a bit and they would talk more freely before a member of their family, so Franz would find out exactly what they felt about things. There was no question of spying, of course — Germany had plenty of spies — von Heiden did not want to know about armaments or ships or anything like that. He wanted Franz to put his finger on the pulse of the people, that was all (von Heiden had always disliked his wife's relations, but that was not the point — the point was that they could be made use of). The idea was well received by his superiors and Franz was sent for and given his instructions. Von Heiden added to these instructions in private and impressed Franz with the importance of his mission. Franz listened and agreed and promised to carry out his father's plan — he was excited and proud of the responsibility with which he was being entrusted.

"Remember," said von Heiden, as he saw his son off at the airport. "Remember that this is just a private visit to your mother's relatives. You will talk with them and discuss with them and what more natural than that you should write to me, your father, and tell me what things they say ?"

Franz understood perfectly.

So it was that Franz came to England, and came with the firm intention of carrying out his instructions to the best of his ability. He had expected to be involved in long arguments about World Affairs, arguments in which he would take his share, explaining and expounding the doctrine of the Nazis in which he had been bred. He had expected that he would have to explain the necessity of the Austrian Anschluss, which had just taken place, and to justify it if necessary . . . but the days went past and no arguments of any description eventuated. He began to think that these people were uninterested in World Affairs — or were they deliberately avoiding all controversial subjects when he was present? He could not tell, but whichever it was the fact remained — and how could he accomplish his mission unless they could be persuaded to air their views and discuss things with him?

Franz had written to his father on arrival, and had written again a week later, and in both these letters he had to apologise for the absence of information. He had assured his father that he was doing his best, but that he found his English relatives difficult to understand, and had expressed the conviction that he would soon be in a position to send the information required.

The nearest approach to a discussion upon World Affairs took place when Franz had been at Fernacres for about a fortnight. He and Wynne and Migs Corbett were sitting under a tree in Fernacres garden watching a tennis match. The garden was now in full bloom, the grass was beautifully green, beyond the lawn was a herbaceous border — a mass of colour outlined against the dark foliage of an ilex hedge. There were antirrhinum of all shades of pink and yellow and there were lupins and long graceful spikes of delphinium, and at either side of the steps which led downwards into the wood, there were masses of mauve and white aubrietia. The garden was large and well-designed — there were other houses quite near of course, but they were screened by trees and it was only in the winter when the trees were bare that a chimney-pot here, or a corner of masonry there, or an angle of gable showed that Fernacres was situated in a residential area and not in the depths of the country. Although the afternoon was warm, it was cool in the shade of the fine old tree and extremely peaceful, but Franz did not feel at peace. He was worrying about his third letter to his father which should have been written yesterday and which was still absolutely non-existent. He had no information at all, and he shrank from the task of elaborating more excuses for his failure to procure it. He decided that he must make an effort to promote a discussion and sitting up suddenly he began to talk about encirclement. It was not very easy to talk to Migs Corbett, for Migs was lying back in his long chair with his hat tilted over his eyes but Franz persisted in his endeavours to interest Migs in this vital subject and at last Migs responded.

"But that's the worst of living in a round world, old boy," he said.

"A round world!" echoed Franz in amazement.

"We're all encircled," exclaimed Migs, waving his hand in an airy manner. "We've all got people living all round us — bound to have, you know. Wasn't it Bismarck who discovered it first?"

"Discovered what?"

"I mean he made that point about encirclement."

Franz did not reply. The finer points of Chancellor Bismarck's policy had not been considered a necessary point of education.

"Clever chap, Bismarck," continued Migs in a ruminative voice. "I forget what he said exactly, but I have a feeling he was a bit anxious about encirclement." Migs shut his eyes, and his voice became more drowsy than usual. "You know all about it, of course . . . never really studied the question, myself."

Franz had always believed — indeed he had been taught to believe — that encirclement was a new danger discovered by his Leader. It seemed strange that nobody had seen fit to instruct him in the pronouncements of Bismarck . . . it seemed even stranger that Migs should know more about it than he — *Migs* of all people! Franz had formed a very low opinion of Migs Corbett for he was the living antithesis of everything that Franz had been taught to admire. He played no games, he took no exercise and, as far as Franz could see, he did nothing at all to justify his existence. He lay about in a deck chair and smoked cigarettes and expected everyone to fetch and carry for him . . . and strangely enough they did it. Yes, even Wynne was ready to fetch a cigarette for

Migs and to put it in his mouth and light it for him.

"As far as I can remember," continued Migs in that sleepy voice which Franz had grown to dislike so intensely, "as far as I can remember Bismarck took a great deal of trouble to make friends with his neighbours, the idea being that nobody minds being surrounded by friends. Encirclement doesn't worry you, does it, Wynne?"

"What d'you mean?" Wynne inquired.

"Ivy Lodge on the east . . . Cherry Trees on the west," explained Migs. "You don't mind, do you?"

"No," agreed Wynne. "No, I like it, really. It's only when horrid people like the Pages come — you know they've bought the Red House — that you begin to feel a bit hemmed in."

"Make friends with the Pages, darling," murmured Migs. "The Pages must have their good points . . . find them out . . . establish contact (even if it means that you have to fondle their Pekes). That's what old Bismarck did, and believe me there were no flies on old Bismarck."

"I believe it might be quite a good plan," agreed Wynne thoughtfully.

Franz decided not to report this extraordinary conversation to his father, partly because he was aware that his father would not understand it, and partly because his own share in the discussion had been so feeble. He realised that the reason he had not been able to stand up to Migs was simply that Migs knew more about the subject than he did . . . there was something wrong here, decided Franz.

They were still sitting under the tree and Franz was still meditating upon his difficulties when an incredibly ancient and battered car drove in at the gate and Roy Braithwaite leapt out, followed more slowly by his friend and shipmate Harry Coles. Franz had met these two young men before. They were officers in the British Navy and therefore were entitled to respect; they behaved like schoolboys of course, but Franz made allowances for them.

"Oh, Roy, how splendid!" exclaimed Wynne, rushing to her brother and hugging him ecstatically. "I was just wondering if you'd come today. How long have you got?"

"Till tomorrow night," replied Roy.

"That's all, but it's better than nothing, isn't it? Could we have somebody in to dance?"

"Of course we could — Nina, and the Audleys — darling Roy, it's so lovely to see you."

"You saw me the day before yesterday."

"I know, but it seems ages."

She stood and looked at him with her heart in her eyes for, to Wynne, Roy was the pink of perfection. She had always thought that if she ever married it would have to be somebody like Roy — only of course there was nobody like Roy, that was the trouble — he was so big and ruddy and smiling, he could share her thoughts and feelings and could laugh at the same absurd jokes. She had loved and admired Roy ever since she could remember; she had always followed his lead and had been greedy for his approbation; she had climbed trees and jumped ditches and had hidden her fear of cows so that he might not despise her . . . Wynne had never minded what she did if only Roy would let her play with him.

"Harry got leave, too," continued Roy, waving casually towards his friend, "so I brought him along — or rather he brought me. That strange contraption belongs to Harry's brother, we're not quite sure what he'll say when he finds he's lent it to us."

"He'll be as sick as mud," remarked Harry cheerfully.

"I'm *sure* he won't mind," declared Wynne. "He isn't using it himself, and you haven't done it any harm at all."

"Not yet," agreed Harry. "As a matter of fact it would be difficult to do it any harm — one dent more or less wouldn't be noticed — but the thing is I bust up his last car for him so he isn't too keen on lending me Agatha. It's silly of course. I can drive much better now (can't I Roy?) but he's prejudiced, I'm afraid."

"Why does he call it Agatha?" inquired Wynne with interest.

"I can't think," declared Harry, "unless it's after some girl or other . . . but I never heard of *anyone* being called Agatha, did you?"

Wynne had not — but she had never seen a car like this, so perhaps that was the explanation. She was beginning to put this somewhat abstruse idea into words when Roy interrupted her.

"Look here," he said, "I'd better get hold of Sophie — will there be a bed for Harry or will he have to sleep on the floor?"

"Anywhere at *all* will do," declared Harry. "I mean I can sleep anywhere — "

"He can sleep anywhere," agreed Roy, "but the place he likes best is the bridge of the Terrible on a cold, foggy night . . ."

"Shut up," said Harry. "That was only once, and I wasn't really asleep at all. I had shut my eyes for a moment because the fog made them prickle . . . you know how it does."

"It will be perfectly all right," Wynne assured them, "I'll find Sophie, and tell her, and arrange *everything*. Harry can have the divan bed thing that we got at Harrods. We'll put it in your room. It's quite comfy because I slept in it myself when Wendy was here . . . or you can sleep in it and let Harry have your bed . . ." she hurried away to make the arrangements and Roy and his friend sat down.

"What a fuss there was!" said Roy, accepting a cigarette from Migs and lighting it with a flick from his pocket-lighter. "Old Harvey gave us leave and Weller was in the most awful rage about it. You know Weller, don't you, Migs?"

"Knew his brother," replied Migs laconically.

"Weller's a most awful swine," declared Harry. "He never wants any leave himself and he doesn't see why anyone else should have it. There he sits like a — like a spider or something — "

"He's more like a cat, I think," objected Roy. "One of those pussyfoot creatures — I don't mean that he doesn't drink because as a matter of fact he puts more through his face than any man I've seen — but he creeps about snoopily on rubber soles . . . and pounces."

"Everybody hates Weller," said Harry.

"He'll get pushed into the sea some dark night if he doesn't look out."

"I'd push him myself for twopence."

The duet finished there, and a long silence ensued. The sun shone and the birds sang and the tennis players rushed about in strenuous combat. Franz ruminated upon what he had heard and wondered whether this was one of the items of interest which he ought to report to his father . . . disaffection in the British Navy

. . . but Franz was no fool and he was aware that people on the verge of mutiny did not usually proclaim the fact at the top of their voices, nor did murderers announce their intentions beforehand with such a cheerful air. . . .

Franz sighed. It was so difficult. What were these people really like inside? They made fun of everything, they insulted each other . . . and laughed; they reviled their superior officers and criticised their government and its administration. To Franz they were like people from another planet and the more he saw of them the more incompetent he was to understand them.

While Franz had been thinking over his problems the conversation had taken another turn.

"I saw you were at Buckingham Palace yesterday," remarked Roy. "How did you get on? Was George in good form?"

"Excellent form," replied Migs. "We had a little chat and I told him some bedtime stories. We parted the best of friends."

"But why — " began Franz, and then he stopped. For one thing nobody was listening to him and for another he did not wish to make a fool of himself. Perhaps he had misunderstood what was said, or perhaps this was one of the occasions when one thing was said and the opposite intended. It could not be true (that was certain) Mr. Corbett could not have been received by King George.

"Hullo!" said Roy. "The set's finished. D'you want to play, Franz?"

"No thank you," Franz replied, rising to his feet. "I have played enough. I think I will go in now."

He left the others to play another set and wandered into the drawing-room to find his hostess. Perhaps she would be able to help him. She was kind and he liked her. She puzzled him, of course, but puzzled him in a different way from his contemporaries . . .

Cousin Sophie welcomed him with a smile. "Have you had a nice game?" she inquired.

"Yes, thank you," Franz replied. "but now I have come to talk to you if you are not busy."

"Of course I'm not busy," declared Cousin Sophie. "I'm doing the bills, that's all, and I hate doing the bills; we'll have a nice little chat until the others come in for tea." She closed her desk with the bills inside and settled herself comfortably in an easy-chair. "What shall we talk about?" she inquired.

Some people might have found the question stultifying but Franz had plenty of material for conversation.

"I have difficulties," he declared. "There are many things I cannot understand. Sometimes things are said that are not true. I do not know what to believe and what not to believe."

"Not true!" echoed Sophie in horrified tones. "But Franz . . . do you mean they tell lies?"

"Not true," repeated Franz doggedly. "Perhaps it is not exactly lies, for nobody is deceived except me."

"I don't understand," declared Sophie hopelessly.

"No," agreed Franz. "It is very difficult. Sometimes they say a thing and it is true, and sometimes they say a thing and it is just the opposite and I cannot make out which it is."

"I don't understand," repeated Sophie more hopelessly than before.

"It is difficult to explain," said Franz, frowning with the effort involved, "but here is one thing, Cousin Sophie. Mr. Corbett has just been saying that he had an interview with your King."

"But he *did*," declared Sophie smiling with relief. "Dear Migs went up to town yesterday and was received by His Majesty at Buckingham Palace, That's *quite* true, Franz."

"It is true?" inquired Franz incredulously.

"Quite true," she nodded.

"That is . . . that is very strange," Franz said.

Sophie took no notice of this assertion, she continued as if she had not heard. "Migs is a Lieutenant in the Westshires — there have always been Corbetts in the Westshire Regiment. Mr. Corbett's brother commanded the 1st Battalion in the war, and *his* grandfather Sir Miguel Corbett, fought at Waterloo — so you see it was quite natural that Migs should go to the Westshires."

"Mr. Migs Corbett?" inquired Franz with the sudden conviction that somehow or other they were talking at cross purposes. "Do you really mean that he is an officer in your army?"

"Yes," said Sophie. "Why shouldn't he be?"

There were so many reasons why he shouldn't be that Franz was at a loss to enumerate them. He grasped at the most obvious. "Where is his uniform?" he inquired.

"It's probably packed away in a box," replied Sophie somewhat vaguely. "He wouldn't want to *wear* it, would he?"

"He wouldn't want to wear it!" echoed Franz in complete amazement.

"No," said Sophie, "no, it wouldn't be comfortable, and it would look so queer..."

"How could anyone know he was an officer?"

"Nobody could, of course, but that doesn't matter. I mean it's much nicer for Migs to wear cool, comfortable clothes when he's on sick leave. Of course he put on his uniform yesterday for the investiture," she hesitated and added, "I don't know if you understand that word, Franz — it means that His Majesty gave Migs the Military Cross."

Franz stared at her in dumb amazement.

"It was nice wasn't it?" she continued. "Poor Migs had such a dreadful time in Palestine — what with the heat and the flies and those terrible Arab Bandits — of course Migs never mentions the subject, but Mrs. Corbett told me all about it."

"I should like to hear about it," said Franz in a subdued voice.

"Would you? Of course Mrs. Corbett could tell you much better than I can, but I'll do my best," said Sophie modestly. She drew a long breath and began the tale. "It was in Palestine," she said. "I told you that, didn't I? Well, one day Migs was sent out with his company to escort a convoy. They weren't expecting trouble because the bandits had been fairly quiet for some time past, but, quite suddenly, when they were going through a narrow pass between some rocks, the bandits swooped down and attacked them. The captain, who was in command of the company, was killed in the first rush and Migs was badly wounded in the leg, but Migs got a man to help him on to a lorry and he fought on, firing at the bandits and encouraging his men. You see, Migs knew how important it was that the convoy should get safely through — it would have been dreadful if it had fallen into the hands of the bandits — it was food and stores and ammunition. They managed to hold off the attacks until reinforcements arrived and drove the bandits away. Poor Migs was very ill for weeks — he was taken to a big hospital at Alexandria — and at one time they thought he might have to lose his leg, but fortunately he's got a very good constitution and after a little his leg began to mend. They sent him home as soon as he was well enough to be moved and he recovered quite quickly. Of course he still has to rest a great deal and he mustn't get over-tired . . . so that was why he went up to town yesterday," said Sophie in a more cheerful tone, "and Mrs. Corbett told me that His Majesty talked to him very kindly and asked him all sorts of things about Palestine and the conditions there."

Franz was so dumbfounded at this tale that he was incapable of speech and, after a moment's pause, Sophie added, "You had better not say anything to Migs . . . he might be annoyed if he knew I'd told you."

"But he is a hero!" Franz exclaimed.

"Yes, I suppose he is," agreed Sophie in a surprised sort of voice, "yes, I suppose you might say he was a hero . . . but as a matter of fact people don't seem to think about it like that, they just do their duty, you see. They don't *like* a lot of fuss."

Franz considered this. "But Cousin Sophie . . ." he began, and then he hesitated. He had begun to realise that there was something here which might give him a clue to these incomprehensible people. He had been looking at them from a wrong angle. He had started with the conviction that Britain was a small cosy place where people lived in comfortable houses and amused themselves and each other. He had forgotten Britain's Empire. No nation could keep an Empire together by living comfortably and cosily at home . . . People like Migs Corbett guarded Britain's Empire. They left their comfortable homes thousands of miles behind them and fought and suffered in deserts under burning suns, and, because this was bred in their bone, they wanted no fuss. It was their duty, that was all.

We would do the same if we had colonies Franz told himself (it was a sore subject of course), but somehow Franz was aware that if a German youth had accomplished anything so spectacular he would enjoy the ensuing "fuss". He would be fêted and acclaimed, and would strut about in uniform with his decoration pinned to his breast for all the world to see.

"It is very strange," said Franz after a little pause, "it has given me a lot to think about, Cousin Sophie."

"Of course it *must* be strange," she agreed. "You must always come and ask me if anything puzzles you, Franz dear."

"Yes," agreed Franz, "thank you, Cousin Sophie, that will be very helpful to me."

"Ask me anything you like," she invited him. "Perhaps there's something else that you can't understand."

She hoped there was for she was enjoying their little chat. It was delightful to be able to explain things to Franz. Her family never came to her to have things explained, but only too often to explain things to her — and that was not nearly so pleasant.

"Yes, indeed," said Franz slowly. "There are many things that I do not understand." There were so many, that he did not know where to begin . . . he cast about in his mind and hit upon the problem of the "bearded pard". A bearded pard was a kind of leopard — so the dictionary said — but it was also the nickname of the chaplain of the Terrible. This chaplain had come over to lunch at Fernacres with Roy, and everyone — or at least all the younger members of the party — had called him the bearded pard, and had called him it to his face . . . and his face was round and fat and pink and as innocent of hair as the face of a two-year-old child.

"Why do they call Mr. Dickens the bearded pard?" inquired Franz gravely.

"Oh, that's a joke," replied Sophie, delighted to find that she could answer the question so easily, "because Mr. Dickens hasn't a beard you see — and of course he's the padre — so they call him the bearded pard."

"It is a joke," said Franz, considering it gravely.

"Yes," she agreed, "just a joke, that's all." She hesitated doubtfully. Now that she had explained it to Franz the joke seemed distinctly poor. She continued, "You see, Franz, when people are very young and happy everything seems a joke. I mean even silly jokes seem funny. It's because they're all so young . . . well, of course, you're young, too, but perhaps you aren't quite so happy."

"I am not unhappy," Franz said thoughtfully. He was not unhappy. Indeed he was much happier in this alien land than he had expected to be. "I am not at all unhappy," he repeated, "and I am not homesick as I had expected. Everyone is very kind and friendly. It is just that I cannot understand when it is a joke and when it is not — that is my chief difficulty. We have jokes, too, but they are quite different from your jokes. Even with you, Cousin Sophie, I am not always sure whether it is a joke or not."

"But I don't know, myself!" she declared. "I talk a lot and I usually mean to be quite, quite serious . . . and then, sometimes, I find I've made a joke, so how could you possibly know? I shouldn't worry about it if I were you."

"No, it is no use worrying."

"Talking helps," she continued in a thoughtful voice, "talking helps a lot if you don't quite know what you mean. It helps me to understand what I mean myself if I talk about it."

"But how — " asked Franz in bewilderment, "but Cousin Sophie, how can you talk at all unless you know what you mean?"

"I don't know," she replied, "I just know that I talk and then the thing comes clear . . . and, even if I don't understand it myself, Dane always understands. That's funny isn't it?"

He agreed that it was.

This conversation, though extremely muddling, helped Franz a good deal and he began to see a glimmer of light where before there had been fog and darkness. He saw that there was a great deal to understand so he was a step further on his way to understanding. He began to look at these people with new eyes and to listen even more attentively to all they said. There was Major Worthington, for instance, Major Worthington was apparently strong and well but he did not work and Franz had put him down as a *flaneur* and had despised him only a shade less than Migs Corbett, but now Franz saw that, as he had been so completely mistaken in the one case, he might be mistaken in the other. For all he knew to the contrary Major Worthington might be another hero in disguise. Franz began to ask discreet questions about Major Worthington and to study him with a good deal of care.

CHAPTER EIGHT

WHEN Roy returned to Fernacres for a spell of leave he seemed to be filled with positively dynamic energy. They played tennis all the afternoon, they danced until midnight, and the next morning at breakfast Roy was still full of vim.

"We'll bathe this morning, shall we?" he inquired, as he dug his spoon into his porridge and cream. "It's a lovely day and we must make the most of our time. Harry and I have got to be back at ten. We could bathe this morning and play tennis in the afternoon and then go on to the pictures. Who's for bathing?"

"It's a splendid idea," declared Wynne, who would have assented with equal fervour to any suggestion of Roy's.

"I think so too," agreed Franz.

"Absolutely O.K.," said Harry, "what time do we start? Where do we go? Is Agatha invited to join the party? She hasn't a bathing suit of course but I bet she can swim."

"Agatha would go to the bottom like a stone," said Roy quite seriously.

"She wouldn't."

"She would."

"I bet you," began Harry, and then he stopped, "oh, well," he said, "oh, well, it's no use betting because we couldn't try it out. I mean Jim would simply kill me if I ran Agatha into the sea. All the same I'm pretty certain she'd float, Roy."

"I'm pretty certain she wouldn't."

This was the sort of conversation that left Franz miles behind. He sat and gaped. They could not be serious in their desire to run the car into the sea and yet they seemed perfectly serious. Harry had now produced a piece of paper and a pencil and he was making careful calculations while Roy looked over his shoulder and objected or agreed. Even Major Worthington seemed interested in the problem of whether or not Agatha would be seaworthy.

"Her body is wood," Harry was saying, "and her wheels too . . . and she's the right shape you see."

"You'd have to know her weight to get at her displacement wouldn't you?" Dane inquired.

"It's her engine," Roy pointed out, putting a finger on the neat diagram which Harry had been making. "She'd go down by the bow, Harry."

Harry pushed the drawing away. His eyes were dreamy; "I've always wanted to make an amphibious car," he said, "what d'you think about it, Major Worthington?"

"There might be something in it," agreed Dane thoughtfully, "for military purposes, or for the colonies — and I believe Russia has been experimenting with an amphibious tank — "

"For *us*," Harry cried. "Don't you see, sir, it would be simply marvellous for *us*. If Agatha were amphibious. I could drive down to Kingsport and straight out to the Terrible. There would be no need to hang about on the quay waiting for the picket boat."

"What would you do with her when you got there?" Dane asked with a humorous lift of his brows.

"Garages on board," suggested Roy, who had begun to visualise the possibilities. "Garages, my boy, and a sort of shutter with a hinge to let down into the sea so that you could drive in."

"Or you could swing them up with derricks," Harry said.

"My idea's better," declared Roy. "Less trouble and more fun. Fancy driving your car straight out of the sea into the Terrible — gorgeous!"

Dane smiled. "There might be some difficulty about garage space," he pointed out, "if every N.O. had a car — "

"I knew there'd be a snag somewhere," said Roy, frowning, "there always is. The amphibious car is not for *us* — Oh, hell, you'd have to wait until you were a post captain at least before you could garage in the ship . . . That reminds me," he added in a different tone of voice, "by Jove I nearly forgot to tell you. The Majestic is coming to Kingsport."

This piece of news brought exclamations of delight from Sophie and Wynne; and Wynne, who was always thoughtful and kind, explained to Franz that Sophie's brother was the Admiral and that he would be sure to ask them to lunch on board.

There was a sudden silence after that and Roy, glancing at the clock, declared that it was high time they were under way. So the four young people rushed off and found their bathing suits and were issued with coloured bath towels and soon they were packed into the old battered car and were on their way to bathe.

They went through the village and along the cliff and then, turning off the main road into a narrow stony lane, they bumped along to a gate. Here they left Agatha and proceeded on foot down a steep path to the shore, and they found themselves in a sheltered cove where a barrier of high rocks stretched out into the sea.

"It's the best place, isn't it, Wynne?" said Roy. "We'll undress and sit in the sun until the spirit moves us to bathe. You can have the cave to undress in," he added generously.

They undressed and sat in the sun. It was sheltered and warm. The rocks were warm to lie on and there were tufts of sea pinks — cushiony tufts of grey, green grass with the flowers standing up on their thin, wiry stems. The sea was blue and purple and green in patches and there was a little fishing boat with a white sail tacking manfully against the breeze.

"She's nice, isn't she?" Roy said, break-

117

ing a little silence. "By Jove, everything's nice. I am happy."

"Summer is the best time," Wynne murmured dreamily. "If it was always summer, and you always had the people you liked best near you, it would be Heaven, wouldn't it ?"

Franz looked at her as she sat there, perched a little above him on a flat-topped rock, with her hand clasped round one knee and her profile outlined against the blue sky. He saw her long slender limbs, the bright gold of her fine silky hair, and the faded blue bathing suit which moulded her slight figure like a glove and he thought that she was the embodiment of summer and all that summer meant. Franz felt sure that she was unique, there was nobody so full of the joy of living, there was nobody so vital. She gave the whole of herself to whatever she was doing or saying and she had always more to give ... she was joy, thought Franz, joy and youth personified. He felt old compared with her, for he had seen so much sorrow and suffering; he had seen fear, too, and fear was ugly. Wynne did not know what sorrow was, Wynne was fearless and beautiful.

Franz felt sorry for himself in a vague sort of way because he realised that he had never been really young — in the way that Wynne was young. He had never been absolutely happy and carefree. Looking at her he caught glimpses of things that were very lovely and desirable, things that he thought existed only in songs and fairy tales . . .

"You're dreaming, Franz," said Roy's voice close to his ear. "What are you dreaming about?"

"He's dreaming about the girl he left behind him," declared Harry.

"No," said Franz smiling, "no, there is no girl that I left behind, I have not got a girl of my own yet."

"Tell us about Germany," said Roy, "tell us what you do — how you amuse yourselves and all that."

"It would not interest you."

"Of course it would interest us," said Roy eagerly. "It's frightfully interesting to hear about other countries. When I look at you and think of all the things you've seen — things that I've never seen and probably never will — it makes my brain reel."

"You have seen things that I have never seen," Franz pointed out.

"Go on," said Harry, "tell us about it. Tell us all about Germany."

It was a large order and Franz found it difficult to begin, but after a few minutes he warmed up to his task. His audience helped him a good deal for it was so appreciative and so interested and alert. It hung upon his words, it asked intelligent questions and it goaded him on when his tale began to flag. Franz, sitting on the warm rock, told these new friends of his all that he thought might interest them about his own country. He told them first about the German summer — the air was so much warmer, and the sun more deeply golden — he told them about the flowers, about the lilacs with their honey-sweet warm smell, and how every cottage garden was full of flowers and almost every house in every town had, at the very least, a window-box of gaily coloured blossoms. In the streets there were fruit trees growing, and in all the squares, so that wherever one went, there were flowers and the scent of flowers and the whole land seemed to grow drunk with their sweetness.

They clamoured for information about what he did, and Franz told them about the house in which he had been born and brought up. It was an apartment or — as his hearers realised — a sort of flat in one of the best districts of Freigarten. The rooms were large and somewhat bare in comparison with Fernacres, but they were cool in summer and were heated in winter by big porcelain stoves. "Tant' Anna" was the doyenne of the house, she had taken the place of a mother to Franz, and had devoted her life to him.

"She is old-fashioned a little," Franz declared, "she does not move with the times, and although she does not say so I believe she often thinks that the old times were better."

"Perhaps they were," suggested Roy.

"No," said Franz firmly, "no, we are much more happy now. Everything is better. You must not think that Tant' Anna complains or that she is not loyal to our Leader — we are all loyal and united — but sometimes when nobody is there I hear her singing the old songs, and afterwards she is sad."

He went on to tell them about the

neighbours who lived in the adjoining apartments — there were the Schneiders who lived below and the Von Oetzens who lived above. The Von Oetzens had no children of their own and they had always been very kind to Franz. They had taken a tremendous interest in all he did. Herr Von Oetzen's pockets were always full of sweets and he had never met Franz on the stairs without sharing them with the boy.

"I am afraid I was very greedy," declared Franz with a faraway smile. "I used to wait until I heard him coming down so that I should be sure to meet him — but it was not only for the sweets that I liked to meet him. He was always so kind to me, so *gemütlich*. It will be pleasant to see him again when I go home and to tell him all that I have seen."

"What about your own friends — I mean friends of your own age?" Roy inquired.

This started Franz off again — as had been intended — and he told them about the Wandervögel, the Youth Group to which he belonged. They were young men and girls (said Franz) who formed a sort of club and went for outings together, walking through the woods with their knapsacks on their backs or rowing upon the waters of the lazy German streams. The croaking of the frogs in the grass, the buzzing of the gnats as they drifted along in the flat-bottomed boats — all these things became clear to Franz as he spoke. He told of the camps on the banks of the rivers, of the tents with their swastika flags, and how they built their fires and cooked and feasted and bathed together and danced in the moonlight; and he told of the new Youth Songs which their leaders had taught them and which they sang as they marched, or as they sat round the camp-fire in the evening, taking parts, and filling the woods with harmony.

It all sounded very idyllic, and Franz was vaguely aware that he was making it sound a great deal more idyllic than it was. He was giving a slightly distorted impression of the Wandervögel Outings, an impression seen through rose-coloured spectacles. He had said nothing of the sordid side, of the intrigues, and jealousies and promiscuous love affairs which flourished like weeds in the hotbed of Nazi Youth. Franz had enjoyed the Outings until he began to discover what lay beneath the surface, but before he left home he had grown tired of them and faintly disgusted, and on several occasions he had made excuses to remain behind. He had grown a little tired of the Youth Songs, too, and had sometimes wished that they could sing some of the songs which had been loved and prized long before the Youth Songs were invented — the songs that Tant' Anna sang when she thought that nobody was listening — songs by Schubert and Brahms and Strauss, lovely melodies and words which touched the heart — but Franz had never dared to put this wish into words for his contemporaries would have laughed him to scorn.

These feelings of doubt and vague discontent were far below the surface, and indeed, if the truth were told, Franz had never before acknowledged them to himself. It was only now, when he looked back and saw it all in perspective, that he knew his own mind. He realised, as he spoke, and described the Wandervögel Outings in glowing terms, that Roy and Harry were made of different stuff — *he* had been faintly disgusted, but *they* would be horrified; *he* had been a trifle bored, but *they* would be bored to death.

"Gosh!" exclaimed Roy, "what tremendous fun! Gosh, why don't we have Outings like that? I'll tell you what, Franz, I'll come over to Germany my next long leave and you can take me on one of those Outings."

Franz looked at him in alarm. "But you would not like it, Roy."

"I wouldn't like it? You bet I would. Why, it must be simply grand."

"You would not like it," repeated Franz. "I know you would not like it . . . there are many reasons why you wouldn't like it at all."

"What reasons?"

"Many," repeated Franz, searching wildly to find at least one fairly presentable reason . . . "For one thing you would not like the discipline. You like doing what you like when you like it."

"He's right," put in Harry. "I thought it sounded absolutely grand, too, but I see what Franz means. These Outings are organised. They all bathe by numbers — one, two, three —"

"No," said Franz, "not quite like that, but we are not so free as you."

"I like to be free," Harry said thoughtfully; "I do what I'm told when I'm on duty but my off-duty time is my own, and I'll take good care that nobody interferes with it."

"It is better to be organised — " began Franz.

"No," interrupted Harry firmly, "no, it isn't . . . nobody can organise me in my off-duty time — not even the First Lord himself. If he were to come down that path," said Harry more firmly than ever, "if he were to come walking down that path and tried to start organising me, I'd show him where he got off."

"Don't be an ass," said Roy.

"I'm not an ass," retorted Harry. "You always say I'm an ass if you can't understand what I mean. There's a very deep meaning here . . . listen, Roy."

"I'm listening."

"Well, look here, I'm going to bathe in a minute — I shall climb out along those rocks and take a header into that lovely green water. I'm looking forward to it with every bit of me. I'm just waiting for the exact moment when I shan't be able to resist it any longer, but — mark this, Roy, because this is really the important part — if the First Lord came down that path and began organising me and telling me I was to bathe immediately, I should simply go and dress, I should do it, not because I'm a contrary sort of person, but because there would be no pleasure in bathing under orders — that's all."

"And quite enough, too," declared Roy.

"That is not our way," said Franz, looking at the rebel with disapproval. "We like to obey our Leader. We are agreed that our Leader knows best what is good for us. He tells us how to exercise our bodies and be fit, he orders all our days."

"And what does your leader think of you?" inquired Harry. "I'll tell you what he thinks in his own words. He said you were 'a great stupid flock of easily driven sheep'."

Franz was somewhat taken aback, he pulled himself together and began to explain how much better it was to have definite rules and to obey them and that no country could be happy and prosperous if everyone did exactly as he liked; but he was aware that his words were falling on stony ground.

"Never mind, Franz, old boy," said Roy at last, "we see your idea, but your ways wouldn't suit us. We're made differently or something. Let's leave it at that."

"But if it was war," said Franz in desperation, "if it was war and each one did as he pleased."

"Oh, *war*!" said Harry. "That's different, isn't it? You'd be on active service, you'd be straining every nerve to win. Nobody would mind being ordered about if it was war . . . By Jove!" exclaimed Harry with shining eyes, "by Jove, what fun it would be! Fancy firing real charges at a real ship and seeing her burst into flames!"

"Oh *don't* talk like that!" cried Wynne, who had been listening to the conversation in silence. "It would be ghastly — I can't bear to think of it."

"There won't be war," declared Roy, patting her leg in a comforting manner. "There *couldn't* be war, and Harry doesn't mean that he really wants war. He only means that when you've practised and practised until you're blue in the face with dummy targets it would be rather exciting to try the real thing."

Franz looked from one to the other as

they spoke. Roy was trying to reassure Wynne — and was actually succeeding in his endeavour — but it was obvious that he, too, was of the opinion that it would be a pleasant change to fire one of his guns at a real ship . . . and, although the sun was still warm upon his back, Franz shuddered involuntarily.

CHAPTER NINE

"THE moment has come," said Harry, rising from the ground, "the absolutely perfect moment for bathing has arrived . . ." He waved his hand and began to climb along the reef.

"I'll show you," cried Roy, leaping to his feet. "There's a gorgeous place for diving . . ."

Wynne and Franz followed more slowly. They saw Harry take a header into the sea and they saw Roy go after him in a neat dive, and when they reached the diving rock there were two heads bobbing about below.

"It's heavenly!" cried Roy, splashing about in the cool green water. "It's marvellous . . . come on, chaps."

Franz stood for a moment on the rock, his hands above his head, and then he swung them outwards and backwards and soared into the air . . . his body seemed to float in the air . . . and then, curving downwards and straightening out, it entered the water without a splash.

Wynne had never seen such a magnificent swan dive. She stood quite still for a few moments and her breath came hurriedly. It was a perfect thing, and so utterly unexpected . . . it had been over in a moment but somehow Wynne knew that it would last forever. She knew that whenever she liked she would be able to shut her eyes and see it happening — the green sea, the brilliant sunshine and that perfectly proportioned body soaring and floating and curving downwards, cutting into the green sea like a sharp white knife.

Roy and Harry had been watching and they, too, had appreciated the performance.

"You old dark horse!" exclaimed Roy — and although Franz did not know what the words meant, he could tell by the tone of voice that this must be the highest praise — "you old dark horse — you never said you could dive. I was hanging about underneath in case I should have to pick up the pieces."

"I have learnt to dive," said Franz modestly.

"By Jove, you have," agreed Roy. "You've learnt to dive, all right. He's learnt to dive, Harry!"

"You've said it," murmured Harry, who was lying on his back in the water and splashing with his legs, "he's learnt to dive. What about us doing a spot of learning?"

Franz was quite pleased to oblige his friends and the morning passed in demonstration and instruction. He was a very painstaking teacher and his pupils were intelligent and keen to learn. They had all made a good deal of progress towards the perfect swan dive before cold and exhaustion compelled them to abandon the struggle.

"You will soon be a dark horse, too," declared Franz cheerfully as he and Roy came out of the water together. "Very soon, with just a little more practice, you will be a dark horse."

Roy gazed at him in surprise. "A dark horse!" he repeated.

"Yes," said Franz, "that was what you said to me. A dark horse is a sea animal perhaps — we call it *Seekalb* — it is very good at diving."

"Oh, a *dark horse*!" exclaimed Roy. "A dark horse — " and stifling an idiotic desire to giggle at the very natural mistake Roy proceeded to explain the meaning of the term.

Wynne had been the first to give in, and she was sitting on the rocks combing her hair when the three young men emerged from their "dressing-room" with chattering teeth.

"You've all been in too long," she said reprovingly.

"I know," said Roy, as he rubbed his hair with his towel, "I know we have, but it was such a marvellous opportunity — having Franz I mean. Gosh, my hair is in a mess! Why didn't I bring a comb?"

Wynne took the hint. She proceeded to part his hair with her own comb and to dress it for him in his usual style. When she had finished the job to her own satisfaction she did Harry's hair as well.

"And now Franz," said Roy.

Franz wore his hair brushed back from his forehead in the continental manner, but Wynne decided to alter that. She did it like Roy's, parting it at one side and combing it across. It had grown a good deal since he had come to England and it was very wet so the new style was easily accomplished.

"There," she said, "what do you think of that?"

Franz was trying to see his hair in the

133

tiny mirror which Wynne had given him; he turned his head first one way and then the other to get the effect. It was rather becoming, he decided, but it made him look quite different. The others evidently thought the same.

"It makes you look more like us," declared Harry gravely.

"It suits you," added Roy.

"I knew it would suit you," said Wynne with a satisfied air, "and of course it makes you look more like us. I don't believe anyone would know that you weren't *all* English." She paused for a moment and then inquired, "Would you mind awfully if we called you Frank?"

There was a short silence. It was Wynne's question but Franz felt that the others were waiting for his answer just as eagerly. He felt that there was more importance in the issue than appeared on the surface.

"Of course we won't do it if you don't like it," continued Wynne, who had become aware of the tension. "We know you're proud of being half German and we can understand it, but I thought perhaps, while you're here with us, it might help you to feel at home. It might help you to feel that you really are one of us — that's all."

"Yes," said Franz slowly, "yes, it is quite a good idea. While I am here I will be Frank. That is settled."

All the young people in the neighbourhood received Wynne's idea with acclamation, and even Dane thought that the change was for the better, but when Sophie Braithwaite was informed that, in future, she was to address her young cousin as Frank, her feelings were exceedingly complex. She would have liked to talk about them — this was her recipe for clearing the mind — but she was afraid of saying something which had better remain unsaid, so she was forced to endure the complexity of her feelings in silence. It was so very queer that Elsie's name had been changed to Elsa and her son's name changed back to Frank. There was a significance in this double — so she felt — but she could not puzzle out its meaning. Quite apart from that, however, Sophie was sure that it was a dangerous thing to change your name. Your name was a part of yourself and had a direct influence upon your personality. She had always felt sorry that her parents had not chosen a more dignified name for her, and still regretted it. What a much more interesting and forceful personality she would have had if she had been christened differently — if she had been given the name of Eleanor, for instance, or Frances. Frances was the sort of name which might help one to rise high above the petty jars and discords of life. But Sophie was equally sure that, once your personality had been formed, no change of name could help you, and indeed who could tell what the result might be — the result of putting a new ingredient into your personality — it might upset the whole balance.

CHAPTER TEN

THE Club to which Dane Worthington belonged, and to which he resorted when he visited London, was small, old-fashioned and exclusive. Dane liked it because it was tucked away in a backwater and was therefore extremely quiet. The club master knew Dane well and was always ready to oblige him and the servants were willing and discreet. Dane arrived at this club early one day and announced that he would stay the night. He was expecting a guest to dinner and would like a private sitting-room — could this be managed? Mr. Dowles said that it could be managed, it was not a very usual request, of course, but as it was Major Worthington ...

"A special dinner," Major Worthington said. "I'll tell you exactly what I want, and Hartley will wait on us."

"I can detail a waiter — " began Mr. Dowles.

"No," said Major Worthington, "Hartley will wait. You can send up the dishes to the landing and Hartley will take over from there. Let me see, what shall we have?"

It was a warm day so the dinner was light and exceedingly well-chosen. Major Worthington was very particular. They would start with grapefruit — and on no account must it be tinned — they would proceed to Sole Mornay and then an Aylesbury duckling with green peas.

"Pêche Melba to follow?" suggested Mr. Dowles with his pencil poised over his note book.

"No, that won't do at all."

"Chicken livers on toast?" suggested Hartley.

"Yes," said Major Worthington. "Yes, chicken livers and be sure they're served really hot. The coffee must be hot, too — *really hot*, Dowles."

The wines to accompany this repast were chosen just as carefully and a box of Havanas was produced by Hartley and placed upon a side table. He was busy arranging the room when Major Worthington came in, dressed and ready to receive his guest. Hartley was smiling to himself.

"What's the joke?" inquired Dane, who

was aware that Hartley did not smile unless the joke were fairly rich.

"It's the flowers, sir," replied Hartley, pointing to the various vases of roses which were disposed about the room.

"What's funny about them?"

"Flowers!" said Hartley. "*Flowers!* I believe Mr. Dowles thinks it's a lady we're expecting."

Dane smiled, too. "He couldn't think that. Bless my soul, the dinner wouldn't do for a lady."

"No, sir."

"No, indeed . . . and the wines, Hartley. Nobody in their senses would waste vintage port on a lady — I'm sure Dowles knows better than that."

"I could tell him a thing or two," said Hartley, grinning broadly, "I could tell him about the dinner we gave in Rome to the Countess . . . it was oysters and champagne and iced strawberry mousse . . . and the little German actress, we gave her Escallopes de Veau à la Reine and Coupe Jacques. Then there was Mrs. Headlington at Cannes — "

"Please!" cried Dane in mock distress. "Please, Hartley, consider my reputation."

"Yes, sir, perhaps I'd better not mention them."

They smiled at each other for they both knew that it was just a game — Hartley would have died rather than allow a single item of information to escape his lips — and he was well aware that, although Dane often extended the hospitality of his board to ladies of doubtful virtue, he did it, not for the usual reasons, but for reasons best known to himself.

There was no time to discuss the subject further for at this moment the door opened and Major Worthington's guest was shown in. He was a tall, broadshouldered man with greying hair and a brown, wrinkled face. It was a remarkable face, strong and rugged, with jutting eyebrows and a jutting jaw.

"Well, Dane, here I am," he said, as he shook hands with his host, "you refused to come to me so I had to come to you."

"You're too well known," replied Dane, smiling. "I don't like being seen in your company."

"You could have come to the side door."

"No, not even the side door. You know

as well as I do that I can only be of use because everyone thinks I'm a harmless sort of fellow — a gentleman at large."

"I'm not complaining. You're probably right. I've noticed that you often are."

"I'm glad you've come," said Dane. "We can talk comfortably here . . . Hartley, you can take Colonel Carter's coat and tell them we're ready when they are . . . and make sure we're private, won't you."

Hartley nodded. He took the coat and hat and disappeared.

"Good man, that," said Colonel Carter, sitting down and accepting a glass of sherry. "I've always envied you that man. He'd be invaluable to me."

"He's invaluable to me."

The Colonel nodded. "Discreet, intelligent, loyal to the bone — you're a lucky devil, you know."

"I know. Hartley is all that, and more. He's clever and has initiative, he can speak German like a native, and he's as brave as a lion. I owe my life to Hartley half a dozen times at least."

For a little while the two men discussed the affairs of the day in a general sort of fashion, but once they were seated at the table they got down to the business which had brought them together.

"Well," said Colonel Carter, "well, Dane, what about it? What about this Franz von Heiden?"

"He isn't what we thought. He has no connection with the Secret Service."

"Sure of that?"

"Perfectly certain. He's here to look at us and to report to his father upon our morale."

They looked at each other and smiled.

"What does he make of us?" inquired Colonel Carter.

Dane took a sheet of paper from his pocket and spread it out on the table. "There you are," he said, "that's what he makes of us."

"A letter to his father!" remarked the Colonel, taking it up.

"A copy," amended Dane. "As a matter of fact, that's the third letter he's written to his father since he arrived. The other two weren't worth bothering about. They amused me, I confess, for they contained word portraits of practically everyone in the household — myself included."

"I should have liked to see what he made of you."

"Oh yes, I daresay — but you know enough about me already," declared Dane with a laugh.

"Did you send on the original letters ?"

"Yes, I did. I thought it better that they should go through and, as a matter of fact, I thought they would do more good than harm. Read it and see what you think."

The letter was in German of course but that presented no difficulties to the Colonel; he took it up and read it carefully and there was the suspicion of a smile hovering about his mouth.

Dear Father,

Thank you for your kind letter which I have read with great attention. I am sorry you are displeased with me but I assure you that I am doing my best. The difficulties have been more serious than I expected, but I am gradually overcoming them and you will find that there is more useful information in this letter than in the others that I have written. I shall send this letter to Herr Müller in London and he will forward it to you in the way you arranged. I shall post it myself to be quite safe and sure though I do not think there is any real need for caution. You say that I am wasting my time but I assure you that I am not. I am studying for two hours in the morning and I listen closely to all that is said. At first I found great difficulty in understanding the English people and in fact I was entirely mistaken about them. I believed them to be lazy and effete and pleasure loving, and much too comfortable in their homes, but now that I am beginning to know them better I have reversed my opinion of them. You will be surprised to hear this I know, but it is true and I cannot say otherwise. I have observed Major Worthington very closely. I still have a feeling that I have seen him before. Do you know whether I met him at any time when I was a child? It is very difficult to discover how the English people are disposed towards our country because they avoid discussion when I am present, but they are exceedingly kind to me and there is no antagonism in them. There was one discussion on the subject of encirclement but it led nowhere. I have told them about our Youth Movement and have tried to interest them in the

Nazi doctrine but they hold different views. They are very content and do not want war but if war should come I believe they would fight well. They are stronger than they look. I have met a young officer of the British Army who has won a decoration for courage — a decoration which is equal to the Iron Cross — and I have met a number of officers of the British Navy. I find them intolerant of discipline and jealous of their freedom but I believe that when they are on duty they obey their superior officers. We are going to lunch on board the Majestic next week — my cousin Sophie's brother is the Admiral and he has invited us — so perhaps there will be more of interest to report in my next letter . . .

"Very funny!" said Colonel Carter looking up. "Very illuminating in its way."

"Very illuminating," agreed Dane.

"I like that young man, I'd like to meet him."

"You can't, I'm afraid."

"Perhaps it wouldn't be wise."

"It would be the height of folly," said Dane firmly.

Colonel Carter left that. He returned to

the letter. "What will Herr von Heiden make of it?" he inquired.

"He won't like it, so he won't believe it," Dane replied. "He will reject the whole thing. It isn't what he expected to hear."

"How do you know?"

"I know him," said Dane. "He has always hated and despised us, and you can tell from the apologetic note in the letter that the news will be unpalatable — poor Franz!"

"Yes," agreed Colonel Carter thoughtfully, "a very conscientious young man. Have you met him before?" he added, tapping the letter with his finger.

"Only once, and he was a child at the time. It's curious that he should remember me."

"What is he like?"

"A nice boy. There's something very disarming about him. He's considerate and kind — kindness is a virtue which you often find in the best type of German — that's what makes it so incomprehensible, so incredible — "

"Yes," agreed Colonel Carter thoughtfully, "yes, they're a strange people — a strange mixture, Dane. You have the best type of German, kind and good and talented — you have Goethe and Schiller. Wagner and Strauss, who saw so much beauty in life and had the genius to convey this beauty to their fellow men and you have the other side of the picture, the German who is dominated by an inferiority complex, who thinks he's being unfairly treated and sees insults where none are intended. It is these men who are taught to believe that, compared with other races, the German is a god and can do no wrong."

"Dangerous," said Dane.

"Dangerous, yes, for they're ready to believe it. They're good soil for it, and always have been. Froissart realised that; he says of them, 'They are a covetous people above all other and they have no pitie if they have the upper hand and are harde and yvele handelers of their prisoners!' "

"Good lord!" exclaimed Dane. "Did Froissart say that?"

They were silent for a few moments thinking their own thoughts. At last the Colonel said in a different tone, "Well, Dane, I think we are agreed that this particular German isn't dangerous, so we can relax our precautions. I'm glad of this — particularly glad — because I want you to go over to Vienna next week."

"Vienna!" exclaimed Dane. "Oh no, I can't. I couldn't possibly."

The Colonel looked up in amazement.

"Don't ask me to go," Dane said, "I couldn't leave Fernacres as long as Von Heiden is there."

"I could order you to go."

"I hope you won't do that."

Colonel Carter shook his head. "No," he said, "no, I shan't order you to go. We're past that, Dane. I haven't forgotten the good work you've done for us . . . at the same time I wish you could go over to Vienna. It's a delicate job and you're the man to do it. Vienna is in a hell of a mess."

"I can well believe it," declared Dane, "but my mind is made up."

"What on earth — " began Colonel Carter.

"I'm sorry," said Dane, interrupting him firmly. "It's extremely kind of you to say I've done good work, and perhaps you won't misunderstand me if I remind you that I'm an amateur."

"I'm willing to give you professional status," declared Colonel Carter.

"I know," nodded Dane, and indeed they had thrashed out this question before, "I know that, and I'm grateful for the honour, but I can do better work on my own. I don't need the pay and I like the feeling that I'm perfectly free, so a roving commission suits me down to the ground. You can't say I take advantage of the fact that I'm unpaid."

"You are taking advantage of it now."

They smiled at each other.

"Never mind, Dane," said Colonel Carter, "I know exactly what you mean and I agree. I acknowledge here and now that you've done better work for us than most of my regular staff. You can do things that they can't do, and you can get in touch with people . . . I don't know how you manage it. I wish I had half a dozen amateurs working for me."

They had finished dinner now and they rose and sat down in the comfortable armchairs by the window while Hartley cleared the table.

"Well, Hartley," said Colonel Carter, "I

think I shall have to send you to Vienna — Major Worthington refuses to go."

"I wouldn't be much use without the Major," Hartley replied. "We work together, you see."

"Yes, we work together," nodded Dane. "It was Hartley who managed to get that letter for us. He'll tell you how he managed it."

"I got it out of the Postmaster at Chellford," said Hartley. "He's a friend of mine, you see."

"It can't be very easy."

"It wasn't, sir. I had to explain a good bit — more than I wanted to — but we wanted to keep an eye on the young gentleman's correspondence and that was the only way I could do it. He posts his own letters."

"Nasty suspicious sort of mind!"

Hartley smiled. "That's right, sir," he agreed, "but not quite suspicious enough, if you know what I mean. If the young gentleman had posted his letters in Kingsport we couldn't have got hold of them anyhow. I've noticed that the Germans are a bit apt to underrate other people's intelligence."

"I've noticed it, too," agreed Colonel Carter.

"For instance," continued Hartley, "for instance, Mr. Heiden makes a practice of meeting the postman at the gate — he does it every morning before breakfast — but he doesn't burn his letters when he's read them."

"What does he do with them ?"

Hartley went through the motion of tearing a letter to pieces. "That's all," he said, "I imagine he's under the impression that nobody in the house can read German."

"Very likely."

"There has been nothing of interest in them," added Hartley, sweeping the crumbs off the table with a folded napkin. "Nothing of any interest at all."

"There won't be," declared Colonel Carter. "There won't be anything of interest, but it's quite good practice for you — carry on, Hartley."

"Is there anything more, sir ?" inquired Hartley, looking at Dane.

"Just be about in the passage," Dane said, "we don't want anyone hanging about out there."

There was a little silence when the man had gone. The window was wide open and the foliage of the plane trees in the square was outlined against the sky. The roar of London came faintly to the ears of the two men sitting there — it was like the far-off roar of the sea.

"So it was a false alarm," Colonel Carter said.

"Yes — in a way — but I'm glad I came home. I want to thank you for releasing me and replacing me so quickly."

"Why were you so worried when you heard that this boy was expected at Fernacres?" inquired the Colonel with interest, "and what are you afraid of *now*? . . . you needn't answer if you don't want to."

Dane smiled at him. "I always forget how extremely perspicacious you are! Yes, I'm still anxious about Franz von Heiden, but . . . but if you don't mind I'll keep the reason to myself for the present. It's a purely private reason."

Blue smoke floated upwards from the two cigars.

"About Vienna . . ." Colonel Carter said, "I'm not going to try to persuade you to go, but you know the place so well — and the people. I'm worried, Dane. All our communications have been interrupted and I've got to reorganise everything."

"There's Mosenstein — "

"That's the worst of it. Mosenstein has vanished. I'm afraid they've got the old man, Dane . . . and he knows too much. He knows all our people and he knows our code."

"Mosenstein!" exclaimed Dane. "I liked the old fellow — it's bad news, isn't it ?"

"Damnable news."

The problem was discussed and debated far into the night and the London dawn had broken before Dane's guest departed. Dane stood on the doorstep of the club and watched him walk briskly down the street and turn the corner and disappear.

CHAPTER ELEVEN

WYNNE had not forgotten her intention of taking Frank to see the Roman Villa at Ashbourne — as a matter of fact she had not seen it herself.

"It's always the way," she said seriously, "people come long distances to look at interesting things but people who live quite near haven't the time or the energy to bother. We must make time, Frank. We'll go today, because I feel if we don't go at once we'll never go. We'll take our lunch with us and be back for tea — Migs and Nina are coming to tea."

Sophie agreed to the plan with her usual affability. "It's a lovely day," she said, "and dear Franz — Frank, I mean — will enjoy seeing the country. Don't forget to point out all the interesting things, will you? Be sure to show him Castle-hill — of course it isn't a bit the same as it was when *we* lived there, but he would like to see it. Show him the gates, Wynne, and you can see the house from the road if you stop at the top of the hill and look back."

They were soon on their way and their way took them past the big cross-roads at the end of the village where Sergeant White happened to be on point duty. Wynne stopped immediately and, drawing it to the side of the road, she beckoned to him.

"Hullo, are you on point duty?" she inquired.

It was quite obvious that he was, but Sergeant White understood what she meant, and he answered her meaning rather than her actual question.

"We're short-handed," he said.

"How's the baby?" Wynne inquired, "and how's the kitten? Has Mrs. White thought of a name for it yet?"

The sergeant leaned on the roof of the small car and looked in at the window. His face was larger and redder than ever.

"It's to be John Martin," he said.

"What!" exclaimed Wynne in surprise.

"John after me and Martin after my brother — John Martin, see?"

"Yes," said Wynne doubtfully, "yes, but — but — "

"He's to be christened on Sunday,"

continued Sergeant White, "and we wondered if you would come, Miss. Mrs. White and I would be very pleased if you would. It's to be at two-thirty just before the Children's Service."

Fortunately Wynne realised in time that it was the baby, and not the kitten, that was to be christened John Martin on Sunday at two-thirty.

"Oh yes," she said, rearranging her ideas, "oh yes — yes, I'd love to come. I'll bring my cousin too, shall I ?"

"If he would like it — " began Sergeant White in a doubtful voice.

Wynne was not listening. The thing was fixed. She continued, "John — yes, it's a *very* nice name. I didn't know you were called John. Have you got another — "

Two cars were now approaching the cross-roads from different directions and the sergeant, observing them out of the corner of his eye, left the conversation in the air and returned to his post.

"Bother," said Wynne, "that's the worst of policemen, isn't it ? He never told me what they were going to call the kitten."

"He is busy," Frank pointed out in a soothing voice.

156

"Bother!" said Wynne again. She let in her clutch and drove on.

They left the village and the sea behind them and striking inland were suddenly in the heart of the country. There were fields and meadows here, and huge old trees, the narrow lane turned and twisted amongst the fields, and the hedges were full of flowers. They passed villages, clustering in sleepy hollows, and fine old inns, and cottages with bright gardens. There was a silver stream, scarcely moving between its rushy banks, and cows standing knee-deep in the cool water. They passed Castle-hill where Sophie's people had lived and Frank's mother had spent so many happy hours, and here Wynne, remembering her instructions, stopped at the top of the hill so that Frank might look back.

He looked back in more ways than one and it seemed queer to him that this fine old house which had been so familiar to his mother should be so utterly foreign to him.

"You would think," he said, as he settled back in his seat and they drove on, "you would think that somehow I ought to remember it a little or at least that it should seem to me a friendly place."

Wynne did not answer but the silence between them was a companionable sort of silence and they both enjoyed it. Frank was busy using his eyes, he looked at everything and tried to take it all in. This country was quite different from his own — the very air had a different quality — but it had its charm. At the top of a steep rise, Wynne stopped the car again and here Frank had his first real view of England. He looked out over a plain and saw fields and trees and woods — green and golden in the strong sunshine. He saw the silver snake of a river wandering in a leisurely manner towards the sea, and, far away over the treetops, the land tilting up gently into hills. The air was very soft; the breeze fanned his cheek; the clouds moved slowly over the shallow, tilted bowl.

"Yes," said Frank, with a little sigh, "yes, it is beautiful, Wynne. I think one could learn to love it very much . . ."

"You ought to love it," Wynne said. "It's your mother's country."

They found the Roman Villa in a field adjoining the road, and leaving the car they walked across to look at it. There was very little to see for the place was even less than a ruin and only the foundations had been laid bare by digging. Wynne and Frank were both disappointed, and they were poking about somewhat half-heartedly when a man appeared from a nearby cottage and came towards them. He was a small, middle-aged individual dressed in grey trousers and a grey tweed jacket so torn and shabby and dirty that at first they thought he was a tramp, but his voice disabused them of this idea.

"You are interested in the Villa?" he inquired in cultured accents.

Wynne replied quite frankly that she, for one, would be more interested if there were more to see.

"Oh, but you don't understand!" cried the man eagerly. "Perhaps — perhaps you would allow me to tell you a little about it. My name is James."

Wynne introduced herself and Frank and replied that if he was not too busy —

"But I am not busy at all!" cried Mr. James. "Let me tell you about it . . . have you ever been to Pompeii? . . . No? Oh you *should* go. If you are interested in the Romans — and of course you must be interested or you would not be here —

Pompeii is the first place to see. You would understand *this* so much better if you had been to Pompeii. Let me describe it to you. It is an extraordinary sight . . . a whole town empty of any living soul . . . a monument to a great people — people who lived their lives like you and me. There it stands just as it was when they were alive . . . the greatest monument in the world. There are streets and shops and villas . . . the villas have gardens full of oleanders and there are fountains."

"I should love to see it," declared Wynne.

Frank felt that he would like to see it too, and perhaps to see it with Wynne. He believed that he could enjoy it more if Wynne were there, and, strangely enough, the idea seemed quite a natural one. Mr. James evidently thought that they would see it together and indeed he spoke as if he expected them to start off for Italy next week.

"There are guides of course," he said, "but you must avoid them like poison if you want to feel the spirit of the place, and to me the spirit of the place is even more important than the actual history — but of course I know that this would be heresy to a true historian, to an earnest anti-quarian. See it by moonlight," Mr. James besought them, "walk down the Street of Tombs, you can get to it by the Herculaneum Gate."

"Yes," said Wynne, "yes, it must be marvellous."

"The Patricians were buried there in their family vaults, and there are little altars over their graves . . . but you must see it all for yourselves."

"Yes," said Wynne again, "yes, we must."

Mr. James smiled at her. "Come along," he said, "I'll show you what we've been doing here. Come and see the mosaic, it's rather fine in its way."

They followed him to the excavations and saw the piece of mosaic pavement which had been uncovered. Mr. James looked at it and then looked at Wynne. "I can't tell you what I felt when I saw that," he said. "I almost wept. It was too marvellous to be true. Do you understand mosaic?"

"No," said Wynne frankly, "as a matter of fact I've never seen one before."

"I'll try to explain," said Mr. James. "Yes — er — I'll try to explain. You realise of course that the Villa was built by a Roman — an exile from his own land — and he built it exactly, or as nearly as possible, like the houses of his own land. These people had their own mosaic made — they themselves designed them — or had them designed — and the mosaic shows who and what they were. Each family had its own — like a crest," said Mr. James, trying to control himself and to confine himself to simple words of one syllable so that this utterly delightful — but alarmingly ignorant girl — could understand what he meant.

"I see," said Wynne, and she bent over and examined the mosaic with added interest.

"This is the peristyle," continued Mr. James, pointing to a broken piece of wall and the fragment of a pillar, ". . . and that, of course, is the atrium . . ."

Wynne and Frank gazed and nodded and agreed. It was quite different now that they had Mr. James to explain it to them — there seemed to be more to see. He was full of enthusiasm and possessed the invaluable gift of being able to communicate his enthusiasm to his hearers. From the few small pieces of coloured pavement and the half-buried fragments of wall Mr. James reared the Roman Villa before their eyes. The man came alive, too — the man who had built it or caused it to be built — he moved about in the beautifully proportioned rooms, he stood at the window which looked out upon this alien unfriendly land and dreamed of Rome. Wynne put these thoughts into words and Mr. James agreed.

"Yes," he said, "yes, I expect so . . . only, of course, we wouldn't talk of — er — rooms and windows — "

"But that's what they are," said Wynne.

When they had seen all that there was to see and absorbed all that Mr. James could tell them Frank and Wynne said goodbye to their new friend and thanked him heartily for his kindness.

"You have made it real," said Frank.

"It just shows how interesting *everything* is when you know about it," declared Wynne.

He left them and went away and they sat down on the grass and ate ham sandwiches and drank coffee out of a Thermos flask. Frank was more cheerful and companionable than he had ever been — he was still wearing his hair parted at the side and it made him look younger. He *seemed* younger, too, Wynne thought, and, because she was Wynne and had no inhibitions whatever, she put her thought into words.

"Younger!" echoed Frank thoughtfully, "I believe I feel younger as well though I didn't notice it until you said. Yes, I feel younger and the heart more light . . . I am beginning to see through you," he added.

Wynne was a little startled. She looked at him quickly and saw that he was smiling at her in a friendly fashion. "See through us!" she said, wrinkling her brows.

"Yes. At first I could not see through you at all. It was like looking at a wall and wondering what was at the other side."

"To 'see through' is rather a horrid expression — it usually means that you see something nasty."

"But I see through to something nice," declared Frank cheerfully.

"That's splendid," Wynne said, "but there isn't any wall really — we're the same all through. We don't put on airs or anything. Besides you're one of the family, aren't you? Come on, Frank," she added, "finish up your coffee, we had better start or we shan't be home in time for tennis. We must have *some* exercise . . ."

Frank chuckled to himself as he rose and followed her to the car. Here was another thing he had begun to "see through". He had been rather scornful of Wynne's air of fragility for, in Germany, the young of both sexes were expected to be sturdy and strong. Wynne looked like a fairy, and wore such an air of slender delicacy that one might imagine a breath of wind could blow her away, but Frank had discovered that her stamina equalled his own — she was practically indefatigable and could play games all day and dance half the night without turning a hair.

"The air of England is very wholesome," said Frank, as he settled himself beside her in the car. He was following out his own thoughts to a logical conclusion but Wynne could not know this.

"Yes," she agreed, "of course it is. You're much fitter than when you came."

He was rather surprised at having the tables turned — but it was true. He had gained five pounds in weight, despite the fact that he was taking even more exercise than he was used to at home. The food was amazingly good, of course, but Frank preferred to ascribe his increased weight and fitness to the English air.

This was the first day that Frank realised how much he was enjoying his visit to his English relatives. He was beginning to feel quite at home with them. They had told him so often that he was "half English" and, every time that they had said it, Frank had denied it in his own mind, but now he was beginning to weaken. It was quite a pleasant thing to be "half English", to have his own small place in the family life of Fernacres. He was still a German Citizen, of course, a loyal member of the Third Reich, but why not accept the good things that were offered to him so kindly and make the best of both worlds?

When they arrived back at Fernacres, Frank ran upstairs two steps at a time, and he whistled cheerfully as he changed into his tennis flannels before tea.

CHAPTER TWELVE

SOPHIE BRAITHWAITE was alone in the drawing-room when Frank came down. She was sitting behind the large silver tray with its elaborate equipment of teapots, cups and saucers and jugs of cream and milk; and the silver kettle upon the spirit-lamp was hissing in a friendly way.

"I heard you whistling," Sophie said. "It was one of Schubert's songs. Your father used to sing it long ago. Come and sit near me, dear."

He flung himself into the chair and smiled at her. He was feeling good. He liked the pretty drawing-room with its flowery chintz covers, he liked the golden sunshine pouring in at the big glass doors, and he had suddenly realised that he liked Cousin Sophie very much indeed. She was part of the pleasantly leisurely air of peace and security which was the flavour of England.

She opened the two silver tea-caddies and measured out, into the two teapots, carefully judged spoonfuls of China and Indian tea and Frank watched her carrying out this ritual and thought about her. . . . She really was an extraordinary woman — extraordinarily unselfconscious and spontaneous — she possessed the extremely useful power of making everybody fond of her and anxious to help her, and she exercised this power unconsciously, which made it even stronger. Wynne's friends might laugh at her and make fun of her, but they took care not to hurt her feelings and they were always ready to post her letters or to change her library books. The servants were her willing slaves. Frank had thought it odd, at first, that Major Worthington should live in the house and look after her affairs, but now he did not think it odd at all — Cousin Sophie had needed a man to look after things; she had needed Dane Worthington, that explained it.

Cousin Sophie looked up and met his eyes. "Did you enjoy yourself?" she inquired.

"Very much," replied Frank. "It was a lovely drive. The English country is very pretty. It has an air of its own. What have you been doing all day, Cousin Sophie?"

"I was *very* lazy. I got a new book from the library and I've been reading all the afternoon."

"It is very interesting ?" Frank inquired.

"Yes . . . no," said Sophie in a doubtful tone. "I mean *you* wouldn't like it, dear. It isn't very *good*, I'm afraid, but it's the sort of book I like. It's about nice people and it ends properly — she marries the right man and they live happily ever after."

"Have you looked at the end ?"

"Of course not, but Elaine Elkington's books are all like that. You can *trust* her to end it all happily — such a comfort! Some of the books nowadays begin quite nicely and cheerfully and then, half way through, they go all wrong and make you miserable. You've begun to like the people by that time, so it isn't fair. *That* book, for instance," said Sophie, pointing to another library book which lay on a side table, "that book began beautifully, and then they had a little tiff — well, of course lovers often have a tiff — and I thought they would be sure to make it up; but they didn't," said Sophie, shaking her head sadly. "They never made it up at all . . . she married *quite* the wrong man, and the really *nice* man went off to Rhodesia to shoot lions. It upset me dreadfully . . . Miss Elkington would never do that."

Frank hid a smile. "But sometimes people do marry the wrong one," he pointed out.

"Yes dear, but that's just why," returned Sophie.

They were silent for a few moments and then she looked at him and inquired, "Are you tired, Frank, dear?"

"No. I am very comfortable, thank you."

"You mustn't let Wynne wear you out. She's so terribly strong, you see, and she never thinks of anyone being tired. The young people are *very* strong, nowadays, and of course it's a good thing, but it's wearing sometimes. I was often tired when I was a girl; I wasn't brought up scientifically, you see . . . certified milk and fresh air and airtex and all that," said Sophie, tipping up the kettle and pouring a stream of boiling water into the Indian teapot. "I mean we never had our windows open at night because the night air was bad for us — so Nannie said — the windows were tightly shut and the curtains drawn and even the chimney was blocked up by a sort of tin thing that you worked with a handle. We wore starched petticoats and flannel petticoats with scalloped edges embroidered with silk, and the milk came in cans . . ." she sighed and added, "I suppose it's a wonder we're alive."

Frank watched the tea being made and listened to the flow of talk. He was feeling in harmony with the world. At first Cousin Sophie's chatter had bewildered him, and then, when he had begun to understand it, he had decided that it was extremely silly, but now he had begun to realise that it was not nearly so foolish as it seemed. There was a great deal of interest in it, and it wandered along in a pleasant, soothing, leisurely way like a little English brook.

She had stopped talking now and Frank wanted her to go on.

"How many brothers and sisters had you?" he asked.

"No sisters," she replied. "Your mother was like a sister to me — but I have two brothers. You'll see Tom on Friday when we go and have lunch on board his ship . . . You know," she continued, "it always seems very funny to me when I see Tom ordering people about and everyone doing what he says. I can't believe it, somehow. You see Tom was always the naughty one of the family — not really *badly* naughty, and in fact he was a model boy compared with Roy and Eric — but in those days lots of things were supposed to be naughty which aren't considered naughty now . . . things like tearing your clothes and getting dirty and being late for meals. One day Tom took the door off the potting shed and used it for a raft; it floated quite nicely down the stream until it caught on a rock and turned over (that was the sort of thing Tom did, and it was very trying for his elders but not really terribly wicked, you know) so Father said that if he wanted to go to sea he had better go . . . and he was sent into the Navy."

"Was he pleased at this?" inquired Frank with interest.

"He wasn't asked," she replied, "it was all decided for him. I sometimes thought that it happened very luckily for Father because there had been a good deal of discussion as to what Tom was to do. Henry was destined for the FIRM almost before he was born, but Tom was a problem. He was full of high spirits and Father was often impatient with him, but I believe he was always Mother's favourite . . . and now, when we go and have lunch with him in his ship and everyone rushes to do what he tells them, it makes me think how proud Mother would be if she could see him . . . though, as a matter of fact, she would be eighty if she were alive and too old to go on board a battleship." Sophie was silent for a moment and then she continued thoughtfully, "Perhaps she *does* see him. You know, Frank, I don't believe that anyone could be really happy and contented in Heaven unless they knew what was happening to their children . . . and of course God wants people to be as happy as possible . . . so I expect Mother knows that Tom is an admiral with a ship of his own and a beautiful dining-room and drawing-room on board . . . but I hope she doesn't know about all the trouble he has had with his wife."

Frank rose to take his cup, and also to hide a smile. "It might be difficult for your mother to know the one thing and not the other," he suggested.

"It might be," agreed Sophie, pausing

and looking a little concerned for a moment, and then she smiled very sweetly and added, "but with God all things are possible, Frank dear."

She was so serene and happy in her innocent belief that Frank felt a twinge of shame for his scepticism. He knew suddenly that he loved Cousin Sophie in the way that he might have loved her if she had been his mother. He loved every bit of her, she was precious to him, and because his feelings were suddenly so strong he bent down and took her hand and pressed it to his lips.

"Dear boy," she said, looking up at him with her heart in her eyes, "it's such a pleasure to have you . . . sometimes you remind me of Elsie . . . I feel I can talk to you."

"I like you to talk to me."

She nodded. "I know. You seem older than the others and more understanding. I wonder why that is."

He certainly felt no younger than Cousin Sophie and it seemed quite natural that they should talk to each other like contemporaries . . .

They were both a trifle embarrassed

when the door was flung open and Wynne ushered in her friends. Frank seized his cup and stood up very straight, and Sophie welcomed the newcomers with a little more cordiality than she felt.

"Darling Nina!" she said, holding out her hands, "and dear Migs too . . . here you are just in time for tea. You know Frank? . . . yes, of course you do, how stupid of me! Sit here Nina so that we can talk. I want to hear about your mother's pelargoniums. How are they? Such a frightful thing has happened to ours . . . a sort of blight or something. The petals are all turning brown at the edges and I'm sure Ellis has done something but I don't dare to tell him. Milk and sugar, Migs? . . . no sugar . . . on, no milk either? Never mind, this cup will do for Dane. Where is Dane? Does anyone know?"

"Here is Dane," said Dane's voice from the window. "I've been looking at the pelargoniums. What is it that 'will do for Dane'? It sounds a trifle sinister."

Sophie waved to him to come in. "It's only tea," she said, "because I forgot about Migs not taking milk. Aren't the pelargoniums wretched?" She poured out another cup and added, "That just shows how mistakes can be made."

"Too much water," said Dane. "Ellis has a passion for watering everything."

"Not that," Sophie declared. "I had left off talking about the pelargoniums, Dane. It's the mistake *you* made. You thought there was something sinister about the tea when it was only because Migs doesn't like sugar or milk and I had very stupidly forgotten. If you hadn't mentioned it you might have gone on thinking that the perfectly innocent tea had something odd about it. You might even have thought I was trying to poison you."

Dane considered the matter gravely. "No," he said, "no, because I'm too useful to you, Sophie. You wouldn't have anyone to add up the books or make out your Income Tax return if you poisoned me . . . besides I don't believe it would ever have crossed my mind. I don't read so many detective novels as you do."

He accepted the perfectly innocent cup of tea and crossed over to the fireplace. There was no fire there, of course, but Dane liked standing, and it was his habit to have his tea with his cup and plate on a corner of the mantelpiece. Migs took no notice of him but Frank continued to stand, for he was too polite to sit down before the older man.

Dane smiled at him across the room. "Sit down, Frank," he said, "you know my bad habits by this time. This is my favourite place and Sophie has given up her attempts to make me behave like a civilised being. I can see you all so well, I can help myself to food when I want it, and I can join in the conversation or withdraw from it as I please."

"You could talk just as well if you sat down, sir," declared Migs.

"Haven't you ever noticed that a man on his legs can talk down any seated man?" inquired Dane. "In an argument the advantage is with the standing man. I'd put my money on him every time."

Migs nodded. "Yes, unless there's a desk in front of the seated man," he said.

Dane admitted this point — he was bound to admit it, for it aroused lively recollections of occasions when he had been forced to stand on the wrong side of a desk. The Headmaster's Study, the Orderly

Room . . . he glanced at Migs and caught his eye and smiled.

After this conversation strayed happily as it always did when Sophie Braithwaite was present. Various points were raised and debated, and, whenever the talk flagged or became dull, Sophie was ready and willing to start a new theme. Frank was to remember this day and this particular tea-party for a very long time; he was to remember it when he was far away, and this was not because it was different from other tea-parties which took place during his stay at Fernacres, but rather because it was typical of every tea-party which took place there.

CHAPTER THIRTEEN

FRANK had surrendered to the kindness of his new friends and for a time he was completely happy. He had never been so happy in his life. They all noticed his changed appearance, his light step, his ready smile, and the gay abandon with which he threw himself into the business of living.

"You're looking so much better, dear Frank," Sophie told him.

"It's the English air," replied Frank.

The sun shone, the birds sang and everything was as nearly perfect as it could possibly be in a very imperfect world.

The halcyon period lasted for nearly a fortnight, as halcyon periods often do, and then it ended abruptly. Frank discovered that he was in love. He discovered it quite suddenly when he was helping Wynne to put on her coat after a set of tennis . . . she slipped her arms into the sleeves and he folded it around her . . . and Wynne looked up sideways to smile her thanks. She was so sweet . . . she was so dear and beautiful . . . he loved her.

Once he discovered that he was in love he realised that he had been in love for some time. He could not believe that there had ever been a time when he was not deeply and tenderly in love with Wynne. He looked back, as all lovers do, and tried to decide when it had happened — had he been in love that day at Ashbourne? Yes, he had, and if he had not been a complete fool he might have realised it then. Had he been in love the day they had bathed with Roy and Harry? Yes, it must have been before that. He thought of the morning when the two policemen had come, he had been in love even then, for he could remember Wynne's slight figure standing in the sunlight outside the open glass doors, and he could remember how his heart had stood still, and then raced madly with fear lest anything should happen to her . . .

Frank was dismayed when he considered the matter. He did not want love, and especially he shrank from the idea of loving Wynne. He remembered the ghastly affair of his father and mother. He was pulled in two directions. Sometimes he almost hated

Wynne for what she had done to him, and at other times he abandoned himself to loving her; but whether he loved her or hated her it was impossible for him to keep his eyes off her. He watched her all the time. She was so lovely, so gay. Her spirit shone through the transparency of her skin like a bright light . . . she lived every moment of her life with childlike intensity. In his love Frank reverted to type and became a romantic, and all the beautiful old songs seemed to express what he felt. "Du bist wie eine Blume," thought Frank — indeed it seemed to him that the poem must have been made for Wynne and Wynne alone. She was like a spring flower — gay and vivid and tender. He spent a few hours translating the poem into English with the vague idea that someday he might show it to her.

"Thou'rt like a little blossom
So pure and fair and bright.
And when I see thy beauty
It sets my heart alight.

I'll lay my hands in blessing
Upon thy golden hair,

Praying that God will keep thee
As bright and pure and fair."

Frank read it over several times and was rather pleased with it. Save for the fourth line, which baffled all attempts at literal translation, he had managed to translate it almost word for word. He had kept the spirit of the thing and it actually went quite nicely with the music. On the whole Frank liked his own fourth line better than the original one, for he did not feel "Wehmut" when he looked at Wynne but rather an uplifting of the spirit. He put the poem away in a drawer and locked the drawer carefully . . . and then he opened the drawer again and took the poem out and tore it up into little pieces. He could never show it to Wynne, he could never tell her that he loved her. It was the height of folly to think of marrying an English girl.

Frank fought and struggled. Sometimes he imagined that he had succeeded in his attempt to tear Wynne out of his heart and then he looked at her and she walked straight into his heart and took possession of it again . . . and the world was transformed . . . and he knew that nothing mattered except Wynne, for she was the other part of himself that he had been looking for all his life. He dreamed about her constantly, dreamed that he was fighting bands of desperadoes single-handed, vanquishing them with his own strong right arm, rescuing her and carrying her to safety . . . and then he woke and knew that he could never carry her to safety. If he took her anywhere it would be into danger and misery — the kindest thing he could do would be to go away quickly, as quickly as he could.

Migs loved Wynne — this was another thing that Frank discovered. He saw Migs look at Wynne and, because he loved Wynne himself, he knew what the look meant. Migs loved Wynne. There was nothing to prevent *them* from coming together. They were both English; they shared the same ideals. These thoughts did not comfort Frank at all. They distressed him more than ever. They tortured him. All that evening he kept pushing these thoughts away out of his mind, but when he went up to bed they were still there. He was almost certain that Wynne did not love Migs — not yet — but if he went away, if his presence was removed they would see more of each other. Wynne would have more time to spare for Migs, and Migs would be there waiting for her.

Frank did not sleep much that night. He slept in short snatches which were full of uneasy dreams. Each time he woke he expected to see the sun shining in at his window and was amazed to find it still dark. He slept and woke again and this time it was light. He lay and listened and heard the garage clock striking five. He was hot and uncomfortable and he felt as if he had been in bed for weeks; there was no more sleep in him. After a few minutes he flung off the bedclothes and rose and leaned out of the window. It was quiet and peaceful. The garden flamed with colour in the early morning sun. There had been heavy dew in the night and the lawn sparkled and steamed gently; a faint breeze blew the light clouds hither and thither in the blue sky. It was so peaceful and beautiful and he had got to leave it all and go away. When he had gone it would look just the same — everything would be just the same — but he would not be here to see it.

"Warum?" said Frank softly under his breath. "Warum?" Why had it got to be like this? Why must he leave this place and these people that he had begun to love? Why couldn't everybody in the world be friendly and kind and loving to each other?

Frank searched in the past for some answer to these questions and the answer came. He remembered a big bare school-room with desks and high windows. It was full of boys. They were sitting there, wide-eyed, listening to a speech on the radio — listening to a voice which was so strident, so emotional, that it seemed to reverberate in some inner part of one's body. Some of the boys had been unable to endure the strain on their emotions and had wept openly. One of them had fainted. They had sat and listened for hours, but afterwards Frank found that he had only a very confused idea of what the voice had said. They were to keep themselves fit so that they would be prepared . . .it was in their hands to make the Fatherland great . . . German blood was pure and untainted . . . the world was jealous of Germany . . . the world was against them. . . .

Frank remembered this as he leant out of the window and for the first time a small wind of doubt blew in his mind. Was it true? Was Britain jealous of Germany, and, if so, why? Was all this stirring up necessary? Wouldn't it be better for everyone if the Leader allowed them to settle down and become peaceful and friendly with their neighbours? These were extraordinary ideas and Frank did not entertain them for more than a moment. They merely brushed across his mind and were gone ... the Leader was always right.

Frank was cold by this time and he crept back to bed, though not to sleep. The Leader was always right, but whether he was right or wrong it was absolutely essential that Frank should leave Fernacres. There was a constriction in his throat at the thought and it was not only because of Wynne — though she was the chief reason of course — he was fond of them all, Cousin Sophie and Roy and Dane — yes, even Major Worthington had a place in his heart.

After breakfast Frank followed Major Worthington to his sitting-room and knocked on the door. He remembered the last time he had been there. He had wanted to borrow some books.

"Come in," said Dane. "Come in, Frank. Do you want another book?"

"No, thank you," said Frank, "I have come to tell you that I must go away. I want you to tell the others. I find it too difficult to tell them."

"I'm sorry," Dane said, and strangely enough he really was sorry. "I'm sorry, Frank. Are you going home?"

Frank shook his head. "Not yet," he said. "My father has written to say to come home but I'm not ready yet. I don't want to leave England until I have done what I came to do."

"What you came to do, Frank?"

"I think you know," said Frank with a faint smile. "There isn't anything wrong in what I came to do. It was just to see what you were like — all of you — and what you think about things. There isn't anything wrong in that."

"No, it was a good idea."

"It was my father's idea but he doesn't think I have carried it out properly. That's why he wants me to come home."

"I thought there was a post in London waiting for you."

"That's closed," said Frank. "It's closed to me because they want me to come home."

He took a letter out of his pocket and showed it to Dane. "It came this morning," he added.

Dane put out his hand to take it. "I am to read it, Frank?" he said.

"It's in German!" exclaimed Frank in a surprised tone.

"Naturally," agreed Dane, smiling.

They stood perfectly still a moment, Dane holding out his hand and Frank hesitating in perplexity.

"Yes," said Frank at last, "yes, I should like you to read it — I can translate it for you if you like."

"I can read it." said Dane.

The letter contained the information which Frank had already given and not much more. It was couched in a somewhat grumbling tone. Franz had been sent to England with a certain object in view. He had been idle and extravagant. It was no use for him to ask for more money to be sent because he had already been given sufficient for his needs. ("You are aware that it is uneconomic to spend German money in another land," Herr Von Heiden pointed out.) Franz need not apply to the legation as the post which had been intended for him had been filled. He must return to Germany as soon as possible.

"Yes," said Dane, handing it back.

"You see?" said Frank eagerly, "you understand what he says? I am to go home . . . but I'm not going. It isn't fair to give a person something to do — a task to accomplish — and then break it off in the middle. I'm not ready to go home yet. I'm just beginning to understand. I am interested."

"What do you propose?" inquired Dane.

"I want to get a post in London," said Frank. "I thought you could help me. I can translate and type letters or add up figures. I could be useful to a big firm with foreign trade."

"I think that could be managed but what would your father say? Won't he be annoyed if you refuse to go home?"

"I can square him," declared Frank (it was an expression he had picked up from Roy and he used it with an air of nonchalance which made Dane smile), "I can square my father — he isn't really so stern as he pretends — and if I get a post and require no more German money he can have no objections, can he ?"

"You've thought it all out, I see."

"Yes," said Frank. He had thought about it for several days but it was only this morning, when his father's letter had arrived, that he had suddenly seen the solution to his problem. He must leave Fernacres but he need not go so very far away and if he went to London there might be a chance of seeing Wynne occasionally. She might come up to London, or he might come to Fernacres for a weekend. He realised that it would be very much better if he did not see her, but he wanted to see her. He realised that it would be much wiser to go straight home but he did not want to go home.

Dane was watching his face. "Wouldn't it be more sensible to go back to Germany as your father says ?" he asked.

"Yes," said Frank. "I mean — perhaps it would be more sensible but I'm not ready to go . . . so if you would be so very kind as to find me a post . . . and there's just one thing more. My father doesn't call himself Von Heiden now. The particle means nothing. So I'm just Frank Heiden." He blushed and added. "There was no need to tell you before, but now that I am to be in an office it will be better."

Dane was rather amused, but he did not show it. He sat down and drew out a sheet of notepaper — "Frank Heiden," he said, writing it down as he spoke, "German, English, book-keeping — is that right?"

"I speak Swedish too," said Frank, "and Finnish, of course. We have some great friends in Helsinki and I stayed with them often when I was a child. I can read and write in French but I don't speak very well. I have a little Italian too. I like languages," he added apologetically.

"Obviously," said Dane, looking at him with a friendly smile. "Well, Frank, I think I can promise to find you a job. I'll get hold of a friend of mine in London who knows about these things."

"And you'll explain it to Cousin Sophie," Frank urged him. "You'll explain how it is, and how much I don't want to go away . . . and Wynne too."

"We'll wait and do that when it's all fixed up," said Dane.

191

CHAPTER FOURTEEN

THE anxiety and distress which Frank had been through, and the pitched battles which he had been fighting within himself had made him a somewhat difficult companion. Wynne was certain that there was something the matter with Frank. He had been so happy and gay and friendly, and then, quite suddenly and for no apparent reason, he had begun to behave in the most extraordinary manner. He was moody and inattentive, he sat and stared into vacancy and jumped when you spoke to him. He had periods of feverish gaiety and periods of hopeless gloom. Sometimes his eyes followed her and dwelt upon her with almost dog-like devotion, and sometimes he would scarcely look at her, and answered her curtly when she spoke to him. There was something the matter — Wynne was sure of it — and so she bore with him as patiently as she could. Perhaps he would tell her about it, and she should be able to help him, or perhaps the trouble would pass and they would be happy again. Wynne was obsessed with Frank and his peculiar moods; she was even more unconscious than usual of her own feelings, so the tremendous discovery which she made was all the more astonishing. It was one of those great discoveries which are so immensely important that it seems as if nobody had ever discovered anything before. Wynne discovered that she loved Frank . . . she loved him dearly . . . it didn't matter whether he was in a good mood or a bad one. It didn't matter whether he was kind and considerate, or as cross as a bear . . . she loved him just the same.

She discovered this world-shaking fact at breakfast when Dane announced that he had found a job for Frank in London and that Frank was going away, and it seemed very odd to Wynne that, despite this amazing discovery of hers, she was able to finish her coffee and leave the dining-room without the others noticing that anything remarkable had happened. Ellis had brought in the flowers as usual and had left the basket on the hall table, and Wynne took up the basket and carried it into the pantry. It was the middle of July so the flowers happened to be roses — roses of all shapes and sizes and colours — Wynne stood and stared at them for several minutes without seeing them at all. The basket might have been full of coal for all she knew.

"Frank," said Wynne to herself, "FRANK," and her heart sang within her. She knew now what had been the matter with Frank, he was in love, too. That's why he was so strange and moody and so unlike himself . . . poor Frank, poor darling Frank!

She took a vase out of the cupboard and began to fill it with roses (there was no water in it but she did not notice that), she put two roses in it and then stopped and her hands fell to her sides. She leaned against the cupboard door and dreamed . . .

The thought that Frank was going away, that he was going to London, did not worry her much. She had always known that he was going to London. He would go away, but he would come back and tell her that he loved her. Wynne had always been happy so she could not imagine any other condition. She had always had everything she wanted, and now she wanted Frank. Dear Frank, so big and splendid, so serious and little-boyish, so kind and good and considerate. Poor Frank, so unhappy because he loved her — how happy he would be when he found that she loved him! Wynne smiled to herself — it was a very sweet smile, mysterious and tender. She looked back and saw that this thing had grown up gradually in her heart. The seed of it had been sown at the very beginning of Frank's visit when he had been so muddled and so hopelessly at sea. She had taken care of him and shielded him; she had taken his part when Migs and the others tried to make fun of him. She had thought that it was like having a very large child to look after — but she had fallen in love with her child.

CHAPTER FIFTEEN

FRANK'S departure from Chellford was in the nature of a triumph. He found that he was a great deal more popular than he had imagined in his wildest dreams. All Wynne's friends had grown to like him. They took leave of him with regret, and declared that they would let him know the next time they were in town and he must lunch with them. The Audleys gave him an immense box of cigarettes, Nina Corbett gave him a tie which she had knitted herself. Migs hit him on the back and said that he would be in town next week and would let Frank know . . . they would dine together at a little place Migs knew of where you could get snails. They would do a show together. Sophie wept quite openly when she said goodbye, and she put her arms round his neck and kissed him. Dane gave him five pounds and insisted that he should take it. "You may need it," said Dane, "and be sure to let me know if you find yourself in any sort of difficulty — I mean this,

Frank," Wynne shook hands with him and said, "You'll come back soon, won't you?"

The house was very quiet after he had gone — even Dane felt the difference. He watched Wynne somewhat anxiously and noticed that she was more frequently to be seen about the house. The weather had broken and it was too wet for tennis — that might be the reason, or it might not. He suggested one morning that they should go for a walk together in the rain and Wynne assented with flattering eagerness.

"We haven't been for a walk for ages," she said. "It's a lovely idea, Dane."

Clad in waterproofs and stout shoes and armed with sticks they set off together along the cliffs. It rained softly but steadily, the skies were grey, and far below them the grey sea heaved and sank and broke against the rocks in white frills. Wynne was rather silent and Dane did not try to talk to her much. Their sense of companionship was too strong and of too old a standing to make silence uncomfortable. After they had gone some distance the slight breeze freshened and the clouds began to disperse. They sat down in the shelter of an overhanging ledge of rock and watched the miracle take place.

"That's why I love the sea," Wynne said thoughtfully. "There's so much weather to be seen, and it keeps changing."

Dane agreed. He looked at her as she sat there beside him and saw the drops of rain like dew upon her eyelashes and upon the two fair curls which had escaped from beneath her black sou'wester. Her expression was dreamy and yet alive as if her thoughts were far away, delightful and secret. What was she thinking about? How was he to find out what she was thinking?

"You know, Dane," said Wynne suddenly, "I believe if I had been to Germany and seen it with my own eyes I should understand Frank better."

"I expect you would," agreed Dane. "Frank is very German in many ways."

"He's English on his mother's side."

"Yes, but does he think of himself as half English?"

Wynne considered this, "I don't believe he does," she said slowly. "He's really and truly German at heart — you can't blame him, can you?"

"Of course I don't blame him," Dane

assured her. "He was born and bred a German and he doesn't remember his mother . . . I remember her quite well."

"You knew her, too?"

"Of course I knew her. We were all great friends — Elsie and Sophie and Tom and I. There were others, too, but we four did all sorts of amusing things together. We had tremendous times." He was silent for a moment and then he continued in a tone of casual conversation, "Elsie was a charming girl — she was very like you, so you will realise what a delightful creature she was!"

"Oh Dane!" cried Wynne, turning and looking at him in surprise, "Oh, Dane, how nice of you!"

"Yes," said Dane, "I don't often pay you compliments (you get quite enough from other people) but I'm going to pay you an even greater compliment now. I've decided to tell you a secret."

"A secret!" echoed Wynne.

Dane nodded. "A secret that I have never told anyone before. Can you keep a secret from Sophie?"

"You know I can," replied Wynne, a trifle indignantly. "You know quite well

I have all sorts of secrets from Sophie. She's a darling pet, of course, but it wouldn't do to tell her everything."

"Yes . . . well, I'm not sure that I approve of that. This secret is rather different. It's got to be kept from Sophie because it would make her very unhappy."

"It's about Elsie — Frank's mother?" Wynne inquired.

He nodded. "I was very fond of Elsie. I wasn't in love with her, Wynne, so don't get that into your head. I was in love with someone else, but Elsie was my very dear friend. She knew about it and encouraged me and did what she could to help me. I was very miserable for a time and she was extraordinarily kind and understanding."

"But, Dane, who was it?"

"No," said Dane, shaking his head. "No, Wynne. That's a different story. I shan't say any more about that so you needn't try to drag it out of me. I only told you about it so that you should understand what I felt about Elsie. This is Elsie's story."

"But Dane — "

"This is Elsie's story," he repeated firmly. "You know a good deal of it already

— how she married and went to Germany and how the war came and we heard nothing of her for years."

"Yes," agreed Wynne, but I always wondered why nobody did anything about her after the war was over."

"Somebody did. I did as a matter of fact. I went over to Germany and saw her. I didn't say I was going — I just went. I thought I would find out all about her and come back and tell Sophie how she was. It was really partly for Sophie's sake that I went — Sophie was so worried about her."

"But you never told Sophie!"

"No, I never told her. I never told anyone at all. Listen Wynne . . . I found the Von Heiden's house quite easily and I went and called. I took Elsie a big bunch of pink roses — they were her favourite flowers and I wanted to take her something that would make her think of old times, I didn't know whether she would be pleased to see me . . . I didn't know whether she might have been turned against her old friends. It was rather a dangerous experiment to walk in on her like that without finding out whether she wanted to see me, but I was young then and I took the risk. As a matter of fact I thought it would be rather fun to surprise Elsie . . ."

"Yes," said Wynne eagerly. "Yes, what fun!"

Dane went on somewhat doggedly and without much expression in his voice. He was finding it even more difficult than he had expected to tell the story to Wynne. "I went up the stairs to the apartment — or flat as we should call it — and I rang the bell. Elsie opened the door — she knew me at once."

"Why, of course she knew you!" cried Wynne. "You were friends . . . it was only five years, wasn't it ?"

"I didn't know her," said Dane in a quiet voice.

"Dane!"

"No," said Dane, shaking his head. "No, I didn't know it was Elsie . . . not at first. I couldn't believe it was Elsie. She was an old woman — old and weary — she had shrunk to half her size, her hair was streaked with grey and her skin was wrinkled and pallid. There was no life in her eyes — they had wept too much."

"Oh, what had they done to her!" cried Wynne.

"Nothing," he said, almost sternly. "They had done nothing to her. It was what she had done to herself."

"What do you mean?" whispered Wynne. "Oh Dane, what *do* you mean?"

"It's so difficult to explain . . . she had married Otto von Heiden because she loved him, and she had ruined him. The mere fact that he had an English wife had ruined him politically and socially and he wasn't strong enough to bear it and make the best of it. There was no harm in the man, he was just weak and he let Fate get him down. He had loved Elsie — we all knew that — but his love hadn't stood the test. The test was too great — he was a proud man, you see, proud of his lineage and his position, and now he was completely broken. Elsie knew that the only thing she could do for Otto was to die and be forgotten. She had known this all along of course. When Franz was born she had been very ill but the doctors and nurses and dragged her back from the Gates of Death — it was her own expression. . .

"She wanted to die," he continued in a low, strained voice. "I've heard other people say that they wanted to die but it

203

wasn't true — they only *thought* they wanted to die which is quite a different thing — Elsie wanted it. Perhaps you will say that she wasn't quite sane. I understood. She loved Otto, but Otto had ceased to love her. She loved her little son but she was actually a handicap to him and it would be still worse as he grew up and went to school . . . an English mother!

"I stayed with her for a little and we talked. She cried hopelessly and helplessly. There was so little strength in her that she wasn't ashamed of her tears and they just dripped down her cheeks like rain. I realised more and more how much she had suffered. The lies that had hurt her, too, lies about Britain, about our cruelty to prisoners, things that she knew must be untrue but were accepted as facts by those around her. 'People looked at me,' she said, 'people *looked* at me, Dane.' I knew then why she seemed to have shrunk. I guessed she had not been out of the house for months — perhaps years."

"Oh Dane!" cried Wynne. "Oh *Dane*, I understand exactly how she felt . . . it's horrible! Why are you telling me all this now?"

"I don't know," he said, turning his head away so that she should not see his face. "I don't know why . . . Of course it has been on my mind, Wynne . . . and seeing Franz here . . . I saw him that day . . .

"Did you ?"

"Yes, he was quite a small child, of course — a dear little chap. He stood beside her and leant against her knee and once, when he saw her tears, he reached up and patted her cheek. She said, 'Franz loves me but he doesn't understand. When he begins to understand he won't love me so much.'"

"Dane, I can't bear it !"

"Poor Wynne, I won't tell you any more."

"But I must know. What did you talk about ?"

"Old times," said Dane. "happy times. She liked my roses. I asked her to write to Sophie but not to mention my visit and she said she would try to write cheerfully — she said she would send Sophie a little photograph of Franz. I would have stayed longer but I didn't want to meet her husband. I had never liked him and I liked him even less than before . . . that's all, really," added Dane. "She died a few months later . . . it was pneumonia. I was glad when I heard she was dead."

Wynne sat very still and gazed out to sea. The clouds were racing before the wind and there were big patches of blue sky between them. "Dane why did you tell me all this ?" she asked again.

"Perhaps I wanted you to understand," he replied thoughtfully, "I like you to be happy and carefree, but . . . but nobody ought to live in a fool's Paradise. There is so much suffering in the world . . . Europe is in a queer state of unrest."

"There could never be another war!" she exclaimed, her eyes wide with horror at the thought. "Dane, you don't mean that, do you ?"

"No," he said, "no, Wynne, of course not."

She stood up and stretched herself. "It's cold," she said. "Summer is nearly over, Dane."

"Yes," said Dane. "Summer is nearly over."

There was a verse from Shakespeare which came into Dane's mind as he followed Wynne up the path . . .

"Rough winds do shake the darling
       buds of May
    And summer's lease hath all too
       short a date."

Dane said it over softly, beneath his breath.
Wynne was his darling bud of May; she
had enjoyed her lease of summer — every
moment of it — but he was afraid that it
was nearly over now.

CHAPTER SIXTEEN

DANE said that Europe was in a "state of unrest" and he had said a good deal less than the truth. He had wanted to prepare Wynne for the worst and then, at the last minute, he had felt such a strong desire to protect her and shield her as long as possible from distress and anxiety that he had drawn back. It was September now — September, 1938 — and the Czechoslovakian crisis was at hand. Dane could not see how war was to be averted. He had met Herr Hitler and spoken to him, he had read his book, and had listened to some of his speeches, and he realised that the German Chancellor was a dangerous man — a man who was a mixture of long-sighted calculation and violent impulses which arose from a temper which he did not attempt to control. This man held the fate of Europe in his hand — it was not a pleasant thought. Dane had nothing to do at the moment, for the Vienna mission had been entrusted to someone else. He was at a loose end and he found it very trying.

Outwardly things went on much the same and Dane had the doubtful satisfaction of knowing that neither Sophie nor Wynne was aware of the tremendous issues at stake. There was no radio at Fernacres (for Dane had always disliked what he called potted music, and was wont to declare that the radio had broken up more happy homes than any other device of man) so the only way in which news came to the house was in the papers or over the telephone. During that tense week Dane almost changed his mind about radio for it would have been a relief to hear the news and to be able to watch the situation developing hour by hour.

"We'll have to get a set, Hartley," said Dane at last, and Hartley replied, "Yes, we'll need it when the war starts."

War — it was a ghastly thought! Chamberlain was straining every nerve to prevent it, and if anyone could avert war Chamberlain would do it, but Dane was doubtful whether it was possible now — there were so many conflicting interests involved. Knowing rather more of the inside condition of Europe than the ordinary citizen, Dane was at once less optimistic and more prepared. He had seen the cloud appear on the horizon when it was no larger than a man's hand, and he had watched it spreading and darkening and blotting out the sun.

One evening Dane was sitting by his fire thinking and smoking — he had been smoking far too much these last few days — he had thought and smoked until his brain positively reeled but he could see no way out of the impasse which had arisen. Chamberlain was doing all that he could — more than anyone could have asked him to do — he had flown to Germany twice . . . he had now gone again for the third time. What was happening there, Dane wondered. Was there any hope at all, or would we be plunged into a prolonged and bloody struggle, unarmed and unprepared.

Dane was tired, but he knew that if he went to bed he would not sleep. He was filling his pipe again when he heard the sound of a motor bicycle coming up the road. It was not a very unusual sound of course, but Dane's nerves were so stretched and his perceptions so heightened that he felt an inner conviction that the rider was coming to Fernacres. His face sharpened into an intense expression, and his hand, outstretched for the tobacco-jar, was frozen into immobility. He was a little like a bird as he listened; his head on one side, his eyes alert.

The bicycle came up to the gate and stopped . . . and, after a few moments, there was a crunching sound on the gravel outside the window . . . then Dane came to life. He rose quickly and ran down the stairs to the side door.

His first idea was that this was a messenger from Colonel Carter (though why Colonel Carter should send a messenger instead of using the telephone was not quite clear) and he put on the light and opened the door and inquired in a firm voice —

"Who's there? What do you want?"

A tall figure in a mackintosh coat stepped out of the shadows into the stream of light and Dane saw that it was Frank.

"Frank!" he exclaimed in surprise, "Frank, what has happened?"

"Good news!" cried Frank, coming

towards him with his hands outstretched. "Marvellous news, Dane."

"What is it?" asked Dane again.

"It's over!" cried Frank, his breath catching in his throat with excitement, "it's all over. We're friends, my country and yours — my two countries — we shall never fight each other again."

Dane took his arm and drew him into the house. "My dear boy," he said, "my poor Frank . . . this has been a bad week for you — "

"But it's all *right*," Frank cried, pushing a sheaf of evening papers into Dane's hands. "Look what it says. Read them, Dane."

They were in the sitting-room now and Frank was still talking excitedly, incoherently, "Chamberlain is back . . . I saw him . . . yes, I was in Downing Street when he drove up in the car . . . he had been to the Palace . . . he waved his hand to us. Oh, you should have seen how he looked — how happy and young . . . you should have heard the cheers. I shall never forget it never . . . never . . . "

Dane had taken the papers and was scanning the headlines.

"You see!" cried Frank. "You see what it says! They've signed a pact — my Leader and yours — Germany and Britain are friends."

"It's wonderful news," Dane said.

"It's marvellous!" Frank declared, his eyes shining like stars. "It's a miracle . . . it's the most stupendous thing that ever happened. He was like a victorious general . . . but much greater, much more wonderful, much more worthy of gratitude . . . He has won a peace, Dane."

"Grand!" agreed Dane, stirred with the boy's enthusiasm. "Grand, Frank."

"Oh, grand!" cried Frank, stretching his arms above his head. "Oh, splendid! There aren't *words*, Dane — I think I went mad when I heard the news . . . I spoke to people in the street . . . I told them I was a German . . . we were shaking hands with each other. Somehow or other I found myself in a bar and we were drinking each other's healths. It was unforgettable!" cried Frank. "We were all crazy with excitement . . . with joy and friendship. Nobody wants war, and nobody who had seen what I've seen could make any mistake about it. All the week people have been going about with haggard, anxious faces, and I have been going about with a leaden heart. I had been living in a sort of nightmare, and then, suddenly, I had wakened and the sun was shining — it was like that, Dane."

"Yes," said Dane — he had been living in a nightmare too.

"And then . . . " continued Frank, "then, in the middle of all the excitement I knew that I must come *here* . . . to my first English friends, to my real friends . . . I couldn't wait till morning. I couldn't wait a moment. I had to come."

"My dear boy . . ." said Dane in a moved voice.

"We're friends now," Frank said earnestly. "Not only for a little while, but for always. Our countries are never going to war with each other again, so . . . so . . ." he broke off and made a gesture with his hands. "You know how it is, Dane . . . I thought of Wynne. I think of her all the time . . . Wynne."

"But, Frank — "

"I know all that you are going to say," declared Frank excitedly, "I've said it to myself a hundred times. I've tried to put her out of my heart . . . but Dane, everything has changed — this, this marvellous thing has changed everything. We're friends."

Dane was looking into the fire. It was nearly out, but a core of red-hot coal still glowed amongst the grey ashes. He watched that red-hot core and did not speak.

"Dane!" said Frank in a lower voice, "I love her too much to risk hurting her . . . that's why I went away. I knew the danger and I had seen the dreadful mess that my father and mother had made of things. Wynne is so lovely, she's so gay and fearless . . . I wouldn't hurt her for worlds. I had made up my mind to go away and not come back . . . but now, now it's all right. There's nothing to worry about any more. . . ."

"No," said Dane at last, "no, Frank, I can't give my consent. It's impossible."

"Why ?"

"Because . . ." began Dane and then he stopped for he did not know how to go on. He saw that if this pact was really a true pact on both sides there was no real reason against the marriage, and yet he was against the marriage with all his heart and mind.

"Dane, why won't you consent?" Frank was asking.

"Because it's such a risk," Dane said, "it's such a terrible risk, Frank. These mixed marriages are rarely successful."

"But if we love each other . . . and I do love her most dearly. Please, Dane, please reconsider it. Think about it for a little — perhaps you would get used to the idea," said Frank hopefully.

He shook his head. "No," he said, "Germany is not a fit place for an English girl. Wynne has been brought up in a free country."

"You're thinking of the Gestapo — the Secret Police — " said Frank eagerly. "But they don't interfere with people like us — people who are loyal to the Nazi Régime — "

"No," said Dane again, "no, Frank, there is only one way in which you could gain my consent."

"I would do anything — "

"You would have to live in this country. You would have to become naturalised — you wouldn't do that, would you?"

Frank's eyes flashed. "That's too much!"

he declared. "You've got no right to ask me to give up my country."

"No right at all," agreed Dane calmly, "and I'm not asking you to do it, Frank. I'm only telling you that this would be the only way to gain my consent. You can't marry without my consent because Wynne is my ward and she is under age."

"You dislike me!"

Dane smiled at him. "No, I like you very much. I have only one objection to you — you aren't an Englishman."

"I can't help that."

"I must think of Wynne," Dane continued. "It's too big a risk, I know, far better than you do, what your mother suffered and endured. Your father was ruined and broken. It was a tragedy, the whole thing. I'm not going to risk another tragedy in this generation."

"But, Dane — "

"Have you thought of your father? Have you considered his point of view?"

Frank did not answer. He was sitting, bent forward in the chair with his eyes fixed on the floor.

"Your father would be even less willing than I am." Dane continued. "He would be dismayed if he had any idea of this. He has managed to live down his own marriage but if you were to marry an English girl it would revive the old story. You know as well as I do that it would affect his position very seriously and would be a bar to his advancement. Do you imagine for a moment, that the Nazi leaders would allow him to remain in his present post if his son married an Englishwoman? Herr Hitler wouldn't tolerate an adviser with such pronounced leanings towards England."

"So you know that, too!" exclaimed Frank. "You know that my father is an official in the confidence of our leader. You seem to know everything."

"Not quite everything," said Dane with an involuntary smile.

"It's true, of course," said Frank slowly. "My father is a trusted official in the party."

"And he wouldn't approve of your marrying Wynne," urged Dane.

"No," said Frank reluctantly. "No, he wouldn't approve at first. I should have to persuade him . . . you see he's always been very bitter against Britain. But if he saw Wynne . . ."

"It would be very unpleasant for Wynne."

"I would prepare the way," declared Frank, with more confidence than he felt.

Dane sighed. "Why did he send you here? I can't understand it."

"There were reasons. I told you the first reason — it was to see what English people were saying and how they were feeling towards our country. There was the language, too. I had always been good at English and I wanted to learn to speak it like a native. The third reason," said Frank, hesitating for a moment and then lifting his head and looking straight at Dane, "The third reason is rather difficult to tell, but I want to tell you everything. I thought if I learnt to speak English really well I might be useful to my country. I thought that some day I might return to England as a Secret Service Agent. I can tell you this because it's over now. I could never do it *now* — you must believe this, Dane."

"I do believe it," Dane said.

"I must tell you," continued Frank rather uncomfortably, "I must tell you that when I came here first I came with bitter feelings in my heart. I was half English but I hated the English half of myself — I wanted to tear it out and throw it away. I had such bitter feelings that it was difficult to be polite and pleasant. I believed that Britain was trying to crush my country, to encircle her and crush her to death. That's what we were told."

He stopped for a moment but Dane did not speak.

"It was funny," Frank said thoughtfully, "it was funny to come here and see everyone so — so unconscious. At first I thought it was because people were afraid to speak their minds when I was there, but soon I realised that they were completely natural. They didn't hate Germany or wish her ill. They were too busy and happy to bother. It was funny, too, to hear people speak openly against their own Government, and at first I misunderstood this and thought England was ripe for revolution — but then I changed my mind. I saw they were loyal in the big things, I saw that they spoke little of their country and their Empire because their feelings were too deep. They were of one race, they were happy and secure. I couldn't go on hating you," continued Frank in a lower tone, "it was impossible to hate people who were so kind at heart. You can't hate people when you understand them."

"That's true," Dane said, the words bursting out of him, almost against his will.

"Yes," agreed Frank. "It's a truth I've found out for myself. It's a pity that everyone in my country couldn't come here and have the same experience . . . my mind has been in a turmoil all these months. I was like a man at sea in a boat with a load of preconceived ideas and prejudices and, almost every day, I cast one or two of them overboard. Soon I had none left. Soon I was beginning to feel proud that half of me was English. I saw then that I could never take up any appointment which would mean that I was working against Britain. I couldn't do it because I was half English myself. I saw that so clearly that I couldn't understand why I had never seen it before."

Dane had listened to the tale with deep interest, and he believed every word of it — indeed it was quite impossible to disbelieve the boy.

"I have wondered what to do," Frank continued. "I haven't written yet to tell my father that my feelings have changed. I haven't written to him at all lately for it has been difficult to know what to say . . . but now," he added, looking up and smiling at Dane with sudden joy, "now it's all right, now there is nothing to worry about any more. We are friends." He held out his hand with a sudden, impulsive gesture, and Dane took it in a firm clasp.

"We are friends," agreed Dane, smiling into his eyes, "and I hope we shall always be friends, Frank."

"You *hope*?" cried Frank. "But it's settled. Our leaders have signed the pact!"

Dane was only too ready to believe that peace was assured but he was older than Frank and more experienced. He was more cautious. Perhaps it was foolish to feel any doubts about the future but there were so many things to take into account. There was the Polish Corridor, there were the German colonies . . . could these and other matters be settled amicably?

Frank had been watching his face, and at last he said, "Dane, what is it? Why won't you consent to our marriage? I swear to you that I'll be good to Wynne. I swear that I'll always love her. She shall come first with me always."

"Wait for a little," Dane said. "There's no hurry. I'm saying this for your own sake as much as hers. See what your father has to say about it. You're both so young . . . No, Frank, I won't agree to an engagement either. I'm sorry about it but I can't."

"May I speak to Wynne?"

"No," said Dane. "No, you must wait for a year at least."

"A year!" cried Frank in consternation. "A *year*! But someone else may fall in love with her — they're bound to. Nobody could help it. I don't know why every man she meets isn't madly in love with her. Why must we wait a year before I may speak to her, Dane? Don't you believe in this pact? I tell you it's true. The two greatest nations in the world . . . and now they're friends for ever. The Fuehrer has said so. Do you think he would go back on his pledged word? Do you think that, Dane?"

"I hope not," Dane said in a low voice.

"I've seen him and spoken to him," cried Frank with flashing eyes. "He's a great man — a genius — look what he has done for us! Look how he has remade our country!"

"He has done wonders," Dane agreed.

They were silent again for a few moments, and then Dane rose to his feet. "I'm sorry, but it must be a year," he said gravely. "I trust you, Frank. If I find you have spoken to Wynne and told her that you are fond of her I shall have to withdraw my consent altogether."

"I won't go behind your back," said Frank in a hopeless sort of voice. "I can't help seeing her if she comes to London but I won't seek her out and I won't tell her that I love her."

"That's what I meant."

"Six months," said Frank in sudden desperation, "I can't wait longer than that. Please, Dane . . . it will be the end of March . . . even that is an eternity."

Dane sighed; he was unutterably weary; the clock on the mantelpiece was striking three.

"Six months, then," he said.

Wynne woke at six. It was not unusual for her to wake early and she often got up and went for a walk before breakfast. She wondered if she should do that today. It was a fine morning. The sun was shining and her blind was flapping in the breeze. She lay still for a minute or two and then she heard someone walking round the house — who could it be? It was a firm, light step — a man's step, but not Dane's. Wynne jumped out of bed and ran to the window. She saw Frank walking across the garden to the garage — Frank!

Wynne's heart beat so fast that she was almost choked. Frank had come back. She had known he would come, of course. She opened the window wider and called him softly and he turned and looked up at her.

"Frank, where have you come from? What are you doing? Are you going to stay?"

It was so like Wynne to ask three questions all at once that Frank had to smile. He did not really feel like smiling at all, but he could not help it.

Wynne beckoned to him and he came back across the lawn and stood looking up at her without speaking.

"Frank!" she said, eagerly. "Are you going to stay?

"No, Wynne. I can't stay. I just came to see Dane about something. I'm going back to London now."

"Now?"

He nodded.

"Oh, Frank, must you go? Can't you stay *one* day?"

"No," said Frank.

"Wait a minute," Wynne said. "I'm coming down."

"No, Wynne — "

She had vanished.

Frank looked up at the window and then at the door. Dane would not like it if he knew that Wynne was coming down to speak to him, but what could he do? He was still hesitating on the path when the door opened and Wynne appeared. She was in her pyjamas and a fur coat, and her hair was standing out in a fuzz of gold round her small rosebud face.

"Come here," she said. "Come and tell me — I can't shout at you, Frank. What have you been doing? Have you got into a scrape?"

Frank came towards her somewhat reluctantly — he was remembering his promise to Dane.

"Is it a scrape, Frank?" inquired Wynne again, examining him carefully.

"No, it isn't," he replied. "No, Wynne, everything is quite all right."

"You had better tell me," said Wynne, shaking her head at him. "I mean I might be able to help you. Roy always tells me when he gets into a mess."

"It isn't anything like that. I just came to see Dane."

"And you were going away without seeing *me*!" exclaimed Wynne in reproachful tones.

"I didn't *want* to," replied Frank. He could have said a lot more if it had not been for his promise. He felt that it was going to be very difficult indeed ... Wynne was dearer and sweeter and more adorable than ever. He looked at her and looked ... It would be the end of March before he could see her again — the end of March! He must look at her carefully, he must fill himself up to the brim with Wynne's dear face so that when he shut his eyes he would be able so see her. . .

Wynne was looking at him too, and the little silence that had fallen was full of significance.

"Well!" said Wynne at last, "well, of course if *that's* all you've got to say after not seeing me for *two whole months* — "

"Oh, Wynne, you don't understand!" cried Frank in dismay.

"No," said Wynne. "No, I don't understand it at all. I thought we were friends, you see."

"Of course we're friends!"

"Funny sort of friends," declared Wynne in a puzzled tone of voice. "Very funny sort of friends, Frank. You arrive here in the dead of night and creep away at the crack of dawn. You don't want to see me or talk to me."

"It isn't that I don't want to see you or talk to you."

"Isn't it?"

"No," said Frank desperately, "No, it isn't. I could talk to you all day, but — but I've got to go."

"Why?"

"I've got to get back — back to London."

"I see," said Wynne thoughtfully.

"You see, don't you?" urged Frank. "I mean I've got to go."

"When are you coming back to see us?"

"I don't know," said Frank. "At least — "

"What about next Sunday?"

This was frightful — it would have been much better not to see Wynne at all. "I'll see," said Frank. "I'm — I'm not sure . . . I'll come back sometime, of course."

"Yes, of course," agreed Wynne in a curiously expressionless voice. "You'll come back sometime when you aren't so busy — when you've got nothing better to do."

"Oh, Wynne it isn't that at all."

"That was what you said."

Frank struggled against the overpowering desire to take her in his arms and end all the misunderstandings by kissing her thoroughly. "I'll come back," he said in a gruff voice, "I'll come back as soon as I can; that's all."

"That's all, is it? inquired Wynne. "It isn't much, is it, Frank?"

"No," said Frank, "I mean yes, it is. It's a great deal if you look at it in the right way; because, if I say I'll come back as soon as I can, it means — well, of course it means that I can't come any sooner."

Wynne saw the point. She nodded thoughtfully. "Oh it means that, does it?"

"Yes," said Frank earnestly. "Yes, that's what it means. So if I don't come for — for a little while — "

"Yes," said Wynne, inquiringly, "yes, Frank, if you don't come for a little while what then?"

"Nothing," said Frank, who had suddenly realised that he was sailing very close to the wind. "Nothing, Wynne, I must go at once — "

"Why need you — "

"I really must," declared Frank, "because if I don't go at once . . ."

Wynne smiled at him. "What would happen, Frank?" she inquired innocently. "What would happen? Do tell me."

"If I don't go at once." declared poor Frank who had almost reached the end of his tether. "If I don't go at once I shall — I shall be late."

He turned away as he spoke and began to walk quickly across the lawn toward the garage.

"But Frank!" cried Wynne, "Frank, come back. Aren't you going to say good-bye?"

Frank stopped and looked back. "No," he said, "No, Wynne — don't let us say,

goodbye. I'll just say, 'Auf weidersehen'
... Auf weidersehen, Wynne!"

"Auf weidersehen, Frank," she replied.

She watched his tall figure stride off across the grass, and there was joy in her heart — of course he loved her, poor darling!

CHAPTER SEVENTEEN

IT WAS a long winter. Everyone felt it long, and to Frank, slaving away in a London office, it seemed that spring would never come. He received several friendly letters from Wynne and replied to them in the same spirit for he did not think that Dane would mind. He wrote these letters with an eye on Dane — as it were — and they were so extremely innocent that Dane might have seen them. He corresponded with his father, too, and these letters were much harder to write. At first, Herr Heiden wrote urging his son to come home, but soon the tone of his letters changed and Frank was aware of the reason. Herr Heiden was still under the impression that his son's prolonged stay in England was to perfect himself in the language and so to fit himself for an appointment as a German Agent. Frank had not the courage to undeceive him. It was weak and cowardly — he knew that well — and he was merely putting off the evil day, but he found it impossible to write and tell his father that his ideas and feelings had changed. Frank wrote to Cousin Sophie several times and once to Dane. He lunched with the Audleys at the Berkeley and went with Migs to the little restaurant Migs knew of where they served snails. It was not a tremendous success because neither of them enjoyed the snails very much but they were both too proud to say so.

At the end of February, when Frank had started to count the days and to tick them off on his office calendar, Roy suddenly walked in and announced that he'd got leave.

He sat on the office table and swung his legs and smiled and waved his hands, and he was so like Wynne that Frank could have hugged him.

"The Terrible's in dock for a refit," explained Roy, "so I've got leave and I thought it would be tremendous fun if you and I did one of those Outings together."

Frank began to explain how impossible this was, but Roy did not listen.

"I don't mean in Germany," he said, "because anyhow I don't suppose they'd let me go abroad without an awful fuss and bother. I mean we could do an Outing here, just you and me — and Agatha. Yes, I've got Agatha now . . . you see Harry's brother bought a new car and he wanted to get rid of Agatha so Harry and I bought her between us. It works out all right really. Whoever gets leave uses Agatha and if we both get leave at the same time we can use her . . . so there you are," declared Roy, waving his hands again.

Roy was so large and so full of sea air and freshness that he made the cramped little office seem smaller and more cramped than ever.

"I wish I could," said Frank, regretfully.

"You can," said Roy, "and, what's more, you must. We'll go to Scotland. We'll go to the West of Scotland. There's a fellow I know who says it's marvellous. You're here to see the country, aren't you? Well then — "

"It's impossible," said Frank.

"Impossible, my foot," declared Roy. "Why, of course they'll give you leave. Tell them your long-lost cousin has come all the way from Kamschatka to see you. Tell them your uncle from America has suddenly turned up. Spin them some yarn or other. They'll fall for it all right."

"They wouldn't," said Frank, with conviction.

"They must be cads, then," declared Roy, "and, as a matter of fact, it's obvious that they *are* cads. What a foul, filthy little hole to work in!"

"Yes," agreed Frank in a thoughtful voice. He had begun to think it over and to consider it carefully. He knew that he was doing good work for the firm — practically the whole of their foreign correspondence was in his hands — but they had refused to raise his salary or to give him a better room. He was overworked and underpaid and for some time past he had toyed with the idea of leaving them and trying to get something better. He was pretty certain that he could get something a good deal better, for the experience had been useful and he had begun to know his worth. He saw, too, that it would be a great advantage if he were free to go on this trip for, when the trip was over, it would be quite natural for him to go back to Fernacres with Roy. He and Roy would walk into Fernacres together and there would be no embarrassing questions to answer. The six months would be over on the 23rd of March and he would then be free — free to speak to Wynne and tell her he loved her. Apart from all this Frank wanted to go with Roy. He wanted to shake off the dust of this horrible office and smell the fresh air again.

"Well?" inquired Roy. "Well, what about it? Do come, Frank, it would be a tremendous spree."

"Can you wait a week?" asked Frank.

"Of course I can," said Roy, "I'll go home. I'd have to go home for part of my leave, anyhow — I mean I want to."

"Right," said Frank, making up his mind to take the plunge. "Right you are. Where do I meet you?"

The Outing started under the most favourable auspices. The sun shone and Agatha behaved beautifully. Roy and Frank took turns at the wheel and they spun up the Great North Road in tremendous style. It was cold, of course, for it was only the beginning of March, and Agatha was extremely draughty, but Roy and Frank were young and hardy; they swathed themselves in scarves and enjoyed every moment.

At Newcastle they turned westward —

not by any preconceived plan, but merely because they happened to take the wrong road and could not be bothered to return.

"It doesn't matter," Roy said, looking at the map, "it doesn't matter a hoot. This road takes us to Scotland too — it goes past a place called Carter Bar."

"Is there a place to stay?" inquired Frank who was busy negotiating the heavy traffic in the Newcastle streets.

"There's Otterburn," said Roy. "I suppose that's a village of some sort . . . then we come to Carter Bar, and then to Jedburgh. Mary Queen of Scots used to stay there," added Roy, announcing this interesting scrap of history with some pride.

He was rather sorry afterwards that he had remembered it for Frank was always eager to absorb knowledge and made so many pertinent inquiries about the unfortunate queen that Roy was completely out of his depth.

"She was married to a fellow called Darnley," said Roy, racking his brains in a vain attempt to satisfy his insatiable companion, "and then there was Bothwell. She married him, too, but that was after they'd blown up the first husband . . . or wait, I believe they stabbed him with knives when he was having supper with Mary in her room . . . but no, that was another fellow. She was very beautiful, anyhow," declared Roy, who was thankful to find something which was beyond all doubt.

"She must have been," agreed Frank.

"And she ended up by having her head cut off."

"Why ?"

"It was Elizabeth," explained Roy. "Good Queen Bess . . . she didn't like Mary for some reason . . . Here's Otterburn," he added with a sigh of relief. "Here's Otterburn, Frank. It looks a nice pub — let's stop."

Frank drew up at the hotel and they went in. It was a very nice pub indeed and the beer was most satisfactory. Two small rooms happened to be available, so the travellers engaged them for the night and having put Agatha safely into the hotel garage they went out for a bit of a walk to stretch their legs. They had not gone far when Roy noticed a small mill and he pointed it out to Frank.

"Otterburn Mill," he said. "They make

tweed there. Let's go in and see what it's like, shall we?"

Frank agreed at once and they turned in at the gate and found themselves in a small shop stocked with woollen goods of every description. The rugs fascinated Roy and after some little hesitation he decided to buy one, explaining to Frank that it was not really extravagant because they were going north and they would probably be very glad of it. Frank was looking at the scarves. There was a soft, blue one — very thick and fluffy — with a fawn pattern on the ends. It was a lovely scarf and it reminded him of Wynne — not that he needed any reminder.

"All right," said Frank. "And I shall have this — how much is it?"

"It's far too light," said Roy firmly. "The colour, I mean. It's really a woman's scarf and it'll get frightfully dirty in about five minutes."

"I know," said Frank, taking the money out of his pocket.

"You'd be far better with a brown one," Roy urged him. "Here's one, Frank . . . or there's a green one with a brown pattern . . . that's a woman's scarf."

"I know," said Frank again.

"Oh, I see," said Roy, and he turned away and completed his purchase of the rug.

"As a matter of fact," said Frank, as they left the mill with their parcels under their arms, "as a matter of fact . . . it's really . . . I mean I bought it for Wynne. Do you think she'll like it ?"

"For Wynne ?" inquired Roy incredulously.

Frank did not reply.

"Good lord !" said Roy. "I never thought that you . . . I mean I never . . . well, of course she'll like it. Any girl would."

CHAPTER EIGHTEEN

FRANK and Roy stayed the night at Otterburn and went on their way the following morning. They stopped at Jedburgh for lunch and to see Queen Mary's house and fortunately for Roy there was a guide to show them round. Roy was able to sit back — as it were — and enjoy the spectacle of another man being pursued and harried by a stream of searching questions upon the fortunes of Mary, Queen of Scots, upon the customs of the day, upon the social, political and religious factors which had conspired to encompass her death.

After that Roy and Frank continued north in a curiously haphazard manner, taking any road that seemed good to them at the moment and staying at various more or less comfortable inns. They were very happy together, talking long and earnestly about one thing and another and incidentally learning to know each other pretty well. They discussed international politics too, but here they did not agree so well and, after one or two somewhat heated arguments which led nowhere at all, they decided to leave such controversial subjects alone.

"We'll leave them to people who know more about them," said Roy, and Frank agreed.

By this time they had penetrated into the heart of the Western Highlands and world affairs seemed very far away. Some days they did not bother to buy a newspaper, for it was not easy to procure one and it seemed more important to buy food for themselves and petrol for Agatha and to find a reasonably comfortable shelter for the night.

They came at last to a small fishing-hotel on the banks of a river and here they were forced to call a halt, for Agatha, who had been going so well and had caused no trouble, whatever, suddenly decided that she would go no farther. . . .

"Well," said Roy as he climbed out of the seat, "well, of course I suppose it's rather decent of her to die here. I mean she might have died in the middle of a blasted heath or something. I wonder what the pub's like."

It was called, "The Argyll Arms" and it

was so clean and so comfortable and provided such an excellent supper at such a
moderate cost that any slight irritation they
might have felt evaporated completely.

"Agatha has chosen well," declared
Frank.

"By Jove, she has," agreed his companion. "There are no flies on Agatha.
We'll have a good look at her inside
tomorrow — she needs greasing, I expect."

"We might stay here," Frank suggested.
"We might do some walking "

"Yes," said Roy, "yes it's a grand idea.
I'm sick of sitting in Agatha all day. We'll
climb that mountain."

They engaged a comfortable room with
two beds in it and unpacked their suitcases
which had never been properly unpacked
since they started. Frank took out the scarf
which he had bought for Wynne and looked
at it . . . yes, it was just as pretty as he had
thought and he was more glad than ever
that he had bought it. How lovely to think
that some day it would be folded round
Wynne's neck to keep her warm . . . his
scarf! He gloated over its colour and its
soft fleecy texture and then he rolled it up

again in the paper and put it carefully in the bottom of his suitcase.

The following day was misty and drizzly, and the mountain which Roy had wanted to climb was completely blotted out. Nobody would have known that there was any mountain there, or that there had ever been a mountain.

"But it *is* there all right," said Roy, "because I asked the innkeeper fellow and he told me its name . . . sounded as if he was gargling."

They spent the day profitably in greasing Agatha and cleaning her carburettor and plugs and tightening up her brakes and she responded to this unwonted attention in a satisfactory manner.

"*There*," shouted Frank as Agatha's engine burst into a rapid staccato — more like the explosions of a machine-gun than those of a petrol-driven motor — "There, Roy, what d'you think of that?"

"Grand," yelled Roy as he washed his hands under the garage tap. "By Jove she'll go like smoke when we leave here and go on."

The air was so soft that Roy and Frank slept late into the following morning and, although the day was fine and sunny and the mountain had appeared again in all its rugged magnificence, they decided that they must put off their climb. They consulted the inn-keeper about this and he agreed that they must get up early — very early indeed — if they wanted to get to the top and back before dark. He suggested that they should take a shorter walk today, they might go over to Inverdrum — it was a "fine wee town" and well-worth seeing. They could buy anything they wanted there or they could go to the pictures.

"The pictures!" echoed Roy. "Do you mean there's actually a picture-house near here — a theatre where they show films?"

The inn-keeper assured him that there was. "It's only four miles by the hill path," he added encouragingly. "I could find out what's on for you."

Roy had only asked the question out of curiosity (it seemed so strange to think of a picture-house in these surroundings) and neither he nor Frank had any desire to spend the afternoon cooped up in a stuffy theatre, but the walk would be pleasant and they could do some shopping . . . yes, they would go to Inverdrum.

"I must get some socks," said Roy. "Mine have all gone into holes."

"I want some handkerchiefs," added Frank.

The inn-keeper was so delighted to find that his suggestion was acceptable that he put on his hat and wound a scarf round his neck and accompanied them for part of the way to point out the path. He was a garrulous soul and anxious to do the honours of his country-side to these pleasant-spoken young gentlemen. He told them the names of the hills and mountains in the vicinity and enlarged upon the historical associations. Then he left them and returned to the hotel and the two young gentlemen walked on. Unfortunately, however, the inn-keeper's directions as to how they were to continue were so detailed and so elaborate that they defeated their object, and when Roy and Frank had walked hard for an hour and a half and there were still no sign of the "fine wee town" they came to the conclusion that they were lost. They did not mind much for the hill was a pleasant place to wander, and the air was soft and clear and fragrant. There was no sound save the sudden cry of a bird and the tinkling of water . . . water running everywhere. It ran in small rocky channels or hidden between overhanging banks of green grass. There was withered brown heather; there were outcrops of rock; there were bushes of bog myrtle and an occasional bush of gorse with blazing golden flowers. Here and there they came upon treacherous patches of moss, some of it brilliantly green and some of it pale pink like the inside of a seashell. There were a good many sheep about, and presently they saw a shepherd wending his way up the hill, so they shouted to him and inquired which way they should go, and how far it was to Inverdrum, and he shouted back to them that they were, "just there, almost", and signalled to them to continue round the shoulder of the hill. . . .

"Gosh, it's magnificent!" exclaimed Roy, sitting down suddenly upon a boulder. "Look at it," he added, "look at it, Frank!"

It was a magnificent view. The hill stretched steeply down to the shores of a big sea loch — a wide expanse of blue water which curved away between the green hills and brown mountains until it was lost to sight. The sun was dipping down into a bank of rosy clouds and the eastern slopes of the hills were faintly shadowed. Below them and a little westwards lay the town which they had been seeking, it was built on the shores of a bay and was sheltered from the winds by rocky promontories. The houses were close upon the edge of the loch, and the waterfront was built up from sea-level with old grey weatherbeaten buildings which looked as if they had been there from time immemorial. A pier ran out into the water, and there was a church spire with a clock; the remainder of the town consisted of small grey houses and winding streets and one or two villas in patches of green garden. To Frank the place looked like a wood-cut from the fairy tale — it had an other-worldly air — and Roy put this feeling into words when he inquired suddenly in a puzzled voice:

"Shall we be able to buy socks there . . . and handkerchiefs?"

"No," said Frank, half laughing and half in earnest, "no, Roy, we shall only be able to buy ingredients for a fairy's spell . . . "

"There isn't a picture-house," declared Roy, "no, there can't be. That's too much for anyone to believe . . . Fancy sitting and seeing Laurel and Hardy, or Greta Garbo and then coming out into the middle of this," he added, waving his arms as he spoke.

"How peaceful it is!" Frank said, in a wondering tone. "How lovely and quiet and peaceful. You could be happy here for ever and ever, I think."

They looked at the scene for a little longer and then went down the hill towards the little town and entered it through an old, half-crumbled archway. The streets were paved with cobbles and their footsteps sounded loud in their ears after the soft ground of the hill. The main street curved upwards from the pier and was lined on either side by tiny shops with strange assortments of goods in the windows. In one shop, for instance, you could buy fishing rods and lines and sinkers, neckties, tartan scarves, picture-postcards, rubber boots, anti-midge lotion, walking sticks and umbrellas, Penguin novels, radio sets, or silver brooches set with cairngorms. You could also have your hair cut and your shoes soled and heeled. Unfortunately Frank and Roy wanted none of these things, they wanted socks and handkerchiefs, and these useful necessities of life were not to be had. They went farther up the street and presently came to a newsagent's shop which was also a post-office. A little group of people were standing outside the door and it seemed to Roy that they were discussing some subject of importance. Several of them had newspapers in their hands and were holding them up and reading them with more than ordinary interest.

"I say, Frank!" began Roy, but Frank had stopped suddenly and was pointing to the poster which was propped up outside the newsagent's door. It was printed in large black letters and announced baldly, "HITLER MARCHES INTO PRAGUE."

"Hitler marches into Prague!" exclaimed Frank in a horrified tone, "Roy — Roy it can't be true!"

Roy looked at it — and blinked — and looked again. "Gosh!" he said, "Gosh . . . we'd better get a paper."

It was easier said than done, for the papers had been sold out on arrival, but a middle-aged man, who was standing near the door, noticed the dismay on Frank's face and offered him his own paper.

"I have read it," he said, in his soft Highland voice. "There isn't much in it at all, and if I want I can see my brother's paper. It is bad news, isn't it?"

The news had come upon Frank with such an appalling blow that he was almost stunned. He took the paper, and, without a word of thanks to the donor, he turned on his heel and left the shop.

"Thank you very much," said Roy, trying to make up for the rudeness of his friend. "Thank you — it's awfully kind of you. He isn't usually like that."

The man smiled. "It's all right," he said, "it doesn't matter. He got a shock — I could see that. Will it be war now, do you think?"

"Heaven knows!" said Roy.

"It will be war," said another man in a confident tone. "I shall be away to Oban tomorrow."

"He is a reservist," explained the first man. "He is in the Argyll and Sutherland Highlanders. I am a fisherman and they will want me, too."

"I am in the Navy," said Roy.

"Is that so?" inquired the fisherman with interest. "You will be having the first crack at them, then . . . but I will be needed, too, for I have a stout sea-going boat. . . . "

"And your friend ?" put in the reservist, "is he a naval man, too ?"

"No," said Roy. "No, as a matter of fact, he's . . . but I think I'd better go after him . . . and see what he's doing."

He tore himself away and ran down the street after Frank.

CHAPTER NINETEEN

FRANK was walking along reading the paper as he went, and Roy soon caught up with him. They walked in silence out of the little town and up the hill. When they reached the top, Roy paused and looked back. The sun had set but the spring twilight was very clear, the sky was lemon and palest green with a purple scarf of cloud low on the horizon. The little town was dark save for a few pinpoints of amber light in the windows of the houses, but the loch still shimmered as if it had absorbed some of the departing daylight and was giving it out again. On the hill and amongst the scattered rocks, bushes of gorse which had blazed like living gold in the sunshine were mere ghosts.

Frank had walked on, and again Roy ran after him. He had not spoken once and Roy had a feeling that Frank did not know he was with him — or perhaps did not care. Roy was quite frightened about Frank for it was so unlike him to be inconsiderate and unsociable and he was almost afraid to speak to him for he did not know what to say. At last, however, he could bear the silence no longer and he called to him to stop, and Frank stopped and waited for him to come.

"Frank!" said Roy. "Frank, it's no good dashing on like that. We can't do anything tonight."

"We can't do anything at all," said Frank, hopelessly, and Roy saw that his face was drawn and haggard with the intensity of his feelings.

"No," said Roy, trying to speak in a matter-of-fact voice. "No, we can't do anything tonight so it's no use racing on like that."

"It's true, I suppose?" inquired Frank anxiously. "I suppose it couldn't be a mistake, Roy?"

Roy hesitated. "I'm afraid it's true," he said, "I'm afraid there isn't much doubt about it, old chap."

"I can't understand it," declared Frank. "It's — it's simply incredible. The Fuehrer guaranteed their frontiers. He promised to respect their independence. What will happen now?"

"I don't know," said Roy uncomfortably.

"We'll just have to wait and see what happens . . . we can't do anything. As a matter of fact we'd better be getting back to the hotel. I want to wire Fernacres where I am in case a message has come there for me."

"A message ?"

"They might recall me," explained Roy in an embarrassed tone of voice. "Of course they probably won't . . . but still . . . "

"Yes," agreed Frank. "Yes, I see."

They walked on in silence for a few minutes and then Frank burst out again —

"They trusted the Fuehrer," he said in a strangled voice. "They trusted him. He promised that he wouldn't interfere with them, he said it was his sacred will to respect the Czechs — his *sacred will*, Roy !"

"He — he's changed his mind, I suppose," Roy said.

Frank did not hear him; he continued, "The Sudetenland was his last territorial claim — those were his very words. He said we wanted to live our own lives and others must have freedom to do the same. Those were good words — why has he gone back on them ?" Frank was silent for a moment and then he cried, "Oh Heavens, what is that man doing to my poor country!"

"It's other people's countries — " began Roy.

"He's ruining us!" cried Frank. "He's ruining himself and us at the same time . . . "

"But Frank — "

"Why do you walk with me? Aren't you ashamed to call me your friend?"

"Don't be an ass. You can't help it," declared Roy more uncomfortably than ever. He was all the more anxious to proclaim his loyalty to Frank because for a moment he had been a trifle — just a trifle ashamed of him. It had seemed so odd somehow — when he was talking to those men at the news-shop — it had seemed so very queer that he should be chumming up with a German. He felt now that he had been disloyal in some mysterious way, disloyal to the very real friendship that he felt for good old Frank . . . and yet what on earth would have been the use of disclosing Frank's identity? "Don't be an ass," said Roy. "You know perfectly well we're friends and always shall be. If Hitler chooses to walk into Prague it's nothing to do with you."

"But it *is*," said Frank in a despairing

voice. "It has a lot to do with me. I am part of my country and that man speaks and acts for me and for all my countrymen. If he lies we are all perjured . . . "

"But Frank — "

" . . . and if we're perjured we're lost. We're *lost*, Roy — don't you understand that ? Who will trust us again ?"

The answer was too obvious, and Roy remained silent.

"There's no sense in it," continued Frank wildly. "Nobody can deal with people in business if they can't trust them. I've seen that again and again in my work. How then can nations deal with each other unless they have confidence in each other's promises ? The thing is impossible . . . it's a madness . . . and what do we want with Czechoslovakia ?"

"He wants the Skoda munitions factories," Roy pointed out.

"He wants them !" cried Frank. "Roy, they aren't his. What would happen if everyone took what they wanted. There's no sense in it at all . . . and the Czechs," added Frank, "the Czechs ! What do we want with Czechs in the German Reich ? They aren't our own people."

"It's all part of his policy," Roy pointed out.

This seemed to distress Frank more than ever. "No," he cried. "No, that's where you're wrong. It was never the Fuehrer's policy to incorporate people of alien blood in the Reich. The Austrians — yes, they are our brothers — and the people of the Sudetenland are Germans like ourselves. This is something new, and different — this was never his aim. He has said so again and again."

"I wish Dane was here," said Roy in heartfelt tones, for he felt that Dane would know what to say to this wild-eyed haggard young man. "I wish Dane was here. Let's go back to Fernacres tomorrow and you can talk to Dane."

"Dane!" cried Frank in horror-stricken tones. "Dane! No indeed, I couldn't face him. I should be ashamed — "

"Oh Frank, don't be absurd!"

"I can't face anyone," Frank declared; "you say it's absurd? How would you feel if it were your country — your Britain — that had done this?"

He stopped and waited for an answer to this question.

"Oh well — *we* wouldn't do it, of course," said Roy. (He was aware, directly he had spoken, that he had blundered badly but he could not unsay the words.)

"No," said Frank softly. "Oh no, of course not. *You* wouldn't do it, would you? It's only 'foreigners' who behave like that — people who can't be expected to know any better."

"I didn't say that," declared Roy.

"That was what you meant."

"I can't help it, Frank. I don't know what to say to you. Everything I say seems to be wrong."

They walked on and, as they walked, they discussed the affair in the same disjointed uncomfortable way.

"Oh hell!" exclaimed Roy at last. "This has bust up our whole trip — I wish Hitler was dead."

"You can't wish it more than I do," replied Frank.

Long after they had gone to bed and had turned out the light and Roy was fast asleep, breathing slowly and easily like a contented child, Frank lay sleepless and tossed and turned. His whole world had fallen into ruins and everything that he had cherished was gone. He had lost everything — his love and respect for his Leader, his pride in the Nazi régime. He had lost his past and his future and . . . yes, he had lost Wynne. How could he ask Wynne to share his life ? He had no life left — no life worth sharing. He felt like a homeless dog. If there were going to be war he would have to go back to Germany and fight for a régime which he believed in no longer. He would have to fight against Britain and therefore against Wynne and all Wynne's people. Even if there were not going to be war he could not ask Wynne to leave her comfortable home — he had nothing to offer her. He was a German and he had been proud of the fact, but he did not feel proud of it any more. He had lost Wynne and all chance of personal happiness, but this was not the thought that distressed him most. This was his own private trouble and Frank was thinking more of his country — his beloved country which had been put to shame.

There was only one man in the world who would understand what he was enduring, and that man — Frank was sure — must be enduring the same bitter pangs. That man had trusted Hitler just as Frank had trusted him, had taken Hitler's hand in friendship and signed a pact with him. That man had been betrayed too. If only I could see him, thought poor Frank (only of course I couldn't see him. They wouldn't let me near him — why should they?) if only I could talk to him and tell him what I was feeling, and tell him that others of my countrymen are feeling the same. I would tell him how I saw him that day, when he flew home from Munich, and how I watched him go into his house and cheered him and blessed him for what he had done. He would understand how I was torn in half between my two countries and how I felt that he had put the pieces together and healed me. He would understand how I feel now — ashamed, betrayed.

Before it was light, Frank had risen and dressed, and when Roy opened his eyes to the morning sun he found the room empty. Frank had gone, and he had left a scrap of paper on the dressing table with a few words of farewell. "I'm sorry to go off like this but you will understand. I must bear this alone."

Roy ate his breakfast in a thoughtful

mood. He was very sorry for Frank but he couldn't for the life of him see Frank's point of view. What was there in this new development to make such a fuss about? Everyone knew that Hitler was a twister — everyone had known it for some time — Hitler and his policy had been discussed *ad nauseam* in every ward-room in the British Navy. Everyone knew that we were re-arming as quickly as ever we could and everyone knew why. It was just a question of time — how long a rope should Hitler be given, that was all. There were people who said we ought to have gone to war with him last September; but very few Service people were such fools. Service people knew just exactly how weak we were last September and were unutterably thankful when Chamberlain managed to snatch the situation out of the fire. What was it he had said — "Out of this nettle, danger, we pluck this flower, safety." Yes, thought Roy, it was great work. But most people had seen pretty clearly that Munich had only put off the day of reckoning. Frank hadn't thought so, of course. Frank had evidently taken the Munich pact at its face value . . . it was bad luck on Frank.

Roy reviewed the situation in a matter of

fact way for he was a matter of fact person and he had been trained to think things out clearly and to act quickly and capably upon his deduction. We're more prepared than we were, he decided, but we could do very nicely with another year . . . in another year we should be ready for anything.

He was somewhat surprised that he had not received a telegram to cancel his leave but decided that it was a good sign. It probably meant that we weren't going to stop Hitler yet. We were going to pay out the rope a bit further . . . after all what could we do for the unfortunate Czechs? We couldn't get near them, could we? France couldn't get near them either . . . but I'd better go home, thought Roy — as he finished his plateful of bacon and eggs and passed on to marmalade — yes, I'd better make for home . . . not much fun going on by myself, anyhow.

Roy went straight home, driving at speed but with considerable skill and judgement; and, spending one night on the road, he walked into Fernacres the following evening as his family was sitting down to dinner.

His family was surprised to see him but

not inordinately so, for Roy had accustomed it to his erratic comings and goings; Barber was accustomed to them too, and a place was laid for him at the table in the twinkling of an eye.

"What a good thing I ordered a chicken!" said Sophie, emerging from the deep waters of her son's embrace with a sigh of satisfaction. "I wonder why I did. Something seemed to *tell* me to order a chicken when I was in Kingsport on Monday, and of course it must have been because you were coming home."

"It must have been a clever something," replied Roy as he sat down and unfolded his table-napkin, "because I had no idea on Monday that I was coming home."

"Then why . . . " his mother began.

"Where's Frank?" inquired Wynne.

"Have you been recalled?" asked Dane.

He answered Dane's question first because it was the easiest. "No," he said, "unless there's been a message here. That's why I wired you. *The Terrible* won't be ready for another week . . . has anyone been recalled?"

"No," said Dane.

"Where's Frank?" repeated Wynne anxiously.

Roy shook his head. "I don't know where he's gone. He just weighed anchor and steamed away in the night — no address given."

"You quarrelled . . ."

"Definitely not. No really, we got on like a house on fire. He's a frightfully decent fellow . . . of course he was a bit worried, and I seemed to say all the wrong things, but I'm sure he knew that I didn't mean to . . ."

"What on earth . . ." began Dane.

"Can't you explain . . ." began Wynne.

Roy had just put a large spoonful of grapefruit into his mouth but, taking pity upon the bewilderment of his relations, he swallowed it whole. "The fact is," he said, "the fact is poor old Frank was awfully upset about this Czech business — absolutely sunk — well, I suppose it was natural, really."

PART TWO

German Interlude

CHAPTER ONE

THE town of Freigarten was looking its loveliest when Franz Heiden swung himself down from the big train on to the crowded platform and wandered out of the station into the familiar streets. It was very odd to be home once more after his long visit to England; it was strange to hear German spoken on every side. He had begun to think in German again — quite unconsciously — and to think of himself as "Franz". He had been away a whole year but he was not happy to return — he felt no surge of joy in returning to his own land. It was a very different home-coming from that to which he had looked forward when he left his native place. There was nobody to meet him. Nobody knew he was coming, so he could not complain — but all the same he felt very sad. He wandered along looking at the people and listening to scraps of conversation as he passed.

It was late in the afternoon and the sun was declining; but, even so, the sunshine was warmer and more golden than the sunshine to which Franz had become accustomed. The trees in the streets were already in bud and there were tulips and scillas in the window boxes. There was a festive air about the city. He noticed flags in the windows and the shops were decorated with coloured paper festoons and he realised that Freigarten was celebrating the great and bloodless victory and the incorporation of an unwilling country in the Reich.

Franz had decided to return to his native place because he felt so uncomfortable in England. After leaving Roy in that unceremonious manner, Franz had taken the bus to Glasgow and from there had proceeded by train to London and on every side he had heard the annexation of Czechoslovakia discussed. His fellow travellers took him for an Englishman and did not mince their words, and their words were all the more weighty and significant because they were perfectly calm. They did not rant and rave against Germany, they did not hate her, they merely judged her and condemned her as they would have judged and condemned any thief or any murderer of innocent men. They discussed the whole affair sanely and dispassionately in a manner that made his blood run cold. Franz had buried himself in his newspaper and had tried not to hear . . . This was bad enough, but it was worse when Franz reached London and encountered people that he knew, for they were aware of his nationality of course. They were so careful not to mention the Czechs to Franz; they spoke of the weather and the latest show at His Majesty's and then remembered an important engagement and hurried away. . . .

It was an impossible position — it was intolerable — his nerves became so tender that he shrank from the kindest word. After two days of wretchedness Franz decided that the only thing to do was to go home . . . and now, here he was in his native city and he felt more unhappy than ever. He saw now that he had not considered the matter properly before rushing home — there were many difficulties ahead. What could he say to his father? How could he discuss the situation with him? His father was a Nazi to the backbone and believed in the Fuehrer as a monk believes in God — there was no chance of his father sharing his views. I should not have come, thought Franz, it was foolish of me — it was madness. Yet where can I go, and what can I do?

By this time Franz had made his way to the big block of buildings where his father's apartment was situated — his feet had led him there — but he hesitated at the main door and putting down his suitcase looked up and down the street. Should he go in and announce his presence or should he stop and reconsider the whole affair while there was still time? His father did not know that he was coming home — nobody knew where he was. He might find a job in an office here — or somewhere else in Germany where he was unknown. He was still hesitating and wondering what to do when the porter who took care of the flats came out of the front door. It was a new man and he looked at Franz curiously.

"Are you looking for someone?" he inquired.

"Herr Heiden," said Franz without thinking.

"He is away," the man said. "Herr Heiden has gone to Prague, but you will find Fräulein Heiden at home. Here, I will give you the key of the apartment; it is on the third floor, but you will have to walk up for the elevator is not working now."

Franz took the key. He thought it strange that the man should offer it to a stranger like this, but everything was so strange that he felt as if he were walking in a dream. He went up the stairs, put the key in the lock and opened the door. Everything was the same . . . that was his first reaction . . . the hall with its polished oak floor, the big, old-fashioned furniture, the mirror with its heavy gilt frame. For a moment Franz felt as if he had never been away, as if he were a schoolboy again, coming home from school . . . and then suddenly, as he stood there looking round, the conviction came to him that everything was not the same. There was a queer silence in the house. The clock was ticking loudly, but there was no other sound at all, no sound of dishes clattering in the kitchen, no patter of feet on the polished boards. Where was Gretchen, the old faithful servant who had been with the Heiden family for so long? Where was

Tant' Anna? There was a cold musty atmosphere in the house instead of the usual pleasant smell of floor polish. At this hour, thought Franz in some alarm, at this hour the house usually smelt of supper — of frying sausage or boiling soup.

It was getting late now and the hall was dark and shadowy. Franz put out his hand to switch on the light and then he changed his mind. He put down his case and walked across the hall and opened the door of the living-room. It was lighter here than in the hall for the windows faced west and the reflection in the sky from the setting sun filled the room with a ruddy glow. At first he thought the room was empty and then he saw the tall figure of Tant' Anna standing against the curtain by the window. She turned suddenly as Franz moved. He could not see her face but he was aware that her whole body had become tense.

"Tant' Anna!" he exclaimed. "Don't you know me? It's Franz."

"Franz!" she said in a sort of gasp. "Franz!"

"I've come home," he told her, going forward to meet her. He took her hands and pressed them, they were hot and dry like the hands of a person with fever. "Tant' Anna," he said again, "you're pleased to see me, aren't you?"

"Yes," she said, "yes, Franz, of course — "

She sat down on the sofa and Franz sat down beside her. For some reason which he could not understand he was frightened — his heart was pounding madly in his breast. There was something the matter, there was something terribly wrong. Tant' Anna had always been a rock in the sea of life — so calm and sure — and he had always leant upon her and depended upon her; but now he saw that she was just an old woman and there was no strength in her at all. He put his arm round her shoulders and the thinness of her body frightened him more than ever. There was nothing of her but bones....

"You are too thin!" he exclaimed involuntarily.

"I am not very well, Franz," she told him in a whisper that sounded like the rustling of dry leaves. "I am not well ... the food is good, Franz, but it does not agree with me. It is because I am ill that I cannot eat the good food."

He knew what was the matter with her now; she needed milk and butter and eggs, she needed soups and nourishing jellies and all she could get was the *ersatz* food of the Nazi régime — but it was a crime to criticise the food.

"The food is good," she repeated. "You must remember that, Franz."

"I shall remember," said Franz, and he gave her a little squeeze to show that he understood.

They sat there for a little without speaking and the red light faded in the sky. Darkness gathered in the big cold room and it was very still. At this hour, at this very moment they would be having tea at Fernacres (thought Franz, making a hasty calculation of the difference in time). They would be sitting round a glowing fire. The tea-table would be spread with its load of bread and butter and cakes — more than anyone could eat. Perhaps Cousin Sophie would be measuring out the fragrant smelling tea — Indian tea into this pot and China into that — she would look up and smile and ask who took sugar and cream, and the cream would come out of the silver jug in a luscious stream. The sunlight would be shining in at the windows glancing on Wynne's gold hair and twinkling amongst the polished silver on the tray. Dane would be there — standing by the mantelpiece as his habit was — and perhaps Migs and Nina. Migs would be looking at Wynne. They would be talking casually and happily as these happy people talked, they would be laughing at jokes that were not really very funny but only seemed funny to them because they were happy and careless. Cousin Sophie would forget again — as she always forgot — that Migs took no milk in his tea . . . Cousin Sophie would be prattling about all that she had done, and about all she meant to do, and Dane's eyebrow would lift a little as he listened and his mouth would quiver at the corners. Franz could see it all so clearly, he was homesick for it. Strangely enough it was Cousin Sophie he saw most clearly of all that little group. (He saw her more clearly than Wynne, for Wynne's face and figure were partially hidden from the eye of his mind by a sort of rosy cloud.) Cousin Sophie in her soft pretty dresses with her soft pretty hair and the sweet trusting expression of her blue eyes. He saw her cherished by her family and her friends and waited upon by her servants with eager care . . .

"Why did you come home, Franz?" asked Tant' Anna at last.

Franz could not answer that. He was afraid to begin to answer it, even to Tant' Anna, for he knew that once he began to speak he might say more than was wise.

"Where is Gretchen?" he inquired.

"She has gone, Franz. She has gone home to her own people. It was better, for now we need not buy food for her."

Franz was silent for a moment, considering the situation carefully . . . "You must leave here," he said at last.

"Leave here!" she echoed in alarm. "Oh, Franz, then it is true. They are coming for me!"

"No," he told her, shaking her very gently. "No, why should they come for you?"

"They follow me," she said, gazing round the darkening room with staring eyes. "They watch me. I have told Otto about it but he says it is imagination . . ."

"So it is . . . just imagination. They have nothing against you, have they?"

"That is what Otto says . . . they have nothing against me; I have done nothing wrong. He says I am afraid of shadows."

"Listen to me, Tant' Anna. It is your nerves, that's all. You are ill and there is nobody here to look after you. I shall get you out of here."

He had formed the plan hastily but it was a good plan all the same. She could go to some old friends in Holland, and from there he could get her to England. He would take a little flat in London and they would live there together . . . he would get another post. He explained this to her and urged her to consent, but Tant' Anna refused. She made all sorts of objections and excuses . . . they could take no money with them; she had no suitable clothes; Otto would want her to keep house for him when he returned from Prague. Franz listened with a sinking heart. He had wanted to do this for her, because she had done so much for him. He had wanted to take her away from here, to work for her, to give her proper food and nurse her back to health. For a moment it had seemed to him that this would make life worth living, it would give him something definite to live for now that all his hopes were in ruins. He listened to what she said and added a number of things which she very carefully did not mention, and he came to the conclusion that Tant' Anna felt too ill to move from the house which she had lived in for so long. She was very ill — he was sure of that — perhaps she really was too ill and worn out to undertake the journey.

They talked for a long time and gradually they began to understand each other's minds and to trust each other completely.

"It is worse since you left, it is much worse," Tant' Anna whispered, her mouth close to his ear, for even here in this empty apartment she was afraid of being overheard. "There is no safety anywhere . . . in the shops, one dare not complain that the meat is not good or the butter rancid."

Franz, listening to this and much more in the same strain, saw that he could open his heart to Tant' Anna without fear, and soon he found himself telling her of his love for Wynne, of his hopes — now blasted — and of his fears for the future of their country.

"You have changed," she whispered.

"Oh Franz, how you have changed! You would never have spoken like this before."

"I have changed because I have seen the truth with my own eyes," Franz declared, and he went on to tell her of his life in England, trying to convey to her the atmosphere of peace and security and happiness which prevailed in Cousin Sophie's house.

"I read your letters to Otto," she said. "He was angry about them, Franz. It was not right for him to be angry and I told him so. You were telling the truth — he should not have sent you to England if he did not want the truth."

Once he had started to speak Franz could not stop, he poured out all his feelings, all his bitterness. He told her many things about German Policy which she could scarcely believe.

"But Franz, that is not what we were told . . ." she would begin in accents of bewilderment.

"You were told lies," declared Franz. "You were deceived. The march into Prague is the beginning of the end. You were told that Britain hated us; it is not true. She hates nobody for she is too great, too secure, too busy with her own affairs; but this betrayal of the Czechs has roused her. She was ready to sign a trade agreement with us but now she is angry."

"She would never fight," Tant' Anna said confidently.

"You have been told that, but it is not true. Britain is re-arming now. I tell you Britain will fight . . . she has strength and power and racial pride, she has money, she has her Dominions and Colonies . . . we are finished."

"Gott im Himmel, do not speak like this to anyone — "

"I would speak if it could do any good," said Franz in a sombre voice. "I would like to speak — to warn my father."

"No!" she cried. "No, Franz, they would kill you. It would be madness."

"The whole world is mad, I think. Why can we not live in peace with each other in our own lands and eat the fruits of the earth? The way was open to peace and prosperity and Hitler shut the door. It will not open again. He has destroyed us and will destroy us further unless . . ."

"Unless what?" she asked.

Franz did not reply.

CHAPTER TWO

IT WAS quite dark now and the stars were shining above the house-tops of the city in a clear, dark-blue sky. Franz had no idea what the time was — they had been talking for hours — but he was very hungry.

He rose and stretched himself. "It is long past supper time," he said.

"I had forgotten," Tant' Anna declared. "I am never hungry now. I will see what there is . . . perhaps there will be an egg or two and I will make coffee for you, Franz."

"I have brought you some good things," he replied. "Wait and I will show you."

He opened his suitcase and took out a roll of butter and a loaf of bread and a large packet of coffee.

"Oh Franz!" she cried. "Real coffee! I have almost forgotten what it tastes like! I have some milk in the larder!"

She fetched the milk and the coffee-pot and began to prepare the feast. "It is a good thing Otto is not here," she declared. "He would not allow us to eat this food.

He would say it was disloyal to the Fuehrer . . . and you must not speak of it to anyone or there might be trouble."

"Surely not!" exclaimed Franz. "Surely nobody would mind my bringing you this food from England."

"I don't know," she replied. "It is so difficult to know what is right and what wrong. You remember the Von Oetzens? Why, of course you do. They were always good to you when you were little. They have had very bad trouble, Franz."

"Trouble!" he echoed in surprise. "*Trouble* — but he was a good Nazi — "

She nodded. "I will tell you about it," she said. "They had an English Professor staying with them during the Christmas holidays. He was studying music here — a kind man with a long thin face and vague blue eyes. When he went back to England he sent a parcel of good things to the Von Oetzens — there was coffee and tinned butter and a warm coat for Frau von Oetzen who feels the cold so much — the parcel was opened and confiscated but that was not all . . . Herr von Oetzen was arrested."

"Arrested!" cried Franz in amazement.

"They said he must have complained to a foreigner that our food was bad and that we had not sufficient clothing. He was taken away one morning just as he was starting for his office. He had no idea what it was that he had done. He did not know about the parcel — did not even know that it had been sent — it was only afterwards he heard. He was away for three weeks and the poor wife — she was nearly insane with anxiety. It was Otto who procured his release."

"Thank heaven for that!" exclaimed Franz.

Tant' Anna nodded. "I was glad too," she declared. "I was glad that Otto had that much kindness left . . . enough kindness to risk a little danger to help an old friend in trouble. There is too little kindness amongst us today. . . ."

"I must see him," declared Franz. "I must see Herr Oetzen at once."

"No, Franz, it will be better not. You are too excited, too apt to let your feelings run away with you."

"I must see him," repeated Franz. "I want to know what happened to him. You will arrange it for me, won't you?"

It was against her better judgement that Tant' Anna at last consented to his persuasions. She was certain that no good could come of it, but she was too weak to withstand Franz. Very reluctantly and with a strange sense of foreboding in her heart she climbed the stair to the Von Oetzens' apartment and arranged that Franz would go up and see him the following afternoon.

Franz had always liked Herr von Oetzen — or Herr Oetzen as he now preferred to be called — but, quite apart from his affection for the kind old man, Franz had a definite object in his desire to speak to him. There were all sorts of vague and horrifying tales about the concentration camps but so far Franz had not obtained any first-hand information about them. He was anxious to know the truth.

When the hour came for his interview Franz went up the stairs rather slowly, he was full of good advice and good intentions; he would be careful; he would say little; he would talk of old times and remind Herr Oetzen about the toffee and the sugar almonds with which his pockets were always filled. Perhaps he would tell Herr

Oetzen how he used to wait for him on the stairs so that he might be asked to share the contents of those capacious pockets . . . it would amuse the old man to hear what a greedy little boy he had been. But these good and wise resolutions did not last long, they vanished when Franz was shown into the comfortable living-room and saw his old friend sitting in a chair near the stove.

"Herr Oetzen!" cried Franz, going forward and taking his hand. "I did not know you were ill!"

"I am not ill, Franz," replied the old man with a faint smile, "and I shall be all the better for seeing you, my dear boy. How well you look!"

Franz could not say the same, for Herr Oetzen's face was grey and drawn and his eyes were red-rimmed and had a strange glazed appearance.

"You are ill," said Franz again.

"Do not worry yourself. I was not very well when I was at Buchenwald, but it is nothing. Tell me about yourself, Franz, and about your stay in England."

"Tell me about Buchenwald," urged Franz.

"It is not a pleasant subject. We shall do better to speak of other things," replied Herr Oetzen firmly.

For some minutes they fenced with each other cautiously, but at last Franz could bear it no longer, his feelings got the better of him — as they had done before — and he began to speak his mind. Herr Oetzen lay back in his chair and listened to all that Franz had to say, and when Franz had finished and had paused, almost frightened by his own words, he leant forward and beckoned to Franz to come near.

"Do not be afraid," he said, in a whisper. "I believe what you are telling me — every word. I was a good Nazi before they arrested me but now I am a good German, which is a different thing. It was neither the injustice nor the ill-treatment that changed me, it was a deeper and more important factor, Franz. There were young guards at the camp, boys even younger than yourself, who had been taken from school and trained to be cruel to the prisoners in their charge. That is the most dreadful thing."

He was silent for a few moments and then he continued. "You and I have come to the same place by different roads. You have seen another happier land which lies outside the shadow of the swastika, and I have been walking in the deepest of the shadows. Our nation is being kept in a state of fear. It is drilled into uniformity. If this goes on much longer it will destroy Germany's soul. A man needs a little piece of personal life . . . some happiness and security . . . without this he becomes an animal, a beast of burden, driven here and there at his masters' whim . . . and the masters, Franz!" added Herr Oetzen, "The masters, what are they? Small men scrambling for power and preferment and caring little who is trampled underfoot."

Franz had not realised this before. He had seen that the foreign policy of his country was suicidal and had deplored its breach of faith, but it had seemed to him that, if the men who were responsible for this could be brought to book, all would be well. He began to realise that it was not Hitler but Hitlerism which must be rooted out before Germany could become whole and sane and able to take her rightful place amongst the great nations of the world.

"It seems hopeless," said Franz at last in a sombre tone.

"Not altogether, Franz. There are still people in the Fatherland who care for truth and goodness, who believe in kindness and gentleness — the Christian virtues. There are hundreds of thousands of them, but the difficulty is to get together . . . and to awaken others to the truth before it is too late."

"Somebody ought to try and work for that. Herr Oetzen, that would be a noble work."

Herr Oetzen lowered his voice even further. "There are men who are doing this work for the Fatherland."

"There are?" inquired Franz in surprise.

"Yes, I know one of them. He was at Buchenwald when I was there. He was released before I was, but before he left he contrived to speak to me about an organisation to which he belonged."

"What did he tell you?"

"It is a league," replied Herr Oetzen slowly, "perhaps you will think it a strange sort of league for it has no name, no badge, no headquarters of any description. You see, Franz, these are the things which lead to detection."

"Yes, but how can it work?"

"It works in small unrelated groups," replied Herr Oetzen, "or rather in groups which are unrelated except for one man. For instance in Group A there is one man who is in touch with one man in Group B and so on. Even if one group should fall into the hands of the Gestapo the other groups are safe."

"Your friend had been betrayed?" asked Franz with interest.

The old man nodded. "Yes, but his release was procured. There are influential people in this league — people in high places who are outwardly good Nazis — indeed you would scarcely believe me if I were to name them to you. My friend was told that he had been arrested by mistake. He was released and went away. He did not know where he was going but he was sure he would be sent out of Germany to a safe place. The league would not employ him any more — so he said — because he had come under suspicion. It was for his own sake and theirs also. They have to be careful, he said."

"It sounds well organised," said Franz thoughtfully.

"I thought so too. Well and wisely organised. There must be a good brain at the head."

"I should like to join them," said Franz quietly.

Herr Oetzen looked at him in amazement. "You!" he cried. "Oh no, Franz, not you. Think of your father!"

"He would not know. He thinks I am still in England — I told you that, Herr Oetzen."

"It is dangerous," declared the old man. "It is dangerous beyond words. No, you must not think of it, my dear boy. I was wrong to mention it to you but my mind was full of it all and my tongue ran away Forget what I have told you."

"I have nothing to live for," replied Franz. "Don't you understand what I feel? My life is over. I do not know what to do or where to turn."

"No, no, Franz, not you!"

"But yes, it is people like myself who should do this work. I am not married; I have no ties; my future is hopeless."

"But, Franz — "

"I want to join these men. I want to help in this work that they are doing."

For a long time Herr Oetzen held out against all arguments and persuasions, but at last he was forced to give in and before Franz left he had obtained certain information which would enable him to get into touch with one of the groups of the league.

"I can tell you no more," said Herr Oetzen with a sigh of weariness. "I trust you, Franz, but I must not tell you more. If you are really set upon this course you can get in touch with Group P — I have told you the way to do it. They will judge for themselves whether you can be useful to them or not."

"Thank you a thousand times!"

"You will be careful," added Herr Oetzen. "You will be very careful not to bring harm to your father or to Fräulein Heiden. I should never forgive myself. . . ."

"I shall leave home," said Franz. "Nobody will know where I am. Do not distress yourself about that."

CHAPTER THREE

WHEN Franz returned to the apartment he found Tant' Anna waiting for him at the door.

"Franz!" she cried. "Franz, you have been away two whole hours. I thought something had happened to you. I wish you would return to England, you would be much safer there. You are so reckless, so impulsive . . . I feel sure that you will get yourself into trouble."

"I am going tomorrow," said Franz, smiling at her, "so you will not be anxious about me any more."

"Going back to England!"

"That is what you want me to do isn't it?" he replied, turning away so that he did not meet her eyes.

She hesitated, for she could not understand this sudden change of plan.

"You will be quite happy about me, won't you?" urged Franz, "you will know that I am safe. In England it does not matter if the tongue wags freely."

"Yes," she said thoughtfully. "Yes, it is

294

the best plan, of course. Otto need never know that you were here."

"You see!" he exclaimed with an assumption of light-heartedness. "It all fits in. I shall have to leave very early in the morning so we must make the most of our time together."

Even now she was only half convinced. "You have some plan," she said doubtfully, "some plan that you have not told me ?"

"But yes," he agreed. "There is work in England for people like myself who are good at languages. Plenty of well-paid work. There is no need for you to worry about me. I shall not be able to write to you, of course, but you will know that I am safe . . . that is what you want, isn't it ?"

"Yes," she said again. "Yes, Franz, to know that you are safe and well is everything."

"We shall have a quiet evening together," he told her, putting his arm round her affectionately, "and then you will go to bed and I shall pack . . . I shall have to leave very early in the morning."

"But I shall get up and make coffee for you!" she replied. "You must have coffee before you go."

Supper was ready and they ate it together beside the big stove, and then they cleared the table and set out the dominoes. Tant' Anna declared that it was like old times, and Franz agreed, but in his heart he did not feel that it was like old times at all. He was different in himself and Tant' Anna was different — the whole atmosphere of the house had changed. It was true, of course, that the room looked the same as ever — though perhaps a trifle more shabby and less well-kept — and the fine old stove was the same, except that the fuel was poor and did not give out much heat. The table was the same table upon which they had always played, and it was the same set of dominoes with a little chip broken off one corner of the double five. Tant' Anna and Franz were both aware of the chip and it had always been a little joke between them. It was still a joke, of course, for, when Franz laid down his three-and-five, he remarked as usual, "How pleased you are! You can get rid of your double-five now"; and Tant' Anna laughed and replied, "My double-five—how could you know I had it!"

She was so natural in her manner that Franz wondered whether she was feeling what he was feeling; whether she realised that this was the last time they would play dominoes together — the last time they would see each other, perhaps. She was old and ill, and he was going away . . . He wondered whether her nerves were stretched as his were, so that every time the old furniture creaked or the door rattled against the jamb his heart faltered for a second and then raced on . . . but, of course she felt it; she had told him that she was terrified of shadows.

Tant' Anna is braver than I, thought Franz, watching the thin hand as it chose a domino from the pile and laid it down. She feels everything and yet she can bear it. Shall I be able to bear my fate so bravely? His heart ached for her, he could do nothing to help her, nothing at all . . . and then he remembered something. It was a small thing compared with what he wanted to do, but he thought it would please her. He went to his room and, emptying his suitcase on the floor, he found the parcel containing the scarf which he had bought for Wynne. Tant' Anna would like it and it would keep her warm.

For a moment he hesitated with the

parcel in his hands (he had bought it for Wynne. He had chosen it for her with so much love, with such pleasure and hopefulness in his heart) and then he carried it into the living-room and laid it on Tant' Anna's knee —

"There," he said. "It is something for you — a little present from me with my dear love."

"A present for me!" she exclaimed in surprise. "Oh, Franz, you should not spend your money on presents . . ."

"Open it," he said, plucking at the string.

She opened it and the scarf rolled out of the paper. It was so thick and fleecy that it unrolled itself . . . it almost seemed alive.

"Oh!" she cried. "Oh, how beautiful! I have never seen anything so lovely . . . it is real wool!"

"Yes," said Franz gravely. "Yes, it is real wool. I saw the sheep in the fields — hundreds of them — and I saw their fleeces in the mill. It is real wool off a real sheep."

"How warm!" she said, stroking the scarf with her thin hands. "What a pretty colour . . . blue like the sky! Oh, Franz, *how* kind of you!"

He felt amply repaid by her pleasure and he tried to tell her so.

"It is beautiful," she said again. She held it up against her face and there were tears in her eyes as she smiled at him. "It is beautiful, my dear . . . it is too good for an old woman like me."

Franz had tears too, but they did not fall. He answered a trifle unsteadily. "Nothing could be too good for you . . . and it will keep you warm."

"Too good . . ." she whispered. "Too pretty . . . Dear Franz, keep it. Put it away safely. You bought it for the girl you love, the little English girl with the blue eyes . . . Keep it, Franz. Perhaps some day you will be able to give it to her. . . ."

He did not deny that he had chosen it for Wynne, for that would have been useless, but he took the scarf and shook it out and wrapped it round Tant' Anna's shoulders. He had imagined himself doing this for Wynne.

"Poor boy," said Tant' Anna, taking his hand and patting it. "Poor little boy! It has all gone wrong for you and I would give my life gladly if I could put it right . . . but you must never bring her here."

He shook his head. He saw that only too clearly.

"No," said Tant' Anna, "no, she must never come here. This is no place for an English girl."

Franz knew what she was thinking — "Tell me about my mother," he said.

Last night they had spoken of the present and the future but tonight they spoke of the past. Tant' Anna began to tell Franz about his mother. There were so many things to tell that once she had started she could not stop, it was like a ball of thread which has been rolled up for years and now must continue unrolling. Franz hung upon her words; he was intensely interested and this was strange because, before he had gone away, the reminiscences of Tant' Anna would have bored him. His feelings towards his mother had changed completely. He had been ashamed of her before; he had been angry when he thought of her because it was her fault that he was not a pure-blooded German. When he had gone to school he had imbibed these ideas from his school-fellows and had decided to put his mother out of his mind entirely, as if by the mere act of forgetting her he could wipe her out of his life; but now he felt quite differently so he wanted to know about her and he asked Tant' Anna all sorts of questions and helped the ball to unroll. What was she like to look at? Was she gay and happy and carefree like Wynne? Tant' Anna told him all she could. She went and got a photograph of Elsie and showed it to him — it was the only picture of his mother in the house for Otto Heiden had been so anxious to forget his young wife that he had destroyed every reminder of her.

Franz took the photograph and looked at it.

"She was just like that," Tant' Anna said. "It was taken before the war — she had been here for six months or so. Otto had it coloured. He used to keep it on his desk . . . and then . . . afterwards . . . he threw it away. I kept it, Franz, because I loved Elsa. I always loved her. I hoped that some day you would ask me about her as you are doing now."

Yes, thought Franz, yes, she was like Wynne. She had the same sweet mouth, the same pretty hair — but Wynne had the look of unconscious courage which has never known fear . . . this was a softer face.

"And here is something that belonged to her," Tant' Anna continued, putting a little gold signet-ring into his hand. "It was given to her by her father — so she told me — and she valued it greatly. She would like you to have it, Franz."

The ring was quite plain and it fitted his little finger — he put it on and looked at it.

"Yes, I should like to have it," he said.

"Poor Elsa!" Tant' Anna said with a sigh. "She was happy here for a little while and then she was not so happy. Even before the war she had begun to wear a bewildered look. She loved laughter and fun, but it was not our kind of fun. It is difficult to explain," she added.

Franz did not need it explained for he knew what it was like to find yourself amongst people whose jokes you could not understand.

Franz was so interested that Tant' Anna went on talking. She wanted Franz to have all the little intimate details that she could possibly give him, because if she did not give them to him now they would be lost for ever. Her head was clear and many things which she had forgotten — or thought that she had forgotten — came back to her out of the past . . . it was almost as if she were dying . . . but I am dying, she thought. Yes, I am dying, for I am moving towards death and in a few months — a year at most — I shall not be here. And Franz, my dear boy that I love so much, I shall never see him again . . . so this is the end of my life. There is nothing more.

Tant' Anna had started to talk with the idea of telling Franz all about his mother, but she went beyond that. The events of her life, big and small, crowded into her mind and she poured them out before him. They were like little pictures — brightly coloured — that was how she saw them . . . Her first sight of Elsa arriving at the door with Otto — Elsa, very fair and straight and slim, wearing the big cart-wheel hat beneath which you could scarcely see her small, scared face. Elsa in the kitchen, trying to cook (as a German wife should), bending over the hot stove until her face was flushed and gold curls in damp rings upon her forehead. Elsa wrestling with the language — phrase book in hand. Elsa calling out for help. "Anna,

Anna, come and tell this stupid girl not to put so much garlic in the stew." "Anna, how shall I get the chimneys swept?" "Anna, where am I to buy linen?" "Anna, how am I to get this dress altered?"

Anna had loved her dearly — this little English wife of Otto's and had always been willing and eager to come to her assistance, and later, when her own trouble came, Elsa had repaid the debt a thousand-fold. Anna's own trouble — it had been heavy and bitter at the time but Anna was not sorry for herself, nor did she feel that her life had been dreary and useless because she had missed the happiness which all women crave. Looking back she saw many happy hours of sunshine and friendship and the scent of flowers. She remembered best of all the scent of flowers in a bouquet which had been brought to her by Frederick before he went to sea. It was in the war, so it was twenty-odd years ago but she remembered the scent of the flowers so clearly that she could smell them now. They were freesias from his mother's garden, sweet and fresh — they were like honey. He had come to take leave of her, and they were to be married when he returned . . . "It is only for seven weeks," he had said . . . but she had never seen him again. He was a U-boat Commander and often she had wondered how he had died. Had he died suddenly, the frail egg-shell cracking and the water rushing in, or had he known that death was coming and waited for it, lying helplessly at the bottom of the sea and the air growing foul? These thoughts had nearly driven Anna mad. Her friends had troubles of their own and had not tried very hard to help her but Elsa had understood. Yes, Elsa, in spite of her own misery, had held out a helping hand . . . It had seemed strange at the time and it still seemed strange to Anna that, knowing Frederick as she did — knowing every turn of his head and movement of his hands — she would never know how he died, or when. One would have thought that she would know the moment when he had passed over and left her alone in this world. It was the uncertainty which had been so hard to bear — day after day going past and hope dying. Hope died so slowly when you were young, and Anna was still looking for Frederick's return long after his mother had discarded hope.

This was Anna's story and this was why she had had no real life of her own. All her life had been centred in Franz and was bound up in him. He had been given into her arms when he was a tiny infant and Elsa was so desperately ill that they had not thought she would live. She had stayed and helped to look after him when he was a baby, and later, when Elsa died, she had looked after him herself. He had drifted away from her a little when he went to school for he had been imbued with the Nazi doctrines which she could not accept. He had been taught to despise gentleness, and to doubt God. Anna was deeply religious at heart and she could not believe that good could come out of such evil as this but although she was very unhappy about Franz there was nothing she could do. Now she felt that Franz had come back to her and was nearer to her than he had ever been since he was a tiny child and had depended upon her for everything, and it seemed very hard that she must part from him, must send him away from her and never see him again.

Tant' Anna was sorry that she had nothing to give Franz — nothing to leave him when she was gone — she had no money, no furniture, no jewellery of any value at all, for anything of value that she possessed had been sold long ago. She possessed nothing in the world but her clothes, which were of such poor quality and so patched and mended that the veriest beggar would have disclaimed them. The only thing that Tant' Anna could give Franz was these memories, and perhaps a little of her hard-bought wisdom which might be of service to him in the dark days that lay ahead.

"Life goes on," she told him. "Life never stands still. We are blind creatures, Franz, and we do not know where we are going. There are long dark tunnels and then we come out of them suddenly when we are not expecting it, and there is light all round us again. Remember this, Franz, the darkness is only a tunnel after all . . . Sometimes we hate and suffer, as we did in the war, and then we find that this was a tunnel too, and that the hatred was based on falseness and the suffering arose from mistakes. It is hatred that is the matter with the poor world today. Remember that, Franz. Hatred is deadly and kills all good things. Hatred blinds us to all that is beautiful . . . and so it is with the Fatherland which was full of so much goodness and beauty. People are being taught to hate. Jesus Christ taught us to love . . . to love even our enemies. It is for our own sakes we must do this, Franz, because hatred is bad for ourselves. If we hate people it does not hurt them at all . . . it hurts ourselves."

Presently Tant' Anna went to bed and Franz was alone in his small, cold room making his preparations for departure. They were rather strange preparations. He examined his clothes carefully, cutting off all the name tapes and laundry marks and the names of the tailors who had made them. He removed the inner soles of his shoes which bore the name of an English bootmaker and substituted pieces of felt cut from the floor of his room. His handkerchiefs were marked with his name so he took a pair of scissors and cut off the corners. His suitcase had his initials on the side and he removed them with a piece of sandpaper. These elaborate precautions might be unnecessary of course, but Franz was taking no risks. Finally, when all was done and his suitcase packed, Franz opened a secret drawer in his bureau and, taking out a revolver slipped it into his pocket. He was ready to go now and he could slip away without saying goodbye. He did not feel that he could bear to say goodbye to Tant' Anna . . . his young face was very stern and grave as he straightened his back and looked round the room for the last time.

The hall was dark but Franz knew every foot of the way; he avoided a loose board and stepped silently across the floor. Pausing for a moment outside her door he thought of her . . . it was as near a prayer as he could manage, for he had not prayed for years . . . not since he was a little child at Tant' Anna's knee . . . perhaps there is a God, thought Franz and, if so, perhaps He will comfort her and give her strength. . . .

The streets were deserted at this hour, and they were dark and damp. There were low clouds in the sky but it was not actually raining. Franz walked down to the bridge with his suitcase in his hand. He walked slowly and looked about him — it was here and at this hour that he would meet the man from Group P.

PART THREE

Rough Winds

CHAPTER ONE

THE sea mist was lying thick in the streets of Chellford, hiding the small grey stone houses with their jutting eaves. It was thickest near the sea where the fishermen's houses were, and it surged and billowed inland up the little river Chell. On the hill, where the larger houses stood, the mist was thin and gauzy and the sun shone through it like a big orange ball. It was rather fun, really, decided Wynne as she came down the hill and plunged into the white clouds as if she were plunging into a pool. She liked the soft feeling of the mist on her face, and the salty taste of it on her lips. The familiar streets and houses were transformed as if by magic and, if she had not known every foot of the way, she might easily have been lost . . . lost in Chellford, that was a strange idea! Several people passed her, but they were like ghosts, they appeared suddenly out of the whiteness and were gone before she had time to recognise them.

The curve of the road brought Wynne to

the Market Place, a cobbled square where, in former days, the fishermen had sold their catches. They did not do that now, but put them in boxes and sent them by train to London . . . it was rather a pity, Wynne thought. The mist was very thick here between the tall narrow houses, and, if Wynne had not known the way so well, she might have paused, but her footsteps scarcely slackened as she cut across the square, leaving the High Street on her right, and turned down Harbour Street to the fishermen's quarters. Wynne was going to see one of her Guides who had failed to turn up at the meeting last night. She was ill — so one of the other girls had declared, and on being asked what was the matter she had replied that it was "just one of Nellie's sick turns".

Fortunately Nellie was not too ill to see Miss Braithwaite and indeed she evinced the greatest pleasure and excitement when Miss Braithwaite appeared.

"There," said Mrs. Gurney as she showed in the visitor. "It's worth being ill, isn't it, Nellie, to have Miss Braithwaite come and see you."

It almost was. Not only was Miss Braithwaite welcome for her own sake, but also for the reason that Nellie would be able to boast of it to her friends. She could imagine herself talking about it in a casual sort of voice. "Oh yes," she would say, "Miss Braithwaite came all the way to see me and brought me things."

"I don't think it's ever worth being ill," Wynne said, as she handed over the bag of oranges and the sheaf of illustrated papers she had brought and looked about for a vase in which to arrange the sweet peas.

"Oh Miss, how kind of you!" Nellie said. "Yes, there's a vase on the mantelshelf . . . and water in the jug . . . Oh my, how lovely they are!"

Wynne took the vase and filled it and began to arrange the flowers. "I picked them myself," she said. "I like sweet peas, don't you — and I like them all different colours. They're so nice to look at."

"Oh, it was good of you to come."

"Of course I had to come. I wanted to see you; besides it's so boring lying in bed . . . you'll soon be better, won't you?"

"Oh Miss!" said Nellie, her eyes clouding with anxiety. "Oh Miss, I don't know what's going to happen — truly I don't."

"What's the matter?" inquired Wynne.

"It's Doctor," declared Nellie in a smothered sort of voice. "Doctor says I did ought to have my 'pendix taken out . . . says that's why I'm having sick turns and all."

"I expect it is," said Wynne, looking at her thoughtfully.

"Mother says it isn't. Mother says I needn't go to hospital if I don't want to . . . Oh dear, it was such a to-do."

"But why?" inquired Wynne. "If you've got to have it out you'll just have to bear it."

"Mother says I needn't . . . Oh dear, I wish they'd let me alone," wailed Nellie.

"Goodness!" exclaimed Wynne. "Goodness me — and you a Guide! Now listen to me," she added, sitting down on the edge of Nellie's bed and smiling at her in a friendly way. "Now listen to me. Having your appendix out isn't anything at all."

"It isn't anything!" cried Nellie in horrified tones. "Why, whatever can you mean? Not anything to be taken away to hospital and be cut up with knives!"

"Of course it isn't *nice*," said Wynne, shaking her head gravely. "Of course it isn't the sort of thing a person would choose to have done to them, but when a thing has got to be done we must just bear it."

"Mother says it's awful," said Nellie, her eyes filling with tears of self-pity. "Mother says I'll never be the same again."

This was the sort of foolishness that always made Wynne angry. Her face hardened a little and her tone grew firm. "No," she said. "No, you'll never be the same again. You'll never have any more sick attacks and you'll never have that horrid pain. You'll be sorry about that, won't you?"

"No . . . I don't know," faltered Nellie, turning her head away. "Oh dear, I'd rather just be left alone. I don't mind having a sick attack now and then."

"Then you're very silly indeed."

Nellie looked up in alarm. (She knew that tone, for she had heard it once or twice before. If somebody was slacking, or not playing the game in the manner in which a good Guide should, Miss Braithwaite used that tone with excellent effect. "Oh well, of course," she would say in exactly that tone. "Oh well, of course if that's what you feel about it I don't know why you belong to the Guides at all!").

"Oh Miss!" exclaimed poor Nellie. "Oh dear . . . I suppose I'll have to go through with it . . . oh dear, I don't want them to cut me open with a knife."

Wynne relented at once. "That's right," she said. "That's *much* better, Nellie . . . and you won't feel anything at all. You won't know anything about it."

"Chloroform!" said Nellie with a shudder.

"Yes, marvellous stuff," declared Wynne. "It's just like going to sleep, and then you wake up and it's all over."

Nellie stared at her with unbelieving eyes. "It's easy to say. How so you know it's like that?"

"Because I've had it myself, of course."

"You've had it! You mean you've had your 'pendix out?"

Wynne nodded.

"Oh Miss — not really?"

Wynne nodded again. "Yes," she said, "and it isn't anything to worry about — honestly it isn't."

She held out her hand and Nellie took it and clung to it like a drowning man. "Oh Miss!" she said, "Oh Miss, I *am* glad you've had your 'pendix out. I'll be like you, won't I?"

"Yes," said Wynne, patting her head.

"I don't mind — really I don't — not nearly so much."

"You'll be good and brave, won't you?"

Nellie nodded, "And I'll think of you," she said. "I'll think of you when I go to the hospital . . . I'll think of you all the time."

"And I'll be thinking of you," said Wynne, nodding her head gravely.

So far so good, but there was a lot more to be done before Wynne could feel that the thing was settled. She interviewed Mrs. Gurney next and spoke to her pretty strongly about the folly of her ways.

"It's very wicked indeed to frighten Nellie like that," declared Miss Braithwaite with flashing eyes.

Mrs. Gurney, a small, ineffectual sort of woman with wispy hair, gazed at Miss Braithwaite in dismay. "Oh dear," she said weakly. "Oh my, I don't know what to do, I'm sure."

"You must do exactly as the doctor says."

"My husband died in hospital," said Mrs. Gurney, wiping a bone-dry eye with the corner of a very dirty apron. "I don't want Nellie to go to hospital, Miss."

"That's just silly," said Wynne firmly. "Nellie will probably die if she doesn't have her appendix out . . . and it will be all your fault."

"Die!" exclaimed Mrs. Gurney.

"Yes," said Wynne. "Your appendix goes bad and poisons you. The surgeon explained it to me. Do be sensible, Mrs. Gurney," she added impatiently.

Mrs. Gurney agreed to be sensible — she was too brow-beaten to do anything else. Wynne was aware, however, that the moment her back was turned, Mrs. Gurney might change her mind — she was that sort of person — and they would be back at the beginning again, so she pursued Doctor Headley all round Chellford and ran him to earth at a confinement case. Nothing was happening at the moment and Doctor Headley was only too pleased to come out on to the doorstep — as he was asked to do — and speak to Miss Braithwaite. He was a newcomer to Chellford and exceedingly young, and he decided instantly that this was the prettiest girl he had ever seen.

"Yes," he said, smiling at her, "Yes, Miss Braithwaite?"

"It's about Nellie Gurney," said Wynne, somewhat breathlessly. "I've fixed it up and they're going to be sensible."

"Oh, good work!"

"Yes," said Wynne. "Yes, they've agreed."

Doctor Headley laughed. "There was an awful fuss this morning," he told her. "I tried to persuade them for all I was worth ...that Gurney woman is an absolute fool."

"Yes," agreed Wynne in heartfelt tones. "Yes, isn't she? And, as a matter of fact you'd better get on with it before she has time to think about it and change her mind again."

"I shall," declared Doctor Headley firmly. "That girl ought to have had the operation weeks ago. I'll get her off to hospital this afternoon. I'll be thankful when I get her safely there."

"Good," said Wynne, who liked quick work. "Good. Well, I've got a lot of things to do — "

She turned and retreated down the steps.

"I say!" said Doctor Headley, pursuing her, "I say, how on earth did you manage it, Miss Braithwaite?"

"Oh, I just told them," Wynne said.

There was tennis at the Audley's that afternoon and Wynne thought of Nellie quite often — as she had promised to do — and that night when she went to bed she thought of Nellie again and wondered how she was feeling, and Nellie's name was mentioned in her prayers.

Wynne was going through a difficult time herself. She was "growing up" and was suffering from growing pains. Life was not all honey and jam. Sometimes she felt radiantly happy and sometimes she felt sad, and there seemed to be no sane reason for these divergent feelings. It was July now and nothing had been heard of Frank since the day he had left Roy and disappeared, but Wynne did not believe that he had vanished altogether from her life . . . he loved her, she knew. When people loved each other they belonged to each other — Frank belonged to her and she to him. Whatever happened there would always be Frank and so she could bear anything, even this strange and prolonged silence. Every day she expected a letter from Frank — or even better, he might suddenly come back — and every morning she got up wondering if she would hear from him today. At night, when she went to bed, she shut her eyes tightly and willed herself to sleep because

Frank might come tomorrow. . . . She was not unhappy — except just sometimes — and she went about as usual and played tennis and enjoyed herself, but the world seemed a trifle unreal to her and Frank became more real. Frank was hers — they were bound up together — and someday he would come back.

Wynne had never bothered much about her personal appearance (she was one of those fortunate people who do not need to bother) but now, when she stood in front of her mirror brushing her hair or powdering her nose, she looked at herself with interest. Frank loved her, and she was dearer to herself because she was precious to Frank.

Her family — Sophie and Dane and Roy — were just as dear to Wynne as ever, but just at the moment they did not seem very real; for Frank coloured all her thoughts. She could have been happy on a desert island with Frank. With Frank's arm round her she could face anything that might come . . . and queer things were coming. The world was not quite so secure and comfortable as it used to be. There were all sorts of strange things going on during that summer of 1939: Gas Courses, where they told you about the ghastly effects of phosgene and mustard gas and lewisite, and First Aid Courses, where they showed you how to bind up broken limbs. Wynne attended these courses — everyone did — and she made copious notes, but somehow or other it was impossible to believe that this knowledge would ever be needed, and she was pretty certain that nobody else believed it either. There was a good deal of laughter and fun at the bandaging lessons and the grim idea at the bottom of all these activities remained at the bottom undisturbed.

Dane had gone away some weeks ago and Wynne missed him — but not as much as usual. Roy's ship was still in the vicinity and he came and went at irregular intervals. Migs had recovered from his wound and was at the Westshire Regimental Depot, helping to drill recruits. He came and went too, and was almost as irregular and unexpected in his comings and goings as Roy. It was a very unsettling sort of time, and the people who remained firmly fixed in Chellford found it difficult to make plans.

If they arranged tennis it had to be in a provisional manner. "I'll come if Migs doesn't turn up," Nina would say, "or if Migs turns up and wants to play I'll bring him . . . he might bring a friend of course, and in that case there'll be three of us."

This presented grave problems for a hostess with only one court and, too often, the tennis party fell through altogether or increased to unmanageable proportions.

Migs was finding life very complicated too. He found himself caught in a snare of his own making. He had always been fond of Wynne in a brotherly sort of way and had had teased her and joked with her and ordered her about in a truly brotherly manner, but now he had fallen in love with Wynne and his dearest wish was to marry her. There was no reason why he should not marry her of course; the match was eminently suitable; but unfortunately Wynne still treated him like a big brother and accepted all his advances in a jocund spirit. Migs had tried his level best to alter the relations between himself and Wynne but without avail — Wynne was quite unconscious of his efforts.

It was all the more difficult because, ever since she was a small child, he had called her, "darling" and had kissed her in a brotherly sort of way. He had told her often that he, "loved her to distraction" and now that these cogent words had suddenly become true there was nothing left for him to say. One day when they were sitting in the Audleys' garden watching a set of tennis, Migs made a special effort to pierce the invisible barrier between himself and Wynne; he began to talk about their friendship and to tell her that on his side this friendship was changing into something deeper. Emboldened by her silence, Migs became quite eloquent, and he assured her that he had loved her for months and that there was nobody like her in the world. When he had reached this point he looked at Wynne to see how she was reacting, and to find out why she had not responded in any way . . . and he saw by the faraway look in her eyes that she had not been listening to a word.

"Wynne!" he exclaimed with justifiable annoyance, "Wynne, what *are* you thinking about ?"

"Nothing special," replied Wynne untruthfully (for of course she had been thinking of Frank). "Nothing special, Migs. Why?"

"Why!" echoed Migs. "Because I was talking to you of course. I wish you'd listen."

"I'm sorry, darling — was it important?" inquired Wynne with a friendly smile.

"Yes, it was," he replied earnestly. "I wish you'd listen, Wynne. I was trying to ask you to marry me."

Wynne threw back her head and laughed delightedly, "Migs *darling*!" she cried. "What a marvellous idea! Did you think of it all by yourself?"

The wretched Migs was about to try to explain that this was not one of his well-known jokes but a *bona fide* offer of matrimony when unfortunately the set of tennis finished and they were surrounded by tiresome people clamouring for tea. There were far too many people about the place, decided Migs, the place was simply infested with tiresome people. He rose and walked away, for he wanted solitude.

It was obvious, of course, that Wynne did not love him, for, if she had loved him, she would have responded differently; but

Migs tried to convince himself that if only he could get her to take him seriously her feelings might change.

CHAPTER TWO

"WHAT'S the matter with Sophie?" Nina inquired — she and Wynne were both shopping in Chellford and they bumped into each other outside the post office.

"What?" inquired Wynne.

"What's the matter with Sophie? She's very piano these days."

"Is she?" inquired Wynne in surprise.

"Yes, of course she is. What's wrong with the sweet?"

"I don't know," said Wynne.

Nina shook her head gravely. "There's something," she declared. "There's a worm in the bud . . . you better find out what it is. We can't have Sophie losing her sparkle . . . I mean life wouldn't be the same at all. Everyone loves Sophie, she's a sort of institution . . . I mean I'd do anything for her."

"So would I, of course," said Wynne hastily.

"But you haven't," Nina pointed out with the devasting frankness of her generation. "You haven't done a thing. I mean you hadn't even noticed that the poor darling lamb was a bit under the weather, had you?"

"She isn't . . . it's just . . ."

"She is. Migs and I noticed it ages ago."

Wynne was taken aback at this attack. She was awakened out of her dreams and, having been awakened, she felt somewhat annoyed with Nina. It wasn't Nina's business to point out her duty to Sophie . . . and anyhow it was all nonsense, it was Nina's imagination. But observing Sophie closely, Wynne was forced to the conclusion that it wasn't all nonsense. Sophie was not so sparkling as usual . . . she was like champagne gone flat.

Something would have to be done about it — that was clear — but Wynne did not know what to do. It was no use asking Sophie what was the matter, as one would have done to a fellow creature of one's own generation. ("Look here, old thing, what's wrong?" one would have said in sympathetic tones and the matter would have been opened up satisfactorily.) Sophie was different. Sophie belonged to a generation which had to be treated with tact . . . "Curse tact!" said Wynne, to herself in disgust.

It was breakfast time and the meal had proceeded in silence. Sophie had been reading her letters with an absence of comment upon their contents which was absolutely unprecedented, and Wynne had been racking her brains for a tactful approach. The bacon had been over-cooked — it was cooked practically to a cinder — but Sophie had made no remark upon this unfortunate circumstance. It's Gladys, thought Wynne to herself (Gladys was the cook). It's Gladys — that's what's the matter — and she heaved a sigh of relief for she had been picturing all sorts of dire calamities.

"Is Gladys behaving herself?" she inquired in a casual tone.

"Gladys!" said Sophie in surprise. "Oh, *Gladys* . . . yes, I think so. She wants to go to her sister's wedding on Saturday so I told her she could have the weekend. Barber and Rose will manage all right — they don't mind a bit."

Wynne became aware that the trouble was not Gladys and she tried another tack. "Anything wrong with Roy?" she asked anxiously.

"Oh, poor Roy!" said Sophie with a

worried frown. "Where did I put his letter? He hasn't a single pair of socks without a hole in them. I don't know what Roy does to his socks . . . I must write to Harrods at once."

Wynne realised that Roy was perfectly sound and well. "What about Dane?" she inquired.

There was a little silence and then Sophie said, "What about him, dear?"

"I mean," said Wynne, feeling sure that she was getting warm, "I mean . . . well, when is he coming home?"

"I don't know," said Sophie shortly.

"He's been away a long time, hasn't he?"

"Three weeks and five days," replied Sophie without thinking.

"Sophie," said Wynne, leaning forward and speaking very seriously. "Sophie, where is Dane? Do you know? Do you know what he's doing or anything?"

"No," said Sophie, and she added, "you must remember to give that jumper to Rose. There's a stitch gone and it will get worse if it isn't mended . . . I told you about it yesterday."

"Yes, but what about Dane?" urged Wynne. "It's funny that he hasn't written."

"He would write if he could."

"If he could!" echoed Wynne. "Why couldn't he write?"

"Sometimes he can't," said Sophie firmly.

Wynne looked at her in surprise — so Sophie knew what Dane did! That was odd. She waited a few minutes and then she asked, "Are you worried about him?"

"It isn't any use being worried," said Sophie, moving her hands vaguely. "He doesn't like being worried about . . . and anyhow it doesn't do any good. I mean I believe it does a person harm if you worry about them. You can pray, of course, and of course I always *do* . . . but, just lately I haven't been able to pray in quite the same way. It's as if there was thick cotton-wool between . . . well, between me and Heaven . . . such a horrid feeling . . ." and she looked at her daughter apologetically.

Wynne nodded. "Yes," she said, "but Dane will be all right — he always is. He's so clever — much cleverer than he looks."

"He *is* clever of course," agreed Sophie, "but still — "

"And he's got Hartley," Wynne continued. "Hartley will look after him all right."

"Yes," agreed Sophie a shade more cheerfully. "Yes, there's Hartley, of course."

"I feel sure he's all right."

"Do you ?"

"I have a sort of Feeling in my Bones . . . yes," said Wynne, feeling her Feeling carefully, "yes, I'm sure Dane's all right."

Sophie smiled. "Well dear," she said, "I must say I'm a great believer in Feelings like that. It was really because I had a sort of Feeling that Dane . . . but perhaps . . ."

"He's all right," Wynne assured her. "It was just that you . . . I mean you were worried about him, and so . . ."

"Yes, of course," said Sophie nodding.

This conversation comforted Sophie a good deal and she decided to take some exercise, so, after she had written a letter to Harrods about Roy's socks, and had seen Gladys to order the food which seemed, on the whole a waste of time and energy when there were only Wynne and herself to eat it, and had listened with an assumption of interest which she was far from feeling to more details about the wedding arrangements, Sophie put on her hat and sallied forth with the intention of walking to the village and posting her letter at the Chellford post office so that it would reach its destination without delay.

Mrs. Audley was working in her garden and she waved to Sophie and signalled with her hoe, and then came down to the gate, hoe in hand, to speak to her.

"I haven't seen you for ages," said Mrs. Audley, "not since the flower show. It was better than usual, I thought."

"Yes," said Sophie.

"You ought to have got a first for your sweet peas."

"We got a third," said Sophie. "And a first for our Gloire de Dijon roses. Ellis was awfully pleased."

"They were beautiful," nodded Mrs. Audley; "so were your sweet peas. Ours were hopeless this year. We didn't show any. It's the first time for six years that we haven't got a first for our sweet peas."

"Wonderful!" exclaimed Sophie.

"What have you been doing with yourself?" inquired Mrs. Audley, smiling at her.

"Oh, nothing," said Sophie. "Just the usual things."

"You ought to come to the bandaging class, Sophie."

"Yes," agreed Sophie doubtfully. "I suppose I ought, but to tell you the truth I think it would be a waste of time. I'm not very clever at practical things."

It was true, of course, and Mrs. Audley knew it, and the thought shot through her mind that perhaps Sophie was right to absent herself from activities which were not in her line. There were people quite as vague and impractical as Sophie who attended the First Aid Classes regularly as clockwork — but what a nuisance they were!

"I shouldn't be any use," continued Sophie earnestly, "because even if I learnt how to bandage properly I should be too frightened to do it when the time came. I should be frightened of doing quite the wrong thing and perhaps making them worse than they were before."

"Perhaps you're right," said Mrs. Audley kindly.

There was silence for a few moments and then the subject was changed.

"How's Wynne?" Mrs. Audley inquired.

"Very well, thank you."

"That's good," said Mrs. Audley. "I

thought . . . I wasn't sure. Of course, it's been very hot lately."

"Oh!" said Sophie, "er — yes . . . yes it has."

"And these young things are so energetic. They *will* dash about in the sun. Are you going to the Corbetts' Sherry Party ?"

They discussed the Corbetts' Sherry Party for a minute or two and then Sophie walked on. She and Mrs. Audley had understood each other perfectly and, as Sophie now perceived, Mrs. Audley was right — there *was* something the matter with Wynne. It was Frank, of course. Sophie had been afraid of that all along . . . terrified of it. That was why she had been quite glad (in a way) when Frank had left Fernacres and gone to London; that was why she had said nothing about his coming back. Wynne had suggested twice that they should ask Frank to come down and spend a weekend, and on both occasions Sophie had provided a water-tight excuse. Then Frank and Roy had gone off together on that trip and Frank had vanished . . . Sophie thought about it and the more she thought the more worried she became . . . Wynne and Frank, Elsie and Otto . . . "Oh *no!*"

cried Sophie to herself, dashing along the road in a sort of blind panic. "Oh no, not that. Please, God, don't *don't* let that happen."

CHAPTER THREE

IT WAS tea-time at Fernacres and Sophie and Wynne were having it alone. Wynne was attired in her Girl Guide Captain's uniform for she was going down to the hall directly afterwards. The girls were going to give an entertainment — a sing-song in the Village Hall — and this necessitated a good deal of extra work for Wynne. Nellie Gurney had had her operation and was almost well again, and Wynne was particularly glad of this because Nellie had a very sweet voice.

"Last year there were such a lot of us," said Sophie as she measured out the tea. "There was Dane, of course . . . he always takes Indian tea . . . and Frank liked it too."

"Yes," said Wynne. She had been lying back in her chair gazing at the ceiling and not listening at all, but at the mention of Frank's name she seemed to prick her ears. "Yes," she said. "Frank likes strong tea . . . and he loves cream buns."

"Nobody eats cream buns now," continued Sophie, "so I told Barber we wouldn't have them any more . . . it's such a waste."

"They eat them in the kitchen, I suppose."

"Why should they?" Sophie inquired. "I mean Gladys can make a cake for them. Do you think Frank has gone back to Germany?"

"I don't know."

"I think he has. Roy said he had given up that job so where else could he go? If he were here — I mean in this country — he would come and see us, wouldn't he?"

"Not unless he was asked," said Wynne.

Sophie was aware of the implication but she ignored it. "My dear!" she exclaimed, "how can we ask him when we don't know where he is?"

"We knew where he was *before*," Wynne pointed out. She hesitated a moment and then added, "Frank is very sensitive, you know. He wouldn't go anywhere unless he was sure he would be welcome."

"Surely he knows us well enough . . . and anyhow he could have written. Why hasn't he written to Roy or somebody?"

"He will write," said Wynne in a dreamy voice. "He will . . . someday."

There was quite a long silence after that. Sophie had time to pour out a cup of tea and drink it. She thought it tasted a little odd and discovered that she must have put sugar into if for there was crusted sugar at the bottom of the cup . . . quite a lot of it.

"At least two lumps!" said Sophie, looking at it in surprise.

"Two lumps ?" inquired Wynne.

"Of sugar," explained Sophie. "So queer of me to put it in when I know I don't like it . . . and so wasteful too. I gave up sugar in the war and I never liked it afterwards. I must have saved hundreds of pounds of sugar by now."

It was rather an interesting point, and they were still discussing the amount of sugar which had been saved by Sophie's abstention over a period of twenty-three years, when Barber came in with the afternoon post . . . and they both saw that a letter from Dane lay on the top of the pile.

Sophie took it and tore it open. "Oh, isn't that nice!" she exclaimed. "He's in Paris . . . and he'll be home on Thursday."

"Lovely!" agreed Wynne, rising and seizing her hat.

"The day after tomorrow," added Sophie with a sigh of relief.

"Yes," agreed Wynne. "Yes, splendid . . . but you'd better buck up before he comes. You're looking a bit under the weather."

The next morning Sophie announced that she was going to Kingsport to do some shopping. "Some things we need . . ." she said in her usual vague way. "It's been so hot lately and there are one or two things . . ."

Wynne was aware that Sophie wished to kill the fatted calf for Dane's benefit.

"You want to buy a duck, of course," she said (it was always a duck for Dane and a chicken for Roy) and she added in a pleasant voice, "I'll take you in the car." It was rather a nuisance of course, but if Sophie wanted to go to Kingsport she must go — Wynne could easily put off the Audleys' tennis —

"No thank you, dear," said Sophie.

"Did you say, *no*?" inquired Wynne, unable to believe her ears.

"I shall go in the bus," explained Sophie. "Rose says there's a bus at twenty minutes past ten — it will suit me beautifully."

"But Sophie darling, you hate buses — "

"It will be a change," said Sophie — and she blushed.

Wynne looked at her in amazement and she perceived that there was a mystery here. It was so unlike Sophie to deal in mysteries that she was quite alarmed. "Don't be silly," she said in affectionate tones. "You know I like taking you, darling, and I can do some shopping, too. How long will you be ?"

"That's just it. I don't know how long," replied Sophie. "It's very kind of you, dear, but I want to be perfectly free and not have the feeling that someone is waiting for me."

Wynne saw the point. "All right," she said, "but you had better hurry. The bus won't wait for you."

Wynne despatched her mother safely and then went on to the Audleys' and played tennis all the morning. She returned home at lunch-time to find that Sophie had not come back — nor was she expected back, for there was only one place at the table. She saw that she ought to have inquired more thoroughly into Sophie's plans . . . it was really most peculiar.

"She'll be home for tea, I suppose," said Wynne as she sat down to her solitary repast.

"I don't know, I'm sure, Miss," replied Barber shortly.

It was obvious from Barber's manner that she had formed an entirely wrong impression of the whole affair, but Wynne could do nothing to clear herself of guilt; she could not very well explain to Barber that she had offered to take her mother to Kingsport and that her offer had been refused. "They're all talking about it, I suppose." said Wynne to herself, as she toyed about with her food under Barber's reproachful eye, "they're all saying I'm a beast not to take her in the car. I wish to goodness I'd been firmer about it."

At three-thirty Wynne was at the gate, peering down the road for the Kingsport bus. She saw it coming in the distance and watched it anxiously . . . but the bus did not stop at Fernacres gate, it swooped past in a swirl of dust and Wynne was left staring after it in surprise and dismay. She was aware that there was not another until five-fifteen and she was quite absurdly worried. "I'm a perfect fool," declared Wynne to herself. "Anyone would think Sophie was five years old . . ." but this reflection did not comfort her much.

There was nothing to be done except wait in patience, and Wynne's stock of patience was not very large. She returned to the house and spent an hour tidying her clothes — it was a duty long overdue. Her chest of drawers looked very nice when she had finished and there was a pile of discarded pullovers and stockings which would gladden the hearts of some of the Guides. She had also found a very pretty blue scarf which had been lost for months.

It was tea-time now, and Wynne had tea by herself (she could have rung up Nina, of course, but she did not feel like company. Besides Nina would be sure to think that she had been grumpy about taking Sophie to Kingsport. She hadn't been grumpy, but Nina wouldn't believe it.) Wynne turned on the radio — a recent acquisition — and listened to a band from Bournemouth but, although they were playing selections from "Iolanthe" — an opera which Wynne adored — she did not enjoy it as much as usual.

At five-fifteen Wynne was once more at the gate and this time the bus drew up and Sophie was helped down the step by the conductor. She was laden with parcels; and more parcels and boxes were handed out to her by the conductor and her fellow passengers, all of whom had obviously become deeply attached to her during the twenty-minute drive.

"Thank you so much," Sophie said. "How kind of you! Oh thank you . . . yes, I shall manage beautifully now . . . I see my daughter has come to meet me. Yes, thank you. Goodbye. Goodbye, and thank you so much, I do hope your cold will soon be better . . ."

"Sophie!" exclaimed Wynne. "Sophie, where on earth . . ."

"My dear, *such* a nice man," declared Sophie, picking some of the parcels off the road and piling them into Wynne's arms. "Such a very *very* nice man . . . but he's had a cold for three weeks. You see, a bus is a draughty sort of place and he can't get rid of it. I told him about Coldine and he promised to get a bottle this evening when he gets back to Kingsport . . ."

"*Sophie*," said Wynne again. She had intended to be very dignified and reproachful, for she really had been extremely worried about Sophie, but it is almost impossible to be dignified and reproachful with your arms full of parcels.

"Yes," said Sophie. "Don't drop the duck . . . I had to bring it with me because it might not have been in time . . . and that's my new hat, so don't crush it."

"*Sophie*, where have you been? Where *have* you been?"

They were both aware that Sophie had been to Kingsport, but that was not what Wynne meant. Sophie knew what she meant of course.

"Oh, my dear!" said Sophie in concern, "were you worried about me? I *am* sorry but I thought I could be certain to get the other bus. It took so much longer than I expected and she wasn't ready to start until half past two."

"Sophie, do stop dithering and tell me what you've been up to."

"Wynne!" exclaimed Sophie. "Really, Wynne! If I had spoken to my mother like that I don't know what would have happened."

They had reached the house by now, and Wynne put down her load upon the hall table. "All right," she said, "if you don't want to tell me, *don't*."

"Wynne, I only — "

"But I don't think it's very kind of you," added Wynne.

"Oh Wynne, darling!" exclaimed Sophie in distress. "I *would* have told you only it seemed so silly, and I was rather ashamed, really. I thought you might think it was a waste of money (it cost *such* a lot) but the girl assured me that it wasn't, and she said I had such a nice skin. She was a most delightful girl — her father is a Colonel in the Indian Army and *she* was out there, too — most interesting, she was. I've got to put one kind of stuff on at night and quite a different kind in the morning . . . Oh dear!" cried Sophie, searching feverishly amongst the parcels, "oh dear, I hope to goodness I haven't lost it."

"Here it is," said Wynne, putting a small parcel marked "Harriet Sherwood" into her hands; "but I can't for the life of me understand why you couldn't *say* you were going to have a facial treatment or a mud pack or whatever it was. It would have saved me a good deal of unnecessary suffering," added Wynne, half laughing and half in earnest.

"I was rather ashamed," repeated Sophie, ". . . besides it was you who suggested it."

"What?"

"Well, you said I looked a perfect fright," Sophie pointed out.

CHAPTER FOUR

DANE was very glad to be back at Fernacres — even more glad than usual — he had been given a task to accomplish and he had accomplished it, but the information which he had procured for Colonel Carter was not the information he had hoped for and the skies over Europe were darkening rapidly. He was aware from the quality of Sophie's welcome that she had been more than usually anxious about him during his absence, and after Wynne had gone up to bed he began to explain to her how impossible it had been to let her know his whereabouts.

"I know," said Sophie quietly. "It doesn't matter, Dane. You're home now — that's what really matters — and I don't want you to feel you have to tell me things, because I know you can't."

"I was at Danzig — it doesn't matter telling you now."

"Will you have to go back?"

"No, not for some time. As a matter of

fact I told Colonel Carter I wanted a long holiday."

"It's lovely to have you home," declared Sophie, smiling at him.

The words were so warmly spoken and the smile which accompanied them was so affectionate that Dane's heart gave a little leap. "Sophie!" he said eagerly, "you really *are* glad!"

"Why, of *course*," she replied, nodding her head.

Dane hesitated — it was as if he were trying to make up his mind to some course of action — and there was a little silence.

At last Sophie said, "Wynne and I have been rather dull . . . but now you're home and Roy's coming tomorrow for the weekend . . . so we shall all be together."

"Good," said Dane.

"And I think it would be fun to go for a picnic, don't you? We haven't had a picnic for ages."

The idea of a picnic — a family picnic — appealed to everyone, and Roy's suggestion that they should hire a boat and row round the coast to the Smuggler's Cave was acceded to.

"Aren't you tired of the sea?" Dane

inquired with a smile, but the question was not taken seriously.

"It will be more fun than going by car," Roy declared, "and it will save us that hot walk up the cliff afterwards. I'll row, of course . . . and be sure to take lots of food. . . ."

There was always far too much food in the picnic basket when Sophie had anything to do with it so Roy's request was unnecessary, and Dane pointed this out and begged that moderation should be observed.

The following day was bright and sunny with a pleasant breeze — an admirable day for the picnic. Wynne ran the party down to the harbour and left them there and went to park her car. She found an excellent parking place in a back street — a parking place to which Sergeant White's superiors could not possibly object — and following the others to the harbour she found them engaged in a somewhat heated discussion as to what kind of craft should be hired. A rowing boat had been Roy's first suggestion, but now he had seen a small sailing dinghy and his heart yearned for her. She was about twelve feet long, her lines were beautiful and she had a brown sail.

"Do let's," he said earnestly. "It'll be *much* more fun."

Dane was quite agreeable to the change of plan but Sophie was dubious; she distrusted sails unless there was "somebody in the boat who understood about them". She was explaining this to her son when Wynne arrived upon the scene.

"But I know about them," Roy pointed out, "and so does Dane. Dane has done a lot of sailing."

"I mean a *man*," explained Sophie, pointing to a disreputable-looking old fisherman with a red nose who was lounging against a bollard on the quay.

"Can you beat it?" inquired Roy with justifiable indignation. "Can you beat it, Dane? Am I, or am I not a naval officer — and what about you? Neither of us are men — Oh no! Sophie would feel much happier with a drunken old longshore-man on board . . ."

"It will be quite all right, Sophie darling," said Wynne, taking the situation in hand. "Roy knows all about it and so does Dane . . . and anyhow we can all swim.

Hop along, Roy, and hire the boat for the day."

Roy hopped along and the bargain was concluded in record time. He brought the dinghy alongside the steps and Sophie was handed in . . . the basket, and various coats and waterproof rugs were handed in after her.

"All aboard," said Dane cheerfully.

Roy had already disposed his passengers in suitable positions and the sail was ready; he hauled up the sail and made the halyards fast; Dane took the tiller; Wynne pushed off with an oar; the little boat slid gently away and the houses at the harbour receded slowly.

At first there was only just enough wind to fill the sail, and there was little noise and scarcely any wake; but when they got clear of the houses they found a quite good breeze and the dinghy responded nobly. She heeled over to it and rose to the waves and there was a pleasant lapping sound of water under her stern.

Roy had constituted himself skipper and Dane was quite pleased for he was aware that Roy was more knowledgeable than he. It was years since Dane had sailed . . . but the feel of the tiller beneath his hand was familiar and enjoyable. They held straight out of the little bay and it was not until they were well clear of the point that Roy gave the signal for the helm to be put over. "Ready about," he said as he let out the sheet . . . the boom swung out and the little boat came round beautifully.

"She's a darling!" exclaimed Roy, and Dane agreed that she was, for she had responded to their combined efforts with the precision of a racehorse.

Dane was steering straight down the coast now, and the wind was aft. They slid along at a good pace and left a creamy wake behind them. The sea was blue, the air was clear and sparkling, and the sun twinkled merrily amongst the waves. Seagulls hovered high above the water and dived suddenly with a piercing shriek and a flash of white wings. Wynne sat near Dane and she leaned over the side and trailed her hand in the water, it was so blue that one might have thought it would stain one's hand. Sophie sat up very straight — she had recovered from her nervous feelings and had begun to enjoy herself — she watched the shore and thought how strange it looked. If she had not known it was Chellford she would not have recognised it.

"And that's why sailors are different," she said aloud.

"Why?" inquired Roy, who was enjoying himself too, and felt in tune with the universe. "Why are sailors different . . . if they *are* different . . . and what are they different from?"

"Of course they are," replied Sophie firmly, "and of course it's because they see the land from the sea instead of the sea from the land. That's enough to make anybody different."

Dane smiled at this very Sophie-ish statement — as usual it contained the germ of an exceedingly interesting psychological problem — but he had no time to think about it seriously for his skipper was speaking to him again.

"Look out, Dane, we don't want to gybe," said Roy anxiously — it would have lowered his prestige and, what was worse, the prestige of the British Navy. "Look out, Dane!"

"Aye aye, sir," replied Dane, bending himself to his task.

For about a mile the cliffs stood up sheer out of the water with tumbled heaps of boulders below, and the waves were breaking amongst the boulders with white spray; beyond the stretch of cliff was the headland with the lighthouse on it, jutting into the sea. The Smuggler's Cave was beyond that again and Roy signalled to his helmsman to keep well out.

"There may be rocks," said Roy, who was a blue water sailor, "there are often rocks round a headland like this — besides we're in no hurry, are we?"

They kept well out and rounded the headland without mishap.

"There's the cove!" exclaimed Wynne, pointing to the narrow strip of sand between the rocks. "There it is, Roy — how fast we've come! There will be lots of time for a bathe before lunch."

It was much too short a voyage for Roy's liking and he suggested that they should sail a bit farther down the coast, but Wynne was anxious to bathe and Dane was aware that their voyage home would take much longer for they would have to tack. He did not want to try the patience of the passengers too severely.

"We'll land, I think," he said. "Let out the sheet, Roy."

Once more the boom swung over and they headed for the shore, gliding very slowly. There was little wind in the lee of the headland, only just sufficient to give the tiny craft way. She slid into the cove and came to rest beside a ledge of rock, and Roy, with Naval celerity, sprang ashore and made fast the painter.

It was here in this sheltered cove that the bathing party had taken place — more than a year ago — and neither Roy nor Wynne had been here since. They looked round them, at the rocks and the sand and the blue sea with its sprightly waves and they both remembered — but with very different feelings.

"D'you remember the last time we were here?" Roy inquired. "We came by road in Agatha . . . I wonder where old Frank is now . . ."

"Yes," agreed Wynne in a non-committal tone, "I remember it quite well."

"Gosh, he could dive, couldn't he?"

"Yes, he dives beautifully," agreed Wynne.

She had not forgotten that first swan

dive which had surprised them all so much. She had not forgotten the grace and precision with which that flashing white body had taken first to the air and then to the water as if both elements were its natural playground. Wynne remembered it as a little picture in her heart and she always would remember it just like that. Coming here today, to the very spot where the little picture had been made, brought it before her eyes with almost unbearable lucidity, and for a moment Wynne wished that they had not come . . . and then she was glad they had, for, even if it hurt to remember Frank so clearly, she wanted to remember him. His image must never fade, it must never lose its bright colours . . . nor the power to make her suffer.

Wynne leapt ashore; Roy and Dane helped Sophie to land and handed out the bulging picnic basket.

"This is nice," Sophie said, with satisfaction. "The sky is *so* blue. I suppose you children are going to bathe before lunch . . . it's lovely just the four of us," she added.

The other three were thinking the same. Roy had invited Nina and Migs but they had not been able to come, and, although he had been sorry at the time, he was glad now . . . Nina and Migs would have made the whole atmosphere entirely different. This expedition had a "family atmosphere" and it made Roy feel extremely young and cheerful.

"We're silly not to do this oftener," he said.

"You're always so busy," complained Sophie.

He took his bundle and leapt away over the rocks, his fair hair standing on end with the breeze of his passage. Wynne followed him more slowly. Dane carried the basket to a shallow cave just above the line of sea-weed which marked high water, and spread a mackintosh rug for Sophie to sit on. Then he straightened his back and looked round. He had been here before, of course, but not for a long time and he had forgotten what a pleasant place it was . . . sheltered, peaceful and extraordinarily beautiful in its own particular way. On the black cliffs there were little ledges, where feathery grasses had taken root, and there were dark fissures, damp with moss and delicate ferns.

Sophie had sat down on the rug and was

watching Roy and Wynne, and when Dane looked at her he saw that her eyes were full of tears.

"Sophie!" he said uncertainly.

"It's just that they're so young," she explained, shaking the tears away and trying to smile. "So young, Dane . . . and there's going to be another war."

"It . . . it looks like it, I'm afraid."

"They're so young," she repeated. "So young and good. It isn't fair. I feel I ought to apologise to them."

"For the war?" asked Dane, smiling a little; "but surely the condition of Europe isn't your fault, Sophie?"

She shook her head. "No, for *having* them, Dane. I wouldn't have had them if I'd known there was going to be another war just when they were grown up."

Dane sat down beside her, his heart was very full of love and tenderness for Sophie. "I understand," he said, "but we can only do our best."

"We should have prayed harder," said Sophie. "Harder and oftener."

Dane was inclined to disagree for he could not believe that God would pay more attention to prayers which were prayed hard and often. The idea was almost an insult to God's intelligence. He, himself, disliked it intensely if people came to him, reiterating their requests, when he already knew quite well what they wanted and had decided either to withhold or to give in his own good time.

"What are you thinking about?" Sophie inquired.

"About Miss Halton," replied Dane with a smile. "She came again this morning and tried to make me sign that absurd petition of hers. She seems to have got the idea of hard and often . . ."

"But it isn't the same!" cried Sophie. "I know I'm not clever enough to argue with you, but it isn't the same."

CHAPTER FIVE

DANE lay back with his hands beneath his head and looked at Sophie's profile outlined against the brilliant blue sky. She had a charming nose — or so Dane had always thought — it was an unusual shape and slightly blunted at the tip. Her skin was smooth and soft, and the few lines which the passing years had written upon her face were all pleasant and kind. On the surface Sophie was vague and sometimes even foolish, but if one took the trouble to look deeper there was treasure to be found. There was goodness and wisdom and, better still, a streak of humour all the more valuable because it was a humour peculiar to herself and because it functioned rarely and at unexpected moments. Everyone was fond of her, but it took a connoisseur to appreciate the subtle and delicate flavour of Sophie Braithwaite — and Dane was a connoisseur. Dane had always loved her of course, he had wanted to marry her twenty-six years ago when he was an undergraduate at Oxford; but an undergraduate is seldom in a position to marry and Dane was no exception to the rule. He had wanted to marry her then, and he still wanted to marry her, and just lately he had begun to hope that Sophie was ready to turn to him. He had begun to hope, but he was not sure and he was very much afraid of putting his fate to the test for, if Sophie refused to be his wife, his position at Fernacres would become untenable and he would have to go. This would be nothing short of disaster, thought Dane, as he continued to observe Sophie's profile against the blue sky; it would be a disaster for himself, because he could not bear the idea of leaving Sophie, and it would be a disaster for Sophie because she would be lost without somebody to manage her affairs.

Dane sighed.

"What are you thinking about?" Sophie inquired.

He smiled at her. "You're very inquisitive this afternoon and that's unusual, Sophie."

"I *feel* unusual," she replied unhappily. "Everything is so — *so* insecure. I don't believe I shall be able to bear it . . . if there is a war."

"Sometimes I feel the same," said Dane gravely, "as if it were too much to bear . . . to go through it all again, only much worse, because now one understands more, and there's none of the glitter and excitement. Now one sees the futility of the sacrifice. . . ."

"Oh Dane!" Sophie implored him. "Please don't. I mean don't be miserable, too. You're always so strong and comforting."

She turned towards him and held out her hand, and Dane drew her into his arms and kissed her . . . he simply could not help it. She was so sweet and dear, so confiding, so near his heart.

Sophie did not withdraw from his embrace, indeed she seemed to like it, but now that Dane had got her, (where he had wanted for so long to have her) in his arms with her dear head lying snugly against his shoulder, he scarcely knew what to do next. Sophie had accepted it all so calmly that he wondered whether she realised what it meant. Perhaps she took this as a brotherly embrace . . . she was such a little innocent.

He kissed her again, more warmly

than before, and again Sophie let him.

"I love you, Sophie," he said.

"Yes dear," she replied, letting her head rest against his shoulder.

"I've always loved you," declared Dane.

"Yes," she repeated with a little sigh. "Yes I know. You've always been so sweet to me, Dane. I don't know what I should have done without you."

Dane wondered what to say next. He wanted to marry her, and there was no reason why they should not marry, but it seemed so crude to put it into plain words. Besides he wasn't sure, even yet, that Sophie understood — and he did not want to alarm her. There was still time to draw back from the edge of the precipice . . . if Sophie had not understood.

"I wish I were younger," said Sophie at last in a dreamy voice. "It's the first time in my life I've ever wished it, really."

His arm tightened round her and he said softly.

"Grow old along with me!
The best is yet to be,
The last of life, for which the first was
made."

She turned her head and looked up at him. "Oh, Dane!" she said. "How clever of you to remember that! It's so *nice*, isn't it? It's almost as if Browning had made it up on purpose for us. You always liked Browning, so I used to read his poems and try to understand them, but I never could understand them unless I learnt them by heart."

"It's the right way to understand them," Dane replied.

"And the next bit," said Sophie. "Say the next bit — it's even better."

Dane said it obediently.

"Our times are in His hand
Who saith, 'A whole I planned,
Youth shows but half; trust God:
see all, nor be afraid!'"

"Dane, He planned a whole," she murmured.

"Yes," said Dane softly. "Yes, Sophie — "

"So we shall be able to bear it."

"Yes."

"Whatever comes."

"Yes," he said.

". . . and we shall be bearing it together."

"Yes," said Dane. He saw now that it was quite all right. Sophie understood . . . he kissed her again.

After a few minutes (in which the fact that Sophie understood became even clearer and was proved up to the hilt) Dane began to inquire into her feelings.

"I knew you loved me," she said, "and of course I've always loved you — I loved you from the very beginning — but you went away and Philip was there all the time. I was a silly little thing," said Sophie shaking her head. "I didn't really understand myself at all, and Philip was there, loving me and wanting me, and he was so like you, somehow; so at last I said I would marry him . . . but, Dane, you mustn't think that I wasn't happy with Philip; I was very happy indeed. He loved me, you see, and I loved him — not in the same way that I loved you, of course, but very dearly all the same, I suppose I must be a most extraordinary person," said Sophie with a sigh. "I mean I've never read in any book about a woman who loved two men at the same time, have you? In books, if the heroine marries a man, she

368

either loves him — and him alone — or else she hates him and is miserable with him. Well, I wasn't. I was happy with Philip for seventeen years."

"Yes," agreed Dane, "and Philip was happy with you. I'm glad to think that, because Philip deserved happiness. I really am very glad, Sophie — I suppose that shows I'm an extraordinary person too?"

"I believe it does," said Sophie thoughtfully. "You ought to have hated Philip, I suppose; but our way is much more comfortable, isn't it?"

Dane agreed that it was.

"And if we're both extraordinary people it doesn't matter quite so much," added Sophie.

After a little while she said softly, "I'm happy . . . but it seems wrong when other people are so sad. Poor Frank, what will happen to him if this dreadful war comes? . . . and poor little Wynne . . . do you think you were right to send Frank away?"

"Sophie!" exclaimed Dane, drawing away from her and looking at her in surprise. "How do you know anything about it?"

"I just jumped to the conclusion," she

replied. "You're always telling me I shouldn't jump to conclusions, but it's very useful sometimes and saves a lot of thinking out. I'm afraid even after we're married," said Sophie gravely, "I'm afraid I shall go on jumping to conclusions."

"Oh Sophie!" cried Dane, laughing. "Oh Sophie darling — you must just go on being exactly the same. I don't want a single hair of you different . . . but I wish you'd tell me how you knew about Frank and Wynne. Has Wynne said anything to you ?"

"No — nothing really, but I was certain they loved each other and of course it worried me, so I knew you'd be worried too. I knew you would be thinking of Elsie and what happened to her . . . I thought of it all the time. It wasn't really very clever of me to guess that you had sent Frank away, was it ?"

"I think it was very clever," Dane said.

Sophie ignored this, she was too intent upon her explanations to notice compliments. "At first, when I thought about it, I nearly *died*," she declared. "It seemed like Elsie and Otto over again . . . it seemed too dreadful for words . . . but when I thought about it a little more I changed my mind."

"Sophie, it *is* dreadful," Dane said earnestly.

"Yes," she agreed. "Yes . . . but Dane *we* can't interfere with their lives. I mean we mustn't do it. We can advise them and warn them, that's all."

"But Sophie — "

"And Frank isn't like Otto," Sophie interrupted. "He's like Otto to look at but he's made of different stuff. He's stronger and better than Otto, he's more reasonable, more considerate and much kinder."

"That's true, of course."

"And Wynne is stronger than Elsie. They're both whole people, Dane. They know what they want and go straight for it. They're quite different from what we were when we were young."

This was true too, and Dane realised that Sophie was right.

"So if he comes back," said Sophie. "If he comes back and they both still want it . . . well then . . ."

"Yes," said Dane.

"But I hope they won't," she added with a sigh.

By this time the younger members of the party had finished their bathe and were ready for lunch.

"Poor darlings!" said Wynne, as she leaped down off the rocks, "Poor darlings, did you think we were never coming? You should have begun without us."

"Have you been sitting there all this time?" inquired Roy, flinging himself on to the ground beside them.

"You haven't been long," replied Dane and Sophie with one accord.

"Two hours," said Roy, looking at his watch. "Two solid hours. What *have* you been talking about?"

It seemed to Dane a reasonable question and he saw no grounds for evading a reply. The news would have to be broken sometime.

"I asked your mother to marry me," he said in a tone which was as matter of fact as he could make it.

"Oh *Dane*!" cried Sophie. "Oh, Dane why — "

"And she was good enough to accept my proposal," added Dane.

For a moment there was incredulous silence, and then Wynne recovered the use of her tongue. "Oh you darlings!" she exclaimed. "Oh, what a fool I've been! Of course that was why . . ." and she flung herself at Sophie and almost smothered her with embraces.

Dane had been pretty sure of Wynne's sympathy — it was Roy who might be the difficulty. He looked at Roy somewhat anxiously to see how he was taking it. Roy met his eyes . . . and looked away.

"Roy," said Dane. "Roy, I hope you . . . you understand. It won't make any difference to anything."

"I can't believe it, that's all," said Roy uncertainly, and Dane saw that his face was crimson with embarrassment. "I can't . . . believe it. You and Sophie have always been . . . I mean you've been *there* . . . and now . . ."

"We shall still be there," declared Sophie, holding out her hands to him. "Roy darling, of course we're there — here, I mean — always and just the same. No difference at all except that Dane can help me to bear things even better than before."

"Bear things?" he said, pulling at a tuft of grass that grew in a crevice.

"Yes, darling," said Sophie. "There's

such a lot to bear . . . war perhaps, and you going away. You've got your own life now, and Wynne has hers. Wynne may go away too, and then what would become of me?"

"But Sophie — " began Roy, raising his eyes and looking at her.

"But Roy, it's right for people to have their own lives, isn't it? You and Wynne have all your lives before you."

"Oh Sophie!" cried Roy taking her hands. "Oh darling, what a beast I am! As long as you're happy — "

"I'm happy," Sophie declared, smiling through tears.

Dane heaved a sigh of relief, for he was aware that the worst was over. Now that Roy had accepted the idea he would soon get used to it and all would go on as before. Wynne helped to ease the tension which ensued, she was so unselfconscious, so unselfish in her delight at her mother's happiness — and Dane's.

"It's perfect," she declared, looking from one to the other with shining eyes. "It really is quite perfect. You're both such lambs and you fit in together so beautifully . . ."

She was opening the basket as she spoke

and beginning to distribute the food, and they all discovered that they were very hungry.

"It's after two o'clock," Roy pointed out as he seized the leg of a chicken and a large ham sandwich.

"And such a lot has happened," added Sophie.

Fortunately there was a large bottle of hock in the basket, so healths could be drunk with proper ceremony and the mere fact of eating and drinking made everybody feel more normal. They laughed and talked, but Sophie talked faster and more fluently than anyone else. She had suffered an emotional strain and had exhibited a good deal of wisdom and understanding and the inevitable reaction had now set in. She talked about a picnic which had taken place when she was a child, and went on to discuss the difference between children then and now . . . and the next moment she had begun to talk about New York.

"But you haven't been there!" Wynne exclaimed in surprise, "so how do you know anything about it?"

"That's the extraordinary part of it," Sophie explained. "I *have* been there but I *don't* know anything about it. I went with my father when I was ten years old, and why he took me with him I can't imagine. It was such a waste," declared Sophie, shaking her head sadly, "such a terrible waste, because I couldn't take it in at all. I was rather frightened, really, because I had never been away from home before, and everyone had told me that I mustn't be a nuisance to Father. Everyone had told me to be good and quiet and to be sure to remember my manners and not to make Father ashamed; everyone had given me so much advice that I was quite bewildered before I started. I was frightened, too, I was frightened of the noise and the bustle and of all the strange people who spoke to me. They were very kind, of course, and they asked me to parties with Father but I didn't enjoy the parties at all — I was shy and tired and very sleepy because I wasn't used to late hours, and all I longed for was bed. I must have been very dull — I expect they thought I was half-witted, don't you?" Sophie paused for a moment and smiled. "You know," she said, "the only thing I remember clearly is trying to darn my stockings — it was a nightmare to me.

The holes *would* come and I didn't know how to mend them, because, of course, Nannie had always mended them at home. They were black woollen stockings and I watered them with tears."

None of the others had heard of this visit to New York before, and when they could get a word in edgeways, they expressed their amazement that Sophie had concealed it from them for so long.

"I don't know why I remembered it," Sophie replied. "Perhaps it was the vegetable salad — though I've often had vegetable salad before and not remembered New York. I don't really remember it *now*," she added, smiling at her family affectionately — "I mean there's nothing of New York in me — there never was — and I'm exactly the same, now, as if I had never been there at all . . . that's why it was such a waste."

CHAPTER SIX

THE ultimatum which Britain had sent to Germany expired on Sunday morning at eleven o'clock and at eleven fifteen Mr. Chamberlain spoke to the people. He did not make a speech, he just spoke to the people of Britain quietly and from a full heart, and the people of Britain listened. There was no excitement, there was no waving of banners, but there was determination. The people of Britain were at one in their determination to fight against aggression in the cause of liberty and justice — it was in this spirit that Britain took up arms.

Dane and Sophie and Wynne were in the Fernacres drawing-room listening to the radio, and it seemed very strange to all of them that war should come like this. It came so quietly in the pretty peaceful room that they knew so well. They listened to Mr. Chamberlain in silence and rose to their feet with one accord at the strains of "God Save the King". When it was over and silence fell, Wynne could bear it no longer and she fled from the room.

Sophie was sobbing quietly and Dane went over to her and took her hand.

"Sophie dear," he said — and then paused, for there was nothing that he could say.

"Never mind me," said Sophie. "I'm just silly . . . I'll be all right in a minute. It's just that I'm so sorry for *him* . . . he's worked so hard for peace. Go after Wynne — go after her, Dane. Somebody must do something for Wynne."

"You must go to her, Sophie."

"No — you," said Sophie. "You're so much cleverer than I am. You'll know what to say."

He put his hand on Sophie's shoulder for a moment and then went after Wynne, for Sophie was right — somebody must try to help her. It was doubtful whether anyone could do much for her but at least he could try. She had run out into the garden and after some trouble he found her in a little ruined summer-house beyond the tennis courts. She was sitting on the bench staring before her with sightless eyes.

"Wynne!" he said a trifle diffidently, for

it seemed improper to intrude upon the privacy she had sought.

"Oh, Dane!" she said, looking up at him and speaking in a low, even tone. "Oh, Dane, I can't understand it . . . I can't even believe it . . . you know about wars."

Dane looked at her tenderly and he realised what she was trying to put into words. She felt that the whole fabric of life had collapsed, and the world, as she knew it, was in ruins. It was strange that he should understand her so well for the problems of one generation are seldom very real to the next and it is often easier for the old to understand the young than for the middle generation to understand either. He saw that perhaps they had been wrong to allow Wynne to grow up in ignorance of the stern realities of life, but he had loved her so dearly — like the little daughter which she might so easily have been — and he had wanted her to be happy and gay and carefree; he had wanted to give her a long lease of summer. She had been happy, there was no doubt, but perhaps the fact that her life had been lived beneath un-clouded skies made it all the harder for her to withstand the tempest.

"You know about wars," said Wynne.

"Yes," replied Dane sadly. Like every-one else of his generation Dane had vivid memories of the last war. He remembered (for he was old enough) the time of peace before it, and indeed it seemed to him that true peace had been wrecked in 1914 and had never been properly mended. It was a wonderfully secure and comfortable and peaceful world that Dane remembered — "In the old days of peace ere ever the sons of the Achaeans came to the land", as the Greek poet had written — Dane had been formed in that peaceful world but he had been hardened in the crucible of war. Yes, Wynne was right, he knew about wars. The last war was clear in his mind and since then, during the last twenty years, he had wandered over the face of Europe and had met and spoken with men who knew how brittle a thing was Europe's peace. He had been in Germany and had observed for himself the frightful industry with which she was re-arming and re-educating her youth, forging her weapons for the conflict which she had now forced upon the world. He had been in Spain, and had seen the terrible results of modern warfare, wrecked cities blazing like devil's bonfires, and homeless starving people. He had been in France and had stood amongst the great fortifications which France had built at the cost of millions — great fortifications hidden beneath fair fields and smiling meadows and amongst the tender green foliage of woods, but all the more strong and deadly and ominous for that . . . France was in no doubt as to her enemy. So, now, when the precarious peace had crumbled, Dane was not amazed; his soul was armoured against the blow; the frightful menace of war had not come upon him unawares.

"It's so dreadful," Wynne was saying in a quiet voice. "It's so dreadful that I can't . . . can't take it in at all. People killing each other . . . there's Roy, you see . . . and . . . and Frank. I suppose I shouldn't be thinking of Frank."

"Why not? He's your friend."

"It seems selfish to think of one's own . . . at a time like this, but I can't help it. Will Frank be fighting against us, Dane?"

She spoke with a gentle docility which Dane found very moving — far more moving than tears. Wynne trusted him, she had always looked to him to solve her difficulties, and he had always been able to help, but now —

"I don't know," said Dane. "We don't know where Frank is, do we? If he is in Germany, I'm afraid he will have to fight."

"He will be fighting against Roy," she said, and there was horror in her voice . . . Roy and Frank, the two she loved best in the world.

"Don't think of it like that."

"But how — "

"Think of it impersonally," Dane urged her. "Not Frank and Roy fighting against each other, but each fighting for his country as a man must do."

"I can't," she said.

There was silence then, for Dane could do no more. The winds were blowing very roughly upon his darling bud of May.

The winds were rough but after the first onslaught Wynne stood up to them manfully. She was more grave than usual, and less ready to laugh, she was quieter and paler and her face seemed to be firming beneath the strain. Dane watched her and he was proud of her courage. He was all the more proud of Wynne because there was no bitterness in her sadness, she was not sorry for herself, she was not rebellious. It touched him very deeply to see her with her mother — there was a new gentleness in their relationship. Wynne was putting her own troubles in the background and was deliberately engrossing herself in Sophie's affairs. It was natural, of course, that Wynne should share in the anxiety over Roy's safety, but it was less natural that she should share in the happiness of Sophie and himself.

One of the matters in which Wynne was deliberately engrossing herself was the problem of Sophie's trousseau. It was a small matter, perhaps, but Dane thought that the mere fact that Wynne took an interest in it showed a noble spirit. Wynne was determined that Sophie should have a "proper trousseau," and she was setting about the matter in her usual energetic way.

"You must have another coat and skirt," she declared.

"But Wynne, I don't need it, and it's war-time," complained Sophie.

"And you must have a pretty frock for the wedding — and a really smart hat — "

"But Wynne — "

"You must," said Wynne firmly.

She ordered hats to be sent from London on approval and tried them on to Sophie's somewhat reluctant head. Dane happened to come in during one of these orgies and found the drawing-room littered with hats and Wynne with a hat in each hand, weighing their merits.

"What on earth — " began Dane.

"She must have a new hat," explained Wynne gravely, "and she won't go to town and choose one so I've had them sent here. Put this one on again, darling, and let Dane see."

"But Wynne, I look a perfect sight — "

"No darling, it's just that you aren't used to it. Look Dane, isn't she sweet in that one."

Sophie had the type of face eminently suited to the present fashion. The perched Edwardian concoction of feathers in soft shades of blue was not what Dane would have called a "hat" but Sophie looked a perfect darling in it, and he said so.

"There," said Wynne as if that settled the matter. "Oh Wynne, I don't think — "

"Sophie, it's perfect . . . not a bit too young."

"Wynne, I'm sure — "

"Honestly," said Wynne. "Honestly it's simply perfect. Wear it a teeny bit more . . . there, like that."

"I think that other hat — "

"No," said Wynne. "No, you can't possibly have that frumpy old brown one. I couldn't let you — not possibly. You're choosing a wedding hat, Sophie."

"I'm glad of that," said Dane. "Perhaps you'll give me some idea of when you expect to be married. How long will it be before that hat goes out of fashion ?"

Sophie sighed. She loved Dane dearly and of course she was going to marry him but there was no hurry about it . . . she was being rushed, she was being harried. Wynne was harrying her into buying unsuitable clothes and Dane was harrying her into matrimony.

"When ?" urged Dane.

"Darling," said Sophie. "Of course I want to marry you but there's no hurry . . . and the war has upset me."

CHAPTER SEVEN

THE war had had very little effect upon the outward appearance of Chellford. It was in people's hearts that the change was wrought and English people do not wear their hearts on their sleeves. Sophie's heart was leaden, and full of anxiety, but Chellford looked as peaceful as ever. Sometimes it was difficult to believe that war had really come and it was all the more difficult because the weather was so beautiful; the sun shone golden in a cloudless sky, the sea was like blue glass. (How *could* one believe that death might rain from that sky at any moment of the day or night, or that death lurked beneath that lovely peaceful sea?) Slowly the trees turned red and brown, orange and golden; slowly the tired leaves fell.

Meanwhile, and in the midst of all the usual daily activities of housekeeping and shopping, the bulletins of the war were issued almost hourly on the radio; the advance of the Germans into Poland, the sufferings of Warsaw, the sinking of ships.

It was the sinkings of ships which affected Sophie most, for everyone is selfish at heart, and although Sophie's sympathies went out to the Poles, her anxiety for Roy's safety was deeper and nearer and more constant. Roy had been transferred to the destroyer, Spark, which was operating somewhere in the North Sea. His letters were irregular, owing to the exigencies of the service, and when they failed to arrive on the usual day a cloud of misery descended upon Sophie and blotted out the world; but when they did arrive they were cheerful, and it was so obvious that the writer was contented with his lot that the cloud lifted and the sun shone once more.

Wynne and Nina and several of their friends had been detailed for duty at the Chellford Hospital. They had so many hours on, and so many hours off. Their duties consisted of scrubbing floors, getting the kitchens into order and putting up extra beds. Fortunately these elaborate precautions were not yet required for there were no wounded to be cared for and the patients consisted of a few soldiers from the nearby camp with chills and sprains and one or two accident cases. All over the country, hospitals were being prepared by England's unpaid army of social workers; they were being prepared not only for fighting service casualties, but also for civilians wounded or gassed in air raids. Everyone seemed to be busy except Sophie, and Sophie had nothing to do. (She knitted socks, of course, but she did not feel that it was enough.) There were no schoolchildren billeted at Chellford, for it had been made a "neutral area" on account of its proximity to Kingsport and the docks. At first Sophie was sorry about this, for she was very fond of children and she had been looking forward to having children at Fernacres and looking after them herself, but after a few weeks of war Sophie received so many letters from her friends in country places telling her of their experiences with "evacuees" that she became resigned to her childless existence.

It was a lonely time for Sophie. Wynne rushed in at odd hours and rushed out again, and Dane was busy with some work which he had undertaken for Colonel Carter. It consisted of reading and summarising Secret Service reports and translating secret documents. In addition Dane had undertaken the duties of an air Raid Warden. He went out every evening to make sure that the inhabitants of Chellford were screening their lights in a satisfactory manner, and that no chinks were showing between their curtains. Sometimes it was necessary to ring the bell and to point out deficiencies in this respect, and he found that people were very pleasant and bore no ill will for the interference with their liberties. He slept with the telephone beside his bed and his A.R.P. equipment ready, for in the case of an air raid he would have to go out and look after the people in his district. He would have to direct stray pedestrians to the nearest shelter and to give warning to the proper authorities of fires started by incendiary bombs or of the presence of gas. So far these duties had been hypothetical, and Dane had become quite used to the sight of the telephone beside his bed and to the horrible significance of his service gas mask leering at him from the chair. He had begun to put his kit ready every night without thinking about it, or what it meant.

It was a curious war, Dane thought. It was so different from what anyone had expected. It was so completely different in every way from the last war. The spirit of the country was different — there was no excitement, no glitter, no bombast — there was just a solid and dogged determination all through the country to fight against oppression and injustice. Migs had summed up the feeling of the younger generation very clearly. He had said one day at tea, "It's as if a dog had bitten you in the dark and you were going after it with a stick — at least that's how I feel." That was how they felt: determined, rather angry, bent on meting out just punishment for unprovoked offence — it was a stick, and not a gun with which Migs was arming himself, and Dane thought this point was particularly interesting.

Suddenly one morning Dane was awakened by the shrilling of the telephone and the warning — which he had ceased to expect — was given him. He leapt out of bed and shouted to Hartley to rouse the household and then dressed himself hurriedly in the various garments which had been waiting for so long. He was almost ready when the horrible wailing note of the sirens filled the air, a ghastly sound in itself and all the more ghastly because of its import.

Dane found all the members of the household in the hall — Sophie, Wynne, Barber, Rose and Gladys — Hartley was there too, marshalling them in a military way.

"All present and correct, sir," said Hartley gravely.

"Right," said Dane, stifling an involuntary chuckle, "right Hartley, carry on."

It was quite light now and the sun was rising as the party moved out of the front door and tailed down the garden to the air raid shelter. They carried their gas masks and bags and cushions. Hartley had an armful of rugs and two of the servants were carrying the picnic basket between them — it was obvious that they were well prepared for a long siege. They were all perfectly calm and collected; they were even — as Dane had observed — a little amused at the absurdity of the proceedings. They might not be quite as much amused if a bomb dropped in their vicinity of course.

Dane decided not to think about that. He could do nothing more than he had done and Hartley would be there to look after them. They would be as safe with Hartley as if he were with them himself. He ran down the drive and out into the road. The sirens had stopped now, for they had given their dread message, and everything was perfectly still and quiet. The sun had risen and was shining brightly; there was a faint breeze and a flock of puffy white clouds was hurrying across the pale blue sky. The birds were singing merrily.

A man came up the road driving a milk-cart and Dane signalled to him to stop.

"Hi! Look here, didn't you hear the sirens?"

"I 'eard them all right," replied the man, looking down at Dane from the cart. "It's practise most likely. They 'ad a lot of prac-tises at it in the summer . . . makes your blood run cold, don't it?"

"It isn't a practice, it's the real thing," said Dane.

"An air raid, is it?" inquired the milk-man with interest, and he looked up at the sky.

"Yes, it *is*," said Dane. "It's an air raid alarm. You'll find a shelter in my garden . . . cut along."

The milkman smiled at him pityingly.

"Thank you, sir, but I can't slack off just for an air raid."

"Don't be a fool," exclaimed Dane, "do as you're told. Take your horse out of the cart and tie it to a tree, and then make tracks to the shelter. Hurry up now, I can't stand here all day."

"No, sir," agreed the milkman amiably, "but I got my work, you see. There'd be trouble if people didn't get their milk in time for breakfast."

Dane gave up the struggle. He dashed down the road after a couple of small boys with sheaves of newspapers under their arms. The boys were more amenable to reason than the milkman.

"There, what did I tell yer?" inquired the younger of the two. "What did I tell yer, Bert? I *sed* that there screaming noise was a hair-raid."

"Come on," said Dane encouragingly. "There's a shelter quite near . . . I'll show you . . ."

They hid their papers under a bush and ran after him across the garden to the square concrete pill-box which had been constructed for the Fernacres household. It was not very large but there was plenty of room for two small paper boys.

"Come in," said Sophie in a cheerful voice. "We're just making tea. Dane, do wait a minute and have some."

Dane did not want tea, but he stooped down and looked in at the door to see how the small party was faring. It was dark inside but an oil-lamp hung from the ceiling on a hook. Sophie was standing beneath it with a tea-pot in her hand and Gladys was boiling the kettle on a spirit stove. The others were sitting on wooden benches and were busy knitting socks . . . five women hiding in a concrete pill-box on a beautiful autumn morning! Five women hiding from a so-called civilised enemy who was coming to drop bombs on their heads!

They all looked up and smiled, for Major Worthington was very popular in the household.

"Everything all right?" asked Dane.

There were murmurs of assent from all except Gladys — Gladys was looking rather worried and distressed.

"Will it be over soon, sir?" inquired Gladys anxiously.

He tried to reassure her. "You're quite safe, here," he said in soothing tones.

Gladys sighed. "If I don't get out of 'ere soon the breakfast'll be late," she declared.

"We can't help that," Dane told her. "It won't be your fault anyhow."

"It'll be Hitler's fault," agreed Gladys in a resigned voice.

Hartley winked at him solemnly.

Dane was chuckling to himself as he ran back across the lawn. He had been warned that one of his chief duties was to "allay panic" . . . it was a dashed funny war! A dashed funny mixture of tragedy and farce.

The signal began to blow just as Dane reached the gate — it was the same siren, but blowing a long, sustained blast on the same note — he turned in time to see the little procession wending its way back to the house; Sophie and Wynne in front, arm in arm, the three servants behind and Hartley bringing up the rear. The two boys came down the drive with large slices of cake in their hands, they collected their papers from under the bush and proceeded on their way rejoicing.

CHAPTER EIGHT

SOMEWHAT reluctantly Dane decided that he must have a radio set of his own. It was really essential, for he was spending far too much time in the drawing-room. He went down to the drawing-room to hear the news, and there he remained, talking to Sophie instead of getting on with his work. Hartley, when approached upon the subject, agreed that it had become necessary; indeed Hartley had said, more than a year ago, that they would need one if there was war.

"As a matter of fact," said Hartley, "I've been keeping my eyes open and there's a friend of mine in Kingsport that has a first-class set he wants to sell."

"Why?" inquired Dane, who was naturally suspicious of someone who wanted to sell a first-class set.

"Been called up," explained Hartley, "and it really is a bargain. We could get it quite cheap and it would cost about forty pounds to buy new. We want a good one," added Hartley persuasively. "One that will get America."

Dane's idea had been much more humble, he had wanted a set which would give him the news — the Home Service Bulletins — and perhaps Paris and Hamburg, but Hartley's suggestions opened up larger vistas and Dane was attracted by them.

"Well, find out about it, Hartley," he said.

He said no more and he was somewhat surprised when he discovered the radio installed in his sitting-room, and a tall youth in battle-dress boring a hole in his window-frame.

"What on earth's the meaning of this?" inquired Dane.

The boy rose from his knees and saluted smartly. "It's on appro., sir," he explained. "You don't need to keep it if you don't like it — Mr. Hartley said it would be all right."

"Oh, he did, did he?"

"Yes, sir."

"What do you want for it?"

"Well sir, you keep it a bit and see how you like it and, if you like it, you can pay me what you think's right."

"But I've no idea . . . What did you pay for it?"

"I didn't buy it, I made it," replied the boy, and his eyes dwelt on the shiny cabinet with regretful affection.

"You don't want to sell it?"

"I do, and I don't," replied the boy. "I can't take it with me, you see — wish I could, I'll miss it more than anything. You can get any station you like on it — America, China, Australia."

"Marvellous!" exclaimed Dane, looking at the little cabinet with something like awe. It really was marvellous. It was the miracle of modern days.

The boy was rubbing the cabinet with a duster, now, polishing it carefully after its journey, and Dane watched him for a few moments.

"Look here," said Dane. "You don't want to sell it — I'll hire it from you at so much a week. We'll find out how much would be fair. Then it will still be yours and you can have it back when you want it."

"Would that suit you?" inquired the boy, his eyes lighting with pleasure. "Would it really, sir? It would be grand for me."

The bargain was sealed, and, after showing Major Worthington how to work the set and displaying its unique advantages, the young man departed.

No sooner had he gone than Dane drew up a chair and sat down and began to play with his new toy. It was a thrilling experience to turn on the tap (as it were) and to find French, German, Italian, Spanish, Dutch and a host of English voices pouring out of the faucet. It reminded Dane of a conjuring trick performed by the great David Devant in which an ordinary-seeming kitchen kettle was made to produce at command a dozen different kinds of wines. It was thrilling, and it was even a trifle alarming to hear those voices. They went on all day (presumably) and far into the night. All those voices pouring out floods of news, alleging this, discussing that, pleading to be heard, shouting for people to listen, filling the ears of their hearers with truth, with lies, with opinions and theories and facts and fancies, with propaganda of every sort and description.

Dane played with his toy a good deal in the next few days and one evening about six o'clock he came upon something especially interesting. He had heard the voice of the friend, and the voice of the neutral, and, stranger than either of these, he had heard the voice of the enemy, but this was the voice of the enemy of the enemy; it was a German voice coming from Germany and speaking to the Germans, and it was giving out Anti-Nazi propaganda. The talk was good and well-reasoned and Dane listened to it with interest. He realised that the speaker knew his facts and had thought them out and discovered their implications, he realised that the speaker knew Britain and understood British policy. Dane thought that even a prejudiced person, listening to this talk, must be impressed with the sense of it and with the sincerity of the speaker's voice, and he wondered how many people in Germany were risking imprisonment, but the speaker was risking death and worse, yet there were no signs of urgency in the voice, no haste or excitement, and occasionally there was even a touch of humour. He must be a brave man, thought Dane, and for a moment or two Dane lost the thread of the discourse in thinking of the man himself. He listened without listening — as it were

— and it was then that he discovered that the voice had a familiar ring. Dane sat up and listened more intently than before . . . it was absurd, of course . . . it couldn't be . . .

He rang the bell in a somewhat urgent manner and Hartley appeared immediately in a large dressing gown, but with his hair sleeked down as usual. Hartley began to explain that he had been in the middle of changing to go out, but Dane signalled to him to be silent and pointed to a chair. Hartley gathered his dressing gown round him and sat down.

The voice went on. It filled the room. It was strong and vibrant but perfectly controlled. Presently the voice stopped and Dane leant forward and turned the switch. There was silence.

"Was it young Mr. Heiden?" inquired Hartley with interest.

"Well, was it?" inquired Dane. "Did *you* think it was?"

"It was like his voice," said Hartley thoughtfully, "but then I haven't ever heard him speak German. It makes a difference."

"Yes," agreed Dane. "Yes, it does. Don't

say anything about it to anyone . . . we'll listen again tomorrow."

They listened for several evenings at the same hour but the speakers were different, and then, on the fourth evening, it was the same man.

Dane tried to clear his mind of all preconceptions; he tried to forget the words and to concentrate on the voice; he tried to imagine that voice speaking English. He tried to imagine Frank sitting in the chair — where Hartley was sitting — he tried to conjure up Frank's figure. Frank had sat in that chair after the pact of Munich had been signed — it was more than a year ago now — and had talked of eternal peace between his two countries. Poor Frank!

This voice was like Frank's voice, and the speaker possessed exactly the knowledge which Frank possessed. The speaker had gone through the same experiences — he was talking about them now — he was telling his hearers how he had gone to Britain with preconceived ideas, he had been like a man at sea in a boat with a load of prejudices and every day he had cast some of them overboard . . . Frank had said that. Frank had used that very metaphor!

It was not impossible that two men should have had the same experiences, but it was most unlikely that two men should choose exactly the same metaphor to describe them.

Dane bent forward and said to Hartley, "It *is* Frank Heiden."

Hartley nodded.

The news that he had discovered Frank's whereabouts was not good news. The boy was in the most ghastly danger and it would be no comfort to Wynne to hear of it. Dane had always believed in keeping bad news to himself, if it was possible to do so, and in this case it was easy. He said nothing about Frank's activities to anyone but he continued to listen to Frank and Hartley listened too. Sometimes Frank spoke for two or three nights in succession, and sometimes there was an interval of one or two or three nights when different voices spoke. One night Dane and Hartley were listening to Frank speaking and a curious thing occurred.

The broadcast was proceeding as usual when suddenly there was a loud report . . . and then two more reports almost simultaneously. The voice faltered and stopped.

There was a cry of "Achtung! Achtung!" There was a crash, a loud crash as if someone had burst open a door . . . then there were two more reports . . . and silence.

Hartley had sprung to his feet with the instinct to help . . . and then, half shamefacedly, as he sat down again. The incident, whatever it was, had occurred several hundred miles away in the heart of Germany but it seemed very real and near in that quiet English sitting-room.

"I thought for a minute — " Hartley began.

"Yes, but we can do nothing," replied Dane. He had had the same impulse — the impulse to leap to his feet and rush to Frank's assistance — but they were absolutely helpless, of course, they did not know what had happened nor where it had taken place.

Dane was very worried. It was foolish to worry because there was nothing to be done, but he worried all the same. He listened the next night and heard the same sort of propaganda, but in a different voice; he listened every night for a week, for ten days, for a fortnight, but Frank's voice was not on the air . . .

405

CHAPTER NINE

THE war was not very old before the weddings began — it is curious that marriage should be an invariable concomitant of war. Wynne's friends and contemporaries rushed headlong into matrimony — Ian Sutherland married Grace Greensleeves, Anne Fulton married Roger Page; there were a dozen weddings in less than a dozen weeks round and about the neighbourhood of Chellford. Some of the young people, who suddenly discovered that they could not live without each other, had known each other from babyhood, and others met for the first time and were engaged before the month was out. It was really rather bewildering and, having regard to the wedding presents, exceedingly expensive. Nina Corbett and Mark Audley had known each other for years, and had never shown any signs of rapture in each other's company; they might have gone on knowing each other for years longer if it had not been for the war. Wynne always declared it was Mark's uniform — he certainly looked very well in it — that had stirred Nina's heart. They discovered that they loved each other one evening and announced the news to their respective families the following morning at breakfast. It was not a good time to choose for an announcement of this nature and neither of the families was as pleased as Nina and Mark had expected. Mrs. Audley put on her hat and coat and hurried round to the Corbetts, and, finding Mrs. Corbett at home, explained to her as tactfully as possible that Nina was too old — she was six months older than Mark — and that anyhow there had better be no talk of an engagement till after the war. Mr. Corbett — when he returned from his office in Kingsport — put on his hat and coat and rushed round to the Audleys and explained with less tact that Mark was much too young. Mark had no money and his prospects were by no means rosy. He had now left the firm of architects in which he was a very junior partner, and he was a lieutenant in the 6th Westshires — a territorial battalion of course. Mr. Corbett declared that there must be no thought of an engagement at present. The families were somewhat annoyed with each other but their views were identical regarding the proposed alliance, and Mark and Nina were informed that there was to be no engagement, at any rate until after the war. They took it surprisingly well. Mark departed with his battalion to Aldershot and Nina went up to London to stay with her aunt.

Two days later the Audleys and the Corbetts received Night Telegraph Letters from their respective offspring (Nina had made the astonishing discovery that you could send thirty-six words for a shilling if you sent them overnight, and as it was war time and economy was essential it seemed an excellent idea). The Night Telegraph Letters consisted of exactly thirty-six words and, as they were almost identical, it was reasonable to suppose that young Mr. and Mrs. Audley had collaborated over their composition, Nina's ran as follows:

"CORBETT, CHERRY TREES, CHELLFORD.
"DARLINGS WE DID NOT GET ENGAGED BUT JUST GOT MARRIED SPECIAL LICENCE THIS AFTERNOON AUNT MONA BLAMELESS WE HOPE WONT MIND VERY MUCH DARLINGS

Mrs. Corbett received this communication after Mr. Corbett had left the house, and she was so appalled, and so angry that she felt that if she did not show it to somebody and talk about it to somebody she would burst. There was nobody except Sophie Braithwaite — everybody else was busy — and, although Mrs. Corbett would have preferred somebody more rational, she decided that Sophie Braithwaite would have to do.

Unfortunately Sophie was even more vague than usual this morning, and did not seem to appreciate the situation at all.

"Dear little Nina," she murmured as she read the Night Telegraph Letter. "Darling little Nina, I do hope she'll be very very happy."

"The duplicity of it!" Mrs. Corbett cried, more angry than ever (for it was absolutely maddening to hear Sophie's fond murmurs when the treatment that Nina deserved was a good spanking). "The deceitfulness of it, Sophie! Nina has thrown herself away, yes, thrown herself away. Mark has no prospects, he's nothing but a boy, and rather a silly boy at that. I'm furious about it and I don't know what Miguel will say. He was strongly against the marriage. Mark had no right to marry her against our wishes, it's a disgraceful thing and I shall tell Mary Audley exactly what I think about it."

"They didn't want it either," said Sophie somewhat tactlessly.

"And why not?" inquired Mrs. Corbett who was much too angry to be reasonable. "Why shouldn't they be pleased? Who are Audleys anyhow? Nobodies, my dear. Miguel can trace his descent back to one of the Knights who came over with William the Conqueror . . . the Audleys indeed," and Mrs. Corbett made that strange sound of contempt which is sometimes written, "pshaw".

"Poor little Nina!" murmured Sophie. "She's such a dear little thing. I do hope Mark will be terribly sweet to her."

Mrs. Corbett began to wish she had not come. She was getting more angry instead of less. "These war weddings!" she cried. "It's a disgrace to the country . . . they shouldn't be allowed. It's just excitement, a kind of intoxication . . . young people seem to think they can do whatever they like just because of the war . . ." she paused and looked at Sophie. "Sophie, you aren't listening," she said.

"Oh yes — yes I was," said Sophie with a vague smile.

Mrs. Corbett was sure that Sophie had not heard a word; she was even more *distrait* than usual, and that was saying a good deal.

"What's the matter with you, today?" demanded Mrs. Corbett.

"I was just thinking . . ." said Sophie, smiling to herself in an infuriating manner.

"Thinking what?"

"Nothing really . . . it's just that there seem to be so many weddings just now."

There had been a great many weddings, but just at the moment there was a sort of lull, and Mrs. Corbett could not think of any which were due to be celebrated in the immediate future. Her curiosity began to get the better of her rage.

"Sophie, who is it?" she inquired. "Who is going to be married next?"

"I didn't say anyone was," said Sophie, and she blushed.

Mrs. Corbett adored gossip and now she was hard on the trail. "My dear!" she exclaimed. "It's Wynne, of course — how thrilling! Do tell me about it. Of course Wynne had heaps of admirers but I didn't know there was anything serious in the air."

"Oh no!" cried Sophie in dismay. "Oh no, it isn't — "

"I shan't tell a soul," Mrs. Corbett assured her. "You can depend on me . . . darling Wynne, I do hope it's somebody really good enough."

"But it isn't Wynne at all," Sophie cried.

Mrs. Corbett did not believe her. "I shan't tell a soul," she repeated, "I shan't tell a single creature."

"Oh dear," exclaimed Sophie. "This is dreadful! I can't let you go on thinking . . . Oh dear, I do wish Dane would come."

"You had much better tell me," urged Mrs. Corbett — it was the tone that a kind but somewhat strict nurse might use to a recalcitrant child — "You'd much better tell me all about it. There isn't any sense in making mysteries. I've always been so fond of dear little Wynne, and so interested in her."

Sophie groaned. "Oh dear, I suppose I shall have to tell you. It isn't Wynne at all. It's me. I'm going to be married this afternoon."

If she had wanted to astonish Mrs. Corbett she would have had her wish in full measure, but she had not wanted to astonish anyone. Dane had at last persuaded her to marry him, and she had agreed on condition that nobody was to be told — nobody at all. She had wanted to keep the whole thing a secret and to keep it a secret indefinitely. Dane had pointed out that this was impossible, and indeed undesirable; if Dane had had his way he would have made a little splash over their wedding, for he was of the opinion that a small party and perhaps a dozen bottles of good champagne would have carried them over what might be a somewhat awkward fence. Wynne agreed with him and did her best to influence Sophie, but their united efforts only procured the disastrous result of reducing Sophie to tears.

"I don't want them to know," she sobbed. They'll say . . . Oh dear, I know quite well what they'll say . . . they'll say we've been living together . . ."

"Well, you have," said Wynne in surprise. "We've all been living together for years and years...."

(Dane felt himself blushing; it was an unusual and distinctly unpleasant experience.)

"No, no," said Sophie, weeping.

"Yes, yes," said Wynne soothingly, "and now that you and Dane are going to be married it will be much better to have a nice party and tell everyone about it. People will talk far more if you go all hole and cornery ... Let's have a party," said Wynne persuasively. "Darling Sophie, do let's have a party and drink your healths and have speeches and things."

"No," said Sophie, sobbing and shaking her head. "No, I couldn't bear it."

Dane saw that it was time to interfere. "Never mind," he said, "Never mind, darling. It shall all be exactly as you want."

"All hole and cornery," added Wynne in some disgust.

So Sophie had got her way, and she and Dane were to be married that very afternoon by special licence at a small church in Kingsport. Nobody was invited and nobody was to be present except the family and the Fernacres servants (Dane had insisted that the servants should be there and he had appointed Hartley as his best man). It was to have been all hole and cornery — as Wynne had said — and now Sophie had let it out herself, and to Mrs. Corbett of all people!

"Oh dear!" said Sophie. "What a fool I am! I always thought I was silly and now I'm sure . . . and how anyone could ever want to marry such a silly fool is more than I can see."

Curiously enough the same idea had occurred to Mrs. Corbett; she was not one of Sophie's admirers. Perhaps this was due to the fact that she prided herself upon having an orderly mind, or perhaps to a somewhat pardonable jealousy. It was galling to find one's young, reluctant to run messages for oneself, not only willing but eager to perform the same tiresome offices for Sophie Braithwaite. Whichever it was, the fact remained that Mrs. Corbett had not much use for Sophie (except of course as an occasional fountain of news) and Sophie had no use at all for Mrs. Corbett. If only it had been Mrs. Audley — Sophie was thinking miserably — but Mrs. Audley would never have screwed her secret out of her like that.

There had been a short but exceedingly uncomfortable silence when the door opened and Dane walked in, and Sophie, who was always delighted to see Dane at any moment, had never been so delighted as now.

"Oh, Dane!" she cried. "Oh, Dane, I've told her about this afternoon . . . I couldn't let her go on thinking it was Wynne, could I?"

"No, of course not," agreed Dane, smiling at Mrs. Corbett — whom he disliked intensely — in his most diplomatic manner, "of course you wanted to tell Mrs. Corbett all about it. She's one of your closest friends, isn't she?"

"She lives next door," agreed Sophie doubtfully.

"One of your closest friends," continued Dane, raising his voice so as to drown Sophie's infelicitous remark, "and of course you've told Mrs. Corbett that we are hoping to have one or two people here afterwards." He turned to Mrs. Corbett. "I do hope you will come — you and Mr. Corbett and Migs if he's available — it's very short notice, but — but with the war, and everything so uncertain," said Dane, searching wildly for some plausible reason why the Corbetts should not have been invited long ago, "and Roy, of course," said Dane, joyfully seizing upon one, "Roy's leave . . . special leave for his mother's wedding . . . but we didn't know whether he would be able to get leave until the very last minute, so we couldn't arrange things beforehand. However, he's coming, and we do hope — both of us — that you'll all come in at about three o'clock and — and have a little festivity. Just a few of us — the Audleys, of course, and the Winslows — but we wanted to ask you first," added Dane with another and even more charming smile.

Mrs. Corbett wavered. "But Sophie didn't mean — "

"No," agreed Dane, laughing a little. "No, Sophie didn't mean to tell you like that. I think she felt that a little note would be more polite and less embarrassing. But now that she has told you, and told you before anyone else outside the immediate family, I hope you'll all come."

"It's very short notice," said Mrs. Corbett, thawing slightly, "and Sophie . . .

really I can't help feeling a little hurt that Sophie didn't tell me before."

"I think I was rather shy," declared Sophie in a very small voice.

Mrs. Corbett smiled at her, not very easily, perhaps, but it was an effort in the right direction and Dane welcomed it as such.

"It *is* a surprise," Mrs. Corbett said, "and I haven't congratulated you . . . I do congratulate you of course, but you haven't told me who you're going to marry."

Dane had not realised this, he rushed in before Sophie could open her mouth, for she was in one of her less tactful moods today — probably owing to very natural excitement — and she seemed to have been putting her foot in it pretty thoroughly. "She's going to marry me," said Dane hastily. "Yes, of course you *must* be surprised, but as a matter of fact we've discovered that we can't get on without each other."

Mrs. Corbett struggled wildly with herself: one half of her wanted to be nasty about it but the other half wanted to be nice. It would be rather amusing to be nasty because she could talk about it —

there were all sorts of amusing things she could say. On the other hand she was aware that Sophie was popular in Chellford, and Dane also. Dane was very pleasant really, thought Mrs. Corbett

Dane was watching her face and he saw there was nothing for it but to go all pathetic as Wynne (would have said).

"We're both rather lonely people," he said, with a sad smile, "and we've decided to grow old together — that's all."

Mrs. Corbett smiled, too — it was a real smile this time. "Oh, I do hope you'll be happy," she said, holding out her hand, "and I'm sure you will. You know each other so well, don't you? You've been living — "

"Thank you," said Dane, grasping her hand and shaking it heartily. "Thank you very much. I'm sure we shall. You'll come to our little party, won't you? . . . Good, that's splendid . . . about three o'clock . . . grand! And Mr. Corbett and Migs too . . ."

His hair was standing on end when he came back to the drawing-room after seeing Mrs. Corbett out, and Sophie knew by this that he really was disturbed, for it was only when Dane was very fussed indeed that he ran his fingers through his hair.

"Oh Dane!" she said. "Wasn't it dreadful? I am so sorry about it. I really don't know why you want to marry such a fool."

Dane took no notice of this — there wasn't time — Mrs. Corbett would spread the news all round Chellford. The town crier was nothing compared with her.

"Sit down and write," said Dane. "Write to Mrs. Audley and Mrs. Winslow and Mrs. Sutherland and anyone else you can think of. I've got enough fizz for them all, thank Heaven for that." He took her by the shoulders gently but firmly and seated her at her desk. "Go on," he said. "*Write* — start now. I'll tell you what to say. Hartley and Ellis can go round on their bicycles and deliver the letters at once."

The wedding party of Sophie and Dane was the first real "party" to take place in Chellford since the beginning of the war, and people, finding it pleasant to put on their smart clothes once more, donned a festive spirit at the same time. There was so little going on in the way of social activities that nearly everyone who had been asked accepted. The younger generation were there in full force — some of them in uniforms of various kinds and colours. Wynne, on hearing of Sophie's indiscretion, had seized on the chance with delight and had spent a profitable hour ringing up all her friends and inviting them to come and drink Dane's champagne.

"It will be much better to have *lots* of people," she told Dane firmly, when he tried to curb her activities, "you want a *crush*, darling."

Dane did not want a crush but he realised that there was some truth in her words.

"You want a crush," repeated Wynne, who was waiting for a call to Kingsport. "Parties always go better if there's no room to move, and that horrible Corbett woman must be swamped . . . and if you haven't anything to do you can run over to Kingsport and buy a cake."

"A cake!"

"A wedding cake, of course. We've got a teeny one, but it won't feed a quarter of the people. Do go, Dane . . . I've got such a lot to do, and Sophie's in the most awful flap."

He went. It was not an easy matter to find a wedding cake ready made, for most people (so he was informed) ordered their wedding cakes some time in advance, but at last, after visiting at least half-a-dozen baker's shops, he ran one to earth. It was not a very grand wedding cake, but it would have to do — after all it was war-time. Dane put it in the car and returned to Fernacres in triumph to find the house in confusion. Wynne was knee-deep in flowers and the servants were rushing about with trays of glasses. Roy had arrived and had brought Harry Coles and two other naval friends who were complete strangers to Dane — he had never seen them before. Nobody seemed to be worrying about them, but they seemed perfectly happy; they had made themselves at home and were listening to the radio in the drawing-room.

"Roy's busy," explained the elder of the two. "He and Harry are moving tables and things and they didn't want us, so we just parked ourselves here. Hope it's all right, sir."

Dane was about to inquire what their names were and to offer them some sherry and a little light conversation when Hartley came for him and bore him away. From then on everything was a rush and a whirl and partook of the qualities of a dream — almost of a nightmare. His search for the cake had delayed him and there was no time to dress and have lunch in a civilised manner — and Hartley was so excited and worried and so terrified that they would be late that Dane could scarcely recognise him as the quiet, capable creature he had known for so long. Dane had never seen Hartley in a state of perturbation — in the tightest corner he was always perfectly serene — and if Dane had not been so perturbed himself, the sight of a perturbed Hartley would have amused him. As it was he was not amused, he was extremely annoyed. He was annoyed with Wynne for sending him off on that idiotic quest for the cake, and he was annoyed with Hartley for trying to hustle him into the magnificent garments which he had ordered for the occasion. He was even annoyed with Harry Coles who had brought up a plate of ham sandwiches and a glass of beer and was trying to induce Dane to partake of some refreshment while he was trying to dress.

"If you think I want beer . . ." said Dane, struggling to force a stud through his brand new collar and breaking his nail in the attempt. "Oh, curse . . . take it away for Heaven's sake. I hate beer at any time . . ."

"You hate beer!" inquired Harry incredulously.

"We ought to be ready!" cried Hartley, jumping about like a jack-in-the-box. "We ought — really — we'll never be there by two o'clock." He pulled his handkerchief out of his pocket and the bright golden ring with which he had been entrusted leaped into the air and rolled away under the wardrobe.

By the time they had moved the wardrobe and recovered the ring it was ten minutes to two, and Dane was rushed downstairs and into the car at record speed.

All this time Dane had not set eyes on Sophie and he was beset by an unreasonable conviction that something had happened to her, that she had changed her mind, or fallen down the stairs or something. He kept on asking where she was, but nobody had time to answer this very natural question. Everyone was quite mad, thought Dane in despair.

It was not until he and Hartley were standing at the altar rails in the little church (empty save for Wynne and the servants and the three young naval officers in the front pews) and he saw Sophie arriving and walking up the aisle on Roy's arm, that the turmoil in his brain subsided and he knew that everything was all right. He had loved Sophie for twenty-seven years and now at last she was his. Her face was rather pale, rather bewildered, and just a little sad, but it broke into a tender and trusting smile . . . yes, everything was all right.

They had all been late for lunch, and late at the church, and now they were late for their party. When they drove up to the house there were several cars in the drive and a cluster of guests standing about and looking at the house in a mystified way. The house was shut up, for all the servants had been at the wedding, and it certainly was a trifle peculiar to be bidden to a party and to arrive at an empty house. Dane did his best to carry off the situation and he was ably seconded by Wynne. Hartley threw open the door and everyone flocked into the drawing-room where the wedding cake was displayed upon a table surrounded by champagne glasses. The popping of corks started immediately and was followed by a buzz of talk and trills of laughter — the party had begun.

Fortunately Mrs. Corbett was not amongst the early arrivals, who had been received — or not received — in such an unconventional manner, she had decided to arrive late so as to keep Sophie on tenterhooks as to whether or not she was coming. She arrived when the party was in full swing and Dane's champagne had done its appointed work. She arrived with her husband and son in tow (Migs had come over from Aldershot for two days' leave) and found the room so packed with a chattering throng of guests that it was scarcely possible to get in at the door, and it was only too obvious that nobody had missed her, neither Sophie, nor anyone else.

Sophie enjoyed the party thoroughly — she was really a very sociable person — but it was not until the guests had gone that she realised how delightful it had been. The guests had gone and Sophie and Dane, in defiance of the customs of civilised man, remained behind amongst the crumbs of wedding cake and the empty glasses in attitudes of complete exhaustion.

"It was nice," said Sophie. "How nice people are!"

"All except Mrs. Corbett," murmured Dane.

"Even Mrs. Corbett . . ." said Sophie, more vague than ever because she was so tired . . . "we wouldn't have had the party, I mean."

"She has her uses," Dane agreed.

CHAPTER TEN

IN SPITE of the war, and the miseries which war had engendered, the world turned on its axis and circled the sun on its appointed course. The world rolled over and the sunbeams crept across its surface and they were no less golden than they had been in the piping times of peace. Slowly the sunbeams climbed up the eastern slopes of the Carpathian Mountains and swept over Western Europe in a yellow flood and they shone upon the garden and cities of the conquered people as warmly and cheerfully as on those of their conquerors. They touched the spires of Prague and threw a mantle of light around Vienna; the Danube caught the sunbeams and sparkled with joy; Breslau and Dresden were warmed and wakened; Berlin was not far behind. The world rolled a fraction further and in the city of Freigarten it was day — but here the sunbeams struggled amongst heavy clouds and a drizzle of rain was falling.

Anna Heiden was glad to see the grey daylight stealing through her windows. The days were long and lonely and tiring but the nights were worse, for they were full of sad thoughts and uneasy dreams. In the daytime she could think of Franz reasonably and almost cheerfully — yes, in the daytime Anna was sure that Franz was in England and therefore safe — but at night she was not so sure, and her fitful sleep was haunted by dreams which still clung about her when she woke.

Otto Heiden had returned from Prague and had been given an important appointment in his native city. He was kind to Anna, and, unless Franz was mentioned he was pleasant and easy to live with. Franz was the bone of contention between them and their arguments about Franz were long and heated. Anna made no secret of her feelings about Franz — he was in England and she was glad, for he was safe in England with his English relations; he was all the safer because he was half English himself.

"Franz should be here," Otto would declare, and the veins would stand out upon his forehead with suppressed fury. "Franz should be fighting for the Reich — it is dreadful that my son — my only son — should be in England now."

He might have said more but he was aware that Anna was ill, she looked so ill sometimes that he was quite alarmed about her; he made a good many allowances for Anna because — in his own selfish way — he was fond of her.

On this particular morning when Anna woke and saw that day had come she was more than usually thankful. Her dreams had been of Franz and they were still with her . . . Franz was in danger, and the danger was all the more horrifying because it was vague and obscure. Her pillow was wet with the tears which had fallen in her sleep — they were still dripping silently like rain — and her familiar room was full of the mists and shadows which had haunted her all night long.

Anna rose and prepared some hot milk, and then she found that she had overheated it so she put it on her window sill to cool. She stood by the window and waited, and looked out at the dull damp morning. There was no sky to be seen and the houses opposite were scarcely visible; it was still very early and Freigarten was not yet properly awake. The world was grey — just as Anna's world was grey — there was no rift in the leaden clouds, no promise of sunshine. The rain was falling steadily as though it would never stop and the window pane was distorted with a film of water.

Anna was still waiting for the milk to cool when she heard the sound of footsteps coming down the street; she stood by the curtain and, holding it a little to one side, looked down to see who it was. There were plenty of troops in Freigarten, and they marched hither and thither in a purposeless sort of way; sometimes Anna saw them marching down the street towards the big new flying field which had just been built, and sometimes they marched up the street to the Barracks in the Square . . . but this was not troops marching, it was three young officers, and Anna realised that they must be flying officers on their way to the flying field. She looked down at the three figures marching along so confidently through the deserted streets and her heart contracted with pity . . . they were going to carry out one of those reconnaissance flights and they might never return.

She could not see them very well because of the uncertain light and the heavy rain, but she could see that all three figures were tall and well set-up in their long military overcoats. The one who walked in the middle was taller than his companions — taller and broader of shoulder — and because Anna Heiden had always liked men to be tall it was the tall one that she looked at. They came down the street marching briskly, and when they were almost level with Anna's window the tall man paused and looked up. Anna could not see his features but something in the poise of his head reminded her of Franz . . . it *was* Franz!

Anna was so sure that it was Franz that she leaned forward to the window and a little cry escaped her lips . . . but the officer had only paused for a moment and he was hastening on.

It was not Franz — no, it could not be. How could it be Franz? Anna knew that Franz was in England — safe in England with his mother's relatives — and even if he were not in England he would not be wearing the uniform of an officer in the Dritte Reich . . . and, even if the incredible had come to pass and Franz had decided to fight for the man he hated, he would not be here in Freigarten, passing the very door, without coming in to see her . . .

The milk had cooled now and Anna took it up and began to drink it. Her heart was beating uncertainly for the little incident had upset her . . . he had been so like Franz.

The tall man in the military greatcoat had paused and looked up only for a moment, but during that moment he had fallen out of step with his companions. He hastened a little and fell into step once more. Anna had been right in her first instinctive thought — he was Franz Heiden.

"What was it?" inquired one of his companions (he was smaller and slighter than the other but he was obviously the senior, for he wore an air of authority and the badges on his uniform proclaimed him to be a pilot captain in the German Air Force). "What were you looking at, Franz? Do you know somebody in that house?"

"I used to live there at one time."

"You were saying 'Auf weidersehen,' " suggested the other companion in a sympathetic tone.

"I was saying, 'Goodbye,' " replied Franz, using the English expression with its air of sadness and finality.

They walked on in silence for a few moments and their brisk footsteps echoed in the deserted streets.

"Is there somebody living there?" inquired the pilot captain. "Somebody that you know?"

"There may be," replied Franz sadly, "or again there may not. She may have ... gone."

He was aware of the glances exchanged between his companions and added, "It was my aunt."

"It was his *aunt*, Max," said the pilot captain in a significant tone.

"But perhaps it really was his aunt," replied the other.

"It really was," said Franz with a faint smile, "and she may be there still. I wasn't sure ... it seemed to me that I saw her figure behind the curtain."

He spoke so sadly that his two companions forbore to tease him any more.

"Some day you will return," declared the young officer who had been addressed as "Max". "Some day when the clouds have passed ... and Rudi and I will be glad to see you again," he added affectionately.

"We shall be very glad . . . if we are alive," the pilot captain agreed.

"Pshut!" exclaimed Max. "What a way to talk, Rudi! We shall all three meet and dine together when the clouds have blown away."

"If we are alive," repeated Rudi soberly.

Franz did not answer. It seemed incredible that the clouds would ever pass, and even more incredible that all three of them would be alive to welcome the sunshine. He was feeling depressed and weary, for he had been through a great deal in the last few months. Now his work for the league was finished for he had become a marked man and the league was sending him out of the country in accordance with its usual policy.

"We shall all be alive," Max declared — he was the optimist of the party — "Look, Rudi, I will make a bet with you that Franz will dine with us before this time next year."

The others laughed shortly and without much mirth.

"It would be a foolish bet to make," Rudi pointed out; "for if Franz and I were not alive we could not claim the money . . . but enough of that," he added in a different tone. "We are nearly there now. You under-stand exactly what is to be done. Franz goes with me through the gate. Max fol-lows. There is to be no talking. The machine will be ready to start. We have discussed it all so often that it should go without a hitch. If the Herr Commandant appears you must be extremely careful. Salute smartly and say as little as you can. Is there anything you want to ask me, Franz?"

"It's all as clear as day," replied Franz. "As you say, we have thought out every detail, and unless the Gestapo have received information I do not see what can go wrong."

"How could they?" inquired Max.

"It is unlikely," Rudi admitted; "for Franz has been well hidden and the fact that we are smuggling him out of the country is known to very few. The thing has been planned as carefully as possible, and for the rest we must trust to luck."

Franz nodded. His luck had held for a long time and indeed it had been so amazing, and he had had so many almost miraculous escapes that "Franz's luck" had become proverbial amongst his companions, but just lately Franz had felt that his luck was deserting him — he had lost his confidence. "We must trust to luck," he said in a sober voice, "but I want to thank you both for what you are doing."

"That is nonsense," Rudi replied. "We are carrying out our orders — besides we are very glad to help you."

"You would do the same for us," Max put in.

"It is good of you all the same," declared Franz, "but remember if anything should go wrong you two know nothing about me — that is understood."

"Yes, it is understood," Rudi agreed.

"But Rudi — " began Max, seizing him by the arm. "But Rudi, surely — "

"It is the order," Rudi explained. "You and I know nothing of Franz; he is merely Fritz Herschel, the expert in photography who is taking the place of Schwarz. We could not help Franz by exposing ourselves and we are valuable to the League. . . . But there is no need to anticipate trouble for every detail has been thought out."

Max said nothing but his young mouth set in a firm line. If anything went wrong with their plans he would not stand aside and let them take Franz. Rudi was a fanatic and nothing mattered to him but the overthrow of the Nazis — Rudi would sacrifice his best friend in the interests of the League — but Max felt that an individual was more important than any league; he could not have explained why he thought so but it was just this feeling that had made him turn against the Nazi régime. If the League was going all Nazi (thought Max) then there would be nothing left for a man to cleave to — nothing that mattered except his own soul.

Franz had some inkling of what was going on in Max's mind for the same idea had struck him once or twice during his work for the League. He said quietly, "We must use their weapons for their overthrow, Max, or at least we must use a weapon equally sharp . . . but we have *chosen* . . . the weapon has not been forced upon us."

Max was silent, for he understood, but Rudi did not understand at all.

"What weapons ?" he inquired.

After a moment's thought Franz replied in a low voice, "The weapon of unquestioning obedience to a guiding mind."

By this time they had reached the solid

brick wall which encircled the hangars and Rudi forbade any more talking. They skirted the high wall, which was further strengthened by a barbed-wire entanglement, and came to the big gates. There were two sentries here, but they were half-asleep on their feet, their bayonets held slackly in their cold, red hands — they were raw-boned country lads, and very young, and their long black coats hung upon their undeveloped bodies like sacks. They came to attention as the three officers approached, and one of them moved forward, but Rudi was a well-known figure and so was Max . . . the third figure, with his collar turned up round his ears, must be one of the other officers of course . . .

Rudi took the salute and passed in (closely followed by his companions). He swung lightly across the puddled road, turned the corner of a hangar and bore straight out across the field without a moment's hesitation. Franz was aware of large buildings on his right — though they were merely a blur of darker grey in the light grey mist — and then he felt the softness of grass beneath his feet and knew that they were on the flying field. The dank mist enfolded them so closely that they might have been alone in a world of mist for all that Franz could see, and in spite of his nervous excitement he found himself wondering how Rudi knew so confidently what direction to take. He decided that it must be that strange instinct which we call a sense of direction which is born in some men — just as it is born in the consciousness of a homing pigeon — and without which no man could ever become a first-class pilot.

Rudi strode on, and suddenly the huge black shape of a Heinkel Bomber loomed up before them. There were shaded lights about her and a small group of mechanics were at work upon her under-carriage.

"What's this?" Rudi inquired in a sharp tone. "What's this, Haller? Is the Heinkel not ready for me?"

The head mechanic turned and saluted. "There is one small adjustment necessary," he declared. "If the Herr Officer will give me ten minutes — that is all."

"Ten minutes!" echoed Rudi indignantly. "Ten minutes — you should have had her ready. You knew the hour. What have you been doing? Do you think I have all day before me? Let me see what's wrong. . . ."

While Rudi was engaged in harrying the mechanics and examining the adjustments which were being made, Max found the parachutes and was fixing his harness securely. Franz took his, but he was clumsy with the unfamiliar gear, and he was still struggling with it when the Commandant appeared out of the surrounding mist. He was a short squat man with a red face and somewhat bleary blue eyes which surveyed the world in a mistrustful manner from beneath his shaggy brows.

"What's wrong?" he inquired irritably. "Why are you not ready to start . . . and who the devil is this officer? I have not seen him before."

"I am Fritz Herschel," said Franz, and he saluted smartly.

The Commandant looked at him distastefully and did not trouble to return the salute. "Explain," he said to Rudi. "Where are Schwarz and Leiss? Who is this man?"

"Schwarz is ill, Herr Commandant," replied Rudi promptly. "He was taken ill last night — and Leiss also. It is thought that they are suffering from some form of poisoning."

"Why was I not informed?"

"The Herr Commandant was out last night," replied Rudi in a gentle tone.

"Hmph," snorted the Commandant. "Yes, I was out. It is not often that I take a few hours off duty and, when I do, something always goes wrong. Continue your explanation."

"Yes, Herr Commandant; this officer has been detailed to take the place of Schwarz; he is an expert in photography — or so I was informed. I have never seen him before."

"Your papers!" barked the Commandant. He was in a particularly ugly mood for he had been at a convivial party the night before and was suffering from reaction. In addition to his physical discomfort he was enduring mental strain, for he disapproved of these long reconnaissance flights over enemy territory and was obliged to dissemble his disapproval. The Herr Commandant was of the opinion that these flights were foolish and wasteful. They wasted men — two of his best pilots had failed to return — and they wasted machines, and they used up precious fuel. He would not have minded so much if the machines had been employed in their proper manner . . . there was some sense in dropping bombs.

The officer who had called himself Fritz Herschel produced the papers which proved his identity, and there was a little silence while the Commandant examined them.

"They are in order," he declared, looking up, and then he added in an unpleasant tone, "Lieutenant Fritz Herschel seems to be having some difficulty with his parachute harness."

Franz felt that every eye in the little group was fixed upon him. His mouth was so dry that he could not speak.

"It is strange," continued the Commandant, "it is very strange, is it not that an officer who is an expert in air photography should be unfamiliar with the harness of a parachute?"

Nobody said a word.

"Do you find it stange?" asked the Commandant turning to Rudi.

"Very strange," agreed Rudi uncomfortably.

Max swung and seized the straps of the

harness. "Heavens!" he exclaimed in an irritated voice, "Heavens, one would think you had never seen a parachute before! It is *this* way . . . and the buckle fastens *so*," he added, pulling and tugging and scolding roughly at Franz.

His rudeness had the desired effect in turning the attention of the Herr Commandant to himself.

"Hullo! Our good Lieutenant Finkel seems out of sorts this morning!" he declared with a grim smile.

"Who would not be?" inquired Max. "It is bad enough to have to fasten one's own harness on a cold morning when one's hands are chilled and slippery with rain . . ."

The Commandant glared at him. "That is enough. It is even a little too much . . . however, I shall let it pass. What are you waiting for? The machine is ready and you are fourteen minutes late."

"I am ready," said Rudi simply.

"Be off, then. You have your orders. You are aware of the penalty if any bombs are dropped upon non-military objectives," growled the Commandant. He was obliged to give this warning to every pilot that left the field, and to give it in person but it was a duty which went against the grain.

"Yes, Herr Commandant," said Rudi.

"And you are aware that the penalty is the same if the bomb is dropped *by mistake*?"

"Yes, Herr Commandant," said Rudi again.

"Be off, then."

The three young men climbed into the machine. Rudi settled himself in the pilot's seat and checked over the controls quickly and capably. Then suddenly the buzz of the engine rose to a roar and the machine quivered and moved beneath them as though it had life . . . and they were off. They taxied across the field and rose . . . and bumped . . . and rose again, and the next moment they were soaring smoothly in the air and the grey mist was below them.

"So," said Rudi. "So . . . you are safe now, Franz. It was a bad moment that, for the Herr Commandant was peevish and a peevish man is hard to deal with."

"Where was the danger?" inquired Max with a chuckle. "The Herr Commandant could do nothing . . . he was feeling sick and it pleased him to make a fuss. I was not alarmed for I knew that the papers were in good order . . . Wilhelm had seen to that."

"It frightens me," declared Rudi, swinging the huge bomber sideways in a sickening roll. "It terrifies me. The only time I am happy is when I am in the air. I believe I am losing my nerve," he added, swooping through a cloud . . .

CHAPTER ELEVEN

FRANZ had not spoken at all for his tongue was still dry and leathery. It might be (as Rudi said) that he was now safe . . . but he did not feel safe. All around them was mist, and the motors filled his ears with a quivering roar. He had flown before, of course, but that was in a passenger plane — a large air liner — and it had felt as safe as a bus in comparison with the Heinkel. Franz had the feeling of tremendous power hurtling him through the air, and there was a horrible singing in his ears. He was suspended in space between heaven and earth, and he was also suspended between the past and the future. The past was behind him — months of strain and peril — and the future was unknown. Between the present and that unknown future there was an ordeal from which he shrank — an ordeal the very thought of which made his blood run cold.

The League to which Franz belonged had various ways of smuggling its members out of the country, some of them had been passed into neutral countries with faked passports, others had been hidden in packing cases and sent by ship, but neither of these methods was any use in the case of Franz for it had been decided to send him to Britain. He had been sent for by the Chief — the master mind who directed all the League's activities — and had had a long and very memorable interview with him. Franz had been amazed at this man's intellect, his capacity and acumen were much above the ordinary level. He had pointed out to Franz that, although his work in Germany was now finished there was a possibility that he could still be of use. Money was what the League needed and the co-operation of others who were working for the same end — the overthrow of the Nazi régime. The Chief had asked Franz pointblank whether he thought that these things could be found in Britain and Franz had replied very thoughtfully that it was possible that they might be found there.

"Well, go and see what you can do," said the Chief — and the interview was over.

The wheels of the League had turned smoothly and rapidly and here was Franz on his way to Britain in one of Germany's

448

newest bombing planes. He was to make a parachute landing in some deserted spot and after that he was to shift for himself. The thing had sounded simple — much simpler than being sealed up in a crate and lowered into the hold of a ship — and Rudi and Max had assured him that there was no difficulty about it and very little danger. Franz had never attempted such a thing before, but every airman had to practise parachute descents and every airman had to make a first attempt—there was no way of learning to do it except by doing it. Rudi and Max had both been very encouraging. Rudi declared that he had lost count of the number of times he had descended to earth in this manner, and that even when he was a novice he had never experienced any discomfort. Max said that he had made twelve descents — he had broken his collar bone on one occasion but that was because he had been clumsy; there was no danger if you remembered to do what you were told. Franz had listened carefully to all this, and he had assured himself that, if others could do it, so could he — it had seemed a comparatively easy thing to do after so many months of danger — but, now that the ordeal was approaching, it seemed neither simple nor easy and Franz began to wonder whether he would ever be able to climb out of the cockpit on to the slippery-looking wing . . . and let go.

He decided very wisely not to think about it until the time came. He would think ahead, he would try to envisage the future which lay beyond; but somehow or other he found it difficult to do — in fact he could not make himself believe that there was any future at all. He decided that he did not mind very much what happened to him. He had nothing to look forward to, and nothing to live for. The love of life was at low ebb in Franz — or so he thought — but it is difficult for anyone to know how much he clings to life until life seems to be slipping from his grasp. Perhaps there was no future for him, thought Franz; perhaps this was the end; perhaps the parachute would refuse to open. . . .

Franz pulled himself together and fixed his mind firmly. He would make the descent and would find himself in England — or possibly in Scotland — somewhere in Britain, anyway; and (if Rudi had been able to manage it) he would find himself in a deserted spot where he would be able to get rid of his parachute without being seen. After that he would make his way to the nearest town and try to get work, so that he could keep body and soul together until he had time to look round. He must not go near Fernacres, of course, nor must he go back to London where he might meet people he knew. He must depend entirely upon himself . . . but, of course, Rudi might not be able to drop him in a deserted spot, and someone might see his descent and be waiting for him when he reached the ground. In that case Franz was aware that he would probably spend the remainder of the war in a British Prison Camp. There was a third possibility to be envisaged, Rudi might not be able to reach Britain without being seen and intercepted by British Fighter machines. The Heinkel might be engaged in an action and driven off or shot down in the sea.

These were the things that might happen, thought Franz, but he could not see them happening. The future was an absolute blank . . . he could see nothing beyond that drop from the clouds which was coming nearer every moment.

They were flying low now; the mist had thinned; and looking down Franz saw the grey choppy waters of the North Sea. The sea looked unfamiliar seen like this — it looked as if the waters had been painted on a flat surface. Suddenly they flew into a thick bank of fog and almost immediately the machine began to climb; again Franz felt that strange pressure on his back as if the back of his seat were pushing him forward and upwards. They continued to climb for so long that it seemed to him they must be half-way to the moon, it seemed to him that he would never return to the earth he knew. Perhaps something had happened to the machine, perhaps it was out of control . . .

"We're climbing," he said to Max in a low voice.

"Yes, pretty steeply," Max agreed. "We shall probably go very high before we reach the British coast so that we shall not be spotted. You need not worry," he added cheerfully, "I never worry when I am with Rudi — he knows what he's doing all right."

"Do you ever worry, Max?"

"Not often," replied Max with a chuckle.

"There is no use worrying if you are an observer, but sometimes when I am with some other pilot I do not feel quite so happy. That's all."

Now they were out of the fog-bank into pale, watery sunshine, and below them the fog-bank lay thick. It was so thick that it seemed solid — almost as if one could land upon it, Franz thought.

Max had been keeping a good look-out, and now he called to Rudi that he had seen a plane — it was a fighter, and it was coming from the west . . . Rudi swung round in a steep bank and continued in a northerly direction. There were so many clouds in the sky that he was not very worried.

"Just as well to be careful," he said. "We do not want to spend the whole war in a British prison. Bread and water and flogging is not my idea of bliss."

Franz objected to this. He was pretty certain that the British Prison Camps were conducted in a proper manner, and was ready to bet that the food would be ample, for he had pleasant recollections of English fare. A lively argument ensued. Rudi declared that he was willing to take the bet, but added that the point could never be settled unless, of course, one of them were unlucky enough to prove it for himself.

He had hardly spoken when another plane appeared suddenly out of a cloud. Rudi put the Heinkel into a steep dive and they roared down towards the fog bank which still shrouded the sea. Franz shut his eyes and gripped the edge of his seat, expecting every moment to feel the cold water splashing round him. They plunged into the fog, and immediately Rudi flattened out and changed direction and they were speeding on . . . and on.

Perhaps Max guessed that the manoeuvre had been a pretty stiff trial to Franz, and that a little pleasant conversation might help to restore his confidence.

"What will you do, Franz?" he asked suddenly. "You have friends in England, of course."

"Yes, but I can't go *there*. It would put them in a very awkward position, wouldn't it?"

"If they are *real* friends . . ." began Max, and then he hesitated. "No, perhaps not," he said. He was silent for a few moments and then he said softly, "You think a lot, don't you, Franz? I liked what you said about the 'sharp weapon'. I would like to know what you think about something else, but I don't want Rudi to hear. Rudi thinks of the one thing only, the overthrow of the Nazi rulers, and he does not care how it is accomplished. Sometimes I cannot help wondering whether it is right to do evil so that good may come."

Franz could not answer that — "Go on, Max," he said.

"We are living double lives," said Max, putting his lips close to his friend's ear. "With one hand we are giving the Hitler salute and with the other we are preparing his downfall . . . We are saying, 'Yes, Herr Commandant' and 'No, Herr Commandant' like good little boys, and all the time we are looking forward to the day of reckoning. Is that right, Franz?"

"No," said Franz sadly.

"Is that, perhaps, the other edge of the sharp weapon?"

"Perhaps," said Franz doubtfully. ". . . it is, at any rate, their own weapon turned against them."

"Himmel!" exclaimed Max, "Himmel, the thing gets on my nerves. It is like —

like walking on a tight-rope stretched above an abyss!"

"Yes," said Franz softly. "Yes, it is like that."

"It was different for you," Max continued. "You were never an officer of the Dritte Reich — not a real officer. Once or twice you have passed yourself as an officer but that is different. I am two men," added Max with a sigh. "I am an officer in two opposing camps . . . I do not like it."

Franz would not have like it either so he could offer very little comfort to Max.

All this time the Heinkel had been speeding north, but now Rudi swung west amongst billowy clouds which looked like a flock of fluffy white sheep. There were clouds all round them and a film of cloud below, and this seemed to be moving in a different direction. Franz looked over the side and suddenly, through a hole in the cloud, he saw land. He realized then that his ordeal was very near. In a few minutes — at any moment now — Rudi would signal to him to go, and he would have to climb out of the cockpit . . .

The cockpit had seemed a perilous place but now it seemed secure — it seemed like home to Franz, so familiar had it become — and he wondered whether he would be able to leave it when the time came, whether his limbs would obey his brain. He went over the instructions which Rudi had made him repeat so often. Yes, he knew exactly what to do, but would he be able to do it ?

There were several different ways of leaving an aeroplane — so Rudi had explained — and it all depended upon how much time you had which method you chose. Sometimes of course the plane was damaged and you had to leave in a hurry . . . but Franz need not worry about that. Franz could take lots of time and do everything slowly and carefully, and, this being so, it was extremely simple. Franz was to climb out of the cockpit through the sliding roof and allow himself to be blown off . . . that was all.

Suddenly Franz felt Max tugging at the straps of his parachute harness, he looked up in surprise and saw Max's face quite near his own, smiling at him.

"Get ready," said Max. "You have to take off that uniform, you know."

Franz had forgotten this. He had his

English clothes underneath the uniform, his English clothes with a little English money in the pockets . . . his fingers were all thumbs as he fumbled with the straps, but Max helped him and, in a few minutes he was ready.

"See that his parachute is properly adjusted," Rudi said.

"I have done so," replied Max.

"Is he ready ?"

"Yes."

Rudi was circling now, circling above a rift in the clouds and looking down.

"Now!" he said in a firm tone. "Now, Franz — and hurry, for there is no time to waste. Help him, Max . . . Help him, and hurry . . ."

Max was already helping him and encouraging him. "It is easy," he was saying, "it is so easy, Franz, . . . there, the roof is open . . . up you go! That's right . . ."

"Hurry, Franz, there is no time to waste," urged Rudi again.

Somehow or other Franz found himself climbing through the opening in the roof. He had known that the wind would be terrific but it was beyond anything that he had imagined — it was like a living force —

it tore him off the roof and swept him backwards over the tail, and he felt himself being whirled into space like a leaf in an eddy. Then he was falling . . . falling . . .

He pulled the ripping bar.

CHAPTER TWELVE

FRANZ opened his eyes . . . and then he shut them again for the pain in his head was so intense . . . there were fiery circles before his eyes, and a roaring sound in his ears. For a little while he lay still . . . he was alive, anyhow, and perhaps in a few minutes the pain would abate . . . he was alive.

Beneath his hands he could feel turf, and the woody stems of heather . . . he was alive and he was on a moor somewhere in Britain. He lay very still, but there was something in his brain urging him to move, urging him to make a bid for life and safety. Slowly Franz turned on his elbow and raised himself from the ground. Slowly he managed to open his eyes and accustom them to the glare. He saw now that he was sitting on a bare hillside and there was mist all around him. There were rocks behind him, and he decided that he must have hit his head on a rock as he came down . . . his head ached terribly. He put up his hand and tried to discover whether his head was cut, but there was no blood to be found. He had hurt his foot too, and already it had swollen badly.

The parachute lay beside him spread out upon the faded heather, limp and helpless-looking. It seemed odd to think that it had been so strong in the air, holding him up, for there was no life in it now. Franz unbuckled the harness and rolled the whole thing into an untidy bundle and hid it amongst a clump of gorse. He took a long time to accomplish this, because every time he moved he felt as if his head would split with pain, but at last it was done. The thing was hidden and unless a careful search was made it was unlikely to be found.

There was a small stream running down the hillside (it was like the streams that he and Roy had seen on their way to Inverdrum) it cascaded over some rocks and fell into a deep pool. Franz dabbled his hands in the water and then he wet his handkerchief and tied it round his head. The cold water revived him a little and he began to follow the stream down the hill. He had no very clear idea why he should follow it but it seemed the only thing to do . . . he wanted to lie down amongst the heather and sleep, but something urged him on, some subconscious feeling that he must go on . . . and on. His head felt top-heavy and full of pain and his foot was so swollen that he could hardly bear to put it on the ground, but he limped on. He limped on until he caught his foot in a wiry heather-stem and pitched forward on his face.

The fall jarred him unbearably and he lay there for some minutes without moving. He was very cold and a deadly feeling of sickness was on him . . . he felt so ill that it seemed impossible to move, but somehow or other he managed to scramble on to his feet, and to limp on.

The mist was thinning now — it was really a cloud which was resting on the hill — and suddenly Franz found himself in bright sunshine. Below him was a road, a narrow strip of grey ribbon winding across the deserted moor. The sunshine hurt his eyes and the whole world seemed to be swaying beneath his feet . . . Franz staggered on. He fell several times and each time he fell it was more difficult to get up again . . . there was a film before his eyes — it was like looking through water — and everything seemed to waver and was distorted. He reached a gate at the roadside and clung to it and then a black curtain swept over him and the world was blotted out.

Franz was floating in empty space. He was floating down through darkness shot with fiery lights, and the parachute was tight beneath his arms. Down, down he floated, alone in illimitable space. Somehow or other he seemed to know that when he reached the bottom it would be the end . . . but I don't want to die, he thought. He reached out and caught hold of the wing of the Heinkel and then Rudi's voice came to him and shouted to him to let go . . . but I don't want to die, he thought. Everything swirled round him and he was falling, falling into space and the darkness was shot with fiery lights. He was drowning now, drowning in a cold, dark sea, and twice or thrice he rose to the surface and tried to grasp the side of the boat, but each time he sank before he could open his eyes. He shouted — or tried to shout — *"Hilf mir . . . halte fest . . ."*

"You're quite safe," said a voice close to his ear. He opened his eyes and became aware of a woman's face framed in a white cap. It was bending over him.

"*Halte fest*," cried Franz again, struggling to the surface.

She seemed miraculously to understand. She was holding him. Her firm hands were cool upon his wrists, and, for a moment he lay secure.

Days passed, and long nights made up of horrifying dreams. He was always falling, sinking, drowning, always knew that Death waited at the bottom of the abyss; he was always alone, and the loneliness was profound, there was no other soul near to help him and encourage him in his struggle . . . Then he would wake suddenly to find the room dark, save for a shaded nightlamp on the table beside his bed, or to find it bright with sunlight and the woman in the white cap bending over him . . . he would clench his hands and try to hold onto life but, before he could grasp it, he would be sinking again. Sometimes when he woke like this he was conscious of whispering voices, or the tinkle of a glass, and once he opened his eyes and saw a bearded face, a kind old face with dark-brown eyes oddly magnified by the lenses of a pair of steel-rimmed spectacles. He was conscious of these things as if they were far away and belonged to another life, or as if they were happening to another person. It was his dreams that were real, and his dreams were lonely and dreadful.

Gradually his conscious moments lengthened and he was able to take in his surroundings: the small bare room, the whitewashed ceiling, the primrose coloured walls, a glass-topped table with some medicine bottles on it, and white jug with a linen cover. There were blue beads on this cover and they jingled against the side of the jug when the cover was removed. His dreams were different now. The nightmare of falling and sinking came less often . . . he was running in a meadow and Tant' Anna was coming towards him. Her eyes were blue, and she was wearing a scarf . . . a blue scarf made of wool . . . and he ran so fast to meet her that he fell. He fell and lay there, floating between two worlds. Now he was swimming in a warm sea with long, even strokes, and Roy was swimming strongly by his side. "You old dark horse," Roy was saying. "You old dark horse, Frank . . ."

There was a jingle of beads and he opened his eyes and saw the woman's face, she had a cup in her hand.

"I'm Frank again," he said and the words seemed to come from a long way off. He could scarcely hear them for the rushing noise in his ears.

"Yes," she said, nodding. "That's nice, you're Frank. What's your other name, dearie?"

He could not remember and the effort exhausted him. He drifted away amongst the shadows.

The next time he woke it was dark, and the nightlight was burning dimly. He heard a rustle beside his bed and a hand felt below his armpit for the thermometer. His brain was clear, now, and he knew that he was ill in a strange place. He was very ill — perhaps he was dying. People often had an interval of complete consciousness and lucidity just before they died. He was dying and he was all alone. There was nobody near him — nobody who cared.

The nurse was looking at the thermometer, her head thrown back a little as if she were long sighted; she examined it carefully and then pursed her lips and began to shake it down. Her eyes fell and focused on her patient's face.

"Oh, you're awake!" she exclaimed. "You'd like a nice drink, wouldn't you?"

"Very ill," whispered Frank.

"Poor boy," she said, smoothing the sheet, "poor laddie! Here's a nice drink."

He would have liked a drink but there was something he must do first, something he must do before he drifted away into that strange dreamland which he had inhabited for so long.

"Write," he said clearly.

She stooped down. "What is it?" she asked.

"Write," said Frank again.

She understood this time and fetched a pad and a pencil, and bent over him so that she could hear what he wanted to say.

"Major . . . Worthington . . . Fernacres . . . Chellford," said Frank.

It was a frightful effort, and it left him weak and trembling . . . he slipped away into darkness again.

Tides of time rolled on. He woke and slept and woke again, and each time he woke there was a cup at his lips. His dreams were fainter and more vague and the real world came nearer, the rushing noise in his ears diminished.

Suddenly the clouds lifted. He woke one morning and found that he felt different, drained of feeling and strength but strangely peaceful. The ceiling was streaked with sunshine. Shadows flowed across it like water. He lay at rest and watched the shadows for a long time.

Somebody said, "He's conscious now. See if he knows you."

There was a movement beside his bed and he turned his head a little on the pillow and saw Dane. Their eyes met.

"Hullo, old chap!" said Dane. "I'm here all right. Don't talk."

He couldn't talk anyhow. There was a queer feeling in his throat and his eyes were full of tears.

CHAPTER THIRTEEN

THE next time Frank awoke it was broad daylight. He woke slowly and easily and the rushing in his ears had almost gone. He turned his head from side to side and found that the pain had almost gone too. He was better — much better — but he felt as if he had been washed up on the shore after a storm.

"Flotsam — no, jetsam," said Frank.

"What did he say?" somebody inquired and a bearded face with large brown eyes swam into view.

"I said jetsam," declared Frank.

"Not bad," agreed the man. "Not bad at all. That's what you are."

"You're real," said Frank thoughtfully.

"Did you think I was just another bad dream?"

"Not a very bad one."

"I'm your doctor, and I'm fairly well pleased with you. You've a grand constitution. See and take care of yourself and do what Nurse tells you."

"You're Scottish."

"Well, what else did you expect?"

"I didn't know where I was."

The doctor looked at him. "I daresay not," he said, "and let me tell you you're lucky to be here at all. Imphm — well, here you are, anyway, and well on the right road."

"I'm hungry," Frank said. "I want something to eat, something solid."

"You do, do you — a beefsteak, I suppose?"

"Bread and butter and tea," said Frank dreamily. "English bread and butter and Indian tea."

"And what's wrong with Scottish bread and butter?"

"I'll tell you when I've had some," said Frank cheekily.

There was silence for a little and Frank lay and looked at the ceiling with its shifting shadows, and presently he heard the rustle of a starched apron and the sound of a tray being set down on the table.

"Here's your bread and butter," said the nurse cheerfully, "and a nice cup of tea. The doctor says it won't do you a bit of harm." She slipped an extra pillow beneath his head and began to feed him dexterously.

"It's nice, isn't it?" she said. "I'm always glad when a patient begins to get solids. You'll feel quite different soon. Your friend is coming to see you in a wee while and you can talk to him for ten minutes. There, it's all finished."

"It was good," said Frank, "just as good as English bread and butter — tell the doctor I said so."

Dane came in and stood there looking at him, and Frank looked back at Dane. Why had he sent that message to Dane? It was so odd, because he had made up his mind firmly that he would hold no communication at all with Fernacres . . . and then he had sent that message. Why had he done that?

"I thought I was dying. That was why," Frank said.

"Why what?" Dane inquired in a bewildered tone.

"Why I sent for you."

"Was that the only reason?"

"Yes," said Frank.

Dane came over to the bed and sat down beside him.

"There's such a lot to tell you," said Frank with a sigh.

"Don't worry," said Dane quickly. "You can tell me gradually when you begin to feel stronger. I'll do most of the talking."

"Did they send for you?" Frank inquired.

"Yes," replied Dane with a smile. "I got a most mysterious letter from Doctor Duthie to say that he was attending a young man in the Cottage Hospital. The young man was too ill to give his name, and he had no papers on him, nor anything which could provide the smallest clue to his identity. In a lucid interval he had mentioned my name and address to the nurse and Doctor Duthie hoped sincerely that I would be able to identify him."

"What else?" inquired Frank, smiling.

"The young man had been brought to Dalfinnan Hospital by a passing motorist who had found him lying at the side of a road, but his injuries did not appear to be due to a road accident. Doctor Duthie was at a loss to account for the injuries sustained by his patient, they consisted of a fractured skull and a — "

"A fractured skull?" inquired Frank in horrified tones.

"He didn't call it that," admitted Dane;

"but I gather that's what it was. You're getting on splendidly now, so there's no need to worry, but you have been very ill indeed. They were glad to shift some of the responsibility."

"How did you know it was me?"

"I didn't know," replied Dane smiling, "but I thought it might be. It was just as well to make sure."

"Have I been talking?" inquired Frank anxiously.

"Talking!" exclaimed Dane. "You never ceased talking for a single moment. Doctor Duthie told me you talked for days, and it was all in a language which he recognised as German — though apparently he could only understand a word here and there --- "

Frank gave a little groan of relief.

"Just as well — eh?" Dane inquired, looking at him intently.

"I'm full of secrets," said Frank wearily, "I've been full of secrets for months . . . full up to the brim. Sometimes I felt as if I might burst . . . Dane, I believe that's what happened," he added in a surprised tone.

"Oh yes," agreed Dane, "there's no doubt about that. You burst, Frank.

We're putting the pieces together again, and soon the cracks won't be noticeable . . . but the point is I had to do something to allay their anxiety. I had to tell them who you were. I took the liberty of saying you were my cousin, Frank Hyde, and that you had been in Germany for months on a Secret Mission."

"Oh, Dane, it *was* good of you!"

"Nonsense — I had to say something. I had to give you some background. I couldn't tell them where you had come from because I didn't know. You're the local mystery, Frank. The police have been making inquiries all over the country but they couldn't find out anything about you . . . in fact you seemed to have dropped from the clouds."

"I did," said Frank with a feeble chuckle.

"You did what ?"

"Dropped from the clouds."

It was at this moment that the nurse bustled in and declared that the ten minutes were up. Dane rose very reluctantly indeed — he felt like a man who has been reading an exciting serial which stops abruptly at the most interesting moment. . . .

"To be continued next week," said Frank, smiling.

Although he was too weak to talk much there were long hours when Frank lay awake, and his brain was so clear — clean-washed like a plate-glass window — that he began to understand many things which he had not understood before. All the strange things that had happened to him (thought Frank) had happened in a natural sequence. He had had the power of choice of course, but, because he was fashioned in a certain way, he had been bound to choose as he had chosen. Everything in himself and everything that had happened to him had built him up into what he had now become. He thought of all that Tant' Anna had told him — it was part of him now — he thought of the suffering which was being endured and he remembered that Tant' Anna had said it was because there was hatred in the world — hatred and mistrust instead of love between man and man.

It was very pleasant to lie still and to feel that he was recovering his strength day by day. It was a rest — he had had no rest for months — it was peaceful and secure. He trusted Dane implicitly. Nothing could happen to him as long as Dane was there. Gradually and bit by bit he told Dane the whole story and Dane listened to it with the deepest interest and attention. He was especially interested in the account Frank gave him of his adventures in broadcasting, and asked all sorts of pertinent questions about the methods employed.

"Yes, it was a van," Frank said, "a huge van which was fitted up like a shop. We sold hardware in the villages. The broadcasting apparatus was hidden in a sort of cupboard in the roof. At night we camped in fields or meadows and opened it up and got it going. There were four of us to each van . . . oh yes, there are several vans and they are all disguised differently . . . each van has two mechanics who understand the technical part of it, one man to broadcast, and one as a sort of odd job man to sell the stores and to keep guard. I was the broadcaster in our lot," explained Frank. "We toured all over the country and scarcely ever spent two nights in the same place, and that's what puzzled the Secret Police. As soon as they had traced the broadcasts to one neighbourhood, and begun to search for us there, the broadcasts began in quite a different neighbourhood altogether . . . It was fun at first," said Frank, thoughtfully, "but after a bit it began to get rather *too* exciting."

"I can well believe it," declared Dane, looking at him in amazement.

"Yes," said Frank. "It wasn't so bad until the war started, but after that we had great difficulty in getting food. We didn't exist, you see. I mean we had no existence on paper and therefore no food tickets. Fortunately there were plenty of rabbits about and I'm afraid we stole an occasional chicken. We had some narrow escapes; one, especially. We were camping beside a stream and suddenly we found ourselves surrounded by a small body of Secret Police. I was in the middle of a broadcast when I heard shots and I looked out of the window and saw our head mechanic fall with a bullet through his head. Fortunately the other mechanic managed to leap in the driver's seat and we charged right through the police and back on to the road. I got a bullet through my arm but it was nothing.

"We got away all right but we realised

that the game was up, as far as we were concerned, so we spent all night dismantling the van and destroying all evidence of the radio apparatus."

"Why?" inquired Dane.

"Those were our orders," replied Frank, "and they were wise orders, because if the Gestapo got hold of one van they would know what to look for and might easily find the others. . . .

"After that I was on a coal barge. It was easier than the van, because we became real people. We had papers and food tickets. We were flesh and blood coal-heavers." Frank laughed a little and added, "You wouldn't have known me, Dane."

"I daresay not," agreed Dane.

"We shovelled coal all day," Frank continued, "and we did our broadcasting in the evening. We were at it for weeks and then suddenly we got word to sink the barge and scatter, so we sank her. . . .

"We took her into the middle of the river and set a bomb and a small fuse and then we swam to shore. Some of us made for one shore and some for the other. They were such good fellows, Dane. All of them were. It was a marvellous experience to live with men like that . . . we got to know each other inside out, and there wasn't one of them that wouldn't have given his life for another . . ."

It was an amazing tale. Dane listened enthralled. He heard all this and much more, and he heard it bit by bit as he sat beside Frank's bed. The fire burnt cheerfully in the polished grate, the clock ticked away industriously on the mantelpiece, and the medicine bottles stood in orderly array upon the glass-topped table; and sometimes, as Dane listened to the quiet tired voice narrating its owner's astounding adventures, he could hardly believe his ears; the tale was so alien to the austere and cleanly comfort and security of the small bare room as to be almost incredible.

The boy had lived through a nightmare — through months of strain and stress and constant dangers — and it seemed odd to Dane that these experiences had left no mark on Frank. He saw Frank sitting up in bed, with his breakfast tray balanced on his knees, he watched Frank cut off the top of his egg with meticulous precision, and lift the silver egg spoon. There he sat, in an ordinary common or garden hospital bed, wearing a perfectly ordinary pair of pink and white striped pyjamas! It seemed incongruous to the point of absurdity that a man who had fought and starved and suffered, and had escaped by a hairsbreadth from worse than death should look and behave like an ordinary person, should be enjoying his breakfast — just as ordinary people enjoyed theirs, only with a good deal more zest than most — should be having his face and hands washed and his hair neatly brushed by a matter-of-fact Scottish nurse.

Dane was all the more able to understand and appreciate Frank's account of his adventures because he had been in a few tight corners himself. He thought about Frank a good deal for he had plenty of time for thought. Frank was indeed a whole person — just as Sophie had said — and he was even more of a whole person now, for he had found himself. Through dangers shared with other men Frank had found that strange happiness of companionship in danger, he had discovered his fellow man. Dane realised this because he had gone through the same experience.

For years he had travelled the world, locked up within himself, exchanging words or signals with his fellows which carried no freight, and then, through dangers shared with other men, he had found companionship — he had become a citizen of the world and all good men and true were his brothers.

Dane had put up at the little hotel at Dalfinnan. He had come by train for the roads were blocked with snow. It was, indeed, the heaviest snowfall that the country had experienced for years, and the hardest frost. There was very little for Dane to do in the hours between his visits to the hospital. The snow was too deep for him to walk very far except on the roads which had been cleared by the snow plough. He found a set of Waverley novels in the little hotel and renewed his acquaintance with them with a good deal of pleasure. He also wrote long letters to Sophie, telling her all his news, and received in return even longer replies. Sophie and he decided that when Frank was well enough to be moved he was to be brought to Fernacres for a period of convalescence. The doctor was a source of companionship and amusement during these long and somewhat lonely weeks, and Dane often dined with him at his house, or entertained him at the hotel in return.

Gradually Frank recovered. He was allowed to get up for a few hours, and he sat in a chair by the window and looked out at the snow. It was melting now, but not very rapidly, it was seeping away into the ground in small streams of water.

CHAPTER FOURTEEN

"SO YOU see," said Frank, after a little silence. "So you see I couldn't let anyone know where I was or what I was doing — besides I didn't want to. I didn't want to see anyone I knew because I was so ashamed. I had trusted Hitler . . . admired him like a god . . . and I felt he had betrayed me. I had to do something to take the bitterness out of life."

"Are you still a member of that league?" Dane inquired, for this was a question which had exercised his mind a good deal.

"Yes and no," replied Frank slowly.

"Perhaps you're not allowed to tell me."

"I may use my discretion . . . and I'm going to use it. I'm willing to tell you everything because I think we can help each other."

"Why should you think that?"

Frank lay back on his pillows and gazed at the ceiling. "You took me in at first," he admitted. "I thought you were a drone, but I saw quite soon that you had a brain

483

and used it. I believe you are in the British Secret Service."

"No," said Dane.

"You have some connection with it, anyhow, I'm sure of that."

"How — ?"

"Little things put together . . . Dane, we're working for the same end."

"Are we ?"

"Well, of course. Isn't Britain's aim the overthrow of the Nazi Government?" He tugged at Dane's sleeve. "Dane, do help me. You'll put me in touch with the right people, won't you ?"

"You seem to think I'm a magician," said Dane, smiling at him.

"Yes, it's a habit I've got into. You always seem to know everything. You turn up at exactly the right moment and smooth out all the tangles. Yes, I'm afraid I've got into the habit of thinking you can do everything."

"I'll think about it," Dane said. "Perhaps I'll wave my wand . . ."

He thought about it a good deal. Frank had said that they were working for the same end. That was not quite true. Dane was under no misapprehension. He was not one of those wishful thinkers who said that we were fighting Hitler, and Hitler alone; we were fighting Germany and fighting for our lives, there was no doubt of that, but of course it was quite natural that Frank should take the other view. At the same time it seemed to Dane that there were possibilities in Frank's suggestion and he decided to write to Colonel Carter on the subject. The letter was not very easy to write, for the matter was so extremely delicate and confidential that he was unwilling to put it on paper and entrust it to His Majesty's mail, but to Colonel Carter a hint was as good as a detailed statement of fact, he was a past master in the art of deciphering cryptograms.

Having dispatched his letter, Dane decided to clear up another matter which had been on his mind for some time. In the course of their conversations together Frank had often said that he wondered what had happened to Rudi and Max. His recollections of those last few moments in the Heinkel were extremely vague, but he had received an impression of urgency and stress in Rudi's voice. "He kept on saying I was to hurry," Frank had told Dane (and had told him more than once). "He kept saying that there was no time to waste. It was odd, because, before, he had always told me I was to do it slowly . . ."

Frank was anxious about his friends — it was quite natural that he should be — and Dane decided to find out what had happened to them. This was not a difficult matter of course, but to clear it up in a satisfactory manner it was necessary that Dane should leave Dalfinnan by the early morning train and return late in the evening. He told Frank that he was going away for the day but did not disclose his reasons, for if he discovered that Frank's two friends had met with disaster — a not unlikely contingency, all things considered — he intended to keep the fact to himself. Frank had enough to bear without the distress of knowing that his two friends had given their lives in his service.

Frank had plenty of time to think during Dane's absence, and, because he missed Dane's visit so much, he realised more clearly than before how good and kind Dane was to stay with him. Dane must be longing

to go home, and of course he ought to go . . .
I must talk to him about it, Frank decided.
He had had his supper and had gone back
to bed, and was lying watching the firelight
flickering on the ceiling when the door
opened and Dane looked in.

"I'm not asleep," said Frank quickly.

"Good," said Dane. "How have you got
on? I hope you've been a good boy and
done what Nurse told you."

"I haven't any choice," declared Frank
somewhat ruefully. "She's very kind of
course, but she rules with a rod of iron."

Dane came in and stood by the bed, he
looked very tall and thin in the dancing
firelight and his shadow was huge and
distorted upon the opposite wall. "I've got
news for you, Frank," he said.

"News for *me*?"

"Yes . . . I don't know whether you'll
think it good or bad."

Frank gazed at him in surprise. "You're
very mysterious," he said.

"News of your friends," explained Dane,
sitting down beside the bed. "Rudi and
Max . . . they're both well."

"How on earth — ?"

"You said once or twice that you

wondered what had happened to them and it wasn't very difficult to find out. They were attacked by R.A.F. fighters and the Heinkel was forced down into the sea, but Max and Rudi were rescued by a fishing-boat and taken prisoner. They're well and cheerful, and they were very interested to hear all about you."

"Dane, do you mean you've *seen* them ?"

"Yes, and spoken to them."

"You spoke to them in German ?"

Dane smiled. "Of course I did. They can't speak anything else. I had a long talk with them — I was able to arrange it — and when they discovered that I was a friend of yours we got on like a house on fire. They're nice fellows, Frank."

"I think your news is good," said Frank, thoughtfully. "They were both feeling the strain pretty badly . . . but they will be a great loss to the league."

"They sent you messages," continued Dane. "Rudi said I was to tell you that you've won your bet, and Max sent you his love, and a mysterious communication about a two-edged weapon . . . he is content to leave this weapon in other hands."

Frank smiled.

"You understand?" inquired Dane.

"Yes," said Frank. "Yes, I understand very well." He was silent for a few moments and then he said, "I have just thought of something. I ought to be there too . . . in the Prison Camp . . . and, Dane, if you think it right I am willing to go. If you think I should give myself up — "

"No," said Dane, smiling. "No Frank, you stay where you are. We may find other uses for you."

The next day was fine and sunny and Frank took his first walk in the garden of the hospital, leaning on Dane's arm.

"You are good to me," Frank told him.

"Not a bit of it. I'm merely exercising common humanity."

"It is a pity that kindness isn't more common," said Frank with a little difficulty. "There is kindness in German hearts, too, but it is hidden from view because kindness has become a crime."

They stopped their slow pacing and looked out over the hedge encircling the little garden. The road passed by on the other side of the hedge and curved away over the moor. The landscape was brown and wintry looking, and there were still

489

patches of snow to be seen, lying on the sheltered side of walls and rocks and in the hollows of the hills, but in spite of this, there was a feeling of spring in the air.

Frank sighed. "I have given up all hope of Wynne," he said in a quiet voice. "I want you to know that, Dane. You needn't be afraid of — of that any more."

"But Frank — "

"No, please listen. I've thought it all out. You were right, Dane. It wouldn't be fair to ask Wynne to marry me unless I were ready to give up my nationality — that would be the only way — and I can't do that. I can't do it because it's part of myself and some day Germany will be a good and great nation. She must be, Dane. There's so much good in her still — courage and kindness and faith — "

Dane was moved. He said, "Everyone knows that, Frank."

"When that day comes Germany will need us," continued Frank in a low voice. "At least I hope she will. I can't desert my country when she is in distress . . . but it may be years before she is free from shadows." He thought on Tant' Anna as he spoke — an old woman frightened of shadows — and his voice was grave and stern.

Dane was wondering what to say in reply when a car drove up and stopped at the gate and a tall, broad-shouldered man got out and straightened himself stiffly, Dane looked at him . . . and looked again . . . it was Colonel Carter!

Dane was so amazed to see Colonel Carter here in Dalfinnan that he was quite bereft of the powers of speech and movement.

When Colonel Carter had finished stretching himself, he turned and looked up at the hospital and then round the garden. The two figures standing by the hedge caught his eye and he waved his hand cheerfully.

"Hullo," he cried, coming towards them across the grass. "Hullo, Dane, there you are! Once more the mountain has had to come to Mahomet . . . and I imagine this is our young friend. I have wanted to meet him for some time but you kept him in your bag . . . supposing you introduce us."

"But how . . ." exclaimed Dane staring at him.

The Colonel chuckled. "It's worth the

journey to see *you* at a disadvantage," he declated. "By Jove it is! To see you standing there with your mouth open just like any ordinary person taken by surprise . . . ha, ha, it's great! Is there any fishing in this part of the country ?"

"Fishing!"

"Yes, fly-fishing — that's what I'm supposed to be doing. I've given myself a week's leave . . . I had to. When I got your letter I was so eaten up with curiosity that I couldn't concentrate . . . you were so damned careful to give nothing away that your letter read like something out of Alice in Wonderland . . . and, while I was still racking my brains over that, the news came in that you were making up to a couple of German Airmen in the Prison Camp at Northtown . . . using my name to get yourself a private interview with them. What are you up to, Dane ?"

"Lord, lord, what a man!" said Dane, laughing heartily.

"What a man, yourself," retorted Colonel Carter. "What are you up to ? What do you think you're doing ? Did I give you leave to bandy my name about Prison Camps all over the countryside ?"

"I found it worked very well — "

"I daresay you did . . . and that's not all by any means. What did you mean by rousing my curiosity, filling my head with your mad hatter allusions and nearly driving me to drink ?"

"I thought you would understand — "

"You seem to think I'm a telepathist or a crossword puzzle fan," declared Colonel Carter with mock fury. "You seem to think I have nothing to do all day but sit and read your letters with a wet towel round my head . . . and here am I — a busy man with weighty affairs pending — here am I wasting my time chasing you all over Scotland."

"There wasn't any need — "

"Wasn't there ? Of course there was. About the only thing I did manage to glean from your letter was that our young friend had turned up again in mysterious circumstances, and I wanted to see him before you shoved him back into your bag. I've come a matter of five hundred miles to make acquaintance of our young friend — and you refuse to introduce us."

"You haven't given me a chance . . . This is Frank Hyde, Colonel Carter."

The Colonel held out his hand and Frank took it. They shook hands gravely.

"Frank Hyde," said Colonel Carter. "I don't know whether this very extraordinary mutual friend of ours has told you anything about me, but he's told me a good deal about you, and, as I said before, I've come five hundred miles for the pleasure of a little chat with you. I'm staying at the hotel in Dalfinnan and I shall come back tomorrow about eleven, if that suits you. Meanwhile perhaps our mutual friend will put you wise about me."

"I think I can guess," said Frank. "I shall be ready at eleven."

It was just as well that Frank was so much better and stronger now for the little chat which Colonel Carter had arranged was neither short nor easy. It was a private chat; Dane was banished from the room, and the nurse was informed that her presence would not be welcome. Frank was somewhat alarmed at Colonel Carter's high-handed manner with his nurse — he had a wholesome respect for this benign autocrat — but she took her dismissal quite meekly and merely remarked as she closed the door, that there would be trouble with Doctor Duthie or she was a Dutchman.

Colonel Carter opened the door again and looked out. "Nurse!" he said. "Nurse, I shouldn't like you to be a Dutchman or a Dutchwoman either — you're quite nice as you are — but if there's trouble with Doctor Duthie send him to me. I'll deal with Doctor Duthie." He hesitated a moment and then repeated the words as if he were pleased with their sound. "I'll deal with Doctor Duthie," he declared. Then he shut the door again, drew a chair up to the table and sat down opposite Frank.

"Now we can talk," he said. "You can tell me everything. Begin at the beginning and go straight on. When you get to the end we'll go back to the beginning and fill the gaps. I shall take a few notes, of course, but don't worry about that. Just go full steam ahead."

The interview lasted for two hours and when it was over Frank felt as if he had been turned inside out; he felt as if there was nothing left in him that Colonel Carter had not seen. In a way it was a tremendous relief to get rid of all the secrets, and to hoist all his responsibilities on to Colonel Carter's broad shoulders.

"That's all," said Colonel Carter at last. "You're free now — do you understand what I mean? You're perfectly free. I don't want you to do anything more. I shall get in touch with these friends of yours in Germany. You've given me all the information you possess."

"You mean I'm to — "

"Leave it all to me. You can do anything you like as long as you keep in touch with Dane. I don't want to lose sight of you, and, as a matter of fact you might encounter difficulties. You aren't registered as a British Subject — "

"No," said Frank, smiling. "I don't exist, but I'm used to that, of course."

"Dane will look after you," declared the Colonel, returning the smile very kindly. "Dane will see that you're all right ... and you must put all these secrets out of your head. Play about and feed up and get well and strong. You've done quite enough for the time being and you're a free man."

Frank stretched his arms. He felt as if he had been relieved of a heavy burden.

CHAPTER FIFTEEN

SOPHIE and Wynne were waiting in Fernacres drawing-room for the car to arrive. Hartley had taken Dane's car to Kingsport to meet the travellers and he was due back at any moment now. Several times they heard a car approaching and Sophie got up and peered out into the black darkness . . . and the car passed the gate and sped on.

"He'll be tired," Sophie said — she had said it so often in the last hour — "Poor boy, how tired he'll be! He must go straight to bed, Wynne. I wonder if I remembered to tell Rose about the hot water bottles."

"You've told her three times," said Wynne.

"Silly of me!" declared Sophie with a sigh.

They had waited and listened, and then, when the car did at last arrive, they were taken by surprise. The bell rang and they rushed into the hall.

It was dark in the hall for the front door

was open and, for a wonder, Barber had remembered the black-out and had put out the hall light before throwing open the door. The car was standing at the steps and Dane was getting out. Behind Dane was the tall figure which Wynne had been waiting to see. She had waited so long — eighteen months — and it seemed a lifetime.

Wynne had thought about Frank so much that her intimacy with him had outrun realities — she knew that he was hers but he did not know it yet — so his greeting seemed cold. It was certainly a good deal cooler than she had expected. He came out of the misty darkness and stood for a moment in the doorway. It was such a long moment that it seemed to Wynne as if he had always stood there and had only just become visible to her eyes. There was bustle all round her, Dane greeting Sophie and answering questions about their journey, and the servants bringing in the luggage, but Wynne did not notice it. She had eyes for one person only.

"Hullo, Frank!" she said.

He came forward and shook hands with her and they went into the drawing-room together. The others were there too, of course, and Wynne greeted Dane in her usual way, but he was not real to her. Frank had come back and he filled her thoughts. Wynne looked at him . . . and looked . . . he had changed, she thought, he was thinner — he had been very ill of course — and he was more self possessed. He was a man. She saw the lines of his features, firm and resolute, and the clean-cut lines of his jaw and forehead. His eyes shone . . . it was almost as if he had fever, his eyes were so bright.

Sophie bustled him off to bed with hot milk and hot water bottles and he seemed pleased to go.

Wynne was happy now, for it was lovely to have Frank here under Fernacres roof, to know he was safe. It gave her a warm feeling as she went about her hospital duties, to know that when she went home Frank would be there. She had thought in those first few moments that Frank had changed and she saw that she had been right. He had been solemn before, and now he was grave. Sometimes he laughed quite heartily, but his usual expression was one of sadness. He seemed to like Sophie's company best — perhaps he was more comfortable with Sophie than with anyone else — Sopnie was a comfortable person. She was kind, but not too kind; she fussed over him, but fussed in a pleasant way. Sophie was so unselfconscious herself that it was impossible to feel awkward with her.

With others, Frank felt a trifle awkward. He felt awkward with Wynne because he was obliged to watch himself so carefully when she was there, and he felt very awkward indeed with Wynne's friends. They were exceedingly nice to him and it was obvious that they were aware of his changed views, but he felt that he was in a false position and his long illness had made him shy. When people dropped in — as they always did at Fernacres — he was apt to disappear.

There was nothing for Frank to do except listen to the radio. He listened to every news bulletin in every language that he could understand — and unfortunately he understood a good many languages.

"You listen too much," said Dane one day when he came in and found Frank listening.

"Yes," agreed Frank somewhat wearily.

500

"Yes, I listen too much for my peace of mind — but I must listen. Dane, it's frightful!"

"All war is frightful."

"The attacks on fishing boats; the sinking of unarmed trawlers, of neutrals, the laying of mines, indiscriminately — these are crimes against humanity, unforgivable crimes. Ships are sunk without warning; there was a lightship attacked. Surely there must be something fundamentally wrong with people who can do these things."

"They're obeying their orders, I suppose," said Dane uncomfortably.

"Should one obey orders which are against all moral laws?" inquired Frank thoughtfully. "That's the question, Dane. That was what Max asked me and I couldn't answer him. I didn't realise all that was happening until I came here and began to listen to the radio, but now I'm beginning to wonder . . ."

Frank had left the sentence half-finished, and Dane was anxious to know how it would end.

"What are you beginning to wonder?" he inquired.

"I'm beginning to think there's more wrong with my country than its Government," said Frank in a low voice.

He was silent for a few moments, but Dane felt that there was more coming and he waited.

"I'm well now," Frank continued, "and I can't — I simply can't sit here doing nothing. Everyone is doing something except me — there's no place for me here." He got up, and began to walk up and down the room. "There's no place for me anywhere, Dane," he said.

"Colonel Carter might find you something to do."

"I thought of that; but it wouldn't satisfy me. I'm young and strong, and I'm a trained soldier. I want to go to Finland . . . It isn't a new idea," explained Frank gravely. "I've been thinking about it for some time, and this morning I had a letter from my friends in Helsinki — I told you I had friends there, didn't I?"

"Yes," said Dane, watching him.

Frank made a despairing gesture with his hands. "They're homeless," he said in a low voice. "Their house is in ruins . . . they've nothing left. The little girl — I knew her as a baby — was killed . . ."

"Terrible! Ghastly!"

"Words!" said Frank. "Words . . . what use are words? I shall go and fight for Finland. I can do that wholeheartedly. Yes, my heart is with her in her struggle."

"Frank, are you sure you want this?"

"Quite sure," said Frank, looking at him with steady eyes. "Quite, quite sure. It's the best thing I could do. In fighting for her I shall not be fighting against either of my countries, but only for what is right. I shall be fighting for an idea, for freedom and justice and liberty . . . Can you arrange it for me, Dane?"

It was Colonel Carter who made the necessary arrangements with the Finnish Legation in London, and Frank hurried them on as much as he could. At first he had been very content at Fernacres, and had thoroughly enjoyed Sophie's petting, the comfort, the security and the good food. At first he had enjoyed seeing Wynne and watching her and had wanted nothing more. But that phase had not lasted long, it had lasted only while he felt weak and ill. Now he was fit and strong again and the mere fact of seeing Wynne was not enough. He loved her more than ever, he adored her. She had changed a little (Frank thought) but then, so had he. It was right that people should widen their ideas and expand their personalities. In the eighteen months of their separation both of them had grown and developed, but they had advanced in the same direction and they were more in harmony than even before. Wynne had been a charming child, now she was a lovely woman, lovely in every sense of the word. She was still gay and laughter-loving, but there was a new gravity in her, a new graciousness, an added poise. Frank loved her so deeply, with every fibre of his being, that it had become torture to look at her and to know that she could never be more to him than a friend. She was his friend and always would be — so Frank hoped — but he found small comfort in that.

It was now the end of February and Frank felt as fit as ever. He was eager to be off. He had got all his kit — Dane had given it to him — and he was waiting for the telegram from the Finnish minister which would give him his orders. A considerable number of volunteers had come forward and arrangements were being made to send them over to Finland. Frank was impatient at the delay. He listened to the news bulletins with growing concern. The Finns had now been obliged to retreat before the advancing hordes of fresh Russian troops, they had evacuated their island fort of Koivisto, they were falling back upon Viipuri. They were still undefeated and were fighting bravely and wisely but they needed men. Frank was only one man, not a very formidable reinforcement perhaps, but he was a trained soldier and an expert skier — one man, but a useful one he hoped. As a matter of fact he felt so strong (strong not only in physical strength but also in determination) that it seemed to him that he would be able to render valuable assistance. The idea was somewhat fatuous and he was fully aware of that, but the feeling remained — the feeling that if only he could get there in time it would make a difference to them.

It was a Thursday afternoon and Frank was sitting in the drawing-room listening to a foreign broadcast which was giving an account of the fighting in Finland. He was alone because everyone else in the household was busy. Sophie always went to Mrs. Audley's work-party on Thursday afternoons. Dane was shut up in his sitting-room, writing, and Wynne was not due to return from the Hospital until six o'clock. Frank knew the times of her comings and goings very well indeed and he was surprised when the door opened and she walked in.

"Hullo, did you get away early?" he inquired. He realised as he said the words that it was a foolish question to ask for it was obvious that Wynne had left the Hospital a good deal earlier than usual.

"Yes," said Wynne, "I just walked out. I just told Sister I was going home. She was rather surprised, but she didn't say much — perhaps she realised it wouldn't be any use." She walked over to the radio and turned it off. "I want to talk to you," she said.

"But you can talk to me any time," said Frank.

"No," replied Wynne, "I never get the chance to talk to you properly, there's always someone about . . . and I specially want to talk to you today," she added somewhat mysteriously.

Frank was surprised. "Today?" he inquired.

"Yes," said Wynne, nodding. "Yes. Do you know what today is, Frank?"

Frank shook his head. He tried to remember the date — was it somebody's birthday? He looked at Wynne and saw that her small face was paler than usual, and there was a determined air about her.

"What is it, Wynne?" he asked.

She did not answer at once, but came over to the sofa and sat down beside him.

"Now we can talk," she said.

He agreed that they could — "But what do you want to talk about?" he asked, smiling at her.

"Frank," said Wynne earnestly. "This is the 29th of February. It's leap year. I know it's rather silly but I thought I'd wait till today. Will you marry me, Frank?"

"Wynne!" exclaimed Frank in amazement.

"We love each other so much," said Wynne going ahead steadily — or as steadily as she was able — "We've loved each other for such a long time now. It's nearly two years since you came here first, isn't it? I want to marry you, Frank. I want us to belong to each other properly. Of course we do belong to each other already, but I want it to be an outward as well as an inward belonging."

"Oh Wynne!" he said, and that was all he could say.

"Darling Frank," said Wynne, turning her head and looking into his face. "Darling Frank . . . it hasn't been easy . . . you might help me. . . ."

He saw that her eyes were full of tears and her lips were trembling, and he was so shaken at the sight of Wynne in distress that all the good and wise resolutions he had made vanished into thin air.

"Oh Wynne, darling!" cried Frank, and he gathered her into his arms and kissed her again and again, on her hair, on her dear soft cheek, on her darling mouth . . .

"We're engaged now, aren't we?" said Wynne, when Frank had finished kissing her. "We're properly engaged, and you can give me that ring you wear on your little finger . . . just to show that we're properly engaged."

She pulled it off his finger as she spoke and slipped it on to her own — it was the little signet-ring which Tant' Anna had given him, his mother's ring —

"But Wynne — " he began.

"Darling Frank," she said, burrowing her fair head into his shoulder. "Darling Frank, I'm so glad we're engaged."

"We must be sensible," said Frank, but he said it in a very feeble tone, for it was extremely difficult to be sensible with Wynne in his arms, and Wynne's golden hair tickling his cheek, and the fragrance of Devonshire Violet bath powder in his nostrils.

"We *are* sensible," declared Wynne in a muffled voice. "We're frightfully sensible, really."

"No, we aren't," Frank told her. "Honestly, Wynne, this is sheer madness. There are all sorts of reasons why we can't be engaged."

"We *are* engaged, darling," replied Wynne, flaunting the ring before his eyes.

"But, Wynne, I'm going to Finland," he reminded her.

She was silent for a moment and then she said gravely, "Yes, I know you are. I'm terrified, of course, but I wouldn't dream of trying to prevent you. I understand what you feel about it; I believe it's the right thing for you to do, and — and I'm rather proud. I shall be waiting for you when you come back."

His arms tightened round her, and he leant his cheek against her hair, and for a few moments there was silence.

"There's Dane," said Frank at last. "What will Dane say?"

"He won't mind," murmured Wynne in a dreamy voice. "Dane thinks the world of you, Frank. He said your broadcasting in Germany was one of the bravest things he ever heard of."

"Dane said that?"

"Yes, he did."

"But, Wynne, I promised Dane — "

"Oh, did you?" she asked, sitting up and looking at him. "Oh, that was why . . . but, Frank, you didn't ask me to marry you. I asked you. So it's all right — you've kept your promise beautifully."

He could not help smiling — but it was rather a sad smile — "Wynne, you don't understand," he told her. "I'm a German, and some day I may have to go back to my own country."

"I'll go with you," she said, looking at him with steady eyes. "We'll always do everything together. It doesn't matter what happens, I can bear anything as long as I'm with you. If you want to go back to Germany we'll go together, Frank . . . if you want to go back."

It was really a question, and Frank, examining himself, found that he could not answer it. He had always intended to go back, but just lately, he had begun to wonder whether the Germany which was enshrined in his heart, had any existence save in his fond imagination.

THE END

ROMANCE TITLES IN THE ULVERSCROFT LARGE PRINT SERIES

OCTAVO SIZE

PINES

www.gapines.org
Pooler Library

Checkout Receipt

You checked out the following
items:

1. **The English air**
   Barcode: 31057902889149
   Due: 8/19/2023

Total Amount Owed: $0.00

> **You Saved**
> **$0.00**
> **by borrowing from the library!**

OTHER ROMANCE TITLES IN THE ORIGINAL ULVERSCROFT LARGE PRINT SERIES

QUARTO SIZE

FICTION TITLES IN THE ULVERSCROFT LARGE PRINT SERIES

OCTAVO SIZE

OTHER FICTION TITLES IN THE ORIGINAL ULVERSCROFT LARGE PRINT SERIES

QUARTO SIZE

A Breath of French Air	H. E. Bates
The Darling Buds of May	H. E. Bates
The Fabulous Mrs V.	H. E. Bates
All the Days of Minnie-Sue	Susan Bell
That Summer's Earthquake	Margot Bennett
The Manasco Road	Victor Canning
Grand Canary	A. J. Cronin
A Bit of a Bounder	Mary Ann Gibbs
The Healing Touch	Philip Gibbs
The Captain's Table	Richard Gordon
Lost Horizon	James Hilton
The Wrong Side of the Sky	Gavin Lyall
At the Villa Rose	A. E. W. Mason
November Reef	Robin Maugham
Jamaica Inn, Vol. 1	Daphne du Maurier
Jamaica Inn, Vol. 2	Daphne du Maurier
The Man from Martinique	Shirley Murrell
House-Bound	Winifred Peck
Lonely Road	Nevil Shute
A Sunset Touch	Howard Spring

Miss Bagshot goes to Tibet *Anne Telscombe*
The Courageous Exploits of Doctor Syn
                              R. Thorndike
Black Lobster   *Donald Weir*

This book is published under the auspices of the ULVERSCROFT FOUNDATION, a registered charity, whose primary object is to assist those who experience difficulty in reading print of normal size.

In response to approaches from the medical world, the Foundation is also helping to purchase the latest, most sophisticated medical equipment desperately needed by major eye hospitals for the diagnosis and treatment of eye diseases.

If you would like to know more about the ULVERSCROFT FOUNDATION, and how you can help to further its work, please write for details to:

THE ULVERSCROFT FOUNDATION
Station Road
Glenfield
Leicestershire